RESURRECTION
BAY

RESURRECTION BAY

A Novel

WAYNE McDANIEL
STEVEN WOMACK

MIDNIGHT INK
WOODBURY, MINNESOTA

FIRST EDITION
First Printing, 2014

Book design and format by Donna Burch-Brown
Cover art: 141299986/Adrian Studer/Flickr Open/Getty Images
       iStockphoto.com/14255516/vm
Cover design by Lisa Novak

Midnight Ink, an imprint of Llewellyn Worldwide Ltd.

Library of Congress Cataloging-in-Publication Data

McDaniel, Wayne, 1955–
Resurrection Bay : a novel / Wayne McDaniel, Steven Womack.
    pages   cm
    ISBN 978-0-7387-4065-2
1. Women—Violence against—Fiction. 2. Serial murderers—Fiction.
3. Retribution—Fiction. 4. Alaska—Fiction. 5. Psychological fiction.
I. Womack, Steven. II. Title.
    PS3613.C38686R4 7   2014
    813'.6—dc23   2014001934

Midnight Ink
Llewellyn Worldwide Ltd.
2143 Wooddale Drive
Woodbury, MN 55125-2989
www.midnightinkbooks.com

Printed in the United States of America

DEDICATIONS

FROM WAYNE MCDANIEL

To Morgan and Abbey
—W.M.

FROM STEVEN WOMACK

For Natasha, with love . . .
—C.S.

ACKNOWLEDGMENTS

Tip of the hat and heartfelt thanks to —

Christopher Schelling, who guided me through this adventure and for his continued support, both personally and professionally.

Terri Bischoff and the entire crew of Midnight Ink, who made the adventure fun.

Nancy Yost and Sharon Brannock who put me in touch with Steven Womack to get this show on the road.

Thanks are also due to my wife, Cynthia, for introducing me to Christopher Schelling and making this happen.

—W.M.

I, too, am grateful to Nancy Yost for introducing me to Wayne McDaniel and being such a fine midwife on this project. And I'm grateful to Wayne for making this the easiest, most pleasant, and downright fun collaboration I've ever worked on.

I also appreciate my agent, Paige Wheeler, for all the hard work she put in on this book and especially for her wise and insightful guidance. I value it, and her, a lot.

Let me echo Wayne's thanks to all the folks at Midnight Ink, especially Terri Bischoff, Connie Hill, and Amelia Narigon.

For as long as I've known her, my wife, Shalynn Ford Womack (a fine writer in her own right), has encouraged me to be the writer I want to be and to find my way back to that life. This book is a first step to that. Her encouragement, guidance, and support mean more to me than I can say. And I hope she knows that without her love— and that of my daughters Isabel, Ava, and Nova—none of this would be worth it in the first place.

—S.W.

PART ONE

Whatever your hand finds to do, do it gladly with all your might, for in the grave, where you are going, there is neither working nor planning nor knowledge nor wisdom.

—God

BEFORE

THE GIRL HAD BEEN dead a long time before he finally stopped killing her.

ONE

Decatur Kaiser embraced the sweetness.

Thirty-six.

For the better part of the morning, he had been sitting on top of the ridge counting M&Ms.

Savoring the addictive sweetness exploding across his tongue, Decatur leaned back in a silent, perfected stillness against an ancient Sitka spruce, the assault rifle balanced delicately across his knees.

He was watching the clearing below him, waiting as a stone waits.

Centered.

Focused.

Cobra calm.

He was something of a legend, back in Anchorage, for the way he could will his body functions down. More still, some said, than death.

Fifteen minutes passed. Shadows had moved, but not Decatur.

Looking down at his watch, he popped another M&M from the brown bag into his mouth. Crunched the delicate, green sugar coating with his teeth.

Thirty-seven.

Decatur looked up.

The aurora borealis, a rainbow of kaleidoscopic lights, mamboed across the brightening sky.

The glowing, flickering panoply of dancing lights and multihued colors rippled and swayed, folded and unfolded, then suddenly disappeared, only to mystically reform in a new shape seconds later. The northern lights—named after the Roman goddess of dawn, Aurora, and the Greek name for the north wind, Boreas—were doing justice to both.

Haphazardly, the first pillars of sunlight began stabbing through the canopy of tangled branches that blanketed Alaska's Kenai Peninsula, revealing its treacherous mountain slopes for opening day hunters who stalked the Alaskan brown bear.

A squadron of gyrfalcons took flight, screeching a greeting to the dawn, their alabaster wings staining the pale sky as they skimmed the hard gray angles of the mountain's saw-toothed summit. Nearby, the air quaked with the perpetual rumble of a river as it pulsated over a serrated cliff then broke on the ragged boulders far below.

Summertime winds, strong and blistering, had powdered the mountain peaks to an ashen hue with a new layer of glacial silt, which was now dark and slippery from the predawn rain.

To the sound of his own deep, measured breathing, Decatur peered downward through the morning mist. When the slopes were steep and slick with rain, not to mention the choking underbrush, swift streams, and unforgiving glacial moraines, some hunters delayed their hunt or returned home.

But not Decatur Kaiser.

Never happen.

This was his summertime project and, once initiated, nothing in heaven or hell or anything in between could ever turn him back.

Decatur was well aware that the legal bag limit for the Resurrection Peninsula was one bear every four years and there was a good reason for that, both for the hunter and the hunted.

The Alaskan brown bear was generally regarded by the world's best hunters as the most dangerous animal to track and kill. A mature male, the largest of its species in the world, could weigh nearly 1,500 pounds with a skull approaching two feet in diameter and a hide that would square out at more than ten feet. While Alaskan brown bears normally avoided human contact, even going out of their way to leave an area with human activity, they could be ferociously hostile when threatened. This was especially true when their food source was disturbed, when breeding in the Spring, when accompanied by cubs, or when surprised or wounded. When provoked, these behemoths could be surprisingly lethal, aggressively attacking with unbelievable speed and a berserking ferocity.

According to Asian lore, the bear's enormous, seven-inch claws could be ground into an aphrodisiac that would enhance sexual power. But to Decatur, the trophy he stalked symbolized a formidable adversary, a kill to validate his skills as a hunter. He already held the number-three position in the Pope and Young records for Dall sheep taken by a bow, and felt this kill could give him another top spot. Another world record.

At the beginning of each hunting season, back in Anchorage, Decatur's wife, Cindy, had continuously warned him about the added danger of getting shot by other hunters. Decatur had simply turned on his award-winning grin and reassured her, "No worry. M...m...more men have walked on the moon than where I go hunting." Decatur stuttered less these days, but when he got excited there was no way to stop it.

Using the topography at the summit of the crest to keep as concealed as possible, Decatur counted another M&M—*thirty-eight*—and crushed it between his teeth, relishing the count almost as much as the instantaneous explosion of sweetness.

Decatur was an addict.

And a counter.

Among other things he was addicted to counting

Found it relaxing. Some people found solace in yoga, others in religion. Decatur found it in counting most anything. People sometimes asked Cindy what Decatur was doing and Cindy would say, "Oh, that Decatur, he's a counter. He's always counting something, but his real gift seems to be subtracting things. He seems to be really good at that," and people would ask, "No, kidding? What's he counting now or is he subtracting?" and Cindy would say, "I'm never quite sure myself, but he's doing one of the two. That's what he does. He's a counter. It relaxes him." And the people would say, "How 'bout that."

Decatur was a man who didn't say much and when he did, he didn't say much.

He always felt his actions spoke louder than words.

Popping M&M number thirty-nine into his mouth, he silently removed a pair of binoculars from his backpack. Slowly, he glassed the landscape below him.

What he saw shook him to the bone.

Emerging above a rock ridge some three hundred yards below him was a fuzzy brown head at least twenty inches in diameter resting on a body that had to be two thousand pounds easy. In eight years of hunting brown bears in Southeast Alaska, Decatur had never seen such a beast. The height, symmetry, and mass of the living juggernaut were incredible. Just a guesstimate, but Decatur figured the bear as at least a 131 on the Boone and Crocket scale and as high as 125 on the Safari Club International, both making it the largest brown bear on record.

Decatur froze as the magnificent beast came up through the mist, then lowered its head and ambled upward. *I know you can't see me,* thought Decatur. *But I know you. I know how you work. You can see movement, but you can't see distinct patterns. I'm sitting in front of you and you're looking right at me and you can't even see me.*

Decatur mentally calculated the shot. The wind was perfect, a light steady breeze from the bear to Decatur.

Then, in the periphery of his binoculars, he caught a second movement. Decatur shifted and refocused his binoculars near one of the small trees in the alpine meadow.

Finally, the prey Decatur had been hunting all morning came into focus.

His real prey.

His trophy.

Decatur moved back behind the rock ledge. The fog had become less dense. He took off his pack and shouldered his 5.56mm Steyr Aug assault rifle. He backtracked into the draw he had just climbed, pushing forward through the thick undergrowth entwined with devil's club, salmon berry and currant, keeping the rock outcrop between him and his prey.

Decatur now found himself two hundred fifty yards from the trophy of his dreams.

Inch by inch, stopping whenever the head came up, Decatur maneuvered to within two hundred yards of his prey.

Unseen at Decatur's feet, another hunt had reached its lethal climax. A jet-black spruce beetle and a ruddy, gray spring Tiphia wasp were locked in a death struggle on the forest floor, oblivious to the giant in whose shadow they battled. Decatur stepped out of his hiding place, crushing both beetle and wasp under the heel of his camouflaged Wingshooter hunting boot.

When Decatur had crept to within one hundred and fifty yards of his target, he smiled. He had patiently tracked his prey most of the night, in itself no easy feat. The time for the kill was almost upon him. But not yet. Only when Decatur was satisfied that all conditions were perfect would he take his kill shot.

Decatur stealthily rose, spidery mist hugging his legs as he moved.

Slipping like a shadow out of the underbrush, he took a position behind a fir tree, using one of the lower limbs for support. As a breeze moved over him, Decatur sighted his scope on the brown bear. A nifty little head shot.

Then, abruptly, all sound in the forest ceased for Decatur. Every bird, every animal, every insect seemed to fall silent. Only the distant pounding of the falling river water penetrated the thick vegetation. In the quiet echo of the thundering pulse, Decatur eagerly moved the scope's crosshairs away from the bear and sighted in on his real prey, making its way across a small stream.

The bold optics of the magnification ring made his target ten times life size.

Decatur slid the simple cross-bolt safety from the right side to the left, revealing the red "fire" dot, reinforcing his hunting mantra: *Slide to the right, ready to fight.*

He took careful aim and a lungful of air, keeping in mind that when a hunter acquired a target, the reticle of his scope's crosshairs will move in a figure-eight pattern with each breath the hunter takes.

Decatur patiently timed his shot so that the reticle was in the top portion of the figure eight while holding his breath. Not during the inhale. Not during the exhale. In between the two.

It's kinda creepy, thought Decatur. *The bullet will travel three times the speed of sound, which means the prey won't even hear the shot that's gonna kill it. It's just strolling through the woods one minute and the next, Bam! It will be no more forever.*

Decatur smiled, then slipped calmly into that Zen-like, tranquil pool of near nothingness where the little bulb on the tip of this forefinger took over as if on autopilot.

He squeezed the trigger—half from instinct, half from conscious decision.

The explosion shattered the early morning silence.

Decatur instinctively knew, as the gun punched into his shoulder and the target in his scope disappeared in the blur of the recoil, that the perfect shot he'd been waiting for all these hours was his.

One hundred and fifty yards away, the bullet drilled the twenty-three-year-old woman in the head and tunneled downward through her spine.

A scarlet rain sprinkled the ground as her legs churned another few unchecked-inertia steps backward and splayed. She was dead before she collapsed face down into the stream. Her head went under. The water turned deep red and, farther away, pink, then puce. Her legs kept jerking.

"Well, well, looks like we have us another winner!" Decatur amusingly said to himself as he watched the water turn different shades of red. Enthralled.

High above a single blue jay cried out, but not in alarm. In the lower branches tree squirrels leaped and chattered, sending twigs and foliage raining down on the forest floor. Closer to the cool, moist earth, insects crawled, squirmed, cackled and buzzed through the curling fingers of mist.

Living fountains of green.

That's how Decatur thought of his killing ground.

"Living fountains of green," Cindy had repeated at the end of last summer. "Sounds romantic." As Decatur proudly attached the stuffed world-record Dall head to the wall in his den, Cindy had asked, "You've got the world record, Decatur. What are you going after next?"

"I've g ... g ... got some ideas," he had excitedly replied.

He couldn't wait until next summer.

Now, high up in the wooded hilltop, Decatur checked the dead woman through his scope. She had been a redhead. *She was certainly a redhead now*, thought Decatur, laughing out loud.

That's strange, he thought still laughing. He realized he had forgotten her name. Didn't really matter to him anyway. Certainly didn't matter to her anymore.

Decatur chuckled again. Then, sitting down crossed-legged on his ass, he raised the Steyr Aug.

Took aim.

Fired a second shot into the girl's lifeless body.

The rifle automatically chambered another round. Decatur aimed and squeezed the trigger.

Again.

Again.

Decatur mentally counted the remaining rounds in his clip.

Sixteen.

Nice.

Always time for a little target practice.

He continued to shoot until his clip pinged empty.

The girl had been dead a long time before Decatur finally stopped killing her.

Decatur stood up. He walked out into the sudden sunlight, the bees droning in the flowers, the bright sun throwing a shimmering trail out over the surface of the bay. The light traveled across the overhead canopy, flinging streamers of gold through the shadowy emeralds of evergreens and poplars. The air carried up from the ground the dichotomous perfume of flowering plants and decaying rot.

Decatur popped another M&M into his mouth.

Forty.

He crunched into the addictive sweetness.

Yep, no doubt about it. Another flawless morning in Resurrection Bay.

PART TWO

Three Years Later
July 3, 1992

The world breaks everyone, and afterward, many are strong at the broken places.

—*Ernest Hemingway*

All human evil comes from a single cause, man's inability to sit still in a room.

—*Blaise Pascal*

TWO

"YOU KNOW, DECK, I could arrest you on a Code Seven-Two."

"S…s…s…seven-Two?" asked Decatur Kaiser, filled with a mix of dread and trepidation.

"Forging artwork," replied Sarge.

A huge smile of relief floated across Decatur's face. "Looks like we have us another winner, huh?"

"I'd say!" said Sarge.

Like a lot of downtown Anchorage, the Heaven Scent Bakery and Soda Fountain at the corner of Ninth Avenue and Ingra was a living piece of the dying past. For the last three years, the locals had depended on the small bakery for everything from morning bagels and donuts to after-school egg creams and cupcakes.

The Optimist Sees the Donut, boasted the hand-written sign taped to the front window, *The Pessimist Sees the Hole.*

Inside, between black-and-white checkered linoleum squares and overhead banks of fluorescents shedding their hollow glow, Sergeant Dick "Sarge" Turnbull was studying Decatur Kaiser's face.

Or, anyway, half of his face, which was all he could see from where he was standing behind the counter. People's faces, Sarge had noticed over the years, were for the most part symmetrical, so it didn't make any real difference. You saw one side of a person, you saw them all. But with Decatur, something was … *askew*.

That was the word, something a little out of line, out of kilter. Just a little off.

And it wasn't just the pockmarks, the residue of what was obviously a terrible case of adolescent acne. Maybe it was just his overactive imagination, but for some reason beyond his comprehension Decatur's face actually seemed more asymmetrical each time he visited his small, but thriving bakery. In his twenty-three years on the Anchorage police department, dealing with everyone from prostitutes to parents, politicians to families, criminals to friends, he had never come across it before.

What he did see was a likeable-puppy-dog of a man in his early thirties who looked as though he'd been manufactured to fit his name. A little below average height. Brownish hair. Pale white skin. Black Buddy Holly coke-bottle-thick glasses. He reminded Sarge of Rick Moranis in the remake of *Little Shop of Horrors*.

Decatur Kaiser was … just there.

An oldie but goodie blared out from wall speakers, taking him out of his reverie. Hurricane Smith. "Oh Babe, What Would You Say?"

Listening to the offbeat riff, Sarge looked out the window behind Decatur. Even though he was born and bred in Anchorage, he never tired of the breathtaking view of his city—a glittering gem nestled in the green and white circular cathedral of the Chugach Mountains. The view took in downtown Anchorage to across the

Knik Arm, where the Alaska Range saw-toothed across the horizon. A little to the northwest, Mount Susitna—"The Sleeping Lady"— jutted up into the clear afternoon sky.

Sarge broke off his gaze as Decatur pushed an enormous cake across the counter toward him. He shook his head, smiling. "I'm telling you, Deck, it's a work of art!"

The mammoth cake was indeed a beauty—expertly decorated in colored icing to mirror the same spectacular view of Anchorage surrounded by a ring of green and white mountains that was presenting itself behind Decatur. Flowery letters screamed out in pink icing:

Happy Birthday Sunny
Welcome to Alaska

Decatur boxed the cake carefully. He pointed through the transparent insert on the top of the box. "Take a look at the border, Sarge." Decatur pointed to small clusters of marzipan flowers in colorful blue, white and yellow icing surrounding the cake's edges.

"Forget-me-nots! Perfect!"

"Just icing on the cake," Decatur replied.

Sarge laughed and groaned at the same time. Decatur, he knew, was proud of his reputation as the King of Corn.

"You've got to tell me your secret. How do you do all this?"

"Ah, you caught me, Sarge, I do have a secret," he confessed. Even though there was no one else in the bakery, he leaned in close toward him. "There's a piece of me in everything I bake."

He gave Sarge a winning grin.

Asymmetric, but charming, nevertheless.

Sarge laughed for a moment, then just as suddenly turned serious.

Decatur's face darkened as he saw the look on Sarge's face. "P...p...problem?" he nervously stuttered. "You got that worried-face look."

Sarge solemnly replied, "Problem is, Deck, I don't know if we should eat it or frame it."

"Well...might find it doggone hard to hang it up on a wall like a trophy." He beamed, then added, "Hope your granddaughter likes it."

"Are you kidding me!? Sunny's going to love it. I mean, they both are, Sunny and her mother! Even though I've got to tell you, just between us, my daughter is having a little trouble adjusting to being back here in the 'Beyond Your Dream' state."

"Tell you what. The birthday girl is what? Thirteen?"

"Yep. Going on thirty."

"Well, you tell Sunny and her mother they are always welcome here for a cup of hot chocolate, a glazed donut, and a listening ear. First visit's always on the house. And I promise not to bore them with any of my hunting stories."

"You know, Deck, I think they could both use that. I'll tell them."

"Just remember," added Decatur, handing him the boxed cake, "every new beginning comes from some other beginning's end."

"You got that right," said Sarge pulling out his wallet. "What's the damage here, Deck?"

Decatur pulled out a large box of donuts from under the counter. "On the house, Sarge, if you don't mind doing me a favor. I'm on vacation all next week and I was gonna take these over for the guys at the station. Would you mind, save me a doggone trip?"

"Hey, you're doing me a solid. And it's on my way."

"Lookit, I've got a half-dozen M&M cupcakes over here," said Decatur checking his counters. "Might as well take them with you and keep the donuts company."

Sarge looked at the M&M covered cupcakes and balked for a moment. "No, no, we're good … the donuts are enough to keep us busy for a while."

"Hey, they're still fresh. Hate to see them go to waste."

"Thanks, Deck, but I'm good to go."

"That's you, Sarge, always on the go. When you thinking of taking a vacation?"

"Yeah, right! That'll be the day. You doing some hunting, are ya?"

"You betcha."

"Well, good luck with that."

Sarge couldn't resist. He dug into the box of donuts, pulled one out and took a big bite. "Damn, Deck, I'm telling you, these are the best donuts ever."

"Hey, I'm like the Colonel—it's those eleven secret herbs and spices." Decatur grinned from ear to ear. "It's the fizz that does the bizz."

Sarge grabbed the cake and box of donuts and walked toward the door. Another of Decatur's homemade signs hanging in the window caught his attention. It read:

Closed Until July 10
Remember 7 Days Without Pastries Makes One Weak

"There you go again, Sarge," said Decatur. "You got your worried face back on."

"Just wondering," replied Sarge, "what the boys at the station are going to do for the next week."

"Just tell 'em they're gonna have to honker down and enjoy the deliciousness now. I'll be back soon enough."

Sarge opened the door to the recorded strain of the Beatles crooning 'A Taste of Honey' and left. He turned. "Catch ya' later."

That'll be the day, thought Decatur.

He grinned, his thin lips stretching from one side of his face to the other. *You enjoy those eleven secret herbs and spices.*

Outside, Sarge lingered a moment to admire the display pastries in the window, then walked past the building next to Decatur's. On the southeast corner of Ninth Avenue and Ingra, stood a boxlike wooden structure with a tile façade. It had been a Laundromat once, but now it was vacant. A dusty "For Rent" sign hung forlornly in the window.

Back in the bakery, Decatur waved through the window once again at Sarge. He smirked, feeling quite smug and sure of himself. He was, after all, a man of his word.

There *was* a piece of himself in everything he baked. Just this morning at five A.M., he'd stood in front of his industrial mixer back in the kitchen and masturbated into the cake batter, the same dough he'd baked into the cake he'd just given Sarge.

"*The jizz that does the bizz,*" he whispered.

Smiling at his private joke, Decatur glanced at the wall clock.

5:15 p.m.

Closing time.

Just as Decatur started to lock up for the week, a distinguished-looking, middle-aged man rushed to the door.

The man, a bit winded, entered the bakery. An ID badge clipped to his jacket identified him as WILLIAM JOSEPH, M.D./PROVIDENCE ALASKA MEDICAL HOSPITAL

Decatur looked up from behind the counter. "Hi ya', Doc."

"Hey, Deck, I was afraid I'd miss you. My wife is making her famous call to the Mexican place so it's my night to pick up dessert. Any prognosis?"

Decatur pointed toward some intricately decorated cupcakes. "Well ... I know Julie likes the White Mountain Chocolate and Tommie's favorite seems to be the Spotted Turtles."

"Deck, I think you know my kids better than I do! Okay, give me a mixed dozen."

"Well, this seems to be a stopping off place after school," said Decatur boxing the cupcakes. "I know Julie is going to be seven soon and Tommie is what ... five is it?"

"On the nose," said the doctor.

Decatur smiled.

Five years old.

What a kick in the ass.

He had shoplifted for the first time when he was five. A five-cent Batman ring with a circular decoder dial. Impossible not to have if you were a five-year-old boy. Without thinking twice, Decatur had simply slipped the ring on his finger and walked out of the five and dime.

The feeling of walking past the woman at the cash register was euphoric, as close to orgasmic as he could come at that age.

It was an epiphany.

He could have anything he wanted and he could have an orgasm for getting it. How could you lose with that combo? Anything he wanted. Whenever he wanted. The world was his oyster. But not the gray slimy kind. This truly was the pot-of-gold-over-the-rainbow kind.

"How are those pills working out for ya'?" asked Dr. Joseph, ushering Decatur back into the present. "We tried the Ambien, right?"

"Yeah, those bad boys work perfect. One pill and I'm out in five minutes. But, like I told you, I only take them when I get a sore throat.

Never could sleep with a scratchy throat." He scooted the box of cupcakes across the counter. "There you go, Doc, just what the donut ordered. Say hi to Katherine and the kiddos."

Dr. Joseph paid, then made his way to the door. Stopped.

"Something w … w … w … wrong?" asked Decatur.

"Just thinking that the trouble with eating anything from here is that five or six days later you're hungry all over again."

Before leaving, he looked up and noticed a small blackboard on the wall. In Decatur's self-effacing, King-of-Corn style, he had written in white chalk:

Buy Our Bread Cakes
I Knead the Dough

"Don't we all?" observed the doctor as he opened the door to the recorded strains of "A Taste of Honey."

What he failed to notice as he left the bakery was that the ID badge on his jacket was no longer there.

THREE

THE NEW AND IMPROVED Sue of the big Blue Zoo ...

Who looks outside, dreams.

Who looks inside, awakes.

Slip into the mind of one of the smartest men who ever lived—in this case she was thinking of Carl Jung—and you'd have a mind so clean you could picnic off it (as her father would say), but when you came out, you'd want to take one long, hot delousing shower. It's so easy to come up with an aphorism, she thought, I mean how hard is that? It's only putting one word after another. But to live it, to make it matter in your life ... that was quite a different beast.

In fact, her father once countered her Jung with his Marx. "Outside of a dog, a book is a man's best friend. Inside of a dog it's too dark to read." Groucho, of course, not Karl.

Who looks outside, dreams.

Who looks inside, awakes.

Outside?

Outside, it was a perfect Magritte afternoon.

Ocean blue skies with bone-white clouds of fluff. Maple trees everywhere, more emerald than green. Perennial flowers exploding the landscape all around in full Technicolor bloom.

The rising mercury in the weathered John Deere window thermometer peaked in the mid sixties. It was the first week of July and the wintertime snows were a thing of the temporal past. Up above, an autobahn of birds chirped, tweeted and cawed their way across the deep blue sky.

It was summertime in Alaska.

A state that has more caribou than people, Sue Turnbull mused, sliding two large frozen pineapple pizzas into the preheated oven. She squeaked the oven door shut and walked over to the window, which in the confines of her one-bedroom trailer required less than three short steps. She drew back the flowered curtain and leaned her hand on the broken latch on the top sash. She felt the grime and dust on the window sill, looked down and saw the shriveled corpses of a few small, dead, unidentifiable insects. She jerked her hand back, wiped it clean on a dish towel, then sat down at the kitchen table and looked outside.

She gazed out at the quintet of mountain ranges that cupped Cook Inlet and Anchorage in an enormous horseshoe, separating them from the five hundred thousand square miles of Alaska on the other side. Sue had read somewhere that forty percent of the state's population was packed into the 159 square miles of the Anchorage bowl.

Opening the window to let in some fresh air, there was one tacit agreement about Anchorage, Sue thought: every view was a perfect view.

She let go of the window and took the three steps back to the oven.

Inside?

Inside the one-bedroom trailer, Sue was trying hard to put the finishing touches on a perfect day. The one thing she held sacred now was the fact that birthdays should be as perfect as possible, especially since her one and only daughter Sunny was turning thirteen today. This was the one day of the year that everything should go right; in fact, it was the one day of the year that she was going to make *sure* it would go right.

Sue looked up from the cramped combination kitchen and dining room area of the trailer, past the island and at Sunny and her four newest girlfriends having a birthday slumber party in the adjoining living room. The girls, already changed into pajamas and socks, had opened the pullout couch, where Sue slept, and covered the remaining floor space with colorful sleeping bags.

Sue allowed herself the luxury of simply gazing out at the girls for a few moments. Sunny had been the biggest surprise of her life, and she wasn't just referring to the surprise pregnancy that brought Sunny into the world. The real surprise had been how much she had grown to love her daughter, to marvel at her, to stand in amazement at how Sunny approached and savored every moment of life. They had been in the rented trailer less than a month, and already Sunny had made instant—and probably lifelong—friends.

I could have never done that, Sue thought, before she broke off and turned back to her work.

Behind her, Sunny, Chris, Roxanne, Mona, and Debbie dabbed on makeup and polished fingernails while Def Leppard's *Pyromania* spun to the next track on the turntable. "Die Hard the Hunter."

Chris tried to play along on a portable Casio keyboard, only making the odd song sound even odder.

"Oh, turn it up! Turn it up!" shouted Mona, pretty in plaid, elegantly ensconced in an arm chair, a princess on her throne. "I was listening to this song last summer in Boston when my Walkman ate my tape!"

"Oh, my God, I'm telling you, Boston is cursed!" blurted out Debbie, shooting up from the pullout couch, digging into a bowl of potato chips. "It's that whole Lizzie Borden thing."

Sue picked up the Polaroid Land Camera from the kitchen table and aimed it toward the living room. She squeezed off a shot.

"Mom, a little privacy please!" pleaded an embarrassed Sunny.

"Like that's going to happen here in the Blue Zoo!' replied Sue.

"Mo-om!" protested Sunny.

Who looks outside, dreams.

Who looks inside, awakes.

The Blue Zoo.

After leaving Seattle a month before, Sue had found the cheapest best place she could afford in Anchorage—a trailer park off Pago Pago Avenue called the Manoogs Isle Mobile Home Park. For whatever reason, the entire motley collection of refurbished trailers had been painted the same dull shade of blue. The name Blue Zoo was soon applied to the trailer park and the name stuck.

Sue ripped the photo out of the camera and held it under her armpit for a thirty-Mississippi count.

Sue remembered once seeing a photograph of a very young Marilyn Monroe in a chorus line with maybe thirty other young women. She couldn't remember the name of the movie, but she always remembered that photo because of all those dancers, one jumped out, literally screamed out, of the photo: Marilyn Monroe.

Same with Sunny, thought Sue looking at the Polaroid.

But Sunny didn't leap.

She soared.

Sunny, like her mother, was strikingly beautiful. Five foot two with eyes of blue. Midwest corn-blonde hair that swept around the smooth curves of her face catching the late afternoon sunlight and shadow, her eyes alive, all full of mischief mixed with intelligence. She was one of those quietly beautiful girls who never have to draw attention to themselves because attention comes of its own accord.

"Sunny" had proved to be a perfect name for her daughter; her zest for life was irrepressible. She was popular and did well in school, interested in creative writing, history, journalism, and, without saying, boys. Good in gymnastics and a whiz at volleyball, she excelled in dance and ballet. Sue Turnbull couldn't be more proud of her daughter or love her anymore. Yet she always found a way the next day.

Sunny was her rock, her compass.

That was Sunny.

Thirteen. A teenager.

Tough and beautiful, she could do no wrong.

Sue, on the other hand, found it increasingly difficult to do anything right.

Sue had just turned twenty-nine a month earlier and up to that time the one word that summed up her life would be *despair*.

Before despair hit her, trouble did. A troubled teenager, she'd run away from home and gotten pregnant at seventeen. The boy who got her pregnant became one with the wind the minute he heard the news. Joined the navy or something. Sue was never sure. She never heard from him again.

Sue didn't want an abortion, never entertained the thought. She ended up in a group home. It was heaven. She had Sunny, a roof over her head and three squares a day. She tried working. Flipping burgers, waitressing, working the counter at a 7-Eleven.

She could keep Sunny away from the Welfare people, but she couldn't give her the things she wanted. They don't call it minimum wage for nothing.

Then she saw an ad in the paper and tried dancing at a club.

The money was good. Real good. Sue moved to a better place; she could afford dance lessons for Sunny, got her a string of great babysitters.

It was pretty clean, all things considered. There was no sex involved, unlike some of the other dancers who made some special arrangements for after the show. You danced on a stage, maybe wiggled around in a few laps, got the customers to buy a few drinks. Went home. Took a long, hot shower. Counted your money. More than enough to pay the rent for a couple of weeks. Not too bad for one night's work.

Then she'd gotten the call from the Providence Medical Hospital in Anchorage telling her that her father had acute appendicitis. Perhaps more surprising than the call, was the fact that he still listed his wayward daughter as his emergency contact.

Sue didn't hesitate a second. She packed up all of their belongings, which took about a half hour, and moved to the first place she could afford in Anchorage—the Blue Zoo.

Looking at the girls in the living room, she thought *Nothing is going to keep this day from being perfect.*

Who looks outside, dreams.

Who looks inside, awakes.

The sound of crunching gravel caused Sue to look out the window.

Outside her father was pulling into the driveway. Sgt. Dick "Sarge" Turnbull. Sarge got out of his cruiser carrying the largest birthday cake Sue had ever seen.

Perfect, she thought.

Sue ripped the blue trailer door open.

She was greeted with a white bakery box of mythic proportions, a bouquet of flowers of matching magnitude, and the world's warmest grin.

Juggling each was her silent fortress. Her father.

A winning smile instantly necklaced across Sue's face.

"You know, I was hoping you'd get the really big cake," she beamed. "I mean, how's my butt going to get any bigger with this little Twinkie?"

She gave Sarge a kiss on the cheek.

"Well, one of us has to be the responsible adult here." Stepping inside, he was assaulted by the music. He took in the five girls sprawled out in the living room, then gave them his best heavy-metal-evil-eye hand salute. "Hi, Ladies! Whoa, Def Leotards. Great group! Party hearty on."

All five girls rolled their eyes.

Sue led Sarge into the kitchen where he carefully set the cake box on the table.

"Oh, much better in here, decibel-ly speaking," smiled Sarge.

Sue returned the smile, then opened the bakery box and looked inside. "Sarge, this is the most amazing cake I've ever seen in my life!"

"That's good, 'cuz I was going for 'amazing'. And these," he said, handing Sue the bouquet of flowers bursting with blue petals, white inner rings and yellow centers, "are for you."

"Oh, my God I can't believe you remembered these! They're my favorite!"

"I remember! Forget-Me-Nots. The Alaskan state flower. They go with the welcome back theme!"

"I can't thank you enough for helping me put all this together. I mean, I come all this way to help you and look who's doing all the help—"

"'Nuff said," grinned Sarge, reaching into a kitchen cabinet. "C'mon, I'll help you with the drink detail."

"Already taken care of. They're swilling down Diet Coke like rock stars in rehab."

Sarge closed the cabinet and turned to watch Sue fill a large vase with water. She gently fit the flowers into the vase and arranged them.

Suddenly, she turned and looked her father straight in the eye. "I feel like my life is turning into a train wreck. On second thought, comparing it to a train wreck isn't really fair to train wrecks, because some people actually want to watch those."

She tried a smile. Failed.

"Somewhere along the ladder of time I lost the bright-eyed, bushy-tailed best of me." She took a deep breath, then faced her father. "I swear, Sarge, when Sunny and I get a real place I'll pay you back for all the—"

"Would you chill? Your tail looks as ... well, I won't go there, but you look as bright-eyed as ever. And you've only been back less than a month."

"I know, it's just that I can be such a dummkopf sometimes—"

"'Dummkopf!" Sarge grinned broadly. "You still remember that from—"

"—Watching *Hogan's Heroes* with you when I was Sunny's age and eating pretzels and drinking root beer! Oh! Remember what show came on after Hogan?"

"Course, I remember. *Mission Impossible!*"

Sarge and Sue did their "routine" as if Sue was thirteen again. Together, in their deepest Peter Graves imitation, they chanted, "They don't call it Mission Difficult, do they? No! That's why they call it *Mission Impossible!*"

They both laughed fondly.

"Man, those were the good ol' days, huh?" reflected Sue.

"No, Sweetheart, these are the good ol' days. I'm just glad you finally got yourself and Sunny back up here. From now on, everything's going to be fine. You have my word on that."

Sarge looked at the refrigerator door. Along with a few classified ads, the door was saturated with photographs. His gaze stopped on one particular photo, a fading snapshot from years ago.

Her mother. Leilani. The aging photo revealed a forever youthful, truly stunning, drop-dead gorgeous woman. She may well have been the most beautiful woman in the world. In Sarge's eyes, she always had been. And now, looking at Sue, he saw where she came from.

Other photos showed Sue in different dancing attire and poses —ballet, jazz, modern. But most showed Sunny growing up, morphing from a beautiful baby into a beautiful young woman.

Sarge nodded toward the photos. "Time to start a batch of new memories, wouldn't you say?"

"I'd say. And, trust me, I'm here to stay this time."

"Speaking of staying, are you sure you can't stay tonight? Nothing says 'a good night's rest' like five teen-age girls on a sleep-over."

"I honestly wish I could, Sarge, but if I don't come up with two hundred bucks for rent by the end of the week, Sunny and I are going to be having sleepovers on the street."

Sarge started to say something.

"And no!" interrupted Sue. "Charity is not an option. I've been tripping over my own two feet for twelve years all by myself. I really have to do this on my own."

Sarge tapped a finger on a newspaper article taped to the refrigerator door. "That's why first thing tomorrow morning, young lady, we're getting you a new job. Got that?"

Sue smiled. "It's a deal. And I promise to brush after each meal." She hesitated a moment, then added softly, "Know what I'm thinking about?"

"Another one of your scathingly brilliant ideas?"

Sue coquettishly nodded yes. "Opening a small dance studio. Teach ballroom, ballet, swing, modern."

Sarge's eyes suddenly lit up. "My gosh, Sue, you're not going to believe this!"

"Believe what?"

"I know the perfect place!"

"Where?"

"Saw it today. There's a vacant store next door to the best bakery in town."

"Next to a bakery, huh? Perfect! Guess I could call it ...'Dance Your Buns Off'."

"Catchy!"

"Or 'Arthur Murray's Dance & Danishes'. Or 'Fred Astaire's & Chocolate Eclairs'. Or maybe—"

"Uh, Sweetheart ... I think you nailed it with the first one. Oh, by the way, the owner of the bakery ... his name is Decatur. He's looking forward to meeting you and Sunny."

"Looking at his handiwork here," Sue said, glancing at the cake, "we can't wait to meet him either."

There was an awkward silence, then Sarge asked, "Speaking of all this dancing—"

"Uh-oh, here it comes."

"Well, a dad has to ask. This dancing you're doing tonight? Like what you did in Seattle—"

"It's just dancing, Dad. I danced three nights a week there and it paid the rent for the rest of the week. Hard to turn that kind of money down. Plus it allowed me to spend more time with Sunny."

"Just gotta remember, Ms. Goodbar, this isn't Seattle anymore. The days are shorter, the nights are longer—"

Sue laughed. "And the men are men and the sheep are very afraid."

"Yeah, well, something like that."

Sarge looked toward Sunny and the girls partying in the next room through the kitchen partition. "You know, Sue, if there's such a thing as reincarnation, I want to come back as Sunny."

Sarge grinned, then, still looking at Sunny in the living room, slowly turned somber. "Just keep in mind—things have changed here in the last ten years. It can be really rough on a person. You don't watch out, you can really lose someone up here."

"Oh, don't worry about Sunny. She can take care of herself."

Sarge took his eyes off Sunny and looked at Sue. "It isn't Sunny I'm worried about."

———

Sunny opened Sarge's gift last.

"Hey, Princess, I believe there's one more." Sue handed Sunny an oblong box wrapped in pink. "It's from Sarge."

"Oh, Sarge, you didn't have to—" started Sunny, reading the card.

"Okay," replied Sarge, grabbing the present out of Sunny's hands.

"No, no, I'll force myself this time," cried Sunny.

"Force away, Sweet Pea," said Sarge, handing her the present. He smiled, wanting to impart some learned, sagacious wisdom of the day. "Do you realize that at any given moment, you're as old as you've ever been?"

Without missing a beat, Sunny saw his adage and raised him an aphorism, "Do you realize that at any given moment, you're as young as you'll ever be?"

Sarge laughed. "Touché, my little Miss Einstein. Happy Birthday."

Sunny carefully peeled back the pink paper from the oblong box with the skill of a spinal surgeon. She opened the box and her eyes became two saucers.

"OHMYGOSH … It's beautiful!" gushed Sunny. "I mean— they're beautiful!"

Sunny's friends "Ooh'd" and "Ahh'd" as she held the gift up for everyone to see. A bedazzling gold Mizpah pendant seemed to supernova from the overhead light. The pendant, the size of a dollar coin, was cut into two halves. Both pendants hung from long, elegant gold chains.

Sarge proudly pointed at the pendants. "One of those is yours and the other is your mother's. See on the back there? Your mother's name is engraved on your half and your name is engraved on her half."

Sunny, beaming, put her half around her neck. The other half around her mother's.

"Now," continued Sarge, "when you put them together, it reads from Genesis 31:49."

Sue and Sunny connected the two halves, then read the inscription softly together. "'The Lord watch between me and thee when we are apart one from another.'"

Sunny hugged her mother and Sarge for all they're worth. "Thanks, Sarge, just what I wanted."

Sarge leaned in toward her, lowered his voice just enough to shut out all the guests. "I've got one other present for you. I want you to always remember, if you ever need someone to talk to … if not as a grandfather, then as an old friend … well, that, Sweetie, is my other present."

Sunny beamed. "Thank you, Sarge."

Sue tapped her glass with a dessert fork and said, "A toast."

"Here, here," piped in Sarge.

"To my daughter on her thirteenth birthday!"

"Oh, gosh, here we go," said a suddenly embarrassed Sunny.

"May she learn the value of an uncluttered room and an organized mind, and may she realize that when it comes to stuffing the toilet bowl with apple cores, that Mom does sometimes know best."

"Mo-o-om!" cried Sunny. "I did that once when I was, like, little!"

"May she always stay true to her loving, caring, and giving heart. And though today she's officially a teenager, may a part of her stay my Baby Doll forever."

Sunny gazed up at her mother. There was love in her eyes.

"Happy birthday, Sweetie," said Sue. "Now let's lug that mother of a cake out here."

The girls laughed as Sue checked her watch.

"Oh, shoot, I have to leave now!"

"Not yet," said Sarge as he lowered the lights and began playing 'Happy Birthday' on the portable Casio piano. He played with gusto and he played beautifully. A couple of girls entered the living room carrying the oversized cake blazing with thirteen sparkling candles.

Sue, Sarge, and the girls began to belt out "Happy Birthday."

"Are ya' ten, are you eleven, are ya' twelve, are ya' thirteen?"

When they finished, Sue turned to her daughter, "Go ahead, Sweetie, make a wish."

Sunny thought for a moment, then closed her eyes and blew out the candles. All thirteen.

With big doe-like eyes, she looked up at her mother. "I wished you didn't work nights, I wished you worked days like a normal mom."

Sarge studied Sue for a moment, clearly concerned.

A passing look of despair and guilt etched its way across her face, but Sue quickly covered it and presented a brave front for her daughter. "Ah, Sweetie, you're not supposed to tell a wish or it won't come true. Save me a piece of cake when I get back, okay?"

Sue grabbed a light jacket and on her way out picked up a pack of Kool Menthols off the island and stuck them in her purse.

Sarge walked her to the door as the girls all said their goodbyes.

"I should be home by six. You can let them stay up as late as you want," said Sue.

"Like they would listen to me anyway," smiled Sarge. "You just be careful. I don't want to wait another ten years to see you."

"Don't you worry about me, I'm not going anywhere. And if you get hungry, I'm pretty sure there's some cake around here somewhere."

Sue smiled, then shut the door behind her, only to open it a second later. Sticking her head back in, she said, "I just thought of something."

"What's that?" asked Sarge.

"It's kinda corny, but it's true."

"I can deal with kinda corny."

Sue beamed her most sincere smile at her father. "You put the 'anchor' in Anchorage."

"Yeah, yeah, yeah, I love you, too."

And with that, Sue closed the door and was gone.

Unable to resist a smile, Sarge shook his head and locked the door behind her.

He looked at the girls in the living room having the time of their lives. Then his glance came to a rest on a newspaper classified ad section taped to the refrigerator door. Several secretarial jobs were circled in red. One distinctive ad that wasn't circled screamed out:

$$$ Earn Big Money Fast $$$
Dancers wanted immediately
Flexible hours
Full & part time
Call Mon.–Sat. From 12–8
No experience needed

In the living room, smoke swirled in midair above the birthday cake. Lingered over Sunny.

Ghostlike.

FOUR

The speckled-granite marquee on green grass gleamed:

Godisnowhere
Now Read It Again

Twenty minutes after closing his bakery, Decatur pulled his Jeep Renegade into the parking lot of the First Methodist Church. He turned off the engine and checked his hair in the rear view.

Decatur's Renegade, like his bakery, was immaculately clean. It had that "just bought" look and smell year round. Like his hair, not a thing out of place. He reached over to the driver's seat and grabbed a large bag full of donuts.

A mahogany echo greeted a rusty shadow as Decatur entered the front doors of the Methodist Church. He made his way down the nave, across the sanctuary, past the Sunday school rooms, and into a large kitchen area tucked into the back. Opening an overhead cabinet as if he was in his own kitchen, he pulled out a couple of large Tupperware containers and began stuffing them with donuts.

Ron Knott, the pastor, entered with an empty coffee cup. Decatur continued to add donuts to containers as Ron walked over to the coffee maker and asked, "Hey, Deck, how you doing?" Pouring himself a cup, he added, "Coffee?"

"Thanks, Ron, but I've got to get the family to the airport by ten. Just dropped by to tell you that I can't teach my Sunday School class this weekend. I've talked with Dale Hubbard, he said he'd cover for me. That okay with you?"

"No problem at all."

"Good, good. And I wanted to get you all squared away with donuts for while I'm gone. Oh! That reminds me, Hunter can't wait for Danny's bowling birthday party. But he did want me to ask you for a birthday present suggestion."

"One word—anything 'Transformers'. You know those robots in disguise things? They look like one thing, but change into something else? Can't go wrong there."

"'Transformers', huh. Thanks, I'll tell Hunter."

Ron took a bite out of a donut. "You know, I think my parishioners come more for your donuts than for my sermons."

Decatur looked up with his 'ah-shucks' face and answered, "Always nice to be welcomed with open Psalms."

"Hey, that's not half-bad. Can I use that sometime?"

"All yours, no charge."

"Guess you're hunting this weekend?"

"Yep."

"Well, good luck with that. Practice makes perfect … You be careful what you practice …"

"You know me, Ron. I'm always careful." Decatur left as Ron put the Tupperware containers inside the refrigerator.

"Transformers," confirmed Decatur at the door.

"Transformers," Ron nodded around a mouthful of donut.

On his way out of the church, Decatur took special care that no one saw him enter the supply room.

Timothy 3:16. God works in mysterious ways, thought Decatur, as he shoved a twenty-pound Worthington propane tank and a canary yellow, ten-gallon plastic can filled with diesel fuel surreptitiously into the back of his Renegade. *Ask and ye shall receive. Luke 11:9.*

Decatur took Luke for his word. For one thing, Decatur simply hated to pay good money for anything. But mainly, it was for the thrill. It was the same thrill he got with a stripper. Decatur recognized these pathological addictions and accepted them. He just had to control them so that he wouldn't end up in prison. What was the point of that?

Just *ask and ye shall receive.*

Decatur opened the door of the Renegade and got behind the wheel, a wet stain slowly growing across the front of his pants. He turned the engine on. Looked at the church. Smiled.

Yep, that fuckin' Timothy had nothing on Luke.

FIVE

As the sundown slowly paled the sky, Sue twirled the radio dial trying to find signs of intelligent life as she drove her sputtering Kia north along Arctic Boulevard.

Somewhere (*was it in San Francisco?*) she had seen a poster that presented the steps of evolution in terms of a tree chart. At the apex of the chart was Einstein, followed by Newton, Michelangelo, Edison, Picasso, and underneath was the rest of humanity. Then came Neanderthal and Cro-Magnon men, followed by Dan Quayle, Milli Vanilli, and various animals and reptiles until the tree ended with a single cell amoeba from the primordial soup. And at the very bottom, underneath it all, was ... the car she was driving ... a candy-apple red Kia she'd bought salvage after a wreck.

If that wasn't enough, on the radio Jim Morrison was forlornly lamenting blissful realms in "End of the Night." Nice cautionary tale, Jimbo and William Blake, thought Sue, but then one of you dudes ended up dying in a bathtub. Guess you should have listened to your own advice and kept your eyes on the road and your hands upon the wheel.

Sue flipped the radio station from the Doors back to a talk station. "… continuing to celebrate our nation's birthday all week, I'm looking for the thirteenth caller who can tell me which American Revolutionary War hero regretted having but one life to give to his country?"

Applying makeup in the waning light, Sue indifferently answered, "Who was Nathan Hale?"

She took a deep breath, thinking that her only ghost of a true regret was in disappointing her father by what she had done to her mother all those years ago.

It wasn't until she was older, maybe ten or eleven, that Sarge told Sue that he had met her mother at a nightclub. He had just gotten off a sixteen-hour shift and stopped in for a beer. The club's owner announced a new, vivacious talent with an exotic Hawaiian name that, he informed the crowd, meant "heavenly flower."

Leilani.

The owner pronounced it slowly, lyrically … *lay-LAH-nee.*

As Sarge was rolling the name around and over his tongue, a spotlight hit the stage.

And then, he saw her.

Breathless. In an instant, all the air seemed to be sucked out of the room. Time stopped.

The spill from the spotlight haloed Leilani's long, luxuriant blonde hair.

Blonde hell, that didn't do it justice. Spun as gold, like sunshine on honey.

Then the damndest thing happened. Leilani's eyes met Sarge's.

And then the second damndest thing happened. Her eyes stayed there.

In that moment, they found an island in each other's smile, a country in each other's eyes.

As time regained its inevitable momentum, Leilani floated up to the top tier of the stage when one of her heels suddenly stuck, then broke off, in between one of the cheaply constructed steps. Not missing a beat, she had calmly, elegantly, walked to the microphone in the center of the stage, continued to make eye contact with Sarge, then belted out the best version of "Downtown" Sarge had ever heard.

It was love at first note.

Not long after they were married it was Sarge's idea to buy a chunk of studio time for Leilani to record a demo tape.

The plan was to cut the demo right after Sue's birth.

———

Sue eased the Kia right on Northern Lights Boulevard and headed west.

It was true. Her only ghost of a true regret was in disappointing her father.

Leilani never recorded the demo.

Sue killed her before she had the chance.

SIX

ANTLERS IN THE CEILING by Hugh Goose D. Moose. *Mad Magazine* had an article back in the late '70s that listed the top 100 books never written.

Antlers In the Ceiling by Hugh Goose D. Moose made it to number two. It was damned funny in the sixth grade and it was damned funny today, smiled Decatur as he made a left onto Creekwood Drive. At the end of the cul-de-sac, he pulled his Renegade up to a posh, two-story, ranch-style house overlooking distant glimmering mountains. He parked in front on the Bible-black asphalt driveway of the two-car garage as the sunset turned opal over Anchorage.

Above him, an expansive rack of moose antlers from his second favorite all-time kill loomed over the garage door.

Antlers In the Ceiling. Still a fuckin' pisser.

Unlocking the garage door, Decatur kicked the dirt from his boots, more out of habit than anything else. Checking both soles and satisfied they were clean, he walked inside, carrying two donut bags.

He locked the door behind him and turned on the overhead lights to reveal the world's neatest garage.

The interior of the garage was a large space, orderly and efficiently saturated with the accumulation of a lifetime. The garage had never been used to park vehicles. Instead, it was painstakingly packed from floor to ceiling, wall to wall, with…stuff.

Besides the palpable neatness, what made this garage different from other garages used for storage throughout America, was that there were at least two of everything.

Puke-green metal shelves lined every available wall, packed to the point of collapsing. Two chain saws, seven stereos, five televisions, numerous VCRs, cameras, lawn mowers, gas grills with propane tanks, snow skis, boots, poles, storage boxes, toys, games, tool kits, jigsaws, cordless drills, grinders, wet/dry vacs, a couple of cross country dirt bikes, go-carts, two three-wheeler ATVs, their seat covers missing, showing bare patches of discolored foam, a half-dozen ten-speed bicycles.

More of a warehouse, than a garage.

And lining one entire wall was a long work bench and various cabinets with all sorts of equipment and supplies for reloading ammunition, including both RCBS and Lee reloading presses, primers, brass casings, heavy metal jacket bullets, FFFG gunpowder, and calipers.

What really excited Decatur each time he entered his garage was the fact that of all the items in his domain, the ones he had actually paid for he could count on one hand. This afternoon, what excited him even more was the box of 5.56mm reloads he had expertly finished first thing that morning.

He selected twenty bullets from the box.

He cherished the feel of the cold steel in his hand, relished the way they metallically clinked against one another. Magic to the touch. Music to the ear.

Lovingly, he slipped the bullets into his pocket.

Lovingly, because he knew that within the next twenty-four hours one of the chunks of lead embedded in the bullet's business end would claim his next trophy.

Decatur took a last look around the psychotically over-organized garage. He had learned neatness and order from his adopted parents. He had never known his biological mother. She had given him up at birth, for reasons that he would never know.

And if he ever found her, he'd make a special bullet just for her.

Turning off the garage light, Decatur entered a small hallway that took him into his living room. The room was dark except for a faint spill of light from the adjoining hallway. The living room, like every room in the house, was extremely neat and showed his wife's love of the homey artifact. Typical of her style, the room was ornate, damask-and-mahogany, thick and warm and ripe. To either side of the red brick fireplace were bookshelves with her collectibles—a statue of an Inuit shaman in traditional costume, a hand-carved Clipper ship, cabinets stuffed with hundreds of glass figurines, several Bibles on various tables. The walls were covered with pictures of children, Cindy's family, and of Christ.

All in all, the living room was antiseptically functional, as if to say, we have children, but they're tidy children, and they know their place. No clutter here.

Books were arranged in the book shelves by color rather than subject or content, which was okay by Decatur. Never much of a reader, he found better things to occupy his time than the pages of a book. *What's the doggone point of a story if it wasn't true*, he'd say.

To him, the problem with stories was that they made too much sense. Reality, on the other hand, never made any sense. In addition, he never understood the obsession people had with collecting books, putting them in shelves like they were trophies. *What do you need it for anyway after you've read it*, thought Decatur.

His trophy collection was much more gratifying.

TV, on the other hand, was different. TV was an electronic fireplace, that and nothing else to Decatur. Something to warm the mind, not fill it.

In fact, the TV was playing in the background now. Decatur knew this one. *The Exterminating Angel*. Public broadcasting. No one was watching. Go figure.

Of all the movies he had seen, this one had had perhaps the most lasting effect on him. But not because he liked the movie's plot or any of the actors, nor did he especially care for the theme or even the soundtrack.

It was to the way the movie was made that he most related.

Cindy had told him that the director of the movie, a Spanish surrealist artist named Luis Buñuel had shot the movie in Mexico but ran out of money midway through filming. In order to complete the movie, Buñuel came up with a novel idea. He simply repeated as many scenes as he could, scenes that he had already shot. Twenty-seven in all, if memory served him.

Decatur liked that kind of thinking. He liked it a lot. Doing things over, repeating them, until you got them right. *Perfection.* Whether it was baking a donut or carrying out his summertime project. *Perfection is what it was.*

And that Edison guy was on the fucking money. Ninety-nine percent perspiration and one percent inspiration. That's exactly what genius was. Getting it wrong until you got it right. Not giving up, not giving in. Ever. No surrender. No prisoners.

Decatur turned the TV off and a light switch on.

His orderly, controlled world was suddenly turned topsy-turvy by the casual chaos of his family life as they suddenly zipped by to and fro in a frenzy.

A small bolt of lightning streaked down the stairs and hurled past Decatur.

"Hi, Dad. Bye, Dad," said the small bolt of lightning rushing by, giving him a quick high-five. Hunter. Four years old. Blonde, precocious. Wearing an overstuffed Batman backpack.

"Whoa, there, little buddy, where's the big fire?" asked Decatur.

"No fire, Dad. Mom told me to hurry up and finish packing or she was gonna give my butt a big blisterin'."

"Okay, buddy, give me a minute and I'll give you a hand. Don't want any blistered butts today, do we?"

"Nu-uh, no way," said Hunter earnestly, then excitedly remembered something. "Oh, Dad! Morgan told me a funny joke today. Wanna hear?"

"You know it, pal."

"What color is poop?"

"I, uh ... I, I don't know. What color is poop?"

"Turd-quoise!" Hunter giggled, scrunching his shoulders together as if sharing a secret.

"Very funny, Dice Man, very funny. But I think we better keep that one to ourselves ... now, go pack, I'll be down in just a minute."

"Thanks, Dad," Hunter said, disappearing downstairs.

Decatur walked down the hall, unlocked the door to his study and entered.

Cindy, a hurricane of a woman sporting a poofy cloud of parachute ball hair, briefly flew by the opened door with all of the urgency and grace of a Category Five. In his peripheral vision, Decatur thought Cindy was carrying their 14-month-old daughter Nadia, but in the blur, he couldn't be sure. Nadia was learning to walk, but mostly she fell.

"Hey, Hon," said Decatur, "you're not going to believe what happened to me today—"

From somewhere outside the study, Cindy interrupted him, as she always did. "Decatur! ... I don't have time to hear what you did today! ... I'm way too busy packing and you're late!"

Cindy rushed past, frantically going from one room to another packing several suitcases, looking for this, packing that, talking non-stop throughout.

"Well, excuse me for talking while you're interrupting me, but—" was as far as Decatur got.

"I thought you were going to be home by six ... But not to worry, I have almost everything under control like I always do ... If you could just empty the trash before it piles up. ... This place is becoming such a pig sty ... I mean, if you can't help me with the shopping, the least you can do is clean up the place once in awhile ... Oh, I told Hunter to finish his packing or I was going to blister his butt ..." Cindy chattered on, mindlessly staccato.

"... " Decatur attempted, but failed miserably.

He merely shrugged it off with inured insouciance. Cindy was too wholeheartedly concerned with herself to be able even to simulate the slightest interest in anyone else. In fact, she had gotten to the point where she not only talked to herself constantly from morning to night, but she had recently begun answering herself so that Decatur no longer needed to respond in the first place. She answered, verbally, for him, even to the point of arguing with herself. At first, Decatur was stunned by her psychotic behavior, but soon became numbed to it.

Quietly shutting the study door, Decatur stood before a mirror on the wall, practicing his boyish grin, scrutinizing his doe-like, innocent eyes. Prepping for the night yet to come. Satisfied with the man in the mirror, he unlocked a desk drawer. Took out a tin of ginger-flavored Altoids.

All the while, Cindy continued to talk non-stop from the other rooms. "... Let's see ... I've got the passports ... The tickets ... Money ... Oh, I filled up the garbage can in the kitchen ... If you could just empty it ..."

Finally, Decatur locked his desk and went downstairs into the sanctuary of his basement den.

To anyone who came down here, it was instantaneously clear that this was Decatur's domain. The den was covered with a menagerie of glassy-eyed, icy stares. Practically every square inch of wood-paneled wall space was inundated with stuffed trophy mounts, the mounted heads of his world records—fish, Dall sheep, mountain goats, even a grizzly bear. Moose racks, caribou antlers, walrus tusks, and beaver and wolverine skins were arranged around the room. What wall space was not covered with a trophy was covered with framed photos of Decatur and his kills.

The black and white checkerboard linoleum floor, polished to a glowing sheen, was strictly utilitarian. An old red couch was hunkered up against one wall, more accustomed to holding toys and Ping-Pong paddles than people.

A black bear rug was in front of the couch, and behind it, in the center of the large basement, was a tiled area containing a Ping-Pong table and a Foosball game.

48

Along the south wall was a large wooden storage crate. The locked doors held the promise of something sacred inside. This was where Decatur kept a small cache of rifles and handguns. Enough to outfit a small army.

Lying on top was Decatur's personal favorite.

A 5.56mm Steyr Aug bullpup assault rifle.

Adopted by the Austrian Army back in the 1970s, the Steyr Aug had a *Star Wars* look and feel to it that Decatur fell in love with at first sight. Not only did it fire 700 rounds a minute, providing the intended victim with enough death to last a lifetime, but it looked damned cool doing it.

Hunter was sitting on the black bear rug watching TV and stuffing toy soldiers into his backpack. Decatur glanced at the TV. A Disney cartoon bear danced across a forest, crooning a cover of Bing Crosby's "Ac-Cent-Tchu-Ate the Positive."

Decatur watched the singing bear waltz across a forest, then looked over at his son. "Golly, that bear can boogie. Watcha' watching there, Little Man?"

Hunter continued to cram soldiers into his backpack. He shrugged his little shoulders. "Dunno, Dad. Some bear cartoon."

"Well, Boogie Bear there has some good advice. 'Accentuate the positive,'" repeated Decatur, watching the cartoon. "Dang good advice."

"What's that mean?"

Decatur tossed some soldiers into the backpack. A couple of snipers and a Bazooka man. "It means you've always got to look for the positive things in life. That makes you appreciate them more for what they're worth. For instance, you finish packing like your mom wants and you don't get a butt blistering. That's a positive.

Something you can appreciate." Decatur smiled, picked up a worn Teddy Bear. "You want to take Fuzzy Wuzzy with you?"

"No, Dad. Soldiers are too old for teddy bears."

"Ah, good to know."

"Hey, Dad?"

"Yeah?"

"Do I really have to go? Did I do something wrong?"

"No, doggone it, of course you didn't."

Hunter's eyes began to tear up.

Decatur took a step toward him. "Hey, Little Man, no nose bubbles ... besides it's Grandpa and Grandma's. You'll have two whole weeks of fun in the sun. Now that's accentuating the positive if there ever was one, you ask me."

Decatur held up one of the donut bags. "Lookit, I made you a special batch of your favorite gingerbread men. I'll put them in your backpack and you can share them with your platoon on the plane. Sound like a flight plan, Little Man?"

Hunter tried to brush away the tears running down his cheeks without much success. "Can I stay here and go hunting with you? Please?"

Decatur managed a curt laugh. "Sorry, Little Man, but you have to go with your mom and baby sister. You have to take care of them, they're depending on you. We've talked about this—it's the man's job to take care of the women."

"If it's the man's job, then how come you don't come with us?"

"You know this is the one week out of the whole year that I get to do something for myself. Something that I love to do. Something that I have to do."

"It's really fun, huh?"

50

"Like you wouldn't believe. I love the hunt. The tracking. The one-shot kill. That's what it's all about. It's in my blood, is all I can say. Nothing like it, you know. Almost like a religion."

He pointed to the largest stuffed head on the wall—an enormous Dall sheep. "That one alone took me two days to track. Biggest dang Dall sheep I'd ever seen. I'd been within a hundred yards of that bad boy a dozen times over those two days. Gee whiz, the snow was up to my kneecaps, but I crept, inch-by-inch, to within fifty feet to get a clean kill. I raised my bow, aimed through the falling snow just to the back of the sheep's shoulder, and let that arrow slide out of my fingers. I watched as my arrow disappeared right into the white cape! A perfect lung shot—a perfect kill!"

He picked a catalog-sized book off the coffee table. "And look at this—"

He opened the book midway and proudly held the page up. "And this, ol' buddy, is Pope & Young. The hunter's bible. They list all the world record trophy animals. Lookit—"

Hunter's eyes lit up as he recognized his father kneeling beside an enormous dead sheep. "That's you, Dad!"

"Yep, the world's largest doggone Dall sheep and that's me next to it. Waited 'most all day just for that one shot."

Hunter looked up at the Dall sheep's head on the wall. "Don't ya' get bored waitin' that long?"

"Tell you a special trick." Decatur placed a handful of Hunter's soldiers along the coffee table. "I line up a bag of M&M's along the railing of the tree stand. One after the other, each one about an inch apart. Every fifteen minutes or so, I treat myself to one M&M, savoring the fact that if I'm patient long enough, something will come along. Always does, never fails. And if it don't, I still got my M&Ms." Decatur winked at his son. "Accentuate the positive."

Hunter took this in, thought for a moment, then looked up at the mounted Dall head and asked, "But don't you ever feel, you know, bad when you kill them?"

"Bad?! Gee whiz, no, not at all. There are so many of them out there waitin' for the takin' and besides, it's not like anybody's gonna miss them anyway."

From upstairs came the strains of Cindy's megaphonic voice. "Decatur! ... Did you pack Hunter's rain jacket? ... We need to pick up some diapers on the way to the airport ... And we need to pick up some snacks on the way while we're at it ... You know how expensive everything is at the airport ... I would never pay those prices ... Come on you two, we're going to be late!"

Hunter sighed. "Dad?"

"Yep?"

"Maybe we should get Mom some M&Ms."

Decatur smiled, then helped Hunter put his backpack on. "Not sure if there's enough M&Ms in the world to do the trick for Mom. C'mon, Little Man. Time to go."

As Decatur picked up the remote to turn the television off, he hit the channel changer by accident. In a grainy, black and white 1950s movie, a hard-boiled detective-type walked up to a film noir streetwalker sauntering under the umbrella spill of a streetlamp. The streetwalker was spilling out of her low cut dress and Decatur instantaneously got a hard on.

He scooted Hunter up the stairs. "You tell Mom we're coming. I'll get the lights."

Decatur watched as the detective slapped the prostitute on her ample butt, threatening her. "Look, Sweetheart, you're a professional. I ain't gonna do nothing that hasn't been done to you before. So, you don't get excited, you don't do nothing stupid. You know there is some risk to what you've been doing. If you do exactly what I tell you, you're not going to get hurt. You're just going to count this off as a bad experience and be a little more careful next time who you proposition or go out with." The detective took a long drag off a cigarette. Coolly exhaled. "You may even learn to thank me."

Upstairs, Cindy badgered on. "Decatur, did you not hear me? … Are you not listening? We're going to be late and we need to stop before we get to the airport and you need to get back here so you can start cleaning up this pig sty…"

"Okay," surrendered Decatur, turning off the light and fondling the bullets in his pocket.

———

"Decatur! Please slow down a smidge, will you? … Hunter, do you have your seat belt on? … Is it on tight? … Now where did I put those tickets? … Decatur, did you remember to pack Hunter's rain jacket? … And don't forget to water my plants…"

Decatur thought of trying to get a word in edgewise as he zipped down Interstate A-1, heading west in his moving, giant slab of American-made steel.

Instead, he checked his watch. A little before 10:00 p.m. The flight was scheduled for 10:35 so there was plenty of time.

Since sunset wasn't until 11:30 this time of the year, it was still light out as he made the turnoff for the Ted Stevens Anchorage International Airport. The traffic was light and he had made good time.

Five minutes later, Decatur pulled up to the curbside check-in. At that moment he became the happiest man on the planet.

As they all got out of the Jeep, Decatur took the luggage from the trunk and placed it near the check-in counter. He gave Cindy a cursory peck on the cheek. "Give your Mom and Dad a big hug for me. Tell them I'll see them at Christmas."

"I'll do that ... now, tell Hunter you love him."

"I've told him enough, he knows."

"Decatur, tell him!"

"Doggone it, he knows already!"

"Decatur!"

Decatur padded Hunter on the shoulder. "Take care of your mother and sister, Little Man." He turned to Cindy. "Well, you better check in. You don't want to be late—"

"—and you don't want to get a ticket from the police," she said, finishing his sentence.

"Nope, I want nothing from the police, dumbass," replied Decatur. The 'dumbass' was, of course, silent and implied.

A car honked behind Decatur. "Okay, I've got to move. Have a good trip." He got behind the wheel and shut his door.

Cindy grabbed Hunter's hand and shouted across the passenger side, "Have a good time ... and don't do anything I wouldn't do!"

"Hey, I'm a baker. What am I going to do?"

Hunter leaned in and looked directly at his dad. "Butcher, baker, candlestick maker ..."

The car behind Decatur honked again, this time flashing its lights. Decatur gave his son a look, then Cindy chirped in, "Have a great time, Hon. And don't forget to clean the kitchen floor. And all those piles. No one likes a pig sty."

"Yeah, right," replied Decatur driving away as she continued to harangue.

Five minutes later, driving east on Interstate A1 into Anchorage, Decatur pulled out the tin of Altoids he had taken from his study and carefully pried the lid open.

He looked down and smiled. The tin was packed with pure white powder. Carefully holding the steering wheel with his left hand, he lifted the tin to his nose and snorted from the large stash of cocaine. As the tremors ran through him, he set the tin down on the seat next to him and carefully snapped the lid shut.

He reared back and shook his head from side-to-side.

A departing Boeing 737 screamed overhead and Decatur thought of Cindy one last time, opening the window and giving a primal scream into the night, "I hope you roast in hell, you fucking cunt!"

This time it was neither silent nor implied.

SEVEN

FUCKIN' A, BETTE DAVIS! was Sue's first thought as she turned right on Eagle Street and headed west on Fourth Avenue. The storefront office buildings flipped past like black diamonds spilling into her peripheral vision and then, just as quickly, disappearing as she sped uptown into the city's Tenderloin District.

Cruising cars and posturing prostitutes working Fifth Avenue were caught in the shining lights as Sue entered the dark side of Anchorage.

"Bette Davis, you knew it, didn't you, Girl? ... What a dump!"

Largely run by the Seattle Mafia, the Tenderloin District was Anchorage's red-light district: a motley, mostly decadent, collection of seedy bars, seedier pool halls, iffy pawnshops, iffier massage parlors, and the world's cheapest strip joints sandwiched and sardined between the Alaska Railroad Station and the "family friendly" motels lining Fifth Avenue. Anchorage International Airport, the main hub for all air transportation into and out of Alaska, was less than ten minutes away, making the Tenderloin District additionally easy and readily accessible.

Like the saying, Sue thought, it was here that *God knows, anything goes.*

It was here that anyone could buy drugs as easily as they could buy women. This was a man's world, a dying-yet-clinging-to-the-vine, last-gasp vestige to the extinct days of the Old, Old West. The strip joints were there for efficient drinking and negotiating propositions and not much else. The one-way streets throughout the five-block area were ideal for cruising and choosing. Oil workers overflowed the bars and university students fell unconscious into nearby alleys and doorways. Pimps in pink Cadillacs and coffin-black Lincolns parked at the ready near every intersection.

Susceptible, and not so susceptible, young women by the score were lured there by promises of big bucks dancing in clubs with names like the Booby Trap, the Great Alaskan Bush Company, Arctic Fox, and the Wild Cherry. As the population skyrocketed in Anchorage during the '80s oil boom, and with it disposable income, these strip joints were skimming off to the tune of over a hundred grand a month in cash.

Business was indeed booming.

And God knows, anything goes.

Sue was aware of the wanton morass she was entering as she drove past the peep shows, the topless bars and the pornographic magazine stands featuring the worst paradigm of child pornography. She hated it, loathed everything about it, but accepted it as an unfortunate means to a better end. And the math was simple. She either came up with two hundred dollars by the end of the week or she and Sunny would be living in her Kia.

Who looks outside, dreams.

Who looks inside . . . when was the last time I was fucking awake?

The darkness of the street outside Sue's windshield was broken by flashing colored bulbs draped on boxlike, single-story buildings covered by tacky, day-glow paint jobs interrupted by caricature figures of big-chested, long-legged, mostly naked women. Signs advertised dozens of topless, energetic dancers, and just in case any passerby was blind or illiterate, there were barkers standing outside promising a bevy of beauties and pleasures inside.

Sue pulled to a stop in the back parking lot of a simple, single-story, shoebox-shaped building that languished in the shadow of Anchorage International. Even in the parking lot, the blaring bass and thrashing drums of '80s big-hair metal rock was near deafening. Sue couldn't imagine a more suitable soundtrack to her new working place. Or a more suitable name. A pulsating neon light over the back door blinked: *Bushwhackers.* Above the pulsating light, in smaller, neon-red letters: *Madame Bleau's.*

She took a deep, reassuring breath and a quick glance to the north toward the Alaska Railroad Station. At this distance, she imagined a train full of happy and excited tourists heading for romantic trips to fascinating attractions like Denali Park and Mount McKinley. Hell, even Nome sounded romantic at this juncture.

Then she looked south, where she'd be spending most of her night—a lurid, violent avenue where women were nothing more than a commodity. A gift with a pulse. That anticipation prompted more ennui and revulsion than enthusiasm and financial grounding as Sue got out of her car.

Nearby, a riproaringly drunk student cursed as he pissed in a doorway spraying his boots and the bottom of his jeans. He was so drunk he swayed as if walking on a trampoline.

At the intersection to her left stood a working woman. Blonde and about eighteen, she was trying to look like she was waiting for the light to turn green, but in fact, was posing spuriously for every passing car.

Then it hit her.

Like some kind of reverse déjà vu.

A sudden, powerful, overwhelming sense of eerie aloneness, as if she were the lone survivor of some unknown apocalyptic event.

Who looks outside, dreams.

Who looks inside, awakes?

Standing in the parking lot, Sue forced herself to take a deep breath, then slowly counted to ten. Then it was time to rejoin what was left of the human race.

The Friday night crowd was gathering outside Bushwhackers when Sue walked in and was greeted by the owner, a woman who went by the first name Marcella. A heavily-made up woman in her forties, Sue had met Marcella for the first time the day before. Sue nodded hello and headed toward the dressing room in the basement.

"Hi'ya, Baby Doll, here ya' go," Marcella said handing Sue a key. "It's locker 22. Lucky 22. Your costume is inside like we discussed. We'll start you off easy. One dance at the end of every hour, just to ease you in. You change and give me a look-see peep before you go on. Oh, and don't forget to knock 'em dead, Baby Doll."

That settled, Sue went downstairs to the dressing room where she took off her street clothes and hung them in the locker assigned to her. Lucky 22. After putting her purse containing a .32-caliber pistol up on the shelf, she slipped into a white terrycloth robe.

Sue greeted the other dancers as they arrived. The women settled down to do their hair and makeup and change into their costumes.

In front of her dressing-table mirror, Sue carefully affixed blatantly-long Catwoman-like eyelashes that accented her soft blue eyes. She opened her robe and slowly lathered her arms, legs, stomach and breasts with glitter body cream, causing her entire body to glow as if it were lit with tiny incandescent lamps underneath her skin.

From her locker, Sue selected a pair of dark stockings, anchored by thick black borders around the top, a black satin G-string, an abbreviated black bustier, and a pair of high-heeled stilettos.

Studying herself in the muted, radiant glow of soft lights framing the mirror, Sue made some adjustments to her lustrous blonde hair and touched up her lips.

Leaning back, looking at the final result, Sue had to admit it.

No doubt about it.

Mirrors never lie.

She not only looked pretty fucking hot, she looked *smokin'*.

Satisfied, Sue found Marcella and did a slow 360 minuet for final inspection. Giving her okay with a smile and a nod, Marcella led Sue upstairs where the pulsating music grew louder by the stair step, until at floor level it reached thunderous proportions. "Pour Some Sugar On Me" by Def Leppard.

They entered the narrow backstage area behind the curtains. Marcella motioned for Sue to come over to her, where they peeped through a crack to take a look at the girl dancing on the stage and at the raucous audience in front of her.

Sue's heart skipped a beat—hell, a couple of them—when she saw the overflow crowd. No way had she expected this big of a mob. A large gathering of young men in army uniforms were milling around the "meat rack," what the dancers called the seats in front of the stage that offered the best view of the girls. Nearby Fort Richardson was hosting the military's annual Brim Frost Exercises. Thousands of young soldiers arrived to test their survival skills in the Alaskan backwoods and after their exercises were finished, many drifted to the Tenderloin District for rest and relaxation. But mostly relaxation.

Rounding out the crowd, Sue noticed, were white-collar businessmen and blue-collar laborers. Both, she knew, were looking for the same thing. The only real difference being the depth of their pockets and how far they would, or could, dig down to get it. Sue watched as a college student nursed a warm beer, while an oil rig manager on the other side of the room dropped a $50 bill for a bottle of wine that she knew cost a couple bucks at the local liquor store.

Sue stepped away from the curtain as three divas in G-strings walked up, all apparently waiting their turn for the stage. The three girls were in deep discussion on the night's potential.

"Didja' see that guy all alone in the back. Whaddaya' think of him?" asked the platinum blonde.

"SLUF," replied the redhead.

"What?" asked the platinum blonde.

"SLUF—short, little, ugly fucker," laughed the redhead.

"Looks like a helpless dork," chimed in the brunette. "If he was a color, he'd be beige."

"If he was a taste, he'd be water," said the redhead.

"If he was a fart," said the blonde, "he'd be silent but deadly."

The girls laughed, then the brunette spotted a table with a group of burly oil rig workers. "What about them?"

The blonde scrutinized the table with professional aplomb. "Yummy, pipe line workers! And you know they just got paid."

"Definite possibilities," concluded the brunette with a nod of her head.

Onstage the music suddenly ended and Marcella looked at Sue. "Knock 'em dead, Baby Doll." And with that Marcella gave her a push past the curtain as yet another headbanger song jolted her senses and rattled her brain. Somewhere overhead speakers cranked up to eleven, a DJ's sonorous voice was booming out, "… and now join me in welcoming a bubbly new talent to Bushwhackers."

The house lights dimmed.

A spotlight blazed Sue on the stage.

The crowd hushed to a whisper.

Sue's heart pounded like a jackhammer.

But she had no choice, this was it.

Over the speakers, the music began to blast, shaking the walls, and Sue began to gyrate.

She soon entered a Zen-like space and thought only about getting her first dance over with. The first one of the night, she knew, was always a bitch. The hardest.

Swaying to the music, Sue began a mental game, something that she had developed while dancing in Seattle. She began thinking about any mundane chore she needed to do—cleaning, laundry, cooking—anything but dancing in front of a hundred drooling men. And she had learned to keep her eyes just above door level, that way she didn't actually see the customers. Her mental trick was to create a private world that would ensure survival in the real one.

And before she knew it, the song was over.

To her astonishment, she ended her set to enthusiastic audience applause, boisterous catcalls and encoring whistles.

Sue took a few moments to gather up the bills scattered on the stage, then looked up, not sure what to do next. Almost immediately, without any fanfare, another dancer began her set.

Quickly throwing on a wrap-around blouse, Sue counted her money. A hundred and change. Hell, at least it was a start. Okay, it wasn't art, but at least she had made it through the first waltz. And it only got easier from there Sue knew.

Since her next set wasn't for another hour, Sue also knew that Marcella expected her to socialize with the crowd, trying to get them to buy as much Bushwhackers' cheap booze as possible.

Walking across the hunter-green Astroturf in the strobing room, a man in a business suit offered Sue some champagne from a bottle sitting in an ice bucket on his table. Flashing a killer smile and letting her Catwoman eyelashes talk for her, he filled a plastic flute and handed it to her. When he turned toward the pulsating light to look at the girl dancing on the stage, Sue poured the glass onto the Astroturf. Speaking through the loud, pounding music, so that the businessman couldn't hear her, she feigned thanking him and moved on.

Sue noticed a man in the back.

Sitting alone.

Nursing a beer.

He was watching the girl pole-dancing on the stage.

Looks harmless enough, thought Sue. *Must be the SLUF the three girls were talking about earlier.*

The man was sitting at a small round table toward the back, a good distance from the stage. It was harder to see the girls from there, surrounded by pools of shadows, but at the same time it was damn near impossible to make out much of the man. Something he apparently preferred in similar situations.

Sue walked over to the shadow man as he was finishing his beer.

"Feel like a fresh one?" she asked.

The man looked Sue over, then replied, "Me? Why, heck, Hon, I'm always looking for a fresh one."

"I was talking about a drink."

"I wasn't," smiled the shadow man.

Before she could respond, the redhead of the diva trio made her way over to the table. She was wearing a tiny white spandex skirt over red fishnet stockings and spike heels. A fine red mesh blouse did little to conceal her breasts as she bent over with a tray of drinks.

Her arms clasped in front of her to squeeze her breasts, inflating them into deeper cleavage, as she put a fresh beer on the table.

Without looking at Sue, the redhead dismissed her with a practiced ease. "I'll take it from here, Sweetie."

Shadow Man looked into the redhead's cleavage and said, "Honey, you can take it any way you want it."

"Ain't that something?" flirted the redhead, looking at Shadow Man. "Any way is how I like it."

"Do you?" replied Shadow Man.

"Very much," she said, licking her lips. "How about a private show?"

Shadow Man stood up and glanced at Sue. "Well, darlin', if you'll excuse us. Maybe we can have a drink later."

"Not a problem," replied Sue.

The redhead led the Chief of Police by hand out of the bar and into a private room.

"First night, huh?"

Sue whirled around to see if the question was directed at her. For the first time, she noticed another solitary man finishing his beer.

She turned to face him, studying him for a moment, noticing the ID badge on his jacket.

"That obvious?" asked Sue over the clamorous din.

The man gave her a charming, killer smile.

"So," asked Sue, "what's a nice doctor like you doing in a place like this?"

"That obvious?" he asked.

She pointed at the clip-on badge partially hidden by his jacket. "Says you're a doctor right there on your ID card. Dr. Joseph..."

The man grinned wolfishly. "Yeah... but it don't say I'm nice."

Looking up through a pair of thick glasses, Decatur Kaiser unclipped the purloined ID badge and stuck it in his jacket pocket. "Doggone it, I always forget to take that thing off."

EIGHT

SUE LOOKED DOWN AND smiled mischievously. "You gonna take that off, too, Doc?"

"Take what off?" Decatur asked.

"Your wedding ring."

"Ah, well, gee whiz, some things you just don't take off."

"Happy marriage, huh?"

"Nope. Damn thing's stuck solid on my finger."

Sue stared down at the man.

His grin was perfunctory and didn't reach anywhere near his eyes. "So, can I ask you a question?"

"Shoot," replied Sue.

"If a man is standing in the middle of a forest talking and his wife is not there to hear him, is he still wrong?"

"Very funny."

"That was one of them rhetorical questions."

"And that was one of them rhetorical answers."

Decatur smiled. "Can I buy you a drink?"

"My boss expects you to," Sue answered, taking a seat. She stopped a passing waitress and took two drinks off her tray. Leaning forward, Sue tore open the brand-new pack of Kool Menthols from her purse and lit one with a match from a Bushwhackers matchbook. She slipped the matchbook inside the plastic cigarette packing, took a deep drag, then let out a long cloud of blue mentholated smoke.

She studied Decatur studying her.

"What?" Sue suddenly asked. "You gonna call me a dummkopf?"

"A what?"

"A dummkopf." Sue blew out more smoke, laughing. "I used to watch Hogan's Heroes with my father. Long time ago. It's something one of the main characters used to say. I guess I picked up that dumb word from him."

"'*Doom*koff.'" Decatur rolled the word over his tongue, misspelling it in his mind. "'*Doom*koff.' I like it."

"Take it, Doc, it's yours. No charge."

"Thanks, I think I will. Now, then … why would I call you a 'doomkoff'?"

Sue held up the lit cigarette. "Well, you being a doctor and all … Aren't you gonna tell me that these things are gonna kill me?"

"Professionally speaking … I don't think you have to worry about that." He pointed at the pack of cigarettes lying on the table. "Mind if I take one of those?"

"Go for it, Doc." She shot the pack across the table.

Decatur took the pack. Pulled out one cigarette. Stood the pack upright on the table. Balanced the cigarette on top of the pack with the skill of a surgeon. He looked up, asking, "Gotta name?"

Sue thought for a moment. "Susie."

"Tell you what, Susie Q. I'll bet you a quarter that I can hit the tip of this cigarette with one finger and that it will flip up in the air, somersault a couple of times, and then land upright on one end. Right here on the table."

"Standing up?"

"Straight as an arrow."

"No way that's gonna happen ... Okay, I'm in. Let's see the Doc operate."

Decatur dramatically eyed the cigarette on top of the pack, moved his index finger slowly up and down, "practicing" his hit.

Then, suddenly, Decatur pulled his hand way back over his head and ...

SMASH!

Completely crushed the cigarette pack with a closed fist. The pack lay there on the table looking like the crumpled corpse of James Dean's Porsche.

Decatur smiled across the table at Sue. "Looks like I owe you a quarter, Susie Q."

Sue was not amused. "You know, Doc, that would be damned funny if cigarettes weren't so expensive."

She stood up to leave.

"Hey, not so fast, Susie Q, not so fast. Maybe I'm not such a 'doomkoff' after all." He pulled three one-hundred dollar bills out of his pocket. "Would, uh, would this make up for it?"

For a moment, Sue's eyes lit up. "Are the Kennedy's gun shy?" Then, some of the fire died in her eyes. "But, I'm guessing you might be wanting some change back, huh?"

"Well, how 'bout you meetin' me in my car in, say, five minutes? It's in the back parking lot, we can discuss your ... deductible ... there."

"Whoa! Slow down, Doc. I only dance here. Nothing else. There's other girls for that."

"Well, technically, what I have in mind isn't a major operation. Just something you could ... wrap your hands around."

Decatur started to collect the three hundred dollars off the table. "Yep, too, too bad."

"Wait."

Decatur's hands froze on the money.

"Just my hands? Nothing else?"

"Just your hands. What I got in mind won't take long neither ... ten minutes tops ..."

He looked her directly in the eyes. "'Sides, I've got a killer day at the office tomorrow."

Sue looked at the money lying on the table. Just within her reach. She could smell the green. It was exactly what she desperately needed with a few bucks to spare.

"Oh," added Decatur, "and I have a rubber on."

"You have it on now!?" asked Sue incredulously.

"I was a Boy Scout. Got all my badges."

A moment, then Sue smiled. "Scout's honor?"

Decatur held up three fingers. "Scout's honor."

Sue couldn't take her eyes off the money lying so lonely there on the table.

She started to say something.

Hesitated.

Wheels spinning.

Confusion and aggravation found a perfect equipoise.

Finally, Sue shook her head and shoved the money back to Decatur. "I can't ... There are other girls here who—"

"Hey, say no more, not a problem." He collected the money and held it up. "Tell you what. I'm going out to my car in the back parking lot. I'll be there for ten minutes..." He paused, staring up at her. "...just in case you change your mind."

With that, Decatur put the money in his jacket and, making his way through the overflow crowd, walked out the back door. He never once looked back at Sue.

As the back door shut behind him, an ambulatory shadow cast by an enormous dumpster moved across Sue. The shadow was human. Almost three hundred pounds of human, moving with a fluidity and grace that belied its massiveness.

"Miss Marcella wants a word with you," said a voice booming from within the voluminous dark shadow.

NINE

Sue looked up to see a bouncer looming over her.

The guy was big.

Statue of Liberty big, only taller and meaner-looking.

The massive creature had a tattooed face and a linebacker's neck and shoulders to compete with Atlas. He wore a tank top, revealing Herculean muscles and forearm hair thick enough to catch flies and the occasional spider. He looked as if he'd get a lot of pleasure going ten rounds with his great grandmother and making sure she'd go the whole ten rounds, just to fuck with her. Afterward, you could take her home in a bag. Paper or plastic, it wouldn't make any difference.

"Give me a minute," said Sue.

The bouncer's shoulders involuntarily spasmed violently at the request. It was a spasm that looked powerful enough to break your wrist if you were touching his shoulders when the ripple erupted.

"Miss Marcella said she wants a word with you now. She didn't mention waitin' for no minute."

"Okay, okay, I'm coming, I'm coming," relented Sue.

The Shoulder's shoulders remained passively quiet as Sue followed him downstairs past the seedy-looking dressing rooms. She could see that his shoulders held the distinct possibility of providing serious trouble in her near future. She imagined the dire consequences of pissing off the Shoulder. She didn't like that mental image at all. No, that would never do. She damned sure was going to keep on the sunny side of the Shoulder. If she had anything to do with it, the Shoulder and she were going to be on each other's Christmas card mailing list, new best buds forever.

Sue had perceptively picked up on the fact that the Shoulder did not like the phrase "Give me a minute." Sue made a mental note to avoid that phrase like the plague. The Shoulder seemed happy with the phrase "Okay, okay," so that was a phrase the Shoulder was going to be hearing a hell of a lot.

Downstairs, Sue and the Shoulder passed by the drab, wooden, windowless rooms, while a half-dozen, half-clad women applied makeup and costumes. They all talked over each other at the same time, their dialogue fast and furious. It appeared that the blonde and the brunette were in mid-argument:

"I don't know what your problem is," the blonde was saying, "but I'll bet it's hard for you to pronounce."

"Well," replied the brunette, "I'll try being nicer, if you promise to be smarter."

Sue and the Shoulder walked past a third girl. She was counting her money. "Hey, is anyone else having a lousy night or is it my velvet pants?"

Ignoring her, the blonde turned to the brunette. "You know, I really do like you. You remind me of me when I was young... and stupid."

"Don't you be looking at me in that tone of voice."

"Hey, you might want to mention it to your boyfriend that there's nothing worse than using someone else's love doll."

"Did anybody hear me?" shouted Velvet Pants. "I didn't make shit tonight. Again!"

"Some days you're the dog, Honey, some days you're the hydrant."

"Well, fuck," said Velvet Pants. "At this rate I'll be in this doghouse for the rest of my life."

"Hey, it takes a dog to know one," burst in the brunette looking at the blonde.

"Fuck you!" said the blonde, flipping her off.

The Shoulder led Sue to a door at the end of the room. He knocked twice and entered.

The room was small, dark, cluttered. A couple of army surplus file cabinets lined one wall, posters of naked women adorned the opposite wall. There were papers stacked in every nook and cranny.

Marcella looked up from her desk. "Hey, Baby Doll. Thanks for coming down. How's the night been to you?"

"Umm, the night's been good. The place is busy and lots of customers—"

"Miss Marcella means how much did you make so far tonight?" translated the Shoulder.

"Oh! The night! Ummm, so-so." Sue hastily collected her money and counted. "One-hundred forty ... one-hundred sixty."

"Not bad. Not bad at all, Baby Doll. Like we agreed, the house takes fifty-percent plus one-hundred dollars for expenses. We're going to need that now, Baby Doll. Upfront."

"Expenses!? What expenses?"

"One hundred for your costume, the locker and security plus ten dollars to the house for every hour you worked."

"What!? No one mentioned that to me—"

"Just did, Baby Doll. So—" Marcella nodded at the Shoulder.

He took the money from Sue's hands.

All of it.

"So," said Marcella, "you end up owing the house ... what?" She turned to the Shoulder. He did the math in his head.

"Sixty bucks," replied the Shoulder.

"Sixty bucks, it is," repeated Marcella.

"I owe you sixty dollars? I ... I don't have that much ... and I owe two hundred for rent tomorrow!"

"Sorry, Doll, but that's not the house's problem. House expects that money by the end of the night. House rules."

The Shoulder loomed over Sue.

Completely at a loss, she looked up as if to plead. "Please, I'll ... I'll—"

Something in the room stopped Sue in mid-plea.

Above Marcella's head was a small basement window with iron bars. And through the bars, Sue could see the back parking lot.

Sullen and defeated, her emotions aborted, Sue said, "I'll have your money in ten minutes."

TEN

THE FULL MOON SLICED its way through the long edge of a cloud to reveal a breathtaking view of Anchorage well past midnight. The alabaster light reflected off the hood of Decatur's Jeep Renegade sitting under a broken streetlight in the back of the rear parking lot.

Slumped down behind the driver's seat, Decatur peered through the windshield, anxiously glancing over the sea of cars.

Centered.

Focused.

Cobra calm.

He checked his hair in the rearview mirror.

Satisfied, he began talking softly to himself. Rehearsing. Practicing a speech. Saying it several different ways with several different inflections and intonations.

"... You might even *learn* to thank me ... You *might* even learn to thank me ... You might even learn to *thank me*."

He settled for the second reading, thinking it had just the right combination of intimidation and optimism.

Pleased with his speech, Decatur flipped the radio on. The Turtles. "Outside Chance." Snappy, killer lyrics with a kickass backbeat.

He opened the Altoids tin and snorted more coke.

Reaching into the glove compartment, he pulled out one of his daughter's Baby Wipes. Scrubbed down the entire length of the dashboard.

Decatur smiled to himself as he used the Baby Wipe. He'd heard a story about Howard Hughes, once the richest man on the planet. A man so rich and strange that he had once declared, "I'm not a paranoid deranged millionaire. Goddamit, I'm a billionaire." Well, back in the early '70s, Hughes had holed himself into the top three floors of one of his casinos in Las Vegas. Why? Because he had a psychotic fear of germs. Every time the billionaire went to the bathroom, he would coat the toilet seat with seven, count 'em seven, layers of tissue paper from a box of Kleenex.

And what did the world's richest man wear on his bare feet?

The world's most expensive shoes?

No.

Howard Hughes wore the discarded Kleenex tissue boxes!

No shit...

Decatur laughed as he pulled out a bag of M&M's. He carefully placed a line of the colorful candies along the dashboard. Ate them one at a time, timing the intervals. Patiently waiting.

Discarded Kleenex tissue boxes!

What a fuckin' weirdo!

———

Sue stepped out of the back door under the piss-yellow glare of a sodium-vapor streetlight, half hoping the man claiming to be a doctor would be gone.

She was dressed back in her work clothes—a white mini-skirt, a black frilly blouse and white high-heels. She tucked her half of the brand-new gold Mizpah pendant around her neck into the blouse.

She scanned the parking lot.

Near the back, a Jeep's headlights blinked on, then off.

My fuckin' lucky night, thought Sue as she made her way through the maze of parked cars.

Decatur got out of the Renegade. Opened the passenger door. A perfect gentleman.

Sue scooted in.

Decatur walked around to the driver's seat. As he did, he looped his key ring around his index finger and began whirling the keys, twirling them around his finger to the rhythm of the backbeat of the radio. Decatur counted three full circles.

On the fourth twirl he got behind the wheel. Closed his door.

Sue stared straight ahead through the windshield.

Sullen.

Nervous. As a long-tailed cat in a room full of rocking chairs.

Numb.

"Three hundred, right?" she blurted out a bit too quickly.

Decatur pulled out three one-hundred dollar bills. Stuffed them into her blouse pocket next to the crumpled pack of Kools. "Money's all yours. Gotta tell you, you surprised me."

"Yeah, well, surprise is my middle name." *But mostly it's dummkopf.*

Decatur hooked his right arm around Sue's shoulders. Began to play with her hair.

Like dancing on the stage, Sue began to mentally/astrally pro-ject herself to anyplace, anytime, anywhere. Anyplace, anytime, anywhere but there.

Sue's hand ran across Decatur's shirt, down lower around his waist, until her hand came down to the seat.

"Condom on?" asked Sue.

"Condom on."

"Put the seat all the way back."

Decatur did as she asked.

"Guess it's time to see what's up, huh, Doc?" Sue leaned over into his lap. Unzipped his fly. For a moment, in the darkness, she wasn't sure what she was looking at. "What the—"

Before she could finish, the fingers of Decatur's right hand tightened around a handful of her hair, then suddenly, savagely, jerked her head back.

Sue looked up in horror.

For the first time Decatur was looking Sue in her eyes. Dead center.

The barrel of a .357 Magnum was pressed against the side of her head. From behind the cold, blue barrel, Decatur snarled in a deliberate voice, "All right, now, you're gonna do just what I say. I'm good at this … done it lots of times before."

He cocked the hammer back on the gun.

Moved the barrel an inch away from Sue's right eye.

"You just take a look down this hole. Tell me what you see."

Sue, speechless, could only stare at him in mute apprehension.

"I'll tell you what you see," gloated Decatur. His words were spoken hard between clenched teeth and with barely moving lips, the lower jaw jutting out, his eyes crazed and vacant of any emotion between narrowed lids. At once surreal and grotesque.

"You see hollow point bullets in there, don't cha'? And you know they'll make a nice hole in you and provide you with enough death to last you forever if you don't listen to what I say. Now, do we have an understanding?"

Wide-eyed, Sue trembled in a frightened, staccato nod.

"That's a good girl. Now, get your ass down on the floorboard. Your face on the seat. Your knees on the floormat. Your arms behind your back."

She hesitated for a moment as she spotted her car in the parking lot, just a few cars away. Her Kia. Then she remembered what those initials stood for in cop speak. KIA. Killed In Action. *Fuck*, she thought. *Define irony...*

Instantly adding injury to irony, Decatur slammed Sue hard across the face with the side of his gun. "I wasn't asking, goddamit! Move your ass!"

He forced her onto her knees on the floor of the front seat. He reached underneath the seat, came up with a pair of handcuffs.

Sue began to beg, pleading, "What are you going to do to me?"

Decatur's face became a grim mask as he grinned at the terror Sue radiated. Thoroughly enjoying every moment, he handcuffed her hands behind her back, snapping them shut, with two explosive clicks.

"Please don't do this... I only came here to dance... I need the money for... I need the money... please... this was my first night—"

"Look, Susie Q, you're a professional," the mask smirked with calm ferocity. "I ain't gonna do nothing that hasn't been done to you before. So, you don't get excited, you don't do nothing stupid—you know there's some risk to what you've been doing. If you do exactly what I tell you, you're not going to get hurt. You're just going to count this off as a bad experience and be a little more careful next time who you're gonna proposition or go out with. You *might* even learn to thank me."

Decatur started the Jeep.

Sue leaned her face on the seat.

Helpless.

Hopeless.

But not yet fucked.

She tried desperately hard to remember the 'rape' lecture Sarge had given her all those years ago and wished now that she had listened more attentively.

What she did remember Sarge saying was that Alaska generally, and Anchorage specifically, had been plagued by the nation's highest incidence of forcible rapes and sexual assaults. In fact, in the early 1990s the state of Alaska had the highest rate of reported forcible rape among the fifty states and Anchorage had the second highest rate of reported forcible rape among metropolitan cities in the U.S.

Sarge had warned her that rape was a crime of violence and control, not about the actual act of sex. Instead, sex was used as a weapon since it was one way in which a man could very directly assert his physical domination and power over a woman. Sometimes the rapist's motivation was directly tied to females, usually an overbearing mother, girlfriend, or wife; sometimes it was in response to his failure to deal with other stresses in his life. By controlling and dominating a woman, the rapist tried to regain control of areas in his life where he felt he was out of control. Lacking the maturity and facility to deal with these stresses in a more constructive fashion, he transformed his emotional impotency into violence, lashing out at innocent women.

On the constructive side, Sarge had reinforced the fact that Anchorage was a relatively small city with not a lot of hiding places and with an excellent police force. His advice was to submit to the rapist's demands, then once freed, to call the police immediately. The police would take it from there.

As the Jeep bounced along, Sue's only consolation was that Sarge was right as usual. It wasn't much, but at least it was something to hang hope on.

There weren't a lot of hiding places in Anchorage.

ELEVEN

DECATUR DROVE OUT OF Anchorage.

"Where, where are you taking me?" asked Sue, true panic beginning to rise in her voice.

"Not much farther," grinned Decatur. "Never was one much for crowds."

Beyond the windshield, the Renegade's headlights were silver swords scything through a winding country stretch of asphalt, the road cloaked on either side by tall evergreen trees swaying eerily in moonlight. The shrieking wind made the branches look like ominous tentacles grappling in the oppressive gloom.

Decatur was gunning the Renegade, sixty-plus on the winding road. Sue, lying face first on the passenger seat, was tossed side to side by the centrifugal force. The handcuffs were closed tight and she was beginning to lose feeling in all of her fingers.

"My hands are really starting to hurt. Could you please loosen the handcuffs? Please?" She turned her head to face Decatur just as a flashing blue light hit his face.

Decatur looked up at the rearview mirror.

The flashing lights were drawing near. A police car with siren blaring sped up behind Decatur's Jeep.

"Oh, fuck!" Decatur pounded the steering wheel, then shouted down at Sue, "Look, if we get pulled over, stay down! Don't say or do anything, or I'll have to shoot him. Understand me?"

Sue tried to look up. Decatur backhanded her across the face with ferocious impatience. "Do you fuckin' understand me?"

She put her cheek down on the cold seat. The blue flashing light bounced off her face. She began to sob. "Yes."

"Good, now stay down and shut the fuck up!" growled Decatur. He looked up at the rearview mirror. The police car was gaining.

Decatur slid the .357 between his legs.

Sue looked on in stunned silence.

The police car came even closer, riding up on Decatur's bumper.

"Oh fuck, oh fuck, oh fuck," chanted Decatur.

Then, at the last minute, the police car pulled aside the Renegade and raced on down the road.

"Well, well, whaddaya' know, Susie Q? My lucky day. Dumb fucking fucks," gloated Decatur contemptuously.

Sue turned her head away from Decatur. Closed her eyes. Blood trickled from her nose.

Decatur made a sharp turn onto a dirt road framed by deep grazing lands and walled in by mountains. Not another car in sight.

The Renegade's headlights illuminated an eerie forest scene; tightly grouped trees and low hanging branches looking oddly skeletal, alive and groping, anthropomorphizing from the darkness as if coming to snatch them. Then a moose jumped across the road, missing the Renegade by mere inches. It bounded back into the woods and disappeared as quickly as it came.

"Holy crap! Did you see that?" asked Decatur, then smiled, realizing what he had said.

"Of course you didn't, the only thing you can see from there is my ass. A moose just darn near hit my Jeep. It was at least a 120 on the Boone and Crocket scale. What a beauty!"

"Sorry I missed it."

"No never mind, you can get up now. We're here."

Sue struggled up to the seat as Decatur pulled the Renegade into the gravel parking area of a small airfield in the middle of nowhere. The snow-capped tops of the Chugach Mountains glowed in the distant background.

Sue took a look at the small airfield. Just a few planes. A hangar. A small office building. An asphalt landing strip. Not much else. The airfield was deserted in the shadowy light.

Sue looked at the half-dozen single-engine planes tied down around the airfield. She looked puzzled. The panic was palpable now, pounding sledgehammer strong by the second.

"What, what are we doing here?" she asked.

Decatur boastfully answered, "You're in for a special treat, Susie Q. I'm the best doggone pilot you're ever gonna meet."

Coming to a stop, the Renegade almost mated with a wing strut on one of the parked airplanes.

Sue looked at the plane. It was a snow-and-sky-blue Cessna 140, a high-wing, canvas-covered taildragger. She had to squint to read the registration painted on its tail, the numbers and letters were miniscule. 773HZ3NO6.

"Why are the markings on the tail so small?" asked Sue.

"Them's the smallest size that aviation regulations allow. Couldn't paint them no smaller without gettin' into some sort of trouble. And we wouldn't want that, would we?"

"But why so small?"

"Well, you know, just in case I do this in the daytime, if I take off and someone is in that office over there, I can simply radio them any random number, and since mine are so small, they can't see 'em to tell if I'm telling them the right numbers or not." He winked at Sue. "Don't want just anybody knowing my business, you know?"

"And what exactly is your business?"

"Lookit, you've got nothing to worry about, Susie Q. You do what I say and everything will be fine. Got it?"

Sue nodded. But there was something else. Something else…

Then it came to her.

"I had a boyfriend who was learning to fly," she said, her voice low, almost accusatory. "Those are too many numbers. That's not right."

Decatur grinned broadly, one side of his face lifting just a touch higher than the other. "Well, check out the brain on Susie-Q! You're right, darling. Let's just call it my idea of a little joke, just between me and myself. Gotta have my fun, ya' know."

Sue stared off in the distance, wishing she could pull herself away from all this.

"Okay, good, now you just stay put. I've got some stuff to do first. Hate to have to shoot you and put some holes in my Jeep."

"I won't make any trouble, just don't hurt me, please."

"Now why would I go and hurt a purty little thing like you? I got much better things in mind. I'll tell you this—we're gonna' be packing this night full of fun."

Sue mumbled something under her breath.

"What was that?" sneered Decatur.

"This isn't fair, there's no justice—"

"Justice?! Of course, there's justice. Where would we be without justice?"

Sue looked at Decatur. A glimmer of hope.

Decatur broke the glimmer with a wicked wink. "'Just us', Susie Q. Just us."

Decatur opened his door and walked to the rear of the Renegade, popped the back open. He pulled out the twenty-pound Worthington propane tank and the canary yellow, ten-gallon can of diesel fuel that he had stolen from the church. He lugged them over to the Cessna 140, unlocked the door and put both tanks in the cargo hold at the back of the plane, balancing the loads so that the weight would be more or less evenly distributed.

Satisfied, Decatur went back to his Jeep, opened the passenger door. "Okay, c'mon, get out."

He helped Sue out of the jeep. Re-handcuffed her so that the handcuffs were in front, then led her to the plane and opened the passenger door.

"Where are you taking me?" begged Sue.

"Get in. I'll be glad to show you," grinned Decatur.

Sue stumbled, then clumsily made her way into the passenger seat. Glancing quickly at the control panel and the windshield, her first thought was that it was much too high. At the angle the plane was resting on the runway, she couldn't see anything, except for the stars in the distant heavens. Another plane, or even a person, could be standing five feet in front of them and she wouldn't even know it.

Decatur shut her door.

Sue watched as he walked around the 140, releasing the plane from its tie-downs. Decatur then did a visual check of the tires, flaps, and tail.

Content that all was in order, he climbed into the pilot's seat, buckled in and checked the controls. "You better buckle up, too. Wouldn't want anything bad happenin' to ya.'"

Sue struggled with her bound hands to secure her seatbelt. As she did, she glanced behind her seat, at the storage area. In addition to the two fuel tanks was a large cardboard box filled with food.

Decatur saw what she was looking at. Beaming, he piped up: "Told you I was a Boy Scout."

He reached into his jacket and pulled out a laminated card. A pre-flight checklist. He read the checklist outloud: "Pre takeoff and cockpit, check. Trim tab controls, check. Throttle closed. Flap controls full forward. Mixture set to idle. Cutoffs—off. Master battery switch off. Instruments checked and set. Elevator set to neutral. Altimeter set to elevation. Aileron set to neutral. Good. Primer closed and locked. Throttle at one inch. Battery on. Starter switch closed. One, two, three, and start."

Decatur put the card back. "Cool beans, looks like we're good to go." He gave Sue a wink. "How about you, Susie Q?" he asked, growing more companionable. "Bet you just itchin' to get upstairs, aren't cha'?"

Sue stared ahead in desolate silence.

She couldn't understand his sudden chattiness, was he just a neophyte pilot or was this some sort of control thing on his part?

However, the more she thought about it the better it was for her. The more he talked to her, the more she became a "someone" to him, instead of a 'something.' It wasn't much, but it was all she had going in the claustrophobic confinement of the tiny plane.

"Okie-dokie, let's get this here show on the road." Decatur looked to his right, then turned to his left. He stuck his head out of the window and shouted out over the dark landscape, "Clear prop!"

Sue prayed that someone outside would hear this useless warning, but of course, there was no one at the deserted airfield but them.

Just her luck that God had gone deaf.

Decatur turned the ignition key.

The engine popped once, with a loud explosion, then immediately died.

Thank you, God! I know you're not deaf. Please don't let it start thought Sue.

"Okay, of course it's not going to start on the first time."

Decatur turned the key a second time.

This time the engine exploded with a thunderous roar.

The power was astonishing. A living, threatening thing, it assaulted Sue's already assaulted senses as it blasted through her body and rattled her ears.

Decatur applied full throttle and the plane began bumping down the runway, slowly gaining speed until she felt the tail lift up off the grass. Now she could see ahead of them into the starry darkness. Seconds later, the plane lifted off the runway.

Sue nervously dug her fingernails into the seat cushion.

She fought a rising panic attack; where was her next breath? She couldn't find it. Her ears popped and were sealed, and her mouth was packed with a large sponge-like ball, which she finally recognized as her cotton-dry tongue. Her head was pressed back and her chin elevated by an unnatural force as the plane climbed.

The noise inside the small plane became deafening, disorienting and claustrophobic.

A steep climb took the plane to a thousand feet. The plane banked sharply to the south.

The red and blue lights of the instrument panel glared in the pitch-black darkness of the airplane cockpit. Sue, lit only by the dim lights, looked out the window.

Up ahead, she could make out the bluffs of the Kenai Peninsula. The bluffs were actually the ends of eskers and drumlins, elongated hills shaped centuries ago by retreating glaciers. Sue had actually skied this jumble of drumlins and eskers on a sixth-grade ski trip. In fact, the only thing Sue remembered about sixth-grade geography was that her teacher likened the esker to the mess left by a drunk simultaneously walking backward and throwing up.

Suddenly, a pocket of outside air, a thermal coming off the nearby mountains, violently bounced the plane up, then just as suddenly slammed it down. Sue screamed.

Over the ear-splitting noise, Decatur merely smirked. "Relax. Just a little thermal. Kind of like a roller coaster, innit? Love those things. Told you we were gonna pack us in some fun."

Decatur tried a re-assuring look. Missed by a mile.

Another air pocket bounce. Her stomach lurched into her chest. Sue quickly scanned the instrument panel.

"Is that ... is that the transponder?" Without headphones, Sue had to shout to be heard. She pointed to a black box on the instrument panel. The box resembled a glorified walkie-talkie with windows to show a four-number code.

"I'll be doggone, that boyfriend of yours, he tell you all about transponders, too?" asked a surprised Decatur.

"I, I told you—he was learning to fly. He'd come home after each lesson and tell me what he'd learned, just to make sure he remembered everything. Said I should know what a transponder was, just in case we were flying together and something went wrong. Let's see," she closed her eyes and tried hard to remember.

"Oh, yeah, you set numbers in those four windows and miles away someone in a control tower can locate you wherever you are, your heading, speed, altitude."

"Yeah, well, we'll be leaving that bad boy off, so you just sit back and enjoy the flight."

Decatur concentrated on his instrument panel, then turned to Sue. "Wanna hear something funny?"

Sue shrugged her shoulders. She really didn't give a shit at this point.

"I don't have a doggone pilot's license," smirked Decatur. "How funny is that?"

Sue gave him a look that could have frozen global warming forever. Not sure if she heard what he had just said, she finally repeated, "You ... you don't have a license?"

"Well ... I did."

"Did?!"

"Bastards took it away because of a medication ... misunderstanding. But nobody pays no nevermind out here to that, anyway."

Thoughts raced behind Sue's eyes, then she resigned herself to a helpless shrug and slowly shook her head. It was the only emotional response she had at that moment.

As the plane jerked forward, something caught Sue's nose.

"What?" asked Decatur.

"I smell ... something."

"What?"

"Donuts ..." Just as abruptly, Sue's train of thought was broken when she spotted what was stashed in Decatur's side door.

The shape was intermittently illuminated by a red strobe light blinking on the wingtip—off, on, off, on ...

It was like a warning sign.

And Sue recognized the shape behind the warning.

It was some type of rifle.

With a long clip. And a lethal look.

Outside her window, Sue watched as Anchorage faded slowly behind her, one light blinking out after another.

She bent her head forward and thought to herself, *This must be what going mad feels like.*

Decatur applied throttle, regained altitude, and concentrated on the instruments and his chart. Outside, the aurora borealis began to paint the night sky. Decatur's plane became a dark, moving speck against the white, snow-capped mountains in the distance.

The first thing Sue noticed, looking down, was a moving carpet of the deepest blue. Once her eyes focused in the nighttime light, she realized they were traveling over an endless expanse of water.

What Sue didn't know was that Decatur had turned the nose of the Cessna 140 south south-east into the Cook Inlet, a vast body of water with mountains to the east and west and an infinite loneliness in between. The mountains were filled with boundless forests, creeks, and rivers.

The loneliness was called Resurrection Bay.

TWELVE

In times of extreme stress, the mind wanders all over the place, making some strange twists and turns in its attempts to escape...

As the engine droned on, Sue fought to take herself someplace else in her head, away from the freezing cold, the noise, the shaking, this sick fuck next to her gazing out of the cockpit with that lopsided sick grin on his face.

Suddenly, she flashed on her first few days back in Alaska, barely a month ago, after all these years away. She had to get used to living near the Arctic Circle all over again. The hardest part of this time of year was watching the sun set at almost midnight. Tonight, she remembered from the little box on the front page of the newspaper, the sun had set at 11:38. It would rise again less than five hours later.

The thickest, heaviest bedroom curtains in the world were sold in Alaska. It was the only way to seal off a bedroom window and get something resembling normal sleep.

But the sunsets and sunrises were, in a word, *magic.*

Suddenly, she flashed on the boy in New Orleans. Years ago, before Sunny, Sue was crashing with a few other homeless kids at a flop in the French Quarter and she'd hooked up with this twenty-two-year-old guy who was an aspiring filmmaker. He'd thrown together a crew, scraped together a couple thousand dollars, borrowed an old 16mm camera and shot his independent zombie movie in an old neighborhood on the backside of the Quarter, across Elysian Fields, near the Faubourg Marigny.

He was sweet, but a complete flake. He never finished his movie, and after they broke up, she never heard of or from him again. He never became the famous director he knew he'd be, but he'd taught her a term she'd always remembered.

Magic hour. That transitional time between night and day at either dusk or dawn, when the light took on a special, luminescent quality that you never saw any other time.

Sue looked out the cockpit window, scanning the horizon for sunrise. Soon, she knew, the magic light of magic hour would be here.

She looked down and tried to focus on the small clock embedded in the instrument panel, but the unremitting vibration of the plane's engine caused the timepiece to jiggle crazily like a shaken snow globe.

They had been flying south at least an hour when the clouds suddenly shredded, then just as quickly, disappeared.

The engine was not so deafening now that cruising altitude had been reached. It was here, at 5,000 feet, that Sue witnessed a truly awe-inspiring vista of Alaskan vastness—the white, mountainous snowscapes on her left and right horizons gradually gave way to vast, verdant landscapes of summertime greens and browns. Pure untamed wilderness as far as the eye could see. Down below, a school of humpback whales broke the undulating waves, their spouts shooting rainbows above the topaz bay.

If it wasn't so serious, it might be funny. Fucking ironic even thought Sue. She had never been claustrophobic before, never afraid of a small closet without a light or being stranded in an elevator, yet here she was, witnessing what looked like half a hemisphere right in front of her, and she found herself struck by an overwhelming sense of claustrophobia. For the first time, she felt the scope of the total isolation, the complete helplessness that surrounded her on every side.

It was also at 5,000 feet that Sue felt the numbing pain of coldness. She remembered once that another ex-boyfriend, the neophyte pilot, had told her that for every one thousand feet higher you flew, the temperature fell by five and one-half degrees.

Sue shivered, then realized that it wasn't the altitude that was making her cold. It was the same reoccurring pins and needles numbness she felt late at night when she woke up somewhere in the vague veil of consciousness unable to escape the nightmare of killing her mother.

Her mind wandered, drifted, to her mother, and how she'd killed her.

Sue was fifteen when she finally found her mother's death certificate. It was there in black and white. Mostly black. Leilani Turnbull had died three months to the day after Sue was born.

But it was Sue's best guess that she had killed her mother six months before that.

Over time, as she got older, Sue had pieced together the missing gaps in her mother's life, the gaps that Sarge had never filled in.

Sue knew from her own experience that the second term of pregnancy, between thirteen and twenty-six weeks, was the moment in which most women enjoyed their pregnancy the most. The sensations of nausea, extreme tiredness, and back pain, which were all very normal in the first term, generally subsided.

Leilani first complained to her OB/GYN of excruciating back pain during her second term, when the pain should have been gone. Her doctor did a preliminary examination and found nothing anomalous. He surmised it was just normal back pain. When the pain persisted, the doctor prescribed some low-grade pain killers and told her to bear it out, that it would pass soon. At this point in her pregnancy, he said, X-rays were not an option.

According to the laconic hospital report, Leilani died three months after giving birth to Sue from HER2-positive metastatic breast cancer. The pain she had been feeling for over six months was revealed as a hole in her L5 vertebra, a hole caused by the undetected breast cancer's spread, first to the spine and then to the brain.

Since pregnancy, Sue had learned, was a state of immunosuppression, Leilani's own protective army was not working full-time to slow the cancer spread. In fact, Leilani's cancer had spread so aggressively that by the time the doctors had been able to take X-rays, it was too late. The damage had been done.

What a lousy deal, thought Sue. *She gave me life. I gave her death.*

Having killed her mother, Sue, from an early age, felt justifiably trapped in a prison of her only vice. Oblivious and yet at the same time calmly aware, she felt her life was just a bright illusion, her world a torn curtain. She continually had the oppressive feeling that something was wrong, something wasn't quite right.

As if to reinforce her insecurity, young Sue remembered her father working a succession of double shifts and weekends. She assumed he was just staying away from her. In fact, her earliest memories were a succession of pre-K day care centers, followed by elementary after-school programs, and finally when she was seven, becoming a latchkey kid. Day after day, week after week, she would return from school by herself to an empty home because her father was away at work.

The effects of being a latchkey child differed with age. Loneliness, boredom, and fear were most common in those younger than ten. In the early teens, there was a greater susceptibility to peer pressure, which resulted in alcohol abuse and smoking.

The positive effects of being a latchkey child, studies showed, included independence and self-reliance, which is what happened to Sue.

That is, until now.

————

They were well into magic hour now. The brilliant light outside cast morning shadows across the interior of the cockpit as Sue watched Decatur unfold and carefully study an aviation chart of the Anchorage Bowl and the adjoining regions.

Out of the corner of her eye, she noticed three crosses circled in red on the chart. The crosses were likewise numbered in blood red—1, 2, 3.

There was a long silence as Sue continued to look straight ahead at the rising sun. Finally, she spoke in the cool, calm calculus of reason and asked the question she needed answered the most. In a weary voice, she asked, "Why are you doing this?"

Decatur folded his chart. He looked through Sue and with eyes cold as dagger icicles answered, "This is what I do, Susie Q. It's what I'm for." He smiled his charmingly patented smile. "'Sides, it beats watchin' TV."

Sue continued to look ahead, wondering how many sunrises she had seen. Wondering if she would see one tomorrow.

"You know how many millions of people wish for immortality who don't even know what to do on a rainy Sunday afternoon?" snickered Decatur with arrogant assurance. "If you disagree with me, then you're just wrong."

Decatur looked outside his window. Down at a glacier below. "Gee whiz, you wanna see something? Watch this!" he palliated.

Decatur banked the plane hard to his left with a sudden, stomach-churning dip. Sue banged her head against the window, but Decatur didn't miss a beat.

Down below, a pack of wolves made their way across the ethereal blue glow of an ice flow that had detached itself from its parent glacier.

Decatur grabbed the Steyr Aug from the door recess.

Cracked his side window open. The cold morning air blasted into the cockpit.

Unfazed, Decatur chambered a round into the assault rifle. Aimed through the open window.

Squeezed off a shot.

BAM!

The sound of the explosion was deafening in the small cabin.

Sue's instinct was to cover her ears, but the handcuffs restrained her. The noise rattled her eardrums.

Down below, one of the wolves was blown off its feet. Crimson blood pooled on white snow.

Decatur was ecstatic. "Well, lookie there! We have us another winner!" He looked over at Sue. "Doggone it—now that's something you don't see every day!"

Sue turned back to her window in bleak silence.

"Told you it beats the crap outta the TV!"

Hard to argue with a psycho armed with an assault rifle at five hundred feet, thought Sue.

THIRTEEN

DECATUR BANKED THE PLANE over what looked like a small cork plugging the heart of Resurrection Bay. Smiling, he proudly pointed toward the remote, desolate island covered in dense forest. "Welcome to my summer house."

Sue gazed down at the water below, the sparkle of diamonds on every wave crest, the troughs of wrinkled cobalt lapping over cerulean, over topaz, over silver. In the first light, the island resembled an emerald gem set in the shimmering azure ring of the endless bay.

Not more than five miles in diameter, Sue noticed there was no landing strip and the 140 had wheels, not pontoons. "There's no place to land," she said more to herself than to Decatur, allowing herself a faint spark of hope.

"Don't you worry yourself none about that, Susie Q. You're in good hands."

Decatur suddenly nosed the plane straight down at the water.

Sue screamed, "What are you doing!?" burying her fingernails deep into the seat cushion.

"See, right there's your problem. You've got to learn to trust me, Susie Q." Decatur cut the throttle back, lowered the flaps, and side-slipped the plane the last one-hundred feet. "What I've done is taken off the standard tires and replaced them with a pair of tundra tires. Just take a look-see out your window."

Sue looked out and saw what he was talking about. The plane did have large, oversized wheels, something she hadn't noticed back at the airstrip. At the same time Sue saw that they were approaching the water all too quickly. "Wheels won't help on water!" She tensed her body and braced herself for the inevitable crash.

Decatur calmly grinned. "You got that all wrong, Susie Q. What them oversized tires are doggone good for is landings on rough terrain and swampy ground. Now you just sit back and watch this. It's called a shoreline landing and no one does it better than this here!"

Decatur throttled back to 40 mph, then raised the nose. The plane's stall warning blared out and it was as though a bassoon had suddenly become articulate, wailing its warning with a syncopated C-sharp.

Sue shrieked as the plane's tires caromed into the water ten feet from a sandbar. Decatur instantly locked the brakes, effectively turning the large tires into pontoons. The plane effortlessly hydroplaned across the water skimming toward the island's shore. The instant the locked tires touched the sandbar, Decatur released the brakes, turning them once again back into proper tires. The plane rolled across the sandbar and came to a rest on the small island near a scrub-brush thicket.

Decatur looked over at Sue, beaming. "Pretty neat, huh?"

Sue struggled to catch her breath. She watched, as if in slow motion, as Decatur killed the engine and slipped the plane key into his jacket pocket. Then he calmly reached over and unlocked Sue's handcuffs. "Now, here's the deal … We're gonna spend the day in our little slice of paradise, have us some real fun, then first thing tomorrow morning, I'll let you go. Only rule is, I get no trouble from you—agreed?"

Sue sadly nodded.

"Good! Now, pop that door handle up and take hold of the back of the seat and the window supports. You'll be able to get out that way."

Suddenly, from out of the wakening blue sky came the droning sound of an approaching airplane from across the bay.

Sue looked out from her open door. A pontoon plane buzzed overhead then banked into a lazy turn and circled back.

Decatur reached over and slammed Sue's door shut. He glared up at the circling plane. "Shit! The sumbitch is going to land!"

Maybe, just maybe thought Sue, trying to suppress a flicker of hope as well as the thought of screaming her lungs out to get the pilot's attention.

"Don't you get no crazy, fucked-up ideas," barked Decatur as if reading her mind. "Stay in the plane, don't let him see you! If he lands, don't say a goddamn word to him. If you raise hell, I'm going to shoot the both of you … Understand?"

"I won't do anything!"

"Good. Now stay down."

Overhead, the pontoon plane continued to circle.

Decatur opened his door and stepped out. He looked up, waving at the circling plane. This time the pilot dipped his wings up and down in a friendly wave, then continued across the bay.

Sue despairingly sunk her head to her knees as the sound of the airplane engine faded away, along with her hopes for salvation.

Relieved, Decatur stuffed the .357 Magnum pistol into his belt. He went around the plane and swung Sue's door open. "Get out."

Sue hit the ground with both knees quivering. Shaky as hell.

"Don't fly much, do you, Susie Q?"

Sue wanted to throw up, but didn't want to give Decatur the satisfaction.

"Here, take these," smiled Decatur.

He reached into the cargo hold and took out the purloined diesel and propane tanks. Dropped them at Sue's feet.

Sue struggled to stand up. For the first time, she took in the island.

The beach.

The dark forests.

The rolling hills.

The shimmering water.

The distant snow-covered mountains across the bay.

Pine trees so massive they reminded her of the cathedral spires she had seen in New York.

It was a landscape like none other she had ever seen—a tapestry rich in colors, dramatic light, and breathtaking perspectives. Disconcertingly, with the temperature in the mid '60s and with no humidity, this was quite possibly the most beautiful place on earth.

The emotional contradiction between the overwhelming beauty in front of her and the impending threat of evil was clearly visible on her face. She brushed a tear from her cheek.

Decatur noticed Sue taking in the scenery. "Sure is breath-taking, huh? They say around these parts is some of the best huntin' ground in the entire northern hemisphere. Know why?"

Sue shook her head no.

"'Cause gettin' to the moon is a helluva lot easier than gettin' here," Decatur chuckled.

He turned toward Sue. Took in a breath of island air so deep he seemed to suck all the air out of the world.

"Man, oh man, how fresh is this air? Clean, pure, virgin, filled with life, filled with hope. Can't you just feel it?" He took in another deep breath.

"Get this, in one of my hunting magazines, this article told how a bunch of scientists had gotten a bunch of Civil War buttons . . . you know, buttons that were on uniforms way back when. Well, in those days, buttons were made by sealing two pieces of tin together. The kicker is, those buttons still held the air that was around back in the 1860s. Can you imagine that? Before smog. Before acid rain. Before car emissions. Well, these scientist tested the air in those buttons and found out that air out here was the same as it was back then. Practically untouched. Imagine that?"

He took another deep breath and new life, an evil vitality, seemed to surge into him.

This was his stage and he owned it.

Having weathered humanity's derision and indifference all of his life, this was his moment in the spotlight, the moment that created him, propelled him, forced him to come back to his private curtain call again and again.

"Welcome to Resurrection Bay at its best, Susie Q. In the wintertime this whole region is completely frozen over, one big damn popsicle . . . "

He slowly let the breath out, relishing in the moment.

" . . . But in the summertime, that's a different story. They don't call Alaska the land of the midnight sun for nothing. This time of the year, we've got us eighteen, almost nineteen hours of daylight up here. Yep, this here is strictly a summertime project."

He snickered to himself.

The callous, careless impact of his throwaway phrase "summertime project" was not lost on Sue. In that instant she saw the cold-blooded cruelty of the man in his entirety. Yet Decatur passed off this casual utterance without a further thought, as if he was buttering a piece of toast.

Before she could process its possible implications, Decatur took the large cardboard box of foodstuffs out of the plane and pointed with his gun. "That way. The path there leads south." He snickered. "South. How's that song go about being in Dixie?" He laughed at the image, then pointed at the two fuel tanks on the ground. "You take those."

Sue looked at the two tanks at her feet. "What are we supposed to do with these?"

"Well, we've got a few things to do before we start packing this day full of fun. You just follow that path there. Think of it as your very own yellow brick road."

"I can't."

"Oh, you can and you will."

"No, I mean I can't walk in the woods with high heels. It's not possible."

"Well, what say we fix that for you? Give me."

Sue hesitated a second, then leaned against a tree. She took off both shoes and handed them over. "Please, be careful. They're expensive."

Decatur smoothly slid a Ka-Bar knife out of his belt sheath. The edge of the seven-inch, razor-sharp blade glistened in the morning sun.

He placed the over-sized blade against the heel of one shoe and, with one fluid motion, cut it neatly off. He repeated the process with the other shoe, then handed them both back to Sue. "Not anymore."

Her mind raced as she tried to take it all in. Suddenly, she flashed on Kathleen Turner's line in *Romancing the Stone*, when Michael Douglas as Jack T. Colton sliced the heels off her expensive shoes as they trekked through the Colombian jungle. *Is nothing I own sacred to you?*

Reluctantly, Sue kept her mouth shut and slipped both shoes back on.

"See, no such thing as problems, only solutions. Now, as I was saying, you get those."

Sue grabbed both tanks and slowly, painfully began lugging them through the path in the forest.

Decatur followed six feet behind.

Already beginning to sweat under the double load, Sue looked out at the bay, intermittently visible through the trees, scrutinizing the forest around her, weighing her odds of escape if she simply dropped both loads and took off running.

"Oh, yeah … You feel free to take off anytime you want. Just keep in mind the nearest town is coupla' hundred miles away."

He acted confused and pointed in one direction as they walked.

"… that way, or is it—"

He turned and pointed one hundred and eighty degrees in the opposite direction.

"… is it that way?" He grinned heartily. "And that ain't counting all that water between here and the mainland. Oh, and then there's them pesky mountain ranges on the other side."

Cackling, he added, "It's big country out here, Susie Q. Even the biggest game hunters don't make it all the way out here. Yep. Big, big country."

I'm so fucked, thought Sue.

"Could eat a body clean up," concluded Decatur.

In the blink of an eye, the forest engulfed Decatur and Sue until they were completely lost to sight in the most isolated, enormous, and inhospitable landscape this side of the moon.

So fucked.

FOURTEEN

Fuck! Could these cans be any heavier? Sue had been struggling through a screen of leaves and branches almost as thick as tapestry for longer than she could remember.

The latticework of trees overhead was one enormous cocoon catching the light and shadowing the ground. The path itself, if you could call it that, was a mat of tree roots and hand-sized rocks, making it very difficult to make steady progress. The likelihood of twisting an ankle was growing with every step she took. Reduced to a beast of burden, her fingers beginning to cramp, her legs aching, her arms on fire, Sue spied a full moon over a distant mountaintop even though it was only breaking dawn. Using the same ploy that she used when dancing on a stage to transport herself to another place and time, the pale orb on its leisurely pendulum way was just the hypnotic suggestion she needed to take her mind off the pain and discomfort.

Full Thunder Moon!

That's what Sarge used to call it, Sue remembered, for the simple reason that thunderstorms were most frequent during this time of the year.

Looking up at the pale blue light brightening the morning sky, Sue wondered what Sunny was doing right now. Was it somehow possible, at this very moment in time, that she and Sunny were looking up at the same moon?

Kinda doubtful thought Sue. Knowing her daughter, she was probably still sleeping in her sleeping bag along with all of her friends.

Sue momentarily smiled, no longer affected by the heavy load she was carrying.

Sunny's birth had changed everything. Exactly thirteen years ago, Sue had moved into the group home with Sunny. Settling into the home, Sue had an epiphany, almost a breakdown.

In one brief moment, she realized that her previous life was over and another one was beginning. She could either go crazy and resent her child or accept the miracle that was Sunny and devote her life to her.

Sue chose the latter.

In Sue's mind, playing like a movie now, she saw herself thirteen years earlier sitting down at the communal kitchen table, putting deep purple ink against light lavender onion skinned paper and starting her first diary entry.

Thinking back, she remembered ending the entry with:

It's a little after six and you wake up and my new day begins. And, no, Sunny, I haven't solved the Middle East crisis, or discovered the missing mass in the universe. I don't even think I recycled the empty two liter Diet Dr Pepper bottle yesterday. But one thing I do know—to the best of my ability, I did keep you alive and relatively happy and content for another day, and for now, that's all I can ask. And hey, who knows, maybe tomorrow, I'll actually take a shower.

For a moment longer, Sue's thoughts escaped their morbid despair as she remembered a smiling, just-turned-three-day-old Sunny, her big blue eyes full of happiness and life.

But those memories were thirteen years old and at least two hundred miles away. The vision faded quickly, and Sue found herself back on the island coming to the end of the path just as both arms began to spasm.

At the end of the path was a clearing.

And in the middle of the clearing, nestled among the endless pine trees, was a two-room cabin. It was functionally constructed with exterior log walls, a low sloping shingled roof and a wide-planked front porch some two feet off the ground. Behind the cabin, forested hills faded, rank and file, disappearing into the pearly mist.

"Home sweet home," beamed Decatur.

Sue wondered if Sunny would ever read her diary. And, if she did, would she care?

FIFTEEN

"I'LL TAKE THAT YELLOW one," said Decatur, grabbing the diesel can from Sue and walking to the side of the cabin. He unscrewed the top from the can and emptied the diesel fuel into the generator. He pushed in the priming bulb, turned the manual selector to choke, then squeezed the safety lever at the handle and gave the pull cord a quick jerk. The generator spurted to life on the first try as Decatur gradually pushed the lever to the run position.

"This bad boy will give us about twenty-four hours of juice so that we don't have to rough it too much," explained Decatur.

Then he climbed up the porch and opened a huge padlock attached to the front door. He pushed the door inward.

Both rusted hinges rasped and groaned, as if an omen of things to come.

"You hungry?" asked Decatur, leading Sue inside.

He flicked on a wall switch next to the door. A circle of muddy light fell on a front room.

Sue took a quick look around the cabin, and although it was lit only by the nicotine brown glow of a table lamp, it was nothing like she had expected it would be.

The cabin had two rooms, both twenty by twenty, judged Sue. Without any architectural partition, the front room was a combination kitchen, dining room, and living room. From what Sue could see of the back room, it looked to her like a bedroom with at least a bed and a couple of dressers.

A rough-hewn oak table seemed to anchor the main room. Over the door, a handheld crossbow and a pair of binoculars. On the walls, a map, a few animal traps, a couple of animal pelts. A black bear rug lay in front of a couch. Overall, the décor was aggressively macho, but at the same time, homey in a rustic kind of Pottery Barn way.

Opposite the couch was an entertainment center housing the usual array of electronic equipment. A combination TV and VCR. A battery-powered boombox. Speakers. A mile of wires.

Sue was equally surprised by how orderly everything was. Nothing was out of place or even placed haphazardly. For that matter, there was no clutter and nothing was excessively dirty. Rather the cabin was redolent of redwood and pine, as well as the faint and not unpleasant smell of ashes from the fireplace.

On the kitchen side were functional cabinets and a sink with a hand water pump.

Decatur noticed Sue looking at the hand pump. He explained, "The water comes from a well. You gotta pump it for a couple of minutes to get it going. You know how that goes, don't you, Susie Q?"

He pointed at the 2-burner gas stove. "Propane's outside in a tank. There should be plenty left from last year."

"Last year?" Sue asked tentatively.

Ignoring the question, as well as the possible insinuation, Decatur set the carton of food on the kitchen table. "Canned food goes in the cabinets above the sink. Dry foods down here. Hope you like steak."

He pulled a small cooler out of the large cardboard box. Inside were several steaks packed in dry ice.

Decatur suddenly knelt down. Opened a cabinet under the sink. Pulled out a length of chain bolted to the water pipe.

A leg-iron shackle was connected to the other end.

In one quick fluid motion, Decatur snapped the leg-iron shut around Sue's ankle.

"You like duck?" asked Decatur as he walked around, setting up house, conversing like nothing out of the ordinary was happening.

To him, this could have been a Walton moment.

"I was gonna bring duck, but I decided on deer steak instead. You like duck? Me, I love duck. Coupla' years back I was duck huntin' in Alabama and I got my three duck limit in about ten minutes, and I was throwing them in the back of my truck when this redneck sheriff pulled up behind me. He walks up to me and says 'I see you've been huntin' today' and very politely I said, 'Yes, sir, and as you can see I only shot the maximum number for the day, sir.' 'Well, yes, I can see that,' the sheriff says, 'but there's just one problem.' 'What would that be, sir?" I asks. The sheriff picks up the first duck and sticks his finger in the duck's ass and pulls it out and smells it and says 'Well ya' see here, this duck is from Tennessee. Do you have a Tennessee huntin' license?' 'Why yes, sir, I do' I says. So I pulled it out of my wallet and show it to the sheriff. Well, the sheriff, he then sticks his finger in another duck's ass and smells it and says 'I'm afraid this here duck is from Mississippi,' thinking that he has me this time. 'You happen to have a Mississippi huntin' license?' To his surprise, I pulled out a Mississippi license. Shocked the sumbitch. Then he takes the third duck and sticks his finger up its ass and smells it. He smiles because he thinks for sure that he's caught a man hunting illegally. 'Now this here duck just happens to be from Canada and I'm bettin' that you don't have a Canadian huntin' license.' 'Well, actually, I do, Sheriff.' So I pull it out and show it to him. Now by this time the Sheriff is both surprised and pissed off. He looks at me and says 'Well, I guess you're free to go, but with all them huntin' licenses, I'm rather curious. Can I ask you where you're from?' So I turn around, pull down my pants, and tell the Sheriff, 'Well, why don't you find out for yourself, jackass.'"

Decatur chuckled. "Ain't that a pisser?"

He looked at Sue for a reaction.

There was none. He gave her a depraved grin.

———

An hour later, Decatur was tearing at his steak with his teeth, gulping its savory chunks down like any other predator.

To Sue, it reminded her of dirty clothes being tossed around inside a dryer. Still chained, she sat across the table from the Maytag man. She picked at her plate, afraid of what he might do if she refused to eat.

There was a long awkward silence, then Decatur looked up. "You know that TV show—*Star Trek*? I was watching it last night. They say the last freakin' frontier is space. 'Space, the final frontier.' Well, they got that wrong. The last frontier is a woman's soul. Now, that, that is a mystery. I think it was Freud who said it best...'you got your whores and you got your women you can marry.'"

Decatur looked at Sue. "I bet Freud would have liked it out here."

Sue said nothing.

"Doggone it, you gotta learn to relax, Susie Q. I mean, think about it, we're only doing what you get paid to do. 'Sides, it's like I told you back before. I just don't like crowds, you know?"

Still nothing from Sue.

"Okay, got me an idea. How about this?" Decatur dug in his pockets. Pulled out three one-hundred dollar bills. "I'll give you an extra three hundred bucks to lighten up and stop worrying so much. Gee whiz, that's six hundred bucks total we're talking!"

He leaned across the table and stuffed the money into Sue's shirt pocket. "Now, try to understand the simple facts here. We're gonna spend the day together, we're gonna get some sleep tonight, and first light tomorrow, we're outta here. It's that simple, Susie Q."

Sue looked him deep in his eyes. She no longer knew exactly what to believe anymore.

"Scout's Honor," grinned Decatur as he took the last bite of his steak. "Doggone, that was good."

Leaning back on two legs of the chair, he wiped his mouth with his shirt sleeve, then pulled out the Altoids tin.

Opening the lid, he snorted an enormous amount of coke.

Sue remained quiet. The chain rattled as she tried to find a comfortable sitting position.

Decatur looked at her, then smiled.

"Well, Susie Q, maybe you got yourself a point there, after all. I mean, nothing spoils a good party like too much talk."

Decatur stood up and walked over to the wall behind Sue. "Guess there's no time like the present to start packing in the fun, right, Susie Q?"

He pulled back a piece of wall panel, revealing a hidden safe behind. Decatur twirled the combination a couple of times back and forth. The door clicked opened.

Inside the safe, Sue could make out a video camera and what looked like four small videotapes.

Decatur pulled the video camera out and eagerly attached it to a tripod standing near the entertainment center. Connecting a cable to the TV/VCR, Decatur asked, "Ever seen one of these bad boys?"

He turned the TV on. Aimed the camera at Sue. She turned her head away.

"This VCR has a 'loop mode' so that you can play the tape over and over for your endless 'video entertainment'. Kinda reminds me of the A/V club back there in high school, you know? Goddamn, did those days suck."

He opened a case of audio cassettes. Began to thumb through them. Each of the tapes reminded him of his high school days. He began to talk, not to Sue, but to himself, as if transported back in time. "If you look at my face, from the pockmarks you can tell that I used to have a tremendous amount of acne. I was addicted to sweets, still am. When I was a teenager, my face was always one big yellow pimple. Consequently, I never had any girls interested in me. I'd ask a girl out, and she'd say, 'Well, no, I'm sorry. I've got something else planned.' I heard that so doggone many times."

Selecting a tape, Decatur opened the Altoids can and once again indulged in a copious amount of coke. "Well, those days are fucking over."

He pushed the audio cassette into the boombox. "And now for a little mood music..."

He stabbed the play button.

Cornelius Brothers & Sister Rose crooned "Too Late to Turn Back Now," one of the loveliest paeans to unrequited love ever recorded.

"Well, Susie Q, guess it's time you earn those big bucks..."

Decatur pulled her over to the bear rug in the middle of the floor. The chain around her ankle clattered as he forced her down onto the rug.

He went back to the camera.

Aimed it at Sue on the rug.

Hit the "record" button.

"Showtime! Which means... it's time you show me what you got, Susie Q."

Decatur moved over to the rug.

Turned toward Sue and fondled her breasts.

His hands were dead things, cold claws, against her skin and hair, and she shivered, trembling because it seemed that some of the coldness of the man was seeping through into her.

Sue closed her eyes and willed herself away.

———

Who looks outside, dreams.
Who looks inside, awakes.

From inside the cabin came a dreadful howl of pain, horror, groans, and screams like the sounds that might have been heard in the windowless gas chambers at Auschwitz or along ancient Transylvanian roads where Vlad the Impaler skewered countless thousands on sharpened stakes.

It was not a cry for help or even a plea for mercy, but a begging for release at any cost, even death.

Outside, the storm clouds, rolling out of the northwest since before dawn, had finally shrouded the sun, displacing the empty blue skies with towering palisades of angry clouds.

SIXTEEN

THE MAGIC HOUR GAVE way to dawn as it began its early walk across the south Alaskan plain. Intermittent columns of struggling sunlight and drizzling rain made their way westward through the umbrella of gray clouds along Highway 1 from Tok Junction to Chickaloon to Valdez. It continued on through and between the concrete waffles of downtown Fairbanks to Palmer and Anchorage, bringing to life the isolated communities, the all-night truck stops, the scattered few highways, all straight and narrow...

The endless ribbon of logging trucks, flat farms with tepees of corn shucks, the quiet shallow mountain streams teeming with salmon and bear, the pin oaks huddled in hummocks hanging onto verdant summer leaves, the land smelling spongy, earthy, in the warm wind and a mist that matched its melancholy with the walking dawn...

On its own time, in no hurry, the sun rose over Decatur's cabin. Ashen fingers of fog slowly retreated from the waters of Resurrection Bay. A flock of geese took flight from its glass-like surface.

Could hell be any worse than the now and real? Sue thought, somewhere way far away inside her own head. Lying helpless on the rug, she felt Decatur enter her again. "Too Late to Turn Back Now" looped endlessly over the speakers.

He was beside her, inside her, his arms wrapped around her, pulling her to him. Sue felt swathed in pure evil. She unconsciously reached up to her hair and resorted to an old childhood addiction, an addiction that began when she was five—*trichotillomania.* The compulsion to pull out one's hair.

Crazed from the guilt of killing her mother, five-year-old Sue, like many with trich, received some sense of relief and satisfaction from pulling out her hair. One strand, one follicle, at a time ...

It was a small, controlled hurt.

Lying on the rug, Sue reverted back to her five-year-old self. Each thread of her hair felt as soft as silk as she sifted it between her fingers. She touched the root of one hair she had been dying to pull for hours. She reached the root and dug her nails into the skin.

There was a slight pop.

She slowly parted it from her head and felt a rush of relief. Her stomach heaved from the clenching, gut-retching urge to continue.

Now she felt relief. Like an ice cold glass of lemonade on the hottest summer day. She stared at the tiny parcel that she just conceived. She told herself: One hair won't matter.

Her left hand slowly started to reach toward her golden dirty blonde hair. She told herself again: One more won't hurt.

She looked down, next to her on the floor, on the rug. Maybe fifty golden hairs were scattered all around her.

She hadn't realized she'd pulled that many out. She began to cry. Fat tears rolled down her cheeks. Sue closed her eyes, fighting back against the tears.

She'd be damned if she'd let him see her cry.

"Too Late to Turn Back Now," looping on the boombox, brought Sue back to the moment.

Decatur, naked, stood up an eternity of hours later.

Sue pulled herself into a fetal position on the bear rug. She had no more tears left, her makeup streaked down her face. Almost apologetically, she said, "I ... I have to go to the bathroom."

Decatur grabbed an old towel from the kitchen sink. Tossed it at her.

An expression of gloating ecstasy floated across his face.

Sue turned away in disgust.

"No? Well, I'm gonna get some sleep. Oh—"

Decatur powered off the boombox, then hit the "play" button on the VCR. "Enjoy the show. It may not be *Gone With the Wind*, but I give a killer performance."

Sue, lying chained and crumpled on the floor, was left all alone to witness her attack over ...

And over ...

And over.

All coherent thought left Sue's mind then. Sue was gone during that time. In her place was a savage thing made of fury and violence.

Decatur, meanwhile, popped a couple of Ambiens and in ten minutes was sleeping like a dog.

Listening to the tape, her eyes shut, all Sue could think was the odorous reek on that animal's soul, as he snored on in the room next to her.

Sue pulled out one last hair and stared it for a moment, caught between her thumb and index finger. She didn't know how, but she knew she was going to end him.

———

"Around mid-morning, the lake disappeared without a trace. A swirling, unstoppable vortex of doom…" The disembodied voice from the television had an unreal quality to it that was beyond the words it was speaking.

The digital clock in the back bedroom glowed 4:32 AM and Sarge could not sleep.

Instead he was trying to drift off by watching television. But the natural disaster special he was watching was having just the opposite effect; he was transfixed by the monumental carnage unfolding in front of his eyes.

"Water and salt would play the key roles in one of the strangest and most spectacular engineering disasters in history." As the TV narrator continued and the images unfolded, Sarge learned that on November 20, 1980, Lake Peigneur in Louisiana had ceased to exist. Ninety minutes after their drill had become stuck, the twelve men working on an oil drilling rig in the middle of the lake—who had wisely abandoned the tilting rig—watched in amazement from the shore, as their 150 foot derrick completely disappeared. Soon the water around that position began to churn. It was slow at first, but it steadily accelerated until it became a fast-moving whirlpool a quarter of a mile in diameter, with its center directly over the drill site.

Acting like a terrestrial black hole, the unstoppable maelstrom of a whirlpool sucked in everything in the lake including numerous boats, eleven barges, 65 acres of surrounding land and, last but not least, the entire liquid contents of the lake.

As Sarge watched in disbelief, there was a soft knock on the bedroom door, followed by Sunny's whispered voice. "Sarge? You awake?"

Sunny stepped into the room, playing with her half of the Mizpah pendant hanging around her neck. "I, uh, saw the light on underneath the door."

"Hey, Sweet Pea, it's your room, come on in. Is everybody else finally asleep?"

"Yeah, I think all that sugar wore them out." She continued to play with the Mizpah pendant, then shyly asked: "Hey, Sarge, that talking-with-a-friend present? Still on?"

"Anytime, Sunny. Anytime. What's on that pretty little mind of yours?"

Sunny smiled, then glanced at the television. Three huge barges disappeared into the whirlpool, one after the other. "Whoa, that's crazy! Whatcha' watching?"

"I've never seen anything like it in all my years. That was Lake Peigneur in Louisiana, back in 1980. There was a salt mine directly under that lake, something like 1300 feet below. Well, some rocket scientists from Texaco put an oil rig in the middle of the lake and began to drill for oil. Due to some kind of miscalculation, the 14-inch drill bit they were using hit the top of the mine and the entire lake ended up in the salt mine below."

"It's weird, isn't it?" asked Sunny, watching a replay of the massive oil rig being crushed, then sucked into the whirlpool.

"You got that right. Something you don't see every day."

"No, I mean isn't it weird how the Earth never opens up and sucks you in when you want it to the most?"

Sarge looked at Sunny, trying to read her face. "You have something you want to share with the rest of the class?"

"It's just that, the older I get, the more complicated everything becomes. I spend all day and night trying to figure things out. I worry about Mom. I really worry about her jobs. I worry about moving so much. I worry about meeting new friends all the time. Who to trust. Who to keep at a distance. It's just, like, the older I get, the more confused I get. It shouldn't be this way. I thought it would get easier the older I got. You know?"

"Between best buds?" asked Sarge.

"Between best buds," replied Sunny.

"Between best buds... I think that's what's known as getting older."

"In that case, I'd like to put the brakes on it, ASAP."

"Don't we all! Hey, between best buds?"

"Between best buds."

"You've always been the one with scathingly brilliant ideas. Got any now?"

Her eyes suddenly lit up. This is just what she wanted to talk to him about. "Just the only one."

"Which is?"

"Well, Mom told you she wants to open up a dance studio, right?"

"Right."

"Okay, I'm pretty sure I can talk a lot of my friends into signing up. They all love to dance. Just add friends, instant business. What do you think?"

Sarge gave her a reassuring smile. "You know what I think? I think that between the three of us there's nothing we can't do!"

"You gonna get all Three Musketeery on me?"

"Well, I guess it beats getting all Three Stoogey on you. So, how about it, Sweet Pea? One for all —"

"And all for one!" Sunny beamed. "So you really think it's a good idea?"

"Did I mention you were always the one with the scathingly brilliant ideas? The funny thing is I was just telling your mom that I know the perfect place. What say we all go over and take a look at it tomorrow? Start a little early on her birthday present."

"Is that a yes?"

"That's a yes."

Sunny gave him a hug, then went to the door. Turned. "Hey, does it ever get easy?"

"What?"

"Getting older. Does it get easy?"

"What do you want me to say?"

"How about a little fib?"

"Between best buds?"

"Between best buds."

"Oh, yeah, getting older is just icing on the cake."

Sunny smiled, then playfully whispered, "Liar, liar, pants on fire…"

She quietly shut the door as the whirlpool in the middle of Lake Peigneur continued its unstoppable vortex of doom.

SEVENTEEN

SUE, STILL LYING ON the rug, felt a nudge on her shoulder.

A tsunami of nausea swept over her as she felt his touch. The repugnant images of the previous night instantly re-loaded themselves as the Cornelius Brothers and their sister crooned on endlessly.

Decatur yawned, then pushed her shoulder again, "Wake up, Sleepy Head."

Sue's eyes were closed tight, but she was awake. In fact, she hadn't slept at all. She felt, and looked, like hell.

"Daylight's a'burnin', Susie Q," noted Decatur as he made his way over to the VCR and stabbed the stop button.

The television hissed with lazy, cobalt static.

"Wakey, wakey," chimed Decatur.

It was the last thing in the world Sue wanted to do, but as always, there was no denying him.

She slumped and her chain rattled, her face flushed and dripping with sweat, stomach aching and empty, the taste of copper on her tongue, gasping into awareness, groaning in the agony, then the hopelessness of her choking confinement. She tightened her hands around her waist and slowly lifted her head. The cotton dryness that was her tongue was a tangible, living thing. She tried to swallow but only made it to a gag, the lump in her throat like a ball of blazing charcoal.

"Time to go, Sleeping Beauty," Decatur said cheerfully, handing her a steaming cup of coffee.

Sue rubbed her eyes, refusing the coffee. "Go ... go where?"

"Home."

"Home?"

"Where the heart is."

"You're ... you're letting me go?"

"Told you all along I was going to let you go. Boy Scout, remember?"

He bent down and unlocked the shackle around Sue's ankle. With his most charming smile he added, "C'mon ..."

He tossed her clothes at her feet. "Get dressed, I'll be outside."

"But—"

"Get up. Get dressed."

There was that undeniable tone of command again.

Decatur opened the door and stood on the porch admiring the agonizingly beautiful morning, leaving the door cracked fully open.

Sue followed in the time it took her to put on her skirt and blouse.

"Where're my shoes?" she asked, looking back into the cabin.

"Beautiful morning, huh? You don't see anything like this in the lower Forty-Eight, do you? Nothing like it at all."

"Shoes?" repeated Sue.

He ignored her. "Oh, I almost forgot ... these fell out."

126

He tucked Sue's pack of Kools into her blouse pocket. "Told you those things wouldn't kill ya."

He stepped around her and went back inside. He reached down and picked the boombox off the floor and walked out onto the porch. He took a seat on a chair, resting his camouflaged hunting boots on the railing, placing the boombox to his side. He took a long drink of coffee and squinted both eyes into slits to take in the magnificent view that surrounded him three sixty. "Nope, nothing like it at all."

"Aren't ... aren't we going to the plane?" asked Sue.

Decatur took another sip of coffee. "It's a beautiful day, innit? Kinda makes me feel all warm and fuzzy on the inside. Kinda like, you know, the feeling when you were a kid on the night before Christmas. That ... anticipation. Knowing something big was gonna happen soon."

He stared at her a moment. "Yep, nothing like it."

Decatur calmly sat his coffee cup down.

He reached out and cradled the Steyr Aug resting against the cabin.

He chambered a round into the assault rifle.

The metallic clicking sound of sudden death shook Sue to the bone.

Sue looked at Decatur as if for the first time.

The truly terrifying thing was that he was so damned icy calm. His voice, like his face, showed a total lack of emotion. In fact, he'd spoken quite rationally, as though they were discussing something as mundane as the weather or a sitcom.

And that's when it finally hit her like a fucking juggernaut.

"How ... how can you do this? How can you hate people so much?"

"Hey, I like people. Some of my best friends are people."

She looked at him, then at the immense woods in front of her, then back at him. "Do I get a head start or do you shoot me here?"

"What kind of man you think I am?" Decatur grinned, cobra calm. The grin coiled into a sneer. "You got thirty minutes ..."

He pushed the timer button on his wristwatch. "Starting now."

Decatur laughed, then went quiet. Then, in the ensuing stillness, Sue came to the realization that Decatur, in the blink of an eye, had transformed her from a living, breathing being with a soul into a worthless, insignificant image. A 'thing' with no more value or worth than a single grain of sand or a piece of garbage discarded in a gutter.

Sue considered making a break for his gun, but realized she would be lucky if she made three steps. Defeated, she started for the woods, then at the last moment, whirled around to face Decatur.

All sense of dignity gone, she dropped to her knees, pleading, struggling to control her terror. "I have a daughter."

Tears streaming down her face, Sue looked up at Decatur. There was absolutely nothing there, only a blank mask.

"I'm ... I'm the only thing she has in this world. She has no one else. No one. Please. Don't do this to her. Please ..."

"While you were asleep," he said slowly, methodically, "I went through a box of old tapes I brought up here. I thought I had it and I was right."

Decatur simply reached down and pushed the play button on the boombox.

He grinned. "This one's for you, Susie Q ..."

Creedence Clearwater Revival's "Susie Q" broke the morning silence through the cheap, tinny speakers on the boombox. Fogerty's cover of the old Dale Hawkins blues love ballad drifted over the landscape and past Sue's ears like some kind of surrealistic, jarring ringing bell. The pinging notes from the opening guitar riff were almost painful.

Decatur tapped his toes to the rhythm, then began to sing along, his voice an off-key soprano, squeaky and out of synch with the lyrics. The song was the story of a forlorn, lonely lover almost begging for affection and devotion, the emptiness beneath the surface lyrics reflecting the empty black hole that Sue knew was Decatur's heart...

Stinging tears flooded down her face as Sue forced her eyes shut. She tried to open her mouth to plead, but the sheer terror closing in on her was too overpowering. No words came out; she was unable to speak as if the wind had been knocked out of her lungs. Only sob after sob racking her body as her face dipped closer to the ground...

Finally, she willed herself to take a deep breath and then it began pouring out.

"Please ... Her name is Sunny ... She just turned thirteen ... She's the best thing—" Sue choked on her own words, hyperventilating. She took a couple more deep breaths, then continued, tears freely flowing down her face, "She's the best thing that's ever happened to me ... Please ... I love her like crazy ... I can't leave her like this ... Please ..."

Decatur, his face a 1,000-yard-stare, continued singing.

"Look!" Sue wailed, raising her voice to cut through the music. "I'll give you my address! My driver's license! Credit cards ... Passport ... You'll know where we live! I won't tell anyone ..."

Decatur sang on, tapping his feet, rocking back and forth with the rifle cradled in his arms like the woman Dale Hawkins, Fogerty, and countless other men longed to hold. Love me. Be true and never leave me …

Unrequited, pure love and longing.

"I … I did everything you wanted last night … I'll do anything you want …"

Decatur stared over the top of her head, his eyes a glassy stare, drifting with the music, the music that called for one lover to *own* another, the way he owned Sue right now.

"Please …" Sue begged over his off-key singing, "You're a good-looking guy … I know! We could date! You were so good in bed … Just take me back and I'll be your girlfriend … I'll do whatever you want … Whenever … Wherever …"

Decatur pushed the pause button on the boombox.

Sue looked up. A slight ray of hope.

"You know, coupla' years back," smiled Decatur, "when I started this here project … the second girl I had out here, well, doggone it, if she didn't say pretty much the same thing you're saying. She cried and she whined and she pleaded and she begged for the entire thirty minutes. I blew her head off. Right about where you are. No fun at all, that one. Now, you want some good advice? The slower you move, the faster you die. Your choice, Susie Q, makes no nevermind to me."

He stabbed the play button again and sang along.

Sue struggled to her feet. Pissed. Fucking pissed. "You stupid son-of-a-bitch! My father's a cop! He'll have every policeman in the state looking for me! He'll never give up! Never!"

Decatur stopped the tape, walked over to Sue.

"See, Susie Q, right there's your other problem. I'm thinking that you're just not … grasping … the gravity of the situation here—"

He grabbed Sue's right hand. Held it up to her face.

"I'm thinking what you need here is … is a little sense of urgency…"

Decatur smoothly pulled the Ka-Bar knife out of his belt sheath.

He placed the over-sized blade against her index finger and, with one fluid motion, cut it neatly off below the last joint.

Sue didn't feel the pain for perhaps a full second before her hand exploded in blinding white light pain. Blood geysered out of the stub, soaking the ground with a liquid crimson pool.

"Now there, you got your urgency," said Decatur, bringing her back to reality. "I'd say you have 'bout twenty-four hours to find a hospital and get this bad boy re-attached. After that, well, after that you might find it hard to play the piano again."

He tossed the finger into the air like so much garbage.

Sue watched in shocked, surreal horror. Then, a heartbeat later: searing, unbearable pain. Sue stared down at her hand as if it were on fire which, she realized a moment later, it was.

She heard herself scream as if it were coming from somewhere far off.

In slow motion, her finger tumbled end over end through the air, cascading a bloody shower, only to bounce on the ground and land next to her bare right foot.

In Sue's shocked mind she could only formulate the simplest of thoughts: *That belongs on my hand, not on my foot.*

Sue hit the ground and grabbed her finger. She looked up, her eyes spitting blue fire. "You fuckin' piece of shit. I don't know how, but you'll pay for this, you mother of fuck!"

She spat in his face, then turned and walked toward the woods.

Decatur chuckled. Wiped his face. Took a long drink of coffee. "Well, well, well … Looks like we've got us a real live one here, folks."

He squeezed the trigger on the Steyr Aug. A 5.56mm bullet knocked dirt all around Sue. She didn't give him the satisfaction of flinching. Instead, she disappeared into the foliage.

"We'll see how fuckin' long that lasts ..." he whispered.

He leaned back in the chair, smiled contentedly and punched the play button on the boombox.

As Sue was consumed by the woods, she could hear Decatur singing again, his off-key, high-pitched falsetto cruelly mocking her.

EIGHTEEN

SUE RAN.

Gilligan's-fuckin'-Island! That's what this is! She thought as she ran for her life. *This place is like goddamned Gilligan's Island gone straight to motherfucking hell.* But in this alternate TV universe, "little buddy" Gilligan was a full-grown psychopathic serial killer with a high-powered assault rifle whose only philosophy seemed to be *I think therefore I kill.*

Hell, thought Sue, *it wasn't psychology, it was psycho-ology.*

Sue ran.

Cradling her bleeding finger tightly underneath her right armpit, she plunged blindly up a hill and through a maze of trees, kicking leaves and dirt in front of her bare feet, feeling the stitch starting to blaze on her right side, tasting burnt metal in the back of her mouth. In the bizarre abyss of iridescent light, the dark shadows from the overhanging tree limbs flickered zebra patterns, shark-like and razor edged, across her face.

Branches whipped out at her, thorns ripped her flesh and clothes as she stumbled and tripped through the thick underbrush. Her breath was driven from her lungs. Blood splattered the ground.

Sue stopped for a moment to catch her breath, leaning her good hand against a tree. As best she could, she began taking stock of what was happening around her, processing everything while at the same time balancing a mixture of panic, pain, confusion, and desperation all at once.

On her personal pyramid of hurt, her finger was at the pinnacle of the pain iceberg. That was closely followed by the fire burning in her lungs and the explosions in her chest caused by her heart pounding so hard she felt as if each beat might knock her down. Below that, at the bottom of the pain pyramid, were her bleeding, bare feet. That and the intrinsic, paralyzing fear of being shot at any moment by a raving motherfuckin' psychopath.

Taking her chances running through an unknown woods was tantamount to suicide, but her options were limited.

She knew if she stopped and waited there, she would die. Fuck that choice.

If she continued to run, then maybe, just maybe there was a chance to live. But where the hell do you run to on an island?

Goddamn Gilligan's-fuckin'-Island.

Sue ran.

Glancing back over her shoulder occasionally, Sue half-expected to hear the shot that would end her.

Her breathing now reduced to a rasp, she thought of the ex-boyfriend who had tried to get her to take flying lessons and of the Cessna 140 parked somewhere the fuck close by. If only she had listened to him and taken a couple of lessons, maybe that would have been enough.

Shit!

A patch of low-hanging, needle-sharp thistles scratched her face and embedded in her hair. Freeing herself with difficulty, ripping out a handful of hair in the process, she trampled onward through the thickening undergrowth and cursed her bloody bare feet. *Where the hell is God when you need him to open a hole in the earth and swallow you whole?*

She continued to run through the woods in a random serpentine pattern, darting a couple hundred feet to her right, then straight maybe twenty feet, then to her left for another forty or fifty feet.

Zigzagging aimlessly, helter skelter.

She was hoping that somehow her ineptness at being a human prey might somehow confound and confuse the man hunting her down. Maybe there was logic in illogical reasoning. She didn't convince herself for a second. She was only prolonging the inevitable. She didn't stand a chance. She was going to die.

The searing pain in her hand told her so. It was bad. Real bad. The worst she had ever felt. The throbbing, pulsing pain seemed to have triggered some primeval part of her nervous system—the one that monitored the odds of her survival. This part triggered bodily reactions designed to forestall death: off-the-scale body temperature, a rush of pure adrenaline, a knife-turning knot in her stomach, full body sweats.

Her nervous system may have sent the memo, but Sue sure as hell wasn't going to let her body pay it any mind.

Through a gap in the tree cover, she looked up and once again saw the glimmering beacon that was the Full Thunder Moon. As she had earlier, she looked at the moon and this time wondered what Sarge was doing at this moment.

Sarge. Her silent fortress.

He always woke up at first light, never one for wasting the dawn. Chances were he was more than aware that something was wrong. Knowing Sarge, he had probably made at least a hundred official calls by now and was following SOP. Standard operational procedures. First calls to Bushwhackers, then double checking with all the other local bars and stripjoints, then to the various police agencies.

More times than she cared to remember, Sue had gotten into trouble during her last years of high school and no matter how bad or how deep the trouble, Sarge had always been there for her. At the time, it was more embarrassing for her than anything else.

God, what she'd give to have Sarge embarrass her now!

Without warning, the wind picked up and a vortex of leaves slammed into her face. Shielding her eyes with her good hand, she couldn't see more than ten feet in front of her face.

A new sense of panic and dread struck her like a dagger deep in her heart.

She was lost.

Completely, irreversibly, hopelessly lost. This wasn't like the neat, checkerboard grids of Manhattan or New Orleans. *This was ten billion trees that all looked the fucking same!*

For all she knew, she was running straight back to the cabin.

Then, something moved in the woods.

A rustle at first, then a snap like the sound of a broom handle broken in a wet towel. Sue strained to see but the whirling blizzard of falling leaves made it impossible to see anything with clarity.

Whatever it was, it was big. And it was heading straight for her. Crashingly fast.

Then she froze in a half-standing, half-kneeling position and scanned the line of trees. She saw nothing but the forest, but the noise was there and getting louder.

Sue stared unblinkingly through the canopy of falling leaves. Motionless.

Then she saw it, a little flicker of movement behind the thick base of one of the tallest trees.

Panicking, Sue surged to her feet.

She lived a year in a moment.

Finding her legs, she whirled around and began to run even faster than before.

In the backwash of sunlight filtering through the overhanging trees, the leaves suddenly parted like the Red Sea and a deer leapt straight toward Sue.

The deer, even more frightened of Sue than Sue was of it, jumped six feet up into the air, missing Sue by inches.

Screaming, Sue lost her footing on a patch of wet moss and fell backward, tumbling down the hillside, ass after teacups.

She rolled to the bottom with a loud thump. Groaning, the air knocked out of her lungs, she rolled onto her side. The attempt triggered a ripple of shooting pain, but she clenched her teeth and rolled again, until she was lying face down on the forest floor. Her finger leaked a river of blood on the ground, the pain beyond words. She tightly clenched both fists, placed them against the ground and groaned as she struggled to push herself up to her knees.

She stayed there a moment as a thin thread of blood poured from her mouth. Then, with another grunt, she willed herself to her feet. Drenched, bruised, bleeding, disheveled.

But she was standing.

Sue wobbled unsteadily and turned in a slow 360-degree circle before staggering into the woods. She bounced off trees and swiped at branches with one hand while she cradled the other under her armpit.

Fuck it. Why am I doing this?

It made no sense to her. She knew there was no hope.

She should lie down and know a last few moments of peace before the eternal darkness took her. But she kept going, driven ahead by the same mysterious impulse that had caused her to get up and start moving in the first place. She still didn't understand it, but it felt important somehow. Some unconscious part of her believed there was something important she had to get to before she died. She walked and walked, she didn't know how long. Seemed forever. There was some amazing reserve of strength she'd tapped, especially considering the ferocious wound inflicted upon her. Her legs felt like rubber, but still she kept forging ahead.

Ten agonizing minutes later Sue struggled to the top of a hill. Making her way to a small clearing, every muscle in her being strained to the limit, she paused against a large boulder to catch her breath, panting.

Holding her hand in pain, she looked down at the ground. Her blood was pooling below in the dirt.

She looked at her hand.

Fuckin' hell …

It was a mess. She'd seen better-looking hamburger meat.

I've got to do something. Think!

She grabbed a stick lying at her feet. Used it to tear the sleeve off her blouse. She fashioned a tourniquet and wrapped it around the finger stump. The rest of the sleeve she used to bandage her hand.

Hey, at least it's something.

Gritting her teeth, taking a deep breath, she trudged on through the woods.

Sunny.

Sunny's why I'm doing this.

Run, she thought.

Run and don't look back.

NINETEEN

No Sue...

In his dream, he saw the whirlpool over and over again, just like in the documentary, that lake in Louisiana, Lake Peigneur, swirling around and around, sucking everything into a dark hole, never to be seen again...

Never to be seen again...

Sarge jerked awake from the dream, startled. Shaken.

He was still in his uniform, the stiff creases in his pants crunched around his knees. He looked around, at first unsure of where he was. Then he remembered.

Sunny's bedroom. He'd gone into Sunny's bedroom to watch television when the birthday party had finally settled down. Now there was only silence. The girls were asleep in the living room.

His neck was stiff, his eyelids crunchy. He looked around the room. He didn't remember turning the television off, didn't remember dropping off to sleep. The room was mostly dark even now, with the light of dawn just beginning to penetrate the thin gauzy curtain over the bedroom window.

Why hadn't Sue come and gotten him?

He slowly, stiffly pulled himself into a sitting position. His long legs had hung over the end of Sunny's twin bed all night, pressing them mid-calf, cutting off his circulation. His feet had fallen asleep, the tingling climbing up his legs as the blood flow restarted.

Damn, he thought. *I really am getting old.*

He sat on the side of the bed, massaging his arms, moving his feet back and forth to restore the feeling. There was a bad taste in his mouth—too much birthday cake and soda.

Sarge sat there for a few moments, then pulled himself to his feet. Momentarily unsteady, he gave himself a second or two. Then he stepped over a pile of Sunny's laundry on the floor and sidestepped the small desk and chair that they'd crammed into the bedroom for Sunny to do homework. He pulled the door open, stepped into the doorframe, and looked out onto the living room.

He smiled. A massive clump of tangled teenage girl was piled in the middle of the living room floor. Legs intertwined, arms splayed out, hair everywhere, all twisted up in sheets, blankets, pillows.

Sarge was suddenly grateful that his granddaughter was so open to people, despite what she said to him earlier. Sunny and Sue had been here such a short time, but Sunny'd made friends in the trailer park quickly enough for a perfect sleepover birthday party. Sarge stood there looking out at her in her nest of friends and smiled.

Then he looked up and the smile instantly disappeared from his face.

No Sue.

If she hadn't come in and awakened him, then she was supposed to be asleep on the couch next to the girl scrum.

No Sue.

Where the hell is she?

He padded past the sleeping girls, through the living room into the kitchen. It was dark, empty, piles of dirty paper plates, cups, and the remains of the birthday cake scattered across the kitchen table.

Sarge looked over at the stove clock, the dim orange glow cutting through the darkness.

6:12.

Sarge turned, scanned the living room once more as if it might have been possible he'd missed her. Then he crossed to the door, pulled aside the curtain on the glass window and stared outside. His prowler with the Anchorage P.D. emblem on the side was still parked there, the morning mist wafting around it. Everything looked gray, shades of smoked gray.

Next to it, an empty parking space.

Sarge struggled to ramp his mind up into high gear. What was the name of that place? That strip club where Sue had gone to work? He struggled, his brain still fogged with sleep and fatigue.

Damn it? What was it?

Then it hit him: Bushwhackers.

Maybe there's an explanation, he thought. Maybe she stayed behind to help clean up, make a few more bucks.

Maybe she met someone, maybe some guy who...

No, damn it! That was the old Sue. That was the Sue from ten, twelve years ago. This is a different Sue, a different...

Then where the hell is she?

Sarge stepped back into the kitchen, reached for the phone.

Dealing with young Sue had been hard for Sarge. All his adult life he'd been protecting people. He was a good cop. Then his wife died and his daughter began to get in trouble. Sue had pushed Sarge as far away as she could, even to the point of running away from home when she was sixteen.

For once, he couldn't protect her. It was the first time in his life he felt ... *powerless.*

Years later, he would understand. She'd only been trying to wash her hands of all the horrible things she felt she'd done. Perpetually haunted by her mother's death and hindered by an inability to forgive herself, she viewed herself as unworthy of anybody's love and trust. The minute someone, anyone, got too close was the minute she would run away.

Sarge thought back to that time, to when he'd buried himself in work to forget. To forget his lost wife and daughter. He worked so hard that he ignored the increasing pains he was suffering, writing them off to stress. He felt lousy, all over, on so many levels. Life was just a pain.

Then one day it hit, hard: he was walking down the hall toward roll call and everything suddenly went black. The last thing he remembered was the sensation of falling.

He woke up in the same hospital where Leilani had died. He and Sue would later comment on the irony of it ...

There was a clear plastic tube in his left arm. An IV pole with several extensions held two bags of liquid (one clear, the other yellowish) that dripped steadily into a reservoir before traveling the length of tube and disappearing into his arm. There were sounds as well: the occasional whirring of a motor locked inside plastic casing, a blood pressure cuff automatically inflating with a sound like a sigh, a quiet rushing. There was a beeping monitor next to the bed. Sarge faded in and out as he watched his heart rate march across the screen, a neon rhythm moving in what appeared to be slow motion.

When he finally worked his way back to consciousness after his emergency appendectomy, he spotted Sue sitting next to him and looked up in bewilderment.

"What, what are you doing here?" Sarge had asked hoarsely, weakly. "How did—"

Sue suddenly buried her face in her hands, burst into tears, and wept uncontrollably. "I'm so sorry, I'm so sorry," she sobbed, over and over.

Sarge looked at his daughter, completely at a loss.

"Sweetie, stop. I'm just surprised. I never expected to see you again. I don't know what I did to you, but I'm the one who's sorry."

Now Sue bawled uncontrollably, bursting forth with twenty-nine years of pent-up grief and guilt. "I didn't mean to kill her! I didn't mean to kill mom! If I could take her place I would—"

Sue was sobbing hysterically now, finding it hard to breathe.

"Kill mom?" Sarge asked, stunned and confused. "*What* are you talking about, Sue?"

"I didn't mean to kill mom! I didn't, I didn't, I didn't..."

"Your mother?!" asked Sarge. "Is this what it's all about? Your mother?"

"I didn't mean to kill her, Dad. I know you blame me for her death."

"Oh, my Lord. Is this what you've thought for all these years?"

Sarge reached out and took her hand.

"I never once blamed you. That thought never once entered my mind because, well, because that's not what happened."

"But all that time you spent away from me?"

"The force was understaffed and I had no choice. Besides, I was cramming in as much overtime as possible, saving up for college and to buy you a house."

The sobs abated for a moment. "Are you serious?"

"And if you really think about it, it was you who was gone most of the time that I was home. I didn't know exactly how to raise a girl, so I thought I would try and do the right thing by giving you your space."

"I was gone so much because I didn't think you wanted me. All this time, I thought you blamed me for her death."

"Never, Sweetie, not once."

With that, the weight of the world seemed to lift from her shoulders. She came to the side of his hospital bed, leaned down into his open arms, and let him hold her.

"Why did mom have to die?" Sue asked through the tears.

Sarge leaned his head back on the hospital pillow and reflected for what seemed a lifetime. Finally, he spoke in a slow, deliberate voice and said, "There are a lot of things in life that'll never make sense. Maybe there are no answers to all the questions, maybe there are no solutions to all the mysteries. It's a sad fact of life, but you simply can't know everything. It's just the way it is, Sweetie. Then you're left with two choices. You can either accept it, that you'll never know, or you can go crazy trying to fix something that can't be fixed. There are some mysteries in life that just can't be explained. Death happens. It sucks. Life goes on."

Sue looked at Sarge and asked, "Do you remember that Christmas when you read the *Gift of the Magi* to me?"

"'Course I do."

"We're that story, aren't we, Dad?"

"Pretty much, Sweetie." smiled Sarge. "Pretty much, except I'm the one who's losing his hair."

A moment, then he asked, "Is Sunny here?"

"Yes, she's watching TV in the waiting room."

"Her birthday's next month, right?"

Sue nodded through the tears. "You remembered."

Sarge leaned away from her, stared directly into her eyes. There was a silence between them that was broken only when he spoke through his own cracking voice: "Sue, come home. Please. Come home."

Sue burst into a fresh wave of tears, but through them a smile as she nodded *yes*.

"Tell you what, I know the best bakery in town. It would be my honor to get Sunny's cake. If that's okay with you. I'll get her the best one she's ever had, anybody's ever had."

Sue smiled. "I can't see any harm in that."

———

Twenty minutes later, Sarge—his face washed and his tie on, although still unshaven—answered the knock on the trailer door. He walked past the still sleeping pile of teenaged girls on the living room floor and pulled the door open.

A sleepy woman in a pair of jeans, boots, and a barn jacket stood on the front steps.

"Sorry to wake you up, Jackie," Sarge said. "I appreciate this, especially on such short notice. Can't leave a trailer full of thirteen-year-olds alone."

Sarge's younger sister Jackie stepped in and brushed a hank of hair off her face. "It wouldn't be so bad if I hadn't been up packing 'til past midnight."

She turned and took a look back toward the dawn sky. "God, I'm so sick of this grayness. I'd give anything to wake up to green grass and blue skies."

Jackie, Sarge suddenly remembered, guilt washing over him for waking her up, had taken a job in South Carolina and was moving in three days. She'd been trying to get out of Alaska for years and her chance had finally come, thanks to a teaching appointment at a community college just outside Charleston.

Jackie turned back to Sarge and stepped through the doorway, pulling the door shut behind her. "What do you think's going on?" she asked, as she pulled off her jacket and laid it on the back of a kitchen chair.

"I don't know. She didn't know how late she was going to have to work, but I know it wasn't this late."

Jackie turned and faced her brother. "What'd you let her do it for? You know how those places are?"

Sarge reached up and massaged his forehead. There was a growing headache between his temples, radiating out into the back of his head.

"She's a grown woman," Sarge said defensively. "She made her own decision."

"I just hope it wasn't one we're all going to regret."

Behind them, there was a stirring. Sarge turned to see Sunny push herself up on one arm, staring at them with one eye still closed.

"What is it, Sarge?" she asked, her voice thick with sleep. Then she opened the other eye and squinted into the dark kitchen. "Aunt Jackie? What are you doing here?"

Sarge stepped over to the girls and went down on one knee next to Sunny. "Honey, I don't want to worry you, but your mother's not home yet."

Sunny's eyes shot open, completely wide awake now.

"Where is she?" Sunny demanded, tension and fear in her voice.

"I'm going to go find that out, Sweetie. Aunt Jackie's going to stay here with you until I get back."

Sunny reached down and yanked herself clear of a tangle of sheets and blankets. Behind her, another one of the girls—Sarge couldn't remember her name—moaned and rolled over.

Sunny pulled herself to her feet and grabbed both of Sarge's arms. "Sarge, where is she?"

Sarge stood up slowly. "Don't worry, Sunny. She probably had car trouble. You know that damned broken-down old Kia of hers."

"Why didn't she call?"

"She didn't want to wake you guys up," Sarge said. "I'm sure that's it. Now you lay back down. Jackie's going to make you guys some breakfast. Right, Jackie?"

Jackie smiled at her great niece. "Sure. What you want? Waffles? Pancakes?"

Sunny turned to Sarge, her jaw tight and locked. "What I want is my mother," she snapped through clenched teeth.

Sarge pulled his utility belt off the recliner, snapped it on, then adjusted his pistol and holster.

"I know, sweetie. I'm going to go get her right now. Don't you worry."

TWENTY

MORNING KNOCKED BACK IN deep cherry and lavender blue.

Warm, thick coffee slid down Decatur's throat. He shivered with equal parts pleasure and anticipation.

Nestling his scuffed boot heels into the rotting railing, Decatur leaned back on a porch chair and savored the flavor of the freshly percolated coffee as much as the warmth of the rising sun on his face.

Decatur looked to his left. The early morning breeze played with the sunlit dust. The wall of evergreens in the distance rippled, reflected in the shimmering bay.

To his right, squirrels argued in the woods.

High above, a kettle of vultures circled, landed and rose again. Decatur liked to think of the rapacious carrions as zombie angels summoned to worship at the all-you-can-eat-shrine of formerly living things.

Thirteen. Thirteen buzzards, Decatur counted. A baker's dozen of zombie angels.

The rising sun, a crimson skull, rose precariously over the highest parapet of the distant mountains, and in its radiating intensity, the hilltops appeared to be ablaze in one enormous funeral pyre.

The dawn had a curious fluidity about it that had to do with the freshness of the morning dew mingled with the evanescence of the fog slowly ghosting, fading away into the new day.

The smell of the morning was just as electrifying, invigorating and life affirming.

Decatur looked at the porch post next to his boots. Over the last three summers he had hacked three large notches into the pine post. This was his penultimate braggadocio. This was Decatur's net worth. It was the equivalent of American fighter pilots during World War II decorating their airplanes with Nazi swastika symbols to indicate the number of kills they had attained, or the Wild West gunslinger who notched his six-shooter for each of his conquests.

Decatur leaned back in his chair and shut his eyes. He wanted to enjoy every sensation, to savor each second.

He took a long, sustained breath, filling his lungs with cool island air. Let it out slowly.

This was a time to feel the space between things, their weight, their presence. It was a moment to watch the shadows dying slowly and coolly as the sun rose and to watch the colors of the forest explode into a Technicolor frenzy. It was a moment to catch the wind, to climb the clouds.

He never felt more alive. Every sense was on high-alert. Sound came as sight to Decatur, as light in kaleidoscopic patterns. Movement became ocular sound. He heard the clouds glide by high overhead; he heard the diesel fuel atomizing before it burst into combustible power in the generator; he heard the wavering, taunting shadows in the latticework of the forest. The flapping of dragonfly wings in the thick buttery sunshine became tiny floating angels with membranes impossibly eye-spotted and stain-glass patterned, purple staring out of cabbage white, chrome yellow over crimson rose.

Touch became smell to him. The feel of the tin coffee cup in his hand had the sweet, joyful aroma of a blueberry muffin on a rainy Sunday morning; the pine wood beneath his boot heels was a sense memory—the syrupy, adolescent-inducing smell of Wrigley's Juicy Fruit gum. The breeze against his face smelled of the electricity in the air before a thunder storm.

Smell transmuted into sound. The smell of coffee made the sound of hobbling horseshoes as they sparked across cobblestone. Smoke from the kitchen was a series of distant explosions, the sound of cannon shots coming from a past century and the cordite from a spent 5.56mm bullet produced a string quartet worthy of a "Pachelbel Canon," plucking and hammering at his heartstrings. The patch of forget-me-not flowers circling the porch had the resonance of eyeballs being shaved with a straight-edged razorblade.

It was mystical.

Magical.

Mysterious and miraculous.

Nothing like it, thought Decatur. *A strong cup of coffee. The good earth beneath my boots. A good fuck. A clean kill.*

This wasn't a moment to hurry.

There was no reason to rush.

There was no doubt about it, this was the best time of Decatur's life.

His motto: *Start the day early and start the day well.* An early kill. Gets one in the mood.

That's when his thoughts turned to Sue and he wondered if he should have given her the full thirty minutes. There had been something in her eyes just before she turned and walked calmly into the woods, not panicking, that told Decatur she might not be as hopeless as he originally thought.

In fact, Susie Q had Sandra Johnson eyes.

Sandra Johnson was the first girl Decatur had ever asked out.

The moment, the entire day actually, was indelibly seared into Decatur's mind. May 30, 1977. It was a lazy Sunday afternoon, not a cloud in the sky, and the marquee above the Ozarks Theater in Walnut Ridge, Arkansas, had screamed in neon: "Time to take to the road, for a quiet little drive in the country ... or not."

Decatur was about to celebrate his fifteenth birthday and all he could think about was asking Sandra Johnson to see *Smokey and the Bandit* with him on Sunday night. The way he had planned it, Sandra might have plans for Friday and Saturday nights, but no one ever made plans for Sunday evening. All he had to do was ask her and seal the deal. How could anything go wrong? If anyone on the planet deserved a break, it was certainly Decatur Kaiser.

Born in the small town of Decatur, Arkansas, fifteen years earlier, he had been abandoned at birth, not even left with a name. Before he was two years old, he had been adopted by an immigrant Polish baker and his wife who had opened up a small bakery in nearby Walnut Ridge and were unable to have children of their own.

I mean, the fuck is that about, Decatur had wondered his entire life. *People don't even give their dogs away to someone they don't know, but my real parents gave me away to strangers I'd never met.* Decatur laughed about it now. He'd joke, "I can't get a damned credit card, 'cus I don't know my mother's maiden name." It was one of his favorite jokes. *You either joked about it or you killed someone.*

Decatur was all about choices.

No one had loomed larger in Decatur's early life than Tadeusz Kaiser, his domineering adoptive father. His adoptive mother Irena, on the other hand, was a frail, soft-spoken woman who always took a backseat to her headstrong husband. It was Irena's idea to name the youngster after the town of his birth. Decatur had always hated the name he was given, but he was grateful as hell that he hadn't been born in Pocahontas or Bald Knob.

As a father, Tadeusz was iron-clad strict and completely closed-minded, a man full of definite ideas, religious intolerance and the highest standards of work ethics. When he discovered that three-year-old Decatur was left-handed, Tadeusz forced him to use his right hand instead. *It was that way with everything*, Decatur reflected bitterly. *He was always pushing me around, telling me what and how to do it. There was never any way but his way. Nothing I did was ever up to his standard. But then, you see where that got him.*

Tadeusz had learned the baking trade in his native Poland before immigrating to the United States at the age of twenty-two. He'd opened a bakery in Brooklyn, New York, in 1960, and married Irena from nearby Greenpoint, who joined in the business. The move to New York had not met Tadeusz's expectations; the lifestyle, high cost, and the endless hustle and bustle of the city had not afforded him the pace and stability of a small Polish-emigrant community that he desired. Then word came to Tadeusz that an expatriate of his, also a baker, was retiring in Arkansas and wanted to know if Tadeusz would be interested in buying him out.

Looking at the photographs that accompanied the letter, Tadeusz made a few calls and was soon sold on the idea. He packed his wife and their belongings and moved that week to the laid back, cotton-picking town of Walnut Ridge, Arkansas.

Luckily he and Irena were skilled bakers, and a good product spoke as well as words on the small town main street. Business soon supplied a comfortable income and two years later, the couple adopted the two-year-old Decatur.

The family lived in a small apartment above the bakery off Main Street, meaning that at two A.M. work would begin, just through the door and down the stairs.

Decatur's training as a baker came at a very early age, before he was in first grade, and his responsibilities and hours increased as he grew older, similar in many ways to what boys experienced on the surrounding family farms. But Tadeusz was never satisfied with Decatur's work. Worse yet, Tadeusz often described him as *less than worthless.*

It was also at an early age that Decatur began to stutter, something he always blamed on his father. As Tadeusz continued to push Decatur, to work him longer hours, to harangue him to do a better job, to do things with his right hand, the resultant stress from all that pressure caused his stuttering problem to worsen.

During his junior high and high school days, Decatur could barely control his speech at all. School became a constant Hell for him; he came to hate the word *school.* He would be talking to someone, trying to say something to a teacher or classmate, but wouldn't be able to get the words out. He'd break out in a panic sweat and walk away, humiliated.

Worst of all was when the girls laughed at him behind his back. That's what hurt the very most. It unraveled him. Shook him to his core. Maybe their taunting might have ended with the simple act of turning around, facing the girls, and laughing along with them.

Perhaps that would have stopped it all there. But Decatur wasn't pliable. He never wavered, never bent, and the festering feelings of humiliation, rejection, and inadequacy escalated into an internal rage he could no longer control.

Then came his addiction to chocolate, which in turn led to another social-scaring problem—his acute acne. It was like a Bizzaro world Rube Goldberg effect gone to hell—the chocolate led to more acne, which led to more stuttering, which led to more consumption of chocolate, which led to more acne, *ad nauseam*.

Outside of school and working in the bakery, Decatur pursued the more solitary activities of hunting, fishing, and archery. The outdoors provided an escape from the oven of shame he found in social situations.

He also began to set fires. And there was always his old larcenous friend—shoplifting.

The one axiom of Tadeusz's that Decatur did follow all his life was never to procrastinate. He promised himself that when he turned fifteen, he would re-invent himself. He could become an adaptable changeling. *Yeah, see me change,* he would fantasize late at night. And the first step in his transformation was to ask out Sandra Johnson right after Sunday school.

There was just something about Sandra Johnson's eyes.

They performed an electric magic in azure. They screamed a knowing. A lust for life. An intelligence. A beauty. An understanding. *You could see it in her eyes,* thought young Decatur. The way she had looked at him in the hall after chemistry class said it all. *She gets it, she understands me!* Her turquoise eyes spoke to him without disdain.

She wasn't the prettiest girl he had ever seen. She wasn't as pretty as Inger Stevens or Sharon Tate or Jayne Mansfield or Faye Dunaway, but three of those were dead. And in the battle for the top spot among the living beauties, Sandra Johnson was a serious contender.

After Sunday School, the breathless changeling asked Sandra Johnson to see *Smokey and the Bandit* with him that night.

Decatur Kaiser's adolescent life came to a sudden and screeching halt when Sandra Johnson declined his invitation.

At that moment in time—Sunday, May 30, 1977, 10:45 A.M.— Decatur Kaiser died. His heart stopped beating. His blood stopped pumping. His brain terminated. His soul iced-over and froze. His world ended. It was if he'd been hit head-on by a freight train. No, that would have been less painful.

Sandra Johnson said she had to study for a geometry test, but Decatur knew better.

It was him, his stuttering, his acne, his dark secrets. He had been wrong all along. Sandra Johnson's eyes weren't magic. Or knowing. Or understanding. Sandra Johnson's eyes were mocking. Scornful. Derisive. Sandra Johnson's eyes were laughing at him like all the rest.

An hour later, after the church service was over, Tadeusz packed his wife and Decatur into the family car and drove the forty miles north to the town of Cherokee Village. The small Ozark town and its scenic overlook were Tadeusz's one sanctuary from his bakery.

After their meal at the state resort, Tadeusz took his family to the scenic overlook, a place he said reminded him of his home back in Lodz, Poland.

The bottomless sinkhole was set back into the woods a quarter of a mile from the resort and was cordoned off with a rope rail guard. There was no one else around, just the Kaiser family, looking down at the vertigo-inducing sinkhole.

Standing there behind the rope, still dying from his recent rejection with Sandra Johnson, Decatur vowed to salvage what dignity he could. He turned to his father and said, "I want to take tonight off and see *Smokey and the Bandit.*"

"You want what?"

"It's a movie. I just want to go to a movie."

"Impossible. Work always comes first."

The "impossible" was not the answer Decatur wanted to hear. In that moment, with that one word, all of the years he had endured of rejection, acne, stuttering, humiliation … all of it crystallized into a moment of sudden singularity.

Decatur snapped.

He pushed his mother off the scenic overlook first.

As a stunned Tadeusz spun around to face his son with disbelief, Decatur gave him a push.

For three seconds, maybe four, two gut-wrenching screams mingled in harmony, echoing up and down the sinkhole as if it were one enormous megaphone.

Decatur couldn't help laughing out loud. It was music to his ears.

The macabre sonata ended with the meaty echoic resonance of hundreds of bones snapping simultaneously.

Bravo, thought Decatur. *Encore!* If only he had those little opera glasses so that he could see the carnage below even better.

Taking a deep breath, Decatur calmly counted to one hundred, then ran back to the resort screaming for help.

When the police arrived, Decatur told them what had happened. That his mother had slipped and fallen and then his father had tried to make his way down, when he, too, slipped and fell. *Such a tragedy!* he bawled behind big tears.

Interviewed extensively by the police, there was no physical evidence to disprove what Decatur had told them. They, however, recommended he see a psychiatrist for therapy. Decatur, learning to play the game, readily agreed.

At the end of four months, the doctors diagnosed Decatur as suffering from a bipolar effective disorder, a variant of a manic depressive disorder. But the doctors distinguished his affliction from the classic manic-depressive, a pattern by the absence of any serious depressive episodes. Decatur's impulses, they said, were poorly controlled during high mood and energy upswings, in which he developed an abnormal preoccupation with a single activity, a socially acceptable example of his monomanic behavior "where he'd be looking to do things no one else had done to consume his energy."

At his last session, the doctors concluded that Decatur's grief period was over and that, with medication and monitoring, he was ready to join the working force as a productive member of society. Decatur was given a *tabula rasa*, a clean slate, to start life anew.

The doctors' only stipulation was that they wanted him to return quarterly to "keep in touch."

Decatur thanked each doctor, pumping their hands energetically, and walked out to the parking lot.

There he opened the trunk of Tadeusz's family car, now his car, and checked to make sure that Sandra Johnson's decapitated head was still there.

There was just something about those eyes.

Getting a huge hard on, he smiled and shut the trunk. *Yep, time to join the working force. Tabula Rasa.*

Decatur's watch beeped.

Time's up, thought Decatur. *This is gonna be some kind of fun.*

Finishing his coffee, Decatur stood up on the porch and slid on a carefully prepared backpack. He reached over and picked up his cherished Steyr Aug assault rifle. Taking a deep breath of air into his lungs, he thought, *No doubt about it, better to die than live without killing.*

As he trekked into the woods, he broke the early morning silence by singing to himself, a lost memory of his childhood, one of the few good ones. His mother—he briefly remembered her squeal as he pushed her off a cliff—had taken him to a revival of *Snow White and The Seven Dwarfs*:

Heigh ho! Heigh ho!
I'm off to kill a ho'!
She thinks she's strong, but it won't be long...
Heigh ho! Heigh ho!
Heigh ho! Heigh ho!
I'm off to kill a ho'!
Her pussy's fine, but it's all mine,
Heigh ho! Heigh ho!

Decatur smiled as he counted slowly to himself.

"1 ..."

"2 ..."

"3 ..."

"4 ..."

"5 ..."

"6 ..."

"7 ..."

"8 ..."

"9 ..."

"10…"

"11…"

"12…"

"13…"

There were thirteen "ho's" in the song. Another baker's dozen. How fuckin' portentous was that?

Decatur whistled a bit of the refrain, then picked up where he left off:

Heigh ho, Heigh ho, I'm off to kill a ho…

TWENTY-ONE

THE HEAVY EARLY MORNING mist was just beginning to break up as Sarge pointed the prowler west and headed toward downtown. High above him, only partially obscured by the clouds, hung a great golden globe ...

The Full Thunder Moon.

Sarge remembered the day just about a quarter-of-a-century ago when he took his beautiful, blonde five-year-old Sue out in the back yard late one night, pointed to the sky, and told her about the Full Thunder Moon, of how a full moon at the height of the summer had to battle the nearly round-the-clock sunlight this far north, and how the moon always won, and how it celebrated by stirring up the summer thunderstorms.

The Full Thunder Moon ...

Sarge wondered if Sue really knew how much he loved her.

It was only a few minutes past seven; the traffic was still light. He took the Glenn Highway all the way to Mountain View and exited onto East 5th.

He made a left on Ingra Street and drove south for four blocks to 9th. At the corner, he glanced over and noticed the Heaven Scent Bakery was closed. Odd ...

Then he remembered. Decatur had closed for the week and gone on his annual hunting trip.

Next to the bakery was the empty space that Sarge had thought of for Sue's dance studio. He suddenly wanted that studio for her more than anything. He was going to help her start that business, no matter what.

He turned right onto 9th and headed west through the still largely deserted downtown streets, past Delaney Park on his left. Across the street, a marquee sign at First United Methodist caught his eye just as he went past.

Godisnowhere
Now Read It Again

Still sleepy, tired, preoccupied, Sarge actually had to read it again to get the payoff.

Minutes later, he turned onto Spenard Road and headed into Anchorage's Red Light District. One bar after another, one strip joint after another. He passed what was perhaps Anchorage's most famous bar, Chilkoot Charlie's—better known as *Koots*—and grimaced. Koots was an enormous place, a maze of rooms and stages where a thousand people might wind up slobbering, falling-down drunk on any given weekend night. The place was famous for its walls plastered with underwear ...

In his two decades-plus as an Anchorage cop, Sarge had probably arrested fifty people there, broken up maybe two dozen fights, and assisted in—at last count—four homicide investigations in the Koots parking lot.

He slowed as he passed the bar, scanning the storefront dives, strip clubs, porno newsstands and tourist clip joints. Suddenly, he found himself going blank, as if he'd forgotten what he was doing or where he was going.

Damn, he thought, *I'm getting too old to stay up all night…*

Then it came right back to him. He'd been by it a thousand times on patrol. And yes, he was tired, sleep-deprived, worried, but lately it just seemed like his memory wasn't what it once was.

A wave of guilt and regret washed over him. Why had he let Sue come here?

A half-mile down, he spotted it: *Bushwhackers.*

He turned into the parking lot and killed the engine. He stared out the windshield at the front of the club. It was nothing special from the street—a brown brick building, single story, with a large neon fluorescent sign announcing the name. Sarge stepped out of the squad car and stood in front of the building for a moment. A sign announced the hours: 10 AM to 5 AM.

Sarge's boots crunched loudly on the gravel as he walked quickly up to the steel, windowless door. He grabbed the handle, pulled.

Locked.

He banged on the door a few times, stood there waiting.

Nothing.

He turned, scanned the parking lot. A battered old Dodge Ram pickup truck was parked in one corner. Probably some mutt who realized he'd had too much to drink and decided for once not to risk driving. Smarter than most…

Other than the pickup truck and Sarge's squad car, the front lot was empty.

Sarge turned and walked the length of the building, then turned the corner into an alley. There was more parking in the back. As he walked the length of the alley, the heavy shadows of the surrounding buildings seemed to engulf him, as if the whole world was turning darker before his eyes.

He came to the back corner of the building, turned into an even larger parking lot than the one in front, and stopped.

Sarge stood there, staring, at what looked like full military attention. To his right, down the alley, he heard a crunching, metallic noise. He turned. A bum pushing a shopping cart stopped, stared at him, then turned the cart around and went the other way as fast as he could.

Sarge turned back to the parking lot.

Yes. There it was. In the far corner ...

Sue's Kia.

Shit ... he muttered. He crossed the lot quickly and stopped by the Kia. It was Sue's all right; he recognized the long, rusty scratch down the driver's side where someone had keyed the car years ago. He saw the balding tires, recognized the faded, blotched paint on the hood.

He leaned down over the windshield and stared inside the car. His daughter was not the neatest person in the world; several empty fast food sacks were crumpled in the passenger's seat floorboard. The ashtray overflowed. A Styrofoam cup was wedged into the cup-holder between the front seats.

Yep. It was Sue's, all right.

Sarge tried the doors. They were all locked. He walked around the car, scanning it, cop-mode. No sign of a break-in, nothing out of order. The car was just there.

Abandoned.

Sarge tried to muster his thoughts, to stay in cop mode. He scanned the parking lot. There were two other cars: an old Honda Civic parked catty-cornered across two spaces and a Lincoln Town-car that looked like it could have been from the Seventies.

Nothing fancy or expensive. He gazed at the mix of gravel and crumbling asphalt that covered the lot. Lots of discarded, mashed cigarette butts, crunched beer cans, broken glass.

He thought again of Sue working here and his stomach knotted up.

There was a door in the back of the building. He didn't know where it led to, whether or not it was an employee entrance or what. He crossed the lot quickly and yanked the door. Like the one in front, it was thick, heavy metal, windowless, and locked tight. There was a white button in a plastic panel to the left.

He pushed the button and thought he heard a faint buzzing from inside. He pushed the button again, holding it down. He slapped the door a couple of times.

Nothing.

Sarge turned, faced the parking lot again. Everything seemed to slow at the same time his senses felt sharper. He felt the current of cool morning air wafting across his face. In the distance, he heard the faint roar of a jet engine as the overnight red-eye from Seattle approached the Ted Stevens airport.

Somewhere blocks away, a horn blared and brakes squealed. Above him, two birds darted back and forth.

Sue. Where is she?

Sarge pushed his sleeve up and glanced down at his wristwatch: 7:22

Shift change was in eight minutes. Sarge was due at roll call.

As he opened the door of his prowler, something crunched lightly under his foot.

Sarge looked down and felt sick.

A couple of M&M candies were stuck to his shoe.

There was not much that could churn Sarge's stomach, but those damn M&Ms were like an instantaneous sensory memory of the past, a Mohammad Ali lightning jab to the gut.

Once his favorite candy, he had just bought a bag as a rookie twenty years earlier when he got the 10-54. Possible dead body.

The dispatcher directed him to an apartment building on 34th Street where the neighbors had been complaining of an over-whelming stench coming from an apartment on the seventh floor.

After getting a spare key from the super, Sarge had taken the stairs up to seven. The smell began to become nauseous—a living evil entity—somewhere between the fourth and fifth floors.

Sarge had knocked on the door, and getting no answer, let himself in.

The obese man sitting in the recliner had been dead for at least two weeks. Even though Sarge saw countless corpses over the next twenty years, this one, his first, stayed with him.

After confirming the 10-54 with his dispatcher, Sarge had stepped outside for a breath of fresh air. Leaning against the seventh floor railing, he had remembered the bag of M&Ms.

Having nothing else to do but wait, he opened the bag and emptied the contents into his mouth.

By the time he swallowed the last candy, the smell from the opened doorway wafted over him like a blanket.

He threw up.

Ever since then, Sarge knew damn well that it was all psychological, but whenever he saw a bag of M&Ms, he was instantly transported back to the smell and taste of that room.

The smell of death. The taste of death.

Since that day, he had never eaten another M&M. He couldn't.

Standing next to his prowler, Sarge looked down at the smashed M&Ms on his shoe.

He felt sick.

TWENTY-TWO

SUE CRASHED INTO TREES, trying to stem the flow of blood that was flooding from her finger, while at the same time running like the wild, wounded, feral creature that she had become. Teetering for a moment, she staggered backward, cracking the back of her head on a tree branch. Before she could recover, an overpowering heaviness permeated her entire body, as if there was liquid lead flowing in her veins, and then her world went blurry.

When things slowly came back into focus, Sue found herself down on one knee and on the funneling, vertigo edge of blacking out. The verdant forest in front of her, only a moment ago vibrant green, now appeared in darkening hues of yellow with little pinpoints of lights dancing all around like a thousand Tinker Bells on acid.

Sue greedily inhaled a lungful of air, grabbed out at a tree branch and pulled herself upright. She leaned against the tree to take in another intake of air, just long enough to gather the last of her strength and regain her vision. Then she shoved herself away from the tree and struggled on through the woods.

The endless maze of spruce and birch became so dense it made the forest dark. Moving from one pool of shadow to the next, her breathing rapid and gasping, Sue limped farther into the shadowy copse.

Shadow and light. Black and white.

She couldn't wrap her head around the fact that one person's hell could be someone else's vacation.

That's what this was to him.

Enjoyment. Gratification. Pleasure. Addiction. Compulsion. Amusement.

There was no guilt. No anguish. It was like swatting a mosquito to him.

There was only one thing that Sue knew for sure. She had survived for at least a couple of hours already. One hundred and twenty minutes. Maybe more. Even though she didn't have a watch, Sue knew at least a couple of hours had to have passed by.

And that was the key.

Just survive this minute, then the next minute, then the one after that.

Take one step, then the next. Don't get greedy.

And she sure as hell was going to survive this too. Fuck die trying. No option there.

Sue tried to remember something/anything from her past that might help her now. There was that one camping trip Sarge had taken her on as a child. He had showed her how to make a compass out of a watch. Little good that did now. First of all, she didn't have a watch. Secondly, what difference did it make if she knew which way was north? It was a fucking island.

Dammit!

She felt lost. Completely, totally lost. She was in a stranger place, a more dangerous place, than Decatur's cabin, and in a more forbidding darkness.

Sue had felt directionless before, but never truly lost. Scared, yes. Anxious, oh yeah. Confused and even overwhelmed. But always before, she had some form of a mental map, with a path plotted if only vaguely, and she had believed that within her soul was a compass that wouldn't let her down. Couldn't let her down. She had been in wrong places at the wrong times before, but she'd always been sure that there was safe passage out.

Once, at a carnival when she was eight, she had gone into a maze made of two-way mirrors. She had walked straight into a mirrored wall. Wham! Knocked her breath out while all of her friends, watching from outside, had bowled over from laughter. She was embarrassed and terrified at first, but she overcame her fear when she realized that it was funny and that there was a safe path through the infinite images of herself, through more fearful reflections and collisions, and through all of the enigmatic silver shadows.

However, there was no map this time.

No safety compass.

This island was the ultimate carnival mirror maze, and she was hopelessly lost in its nautilus chambers, with no one to turn to for comfort, no hand to hold, no silent fortress of a father to take her home.

Sue continued to fight her way through a spider's web of thick, snakelike vines. The pattern had such enigmatic depth that she was almost convinced she might be able to part the thorny vines and step out of the nightmarish arbor into a sunny realm where, when she looked back, this horror did not exist. Like the cabinet in Narnia or the looking glass in Alice in Wonderland. *Why didn't those things work in the real world?*

Breaking into a small clearing at the top of a hill, Sue came to a sudden stop.

Oh, Fuck me!

Taking a quick glance around there was no doubt about it. Rage and frustration flashed through her eyes as she grimaced with pain. Her legs buckled. She went down on both knees, screaming, "Oh God...no...no..."

The small clearing.

The boulder.

The bloody stick she used to rip her shirt and bandage her hand.

They were all right in front of her.

I've been walking in a circle!

Sue looked hollow and defeated, and she was.

TWENTY-THREE

In the Gospel According to Decatur, being good at being Decatur required obeying four simple commandments.

The First Commandment: Thou shalt not get fuckin' caught. Summertime projects would be impossible from prison, so getting caught was not an option. That's why trolling stripjoints for whores who would never be missed was his way of being faithful to the First Commandment.

The Second Commandment: Thou shalt not leave any trace of a summertime project behind. Without a body, there is no murder. Flying out to the middle of Resurrection Bay pretty much takes care of the Second Commandment.

The Third Commandment: At all times, thou shalt wear one big-ass, shit-eating grin. A killer smile combined with the coy aloofness of a good ol' boy facade can take a person to the top. The very top.

The Fourth Commandment: Thou shalt have no other Commandments before me. There was no Fourth Commandment. Hell, Commandments One, Two and Three pretty much covered everything.

Being Decatur Kaiser and adhering to these guidelines required him to be prepared, organized, and meticulous. First-rate stalking and hunting skills were all important, both in the city and in the woods. Persistence was also key in both places. Hell, thought Decatur, he needed the patience of a fucking saint. Thank God for M&Ms. And, of course, maybe the most important attribute of all, the lure—the all-important, award-winning smile.

Decatur practiced his patented smile at the woods.

The wind answered back. Like always ...

———

Not long after the death of his parents, Decatur had shown up early to one of his psychiatric sessions. The doctor's office had been empty and he noticed a file on top of a stack on the desk.

It was his file. *This is your life.*

Decatur, of course, leafed through it.

The first thing that came to his attention was the doctor's opinion that: "He is surprisingly articulate and speaks with ease *but only* when comfortable with a conversant. This is evident after subsequent appointments, when his demeanor is relaxed and unharried. This after struggling with acute stuttering from the age of two. It is possible, and quite probable, that his adopted father exacerbated his language disability."

Well, no fuckin' shit, Sherlock ...

Decatur continued to read more about himself until he came to a word he didn't recognize. "The patient seems almost solipsistic in his belief system, which could explain much about his actions and their consequences."

The word *solipsistic* jumped out at him. What kind of disease, physical or mental, was that? Decatur knew, with his million dollar smile and his good ol' boy sympathies, he could fake the doctors out on the rest, but *solipsistic* was clearly beyond his frame of reference.

Not understanding a fucking word of what he had just read, Decatur turned to Webster's and found:

sol·ip·sism (sŏl´ĭp-sĭz´əm, sŏ´lĭp-)
n. Philosophy
1. The theory that the self is the only thing that can be known and verified.
2. The theory or view that the self is the only reality.

Now that finally made complete sense!

Solipsism. The belief that you are the only one in—and the center of—the universe. Everyone and everything, the moon, the stars, were created by you and revolves around you.

Worked for him. It was a religious epiphany, a moment of revelation. Decatur had finally found Jesus.

And Jesus was him.

Decatur was willing to tempt his new religion, but not push it. After the tragic death of his parents, and the mysterious disappearance of Sandra Johnson, he decided it was time to relocate and reinvent.

Decatur realized he needed two things, just in case that new theology thing didn't work out.

He needed a better killing field.

And he needed a "shield," a facade of respectability to fool law enforcement.

Enter Cindy.

Purely by chance, Decatur met the sister of a friend while taking a cake-decorating course in nearby Jonesboro, Arkansas.

Her name was Cindy.

She was a senior at Arkansas State and was finishing her college courses to become a special education teacher.

Cindy was a few years older and a couple of inches taller than Decatur. In fact, at one inch shy of six feet, with flaming red hair and glistening orthodontic braces, she was always the odd, tall girl in school. Pencil thin, the boys would joke that she would disappear if she turned sideways. Heavily freckled, the same boys would shamelessly offer to draw obscene connect-the-dots pictures on her face. Even her voice had an awkwardness that conspired against her. When she opened her mouth, she sounded like the chance meeting of a fingernail against a blackboard and a dentist's drill on an operating table. Cindy was the one who always walked stoop-shouldered in the school hallways and classrooms, a full head taller than any of the boys, awaiting the invitation for a date that never came. Never one of the pretty girls, or one of the athletic girls, or one of the popular girls, it only made it worse that she was the smartest girl in her grade.

But Decatur saw possibilities in Cindy.

Shield potential.

On their first date, he confided to Cindy, "When I was in high school I used to stutter so bad that I couldn't answer a question if the teacher called on me. It didn't matter if I knew the answer or not. The kids made fun of me all the time. I used to run away from them, and avoid them rather than try to have a conversation."

This was the main reason why Cindy fell in love with him so quickly and so deeply. She instinctively wanted to help other people. It brought out her inner nurturing mother.

Then, too, Decatur was the first man who ever paid attention to her.

Their romance quickly bloomed.

When Decatur finished his cake course at the beginning of the summer and Cindy received her BA, he asked her to marry him at the scenic overlook outside Cherokee Village.

She eagerly agreed.

Immediately after they married, Decatur suggested moving to Alaska and a chance for adventure. At the time, she would have followed him to the end of the earth. Without hesitating, she said yes and they packed the few belongings they had.

Business and career-wise, Alaska proved to be a wise move. Both Decatur and Cindy had the one skill-set essential in making a success in such a tough frontier: readily marketable expertise. There would always be a high demand for skilled teachers and bakers.

The births of Hunter and Nadia followed soon after. It had taken less than two years for Decatur to molt off his old skin and transform himself into a successful businessman, loving husband, and nurturing father.

In Anchorage, Decatur had used everything—his family, his job, his religion, his outstanding community work—to create his perfect shield. He was, after all, known around the city as a well-respected family man, hardworking, an owner of a house and two cars, an active member of several sport organizations, and a regular member of the Methodist Church. Playing to the myth that sports automatically builds character, Decatur even became something of a legend for his trophy-winning deer and moose hunts.

Beside that, killing was just plain fun.

Hiding behind decency, his family his prop, Decatur had found his impenetrable shield.

And, in Alaska, he had found his perfect killing ground.

Decatur reached for a clump of bushes with some broken ends. A few drops of fresh blood lay nearby. Decatur looked up at the path she had taken, thinking it was going to be a turkey shoot, with Susie Q as the turkey.

"Gobble, gobble. Turkey shoot all the way..."

Decatur pushed his way into the brush.

He smiled and took a long drink from his canteen.

Killing, like religion, was thirsty work.

TWENTY-FOUR

Two hours and ten minutes later, Sarge was back in the front parking lot of Bushwhackers, only this time he had to search for a parking space.

Sarge shook his head. 10:10 in the morning... Who goes to a strip club this early in the morning? Place's been open ten minutes and the parking lot's packed.

Sarge shifted the prowler into park and switched off the ignition. As the engine spun down to silence, he reached up and adjusted the rearview mirror. He stared into the mirror at the image of the club's front door. Two young enlisted guys approached the entrance and opened the door. A burly guy in a wife-beater T-shirt on a stool stopped them, eyed them for a second, then waved them in. Already, from inside the club, heavy metal music blared out into the bright sunny day that had just emerged from the morning fog.

Sarge spotted the security guy eyeing him. No doubt he was already letting his boss know that APD was parked in the lot. Sarge thought he probably should get on this.

He sat there anyway, a burning in his chest as he remembered the last hour he'd spent at headquarters. After roll call, he'd walked down the hallway to the large room full of jammed desks that the plainclothes guys called home. Only one desk was occupied at the moment. Detective Pat Murphy was part of the three-man team that worked missing persons. Murphy was young, smart, with thinning hair and just the beginnings of what would someday be a world class paunch. Sarge hadn't had many dealings with him, but he seemed okay.

"Detective Murphy," Sarge said.

Murphy looked up from the morning paper and set his coffee mug down on the worn, stained wooden desk.

"Sergeant Turnbull," he said, grinning. "Mr. Donut Man. Good morning. Say, there's a few left." Murphy pointed toward the other side of the room.

Sarge turned, spotted the box of donuts he'd brought in yesterday. There were three left, along with a pile of crumbs.

"No, I'm good. Thanks, anyway."

"So, what can I do for you this fine morning?"

Sarge shifted his utility belt and sat down in the visitor's chair. He leaned in, and without meaning to, lowered his voice into what almost felt like a conspiratorial manner. "Got a personal matter I want to run by you. Maybe we can sort of keep this one in the tent, okay?"

Murphy shrugged. "Sure, Sergeant. What's on your mind?"

Sarge paused a moment, then exhaled a long breath of air.

"My daughter, Sue, moved back up here from the mainland a couple, maybe three weeks ago. She and my granddaughter are staying out off Pago Pago at that trailer park."

Murphy nodded. "Yeah, Manoogs Isle." He stared at Sarge for a moment. "Kind of a rough place to put your daughter, Sarge."

"I didn't put her there. Sue's as stubborn as a mule. I tried to get 'em to bunk in with me, but she said she didn't want to be a bother. She wants to be on her own, doesn't want to be a burden to anybody."

Sarge reached up and rubbed his eyes. He really was tired.

"I couldn't even get her to take money from me," Sarge admitted. "Hell, I work at APD, so it's not like I have any money anyway."

Murphy smiled, shrugged. "Tell me about it."

"But she insisted she was going to get a job, make it on her own. Only as you well know, there ain't a lot of lucrative jobs out there right now. So she answered ..."

Sarge hesitated for a moment, trying to find the words that would make him feel less ashamed, less guilty.

"... she answered one of those ads. "

Murphy perked up at that. "Ads? You mean—"

Sarge nodded, looking down at the floor.

Murphy leaned forward, lowered his voice now.

"Which one?"

"That joint about a half-mile or so down Spenard past Koots. Bushwhackers."

"Bushwhackers," Murphy whispered.

"Yeah," Sarge answered. "Bushwhackers."

Murphy leaned back in his wooden desk chair, raising an audible creak from the ancient wood. "So you're telling me this, why?"

"Last night was her first night," Sarge said. "I stayed at the trailer with my granddaughter. It's her thirteenth birthday and she had a few friends over for a party."

Murphy's forehead creased. "Your daughter went to work at a strip club on your granddaughter's thirteenth birthday? Wow, some role model."

Sarge felt his back stiffen. "Hey, it's not like that. My Sue's a good girl, she takes care of her kid. Always has. She just needed a quick few hundred by the end of the week to make rent."

"And did she get it?"

"I don't know," Sarge said slowly. "She never came home."

Murphy let out a low whistle. "So where the fuck is she?"

"That's what I want to know," Sarge said. "When I woke up and she wasn't home, I called my sister. She's staying with the kids. I drove down to the club. It's closed, shuttered up tight. But her car's in the back parking lot, locked. No sign of a break-in, disturbance, anything."

Murphy settled back even farther in his chair and stared at Sarge. He seemed to be lost in thought for a moment.

"Sarge, I hate to ask this, but I gotta," he said. "She done this kind of work before?"

Sarge's jaw clenched and he felt the skin around his forehead tighten. "Yeah," he answered. "I think so. We don't talk about it much."

Murphy sat forward in his chair and put both hands palm-down on the desk.

"Sergeant Turnbull, I don't mean any disrespect by this, but you know how this works. Girls in this line of work don't always keep to what you and I would call a regular schedule. Maybe one of the other girls offered to take her out for breakfast after they got off work. Maybe she met someone, and one thing led to another and—"

"Hey," Sarge snapped. "That's not my Sue, damn it."

"Okay," Murphy said, holding his palms out to Sarge. "I take it back. But you never know. She could be sharing a cup of coffee and a long talk with a friend. She could have taken a walk in the park."

"C'mon, Murphy," Sarge said. "If you knew Sue, you'd know she wouldn't do that. She'd have headed straight home."

"That's just it, Sergeant, I don't know Sue. I just know how the women in this somewhat rarefied line of work can get a little distracted from time to time. Hell, sometimes they just go from one city to another, moving around. They disappear. Nobody ever sees 'em again. Unfortunately, nobody really misses 'em either."

"That's not her."

"Okay, it's not her," Murphy said, nodding. "But my guess is she's gonna show up at that trailer door in a few hours with a sheepish grin on her face and a whole lotta 'splainin' to do. So why don't you just go do your day and sit tight. This'll work out."

"I want to file a report," he said.

"C'mon, Sergeant. You know the rules. We can't do anything 'til she's been gone forty-eight."

"Even for personnel?"

Murphy hesitated, his lips pursed tightly. "C'mon, Sarge, don't put me in this position. Tell you what ... When Larry and Woody check in, I'll run it past them and we'll call the hospital and run the usual checks. I'm not going to fill out any paperwork, though. I don't need the lieutenant's foot up my ass again. You live with that for a while?"

Sarge nodded as he stood up, his full six-feet-two towering over Murphy. "Okay, if that's the best deal I can get, I'll take it."

"Try not to worry," Murphy said. He reached into his desk and pulled out a yellow legal pad. "Write down her stats, okay? Full name, DOB, social and a description. We'll get to work. It's probably a waste of time. She'll be back soon, more than a little bit embarrassed."

Sarge pulled his pen from his uniform shirt pocket. "From your mouth to God's ear."

As Sarge reached for the legal pad, his glance stopped at one of the corkboards on the wall behind Murphy. Three five-by-seven glossies of three women centered the board. The one at the right was a young redhead with almost Hollywood good looks. The other two were equally attractive blondes.

"They missing?" asked Sarge.

Murphy shrugged and nonchalantly replied, "Only God in his infinite wisdom truly seems to know."

Sarge gave him his best 'what the fuck' look.

"Just three whores that we can't find," amended Murphy. "Hell, even if we had the resources—and we sure as hell don't—I don't see any sense in wasting taxpayers money on them. Chances are they're just turning tricks back on the mainland."

Sarge just stared into the eyes of each of the women, ignoring Murphy.

"What are you so hot and bothered about, Sarge? They're whores. They don't leave a change of address, you know?"

Sarge took a minute. Then the words came softly, "What if there's someone out there? Someone doing this? Think about it . . . What if we taught him everything he needs to know."

"What are you talking about, Sarge?"

"What if we taught him who to kill?" Sarge studied the three photographs. "Prostitutes. Just like you said, nobody gives a shit about a prostitute. You said that, right?"

Before Murphy could talk, Sarge continued, "And what if we taught him how to kill? Never leave a body or a crime scene. How perfect is that?"

———

Sarge stepped out of the squad car and locked the door behind him. He walked quickly across the parking lot and opened the front door to Bushwhackers. A cloud of blue cigarette smoke, stale beer vapor, and stink gushed past him, tsunami'd along by Quiet Riot's cover of "Cum on Feel the Noize' at Warp Factor 12. The burly guy in the yellowed wife-beater didn't even get up off his stool.

Sarge glared down at him. Guy needed a back shave; guys this hairy shouldn't go out in public uncovered.

"Yeah?" the guy said, all surly and shit.

Burly and surly, Sarge thought. This guy's a catch.

Sarge refused to try and outshout Quiet Riot. "Sergeant Turnbull, APD," he said in a normal voice. "I'd like to see the manager."

Burly Guy squinted, shook his head, raised a hand to his ear, shrugged.

"Sergeant Turnbull, APD," he repeated. "I'd like to see the manager."

Burly Guy shook his head again. "Can't hear you," he mouthed. He raised a hand, cupped it to his ear again, then dropped it.

Sarge's hand shot out, grabbed the guy's ear, hard. One quick twist and Burly Guy was howling. Sarge walked back out into the parking lot, dragging him behind. Sarge lowered his arm, the ear still clamped in his palm, so Burly Guy had to bend over as he exited the club.

Outside, Sarge raised him back up and slammed him against the bricks.

"Now, one more time," he said calmly, letting go of the ear. "I'm Sergeant Turnbull, APD, and I'd like to see the manager."

Burly Guy was sweating, panting. He reached up, grabbed his ear, massaged it.

"You must have a death wish, asshole," he hissed.

Sarge exhaled a weary breath. "You know, ordinarily I wouldn't give a shit, but it's just too early in the day to put somebody in the E.R. So you get me the manager, Sparky, before I call for backup and both our mornings are ruined."

Burly Guy straightened up, scowling, and nodded toward the door. He stepped around Sarge, opened the door, held it open politely for him.

"Thank you," Sarge said, entering the club.

The crowd inside barely noticed as the Burly Guy led Sarge through the main part of the club. Onstage, a naked young blonde who looked not much older than Sunny, let alone Sue, wrapped herself around a brass pole and lifted her legs in the air until she was upside down. The boys in the front row yowled and stomped as she spread her legs in a pubic *V for Victory* sign.

Burly Guy pushed his way through the crowd, Sarge close behind, and through a pair of double doors next to the DJ's booth. The next thing Sarge knew, they were down a flight of stairs and headed down a dimly lit hallway. They passed a room full of semi-nude women getting ready for work, chattering and complaining in a cacophony of noise, and stopped at a doorway at the end of the hall.

Burly Guy knocked twice, the rap echoing off the cheap, hollow-core door. The door opened and Burly Guy had to look up at the face looming above him.

At six-foot-two, Sarge rarely found himself in awe of physical size, but the guy standing in the doorway was the biggest human being he'd ever seen outside of a movie. His shoulders almost as wide as the doorway itself, the guy had to weigh three hundred if he was an ounce.

"There's a police officer here who would like a word with Miss Marcella," Burly Guy said, a level of respect in his voice Sarge hadn't heard before.

The massive hulk looked up and down at Sarge. He almost looked like the guy with the teeth from the James Bond movies, Sarge thought. Which one was it?

Hell, he couldn't remember.

"Back up front," the Hulk said to Burly Guy. Then he held the door open for Sarge as Burly Guy skulked away as quietly as possible. It's not hard to figure out the politics of this place, Sarge thought.

Sarge entered a small office with a cheap, fake wood desk, an even cheaper Big Box store-quality desk chair, and a row of filing cabinets. Across the opposite wall was a vinyl sofa. The Hulk sat down on the sofa and nodded toward the desk.

Behind the desk sat a middle-aged woman wearing so much makeup it had to have been slathered on with a putty knife. Add to that a huge bouffant of coal-black hair stiffened with enough hair spray to shellac a yacht and Sarge had a complete picture of a woman who'd graduated from strip club employee to strip club owner.

"What can I do for you, officer?" the woman asked. She wore a flower print dress that billowed down over her own broad shoulders and enormous breasts.

Sarge stepped over in front of her desk. "It's Sergeant," he said. "Sergeant Turnbull, Anchorage Police Department, and you are?"

The woman glanced over to the couch, then back at Sarge. "My name's Marcella, Marcella Bluwinski."

"Madame Bleau," Sarge commented. The woman nodded.

"Last night, you hired a dancer, name of Sue. Blonde hair, attractive, thirty."

Marcella Bluwinski smiled at him. "You just described most of my girls, Sergeant. Attractive blondes are my stock in trade. Can you be more specific?"

"You don't remember her? She started last night."

"I hire lots of girls. They come and they go."

"She started last night," Sarge said again, more insistent this time. "I think you'd remember her. Mind checking your records?"

Marcella turned to the couch. "How many girls did we hire last night?"

The hulk on the couch shrugged. "Five, six maybe?"

Marcella smiled. "I follow all applicable labor laws, Sergeant Turnbull. All my employees file W-4s with me and at the end of the year, I mail them out a 1099. I probably send out three hundred 1099s. Two-hundred-ninety-nine of them bounce back from the post office as undeliverable. This is a come-and-go business, Sergeant Turnbull, if you get my drift."

Sarge glared across the desk at her, bile rising in his throat, anger like a fist inside his chest squeezing his heart. The thought of Sue working for this woman . . .

"She started last night," Sarge said again. "And she never came home. Her car's still in the parking lot."

"What's her full name, Sergeant? I'll check my records. If she used her real name and real address, maybe we can work with you."

Sarge gritted his teeth. "Her name was Turnbull, Sue Turnbull."

It took a beat or two for that to sink in, then Marcella turned to him, looked up and smiled. "This isn't an official investigation, is it Sergeant?"

"She's my daughter," Sarge said coldly.

Marcella smiled at him again. "You're wasting my time, Sergeant. I have a business to run. William, will you show Sergeant Turnbull to the door?"

The Hulk stood up. Sarge turned to him. "Sit the fuck back down," he ordered. As emphasis, he casually laid his right hand on the butt of his 9mm Sig Sauer.

The Hulk looked over at Marcella. She nodded. He sat back down.

Sarge turned to her. "It's not official yet," he said. "But I can make it official. And I will. I'll make your life hell."

Marcella surprised him by breaking out into giggles. "My life hell?" she laughed. "I hate to sound like a movie cliché, Sergeant, but you don't have any idea who you're dealing with. I have some very good friends down at APD. Some of my best customers are APD. So before you start beating your chest and shaking your dick at me, I think you should rethink your position."

Sarge stood there silently for a moment. His mouth was suddenly parched. He tried swallowing, but couldn't raise enough spit.

"She's my daughter," he said, his voice breaking.

"Yes, and the truth is, I do remember her. Blonde, thin, very good looking. A real little firecracker. I thought she was going to work out. Actually had high hopes for her. But near the end of her shift, she hadn't earned enough to pay the house cut. She still owed me sixty dollars. Said she'd be back in thirty minutes with the cash. She never showed up. I figure she just split. Girls do that all the time when they can't cut it."

Sarge's eyes widened. "She owed *you?* But she was working for you."

"Our girls are all independent contractors," Marcella said. "They pay to work here. How do you think we make our money? Slinging drinks for the enlisted boys?"

Sarge stood there, stunned, silent.

"If she shows up," Marcella offered, "I'll tell her to call home. Other than that, I can't help you. William, I think you can show Sergeant Turnbull to the door now."

———

Sarge walked out the front door of Bushwhackers. His eyes burned from the combination of cigarette smoke inside the club and the fierce sunlight outside. Almost as an afterthought, he walked around to the back parking lot. The Kia was still there.

If Sue didn't show up soon, he thought, he'd have to have it towed to his house. She'd need it when she came back. He'd have to take care of it for her.

He walked back to the front parking lot, unlocked the prowler, and climbed in. He twisted the key in the ignition and the car fired up. As it did, the two-way sparked to life as well.

"10-Alpha-Romeo, Dispatch," the radio crackled. "10-Alpha-Romeo. 10-65?"

Sarge held the mike to his mouth and keyed it. "10-Alpha-Romeo. 10-65, I copy."

"Sarge," the scratchy voice said, "where you been? We been trying to raise you. Over."

Sarge pressed the mike key. "Sorry, Frieda. I went early 10-40. Didn't get any breakfast this morning. Over."

"Well, you're supposed to call in when you 10-40. Listen, the Chief's raising hell. Wants you in his office posty-hasty. Like right now, 10-46, urgent. I'd 10-19 my ass right down here if I was you."

Sarge turned back toward the front door of Bushwhackers. Bitch hadn't even waited until he left the parking lot before calling his ass in.

"10-4, Frieda," Sarge said into the mike. "I'll be there in fifteen."

Sarge backed out of the Bushwhackers parking lot and melded into the thickening traffic on Spenard Road.

Sue was missing. Sunny was terrified. His sister was moving back to the Lower 48 in a few days. And now he was in deep shit with the Chief.

Sarge had a real bad feeling about all of this.

TWENTY-FIVE

SOMETHING WAS BEGINNING TO smell funny and not ha-ha funny. More like a-slab-of-salmon-left-out-on-a-kitchen-cabinet-for-a-couple-of-days funny.

Sue, struggling through a thicket of thorns as razor sharp as barbed-wire, was really beginning to worry about her finger.

Only a minute earlier, she had come to a stop at the crest of a small hill to catch her breath. She had rested her hands on her knees and looked down. She could no longer tell if the blood pooled below was from her finger or from her shredded feet.

She felt numb. One half of her body was screaming, telling her that she was hurt, hurt bad. The other half of her body was screaming, yelling at her to start running again before she was shot, shot dead.

For the first time since 10th grade, Sue did the geometry. Like the points on a compass, there were 360 possibilities open to her.

North.

South.

East.

West.

And *all* points in between.

The bitch was she had no idea which way north, south, east, or west was. And even if she did, what then?

Her own personal compass needle was wobbling and wavering, spinning madly out of control.

This can't be fucking happening!

Then a thought hit her. What if Decatur was doing to her what he had done to her all night long? What if he was still fucking with her? Nobody hunted down another human being for sport. Sure there was that short story she had to read in school. *The Most Dangerous Game*, that was it. But that's all it was. A stupid story. No one did this for real.

That had to be it. What if all this was just a mind fuck to him? What had he said in the car right before he handcuffed her? She closed her eyes tightly, then it all came back as she remembered his bad breath in her face, then his warning, "You know there's some risk to what you've been doing. If you do exactly what I tell you to do you're not going to get hurt. You're just going to count this off as a bad experience and be a little more careful next time who you proposition. Hell, you may even learn to thank me."

Well, it was a possibility, but Sue sure as hell wasn't going to stick around to find out. Taking a deep breath, she opened her eyes and began running once again. Any distance between her and that *thing* was a good distance.

Sue's face slammed hard into the ground.

What the hell?

Sue knew for certain that she had not tripped over her own two feet. Even though she was physically and mentally drained, she had been pummeled to the ground. More embarrassed than anything, she wondered if she had been shot and not known it?

What the fuck slammed me into the ground? Still sprawled out on the dirt and grass, she looked back at her shredded feet.

Jutting out of the forest floor was a pair of hiking boots, yellowed with time and worn by weather.

Sue looked at her bleeding feet.

Thank God for some good luck!

Without hesitating, Sue grabbed one of the boots and shimmied her foot inside. Amazingly, it was close to her own size.

"Thank you, God … Thank you, God … Thank you, God!"

Limen!

It was only yesterday morning that Sue had gone over the newspaper's word of the day with Sunny, a shared breakfast ritual. The word was 'limen.' It meant, Sue remembered, the smallest detectable sensation. Sue thought hard and remembered the sentence the newspaper had printed for an example. She had, as she always did, read it out loud to Sunny, this time a quote from Thomas Pynchon. "Such to the dead might appear the world of living—charged with information, with meaning, yet somehow always just, terribly, beyond that fateful limen where any lamp of comprehension might beam forth."

Sunny's response had been to laugh. "*Limen*. I've got a better sentence for you that makes more sense. "

"What's that?" asked Sue, wishing that she hadn't.

"When life gives you limens, make—"

"Don't say it," snickered Sue.

"Limen-ade!"

Well, when life gives you limens—thought Sue as she yanked the second boot out of the dirt.

Then she heard the scream.

"HOLYFUCKINGSHIT!..."

It took a moment for Sue to realize it was her own unsuppressed scream echoing through the forest like cathedral bells.

Foot bones with decaying, meaty muscles poured out of the boot and plopped down onto her leg.

A sweetly revolting, hefty, hugging stench and a frenzied swarm of bloated flies hovered over the few remaining pieces of decaying flesh loosely held together with a woman's tarnished anklet.

The sudden smell was overwhelmingly nauseating. Sue had smelled some pretty awful things in her life, but nothing came remotely close to this. This was something altogether different, something in its own class.

The odor was the putrid essence of evil.

My God, thought Sue, looking at the discolored anklet wrapped around the maggot-infected, rotting flesh, and she knew without a doubt, *that fucker has done this before!*

Nothing in her life could ever have prepared her for this. This was visceral. Tangible. Touchable, physical, real. The woman who died in front of her had probably been much like her. A woman who had almost certainly endured the same pain, the same terror, the same hell that she had. The two women were inseparable now. They were one and the same. Two lost souls bonded forever together in insanity and suffering.

Staring down at the rotting flesh and the pallid bones, Sue suddenly felt less alive than ever before. Sue realized that a part of her had died along with the unknown woman whose boots she was now wearing.

She tried to console herself by rationalizing that whatever was left in the ground no longer belonged to anything in the human race. The soul was long gone, and the decaying bones were only leftovers on a long journey to ashes and dust.

Then the harsh, panic-attacking reality sat in. Sue knew she was looking at her own fate. There was no place to run. No place to hide. No one to help. No one to care. There was only nothing.

Dazed and defeated, Sue stumbled back against a tree. Slumped all the way down to the ground. Pulled her knees up tight against her chest. Hugged herself. Began to rock. Back and forth. Back and forth. Back and forth. All she wanted to do was cry.

And she did.

TWENTY-SIX

DECATUR GRAVITATED ALONG SUE'S trail with instinctual insect ease.

Disturbed sticks and stones here, a pool of blood there, disturbed blades of grass everywhere.

Jesus, Decatur thought, *why doesn't she just put up a billboard? They're all so damned predictable.*

They run.

They cry.

They get lost.

Then they die.

So predictable.

And, God, how he loved every second of it.

Decatur spied more blood on the gnarled dogwood tree to his right. The crimson goo on the white berries made a stunning contrast against the tree's emerald-green foliage.

It was Sue's blood. Fresh, not yet congealed. No doubt about it, he was getting closer by the minute.

Reaching out, rubbing the liquid between his fingers, Decatur brought the blood to his mouth. The smell was sourly sweet, with a hint of metal. Copper, maybe iron.

And the taste was glorious.

Decatur continued on, easily tracking Sue's trail leading down the hill. He could clearly see where she had taken a fall.

So predictable...

Then he noticed something new.

Something familiar, yet oddly peculiar.

She was now wearing... boots.

TWENTY-SEVEN

WHOEVER SAID THAT NOTHING good ever came from a pity party probably was not wearing a pair of hiking boots pulled from a dead girl's rotting body.

With her back, and butt, against the tree, the simple truth came to Sue. *When no one is joining in on your pity party, maybe it's time you left, too.*

Which is what she did.

She dried her tears, picked herself up, then picked a direction and started walking. *I mean, what the fuck? I spent thirteen years finding a way to raise a girl. On my own. If I can do that, I can find a way out of this, too. On my own. Fuckin'A.*

Half an hour later, plunging through the never-ending woods in a stunned silence, Sue heard the soft parade of trickling, flowing water.

Wedging her way through a thick line of trees, the forest suddenly parted and she saw the glistening creek winding its way through the woods.

Sue judged the creek to be maybe twenty, thirty feet at its widest and looked no deeper than her waist at its deepest. Sprinting out of the woods and into the partial clearing of the muddy bank, she took a careful, backward glance for Decatur. Nothing. That, of course, she knew didn't mean a lot. These were his woods. His back yard. His killing fucking ground.

But what she did see, shocked her.

Her bootprints, maybe ten of them, leading from the woods directly to the creek bed, were indelibly imprinted in the mud like a road map to her feet. She was making this way too easy for him. Time to change the game.

Then she turned and looked at the meandering creek. *Perfect!* It would be a piece of cake to wade into the middle, then head either upstream or downstream, and in the process lose her telltale boot-prints. *That's how they did it in the movies, right?* she thought. *If it's good enough for the movies—*

Sue took one step into the creek and the crystal-clear gurgling of water stopped her dead in her tracks.

She hadn't realized how thirsty she was. With all of the running she had done, she must have sweated off ten pounds easy. And she hadn't had anything to drink since ... hell, she couldn't remember when.

With one foot in the water and one foot on the bank, Sue knelt down on her hands and knees at the edge of the creek.

For a moment, she looked down at the thing reflected in the ripples of the water. The image was distorted and dopplered. Then, for a brief moment, the ripples subsided and the reflection became clear.

Sue no longer recognized the crazed face staring back at her.

But she had more pressing matters at the moment than her reflection. Cupping both hands into the remarkably cold, crystalline liquid, she lifted them to her mouth. As her hands came up out of the creek, though, all the water drained out through the place where her finger used to be. The water felt good on the wound, but that didn't help her thirst.

Sue leaned over even farther down toward the water and jammed her hands together in such a way as to seal the gap between her fingers, then drank with abandon. Without a doubt, it was the best drink of her life.

Bending down, cupping another handful of water, she looked at her newly-found boots and couldn't help but wonder if the girl who owned them had gotten this far.

That's when something reached down and nudged her on her shoulder.

"FUCK!"

Sue jerked around, screaming, tumbling backward into the rippling creek.

For the first time, she knew that this was how she was going to die.

When no death shot followed, she awkwardly regained her balance, then shielded the sun with her wet hands and spotted what had reached out and touched her shoulder.

It was a low-hanging willow branch undulating in the wind near the water's edge.

For a moment, Sue trembled on the edge of a major meltdown. In that moment, surrender was an option, defeat a possibility, death an inevitability.

Why the fuck continue to run? Why hide? That fucker behind me is a million times better than I am at this shit. He is going to find me and then he is going to kill me. That's what he does. Even if I do lose my bootprints in the creek, so what? I'm still stuck on this fuckin' island!

For a moment, death seemed a welcome respite. Up until now, she'd been able to suppress all memories of the previous night in the cabin for much of her pointless flight.

But in that helpless moment it all came back in a flood.

In vivid, Imax 3D Sensurround memory. The touch of his cold, slimy, sweaty fingers and skin against her own. His nauseating, un-washed-man/musk stink. His acne-scarred face, a lunar landscape, pressed up against hers, stealing her breath and violating her vision. The sweat dripping from his forehead and above his lip. His mouth twisted and leering, making his face even uglier. His penis with its awkward arch, the tip which was either deformed or mutilated.

"Stop!" she screamed at herself, her voice fragile, on the cusp of breaking. "Think, dammit! You're better than this. You've been in trouble before. Just work the problem. Think!"

Sue looked up at the branch and an idea took form. Looking to her right, she saw that the flowing water bent around a corner about one hundred feet downstream.

She gritted her teeth. Resolute, defiant. Her body shaking, she stood up.

Empowered, Sue drew herself to her full height. Soaked in both sweat and cold water, bleeding. Hands trembling. Teeth chattering.

You are better than this.

Be the woman you know you are.

She shouted out to the forest, taunting her stalker, "Okay, god-damit, you wanna fuck, I'll fuck with you!"

Humpty Dumpty may be broken, but by God, I'm sure as shit put-ting the pieces back together again.

Reaching into her blouse pocket, she pulled out the pack of cigarettes. The matchbook was still inside the plastic cover. Both were dry.

Thank God, I need this!

Putting a cigarette in her mouth, she struck a match and lit up. She inhaled, then blew out a plume of smoke.

She dropped the smoldering match into one of her footsteps stamped into the muddy bank.

Continuing to smoke, she waded into the middle of the creek. She began walking downstream. The cool, clear water had an instantaneously energizing effect on her body and a revitalizing, almost baptismal, effect on her spirits.

Blue smoke trailed behind her, like a ghost ... An apparition.

For the first time since yesterday, Sue felt a glimmer of hope. She began to breath again.

Be the woman you know you are.

For the first time since yesterday, Sue felt liberated—*deus ex Kools Mentholis.*

TWENTY-EIGHT

Okay, just where in the fuck did Cinderella get those hiking boots screamed Decatur to himself as he stared down at Sue's tracks.

His brow wrinkled in bafflement. His smile suddenly became strained across his face.

Had he been a drinker, Decatur would have pulled out a half pint of Wild Turkey and kicked it back with one long chug. Savoring the burning sensation in the pit of his stomach, as well as the one shooting toward his head, he would have tossed the empty bottle onto the ground as he pondered the origin of the boots while the bottle turned to dust in just a few million years.

Unfortunately, he didn't have that much pondering time.

Decatur looked up.

That girl! The one from last year! In the parking lot, before he 'cuffed her, she said something about breaking one of her heels while dancing and hoped he wouldn't mind her sexy footwear. That was it! They had to be her boots.

Looking up from the bootprints, Decatur spotted a broken branch stained with blood.

Decatur tasted the blood and smiled.

Except for the now bootless girl who didn't run, this one had to be the easiest one yet.

Dammit, maybe I shoulda' given her an hour head start, maybe that would have made it more fun.

Decatur effortlessly followed Sue's trail out of the woods and toward the creek. There her bootprints were clearly visible in the mud near the bank. The prints were deep, made in the soft, pliable mud, not yet dried in the summer sun. Decatur knew she was close. Very close.

A blind Cub Scout could track this one.

Then Decatur noticed something in one of the footprints. Something not indigenous to his island. He reached down and picked out a match. A burnt match. Decatur grinned, then dropped the match back into the oozing indentation.

Decatur followed the remaining bootprints until they disappeared into the creek.

Standing in the shallow water, he looked to his left, then his right, not sure which direction she had chosen. Or maybe she had simply crossed the creek and continued straight ahead. Hard to tell.

Then he saw it.

Decatur couldn't believe his luck.

A lazy cloud of blue smoke drifted from behind the bend in the creek one hundred feet to his left.

Gobble, gobble, thought Decatur. *The easiest one yet ...*

He waded into the middle of the creek. The gurgling, blue-gray waters covered all traces of his moving as he silently made his way toward the smoke.

As Decatur rounded the bend, he unshouldered the Steyr Aug.

Not much longer now, gobble, gobble...

He chambered a round.

It didn't matter to Decatur if she heard the metallic click of death, there was no place to outrun a 5.56 lead slug.

Then he spotted blue cigarette smoke pouring from behind a large pine tree not more than twenty feet away. A turkey shoot is what it was.

Decatur called out calmly, "You know something, Susie Q? I might've been wrong after all. You know, about those things not killing ya—"

Decatur circled around the tree.

Rifle drawn.

Finger on the trigger.

There was no way Sue was going any farther.

Her days were numbered.

Hell, her seconds were numbered.

Decatur cautiously made his way around the tree.

Son-of-a-bitch!

Five lit cigarettes were attached to the tree bark.

Sue was nowhere in sight.

"Well, well, well, whaddaya' know," said Decatur admiring Sue's handiwork. "Looks like we do have a live wire here, folks."

TWENTY-NINE

SPLAT!

A single drop of blood splashed crimson onto the burnt match embedded in Sue's muddy bootprint.

There was only the sound of water gurgling in the creek as a second drop followed, splattering the discarded match.

Then a third...

As quietly and as quickly as she could, Sue shimmied her way down from the top of the ancient oak tree, limb by limb, until she finally reached the very branch that had tapped her on the shoulder earlier and given her such a scare. Now, she found both refuge and resourcefulness in the branch as she used it to stealthily lower herself into the creek, a couple of feet from the shore.

Ten minutes before, after attaching the five cigarettes to the pine tree downstream, Sue had doubled back through the middle of the creek until she reached the oak tree that had easily taken a year off her life. Clutching the overhanging branch, she had clawed and climbed her way to a fork near the top. There she had prayed that the oversized, flowing leaves would provide her with the safety of concealment.

Not daring to move, she had waited, her stomach knotting and churning while she desperately tried not to push the ejection button.

Then he was there.

Like an apparition appearing out of a foggy mist, Decatur, in his expertly camouflaged clothing, materialized out of the forest. One moment he wasn't there, then the next he was. With predatory ease, Decatur seemed not so much to walk through the forest, but rather moved *with* it.

Sue watched open-eyed from her perch, not daring to breathe. She had to bite her lower lip to keep from shouting out, calling him every scatological vulgarity known to sailors and bad golfers. But she remained a human statue as she watched Decatur reach down and pick up her discarded match. *Good!* She watched as he smiled, watched as he turned and saw the cloud of smoke in the distance, watched as he slowly waded into the water. *It's working!* Watched until he had disappeared around the bend. *You're all mine now, bitch!*

The second he was out of sight, Sue laddered her way down the tree. Every branch seemed to claw into skin, but she kept telling herself that a small cut to her arm was better than a big bullet to her head.

Now, standing in the bubbling creek, she bent down, picked up a stick floating by and used it to scribble something into the mud bank.

Satisfied, she allowed herself a small smile.

A small victory.

Then she began walking backwards onto the mud bank, one backward step at a time. Looking over her shoulder, she carefully stepped into her tracks, retracing them back into the woods. It was the same way that kid had done it in *The Shining*, the movie that she and Sunny had watched, when was it, a month ago, two months?

Sue knew that she hadn't been careful with her tracks before, now she was going to take care of that. Looking in front of her, she was leaving no new footprints for Decatur to follow.

Small victories are what they were.

After twenty backward steps she entered the tree line, then turned around and ran into the soft asylum of the woods.

Overhead, the summer sun grew warmer. Sweat poured off her nose and chin. Her hair began to mat in her face, obstructing her vision. Taking a moment, she stopped to gather her hair behind her head, twist it, and, using a twig, secured a loose knot at the back of her head.

Running again, she darted between the trees in a random serpentine pattern, zigging a hundred feet to her right, then zagging another thirty or forty to the right, and so on. Her gaze was constantly scanning, rapidly inspecting the terrain immediately ahead of her for both obstacles to avoid and resources to use. She managed to avoid numerous needle-spiked, thorny branches and above-ground roots with an astonishing agility and an almost balletic elegance and grace. All that time spent in dance classes was now paying off in ways she never would have thought imaginable.

The farther she made it, the greater the insights came to her in rapid succession.

They say all soldiers find God in a foxhole.

Sue had found hers now and it was all King James version.

Hardcore Old Testament.

An eye for an eye.

A tooth for a tooth.

A ring finger for a ring finger.

She was in. Soul for a soul.

To hell with turning the other cheek. Fuck that.

She wanted Decatur skewered and roasting on a spinning spit over a roaring fire, roasting like the pig he was. Burning until his skin fell off, his eyeballs boiled and his balls exploded.

The last thing in the world that Sue wanted was to see him sent to a maximum-security state prison for three hundred years plus life, there to be observed and studied and advised and re-educated on how best to increase his self-worth, given his own cell to keep him away from the general population, his own color TV to watch daytime soaps and nighttime sitcoms, three squares a day and a feast of hot turkey and sweet potato pie at Thanksgiving and Christmas.

And who knows what other amenities the monster would enjoy during his lifetime of incarceration.

A couple of years ago, someone had smuggled a camera into the Stateville Correctional Center in Crest Hill, Illinois, and caught a day in the life of prisoner C-01065.

Richard Speck.

The footage soon found its way into a TV special, enraging most everyone who had seen it. In 1966, 24-year-old Richard Speck had almost single-handedly ushered in the age of mass killing when he broke into a Chicago townhouse and had systematically tortured, raped, and murdered eight student nurses inside. As shocked as Sue was by this heinous act of senseless savagery, she was just as shocked by the way Speck was surviving inside Stateville Prison.

Correction, he wasn't surviving, he was thriving.

The smuggled film showed Speck eagerly performing oral sex on another inmate, snorting from a huge pile of cocaine, parading around in silk panties and sporting female-like breasts grown, as he bragged, using smuggled hormone treatments. When asked if he worried about disciplinary action, he replied, "How am I going to get in trouble? I'm here for 1,200 years!"

From behind the camera, a prisoner asked Speck why he killed the eight nurses. Speck shrugged and joked, "It just wasn't their night." Asked how he felt about himself in the years since, he said "Like I always felt ... had no feeling. If you're asking me if I felt sorry, no."

Then Speck turned and looked directly into the camera. He concluded the interview by smiling and boasting, "If they only knew how much fun I'm having in here, they'd turn me loose."

"If they only knew how much fun I'm having in here, they'd turn me loose." The boast echoed in Sue's brain with numbed, unrestrained anger.

Fuck that, big time thought Sue. And Speck wasn't the only sick fuck she knew about.

Having just come from Seattle, Sue was familiar with at least three more. First there had been Bundy.

Did custody deter him from killing? *Fuck no.* He had escaped from a jail in Colorado, then went cross country to Florida where he killed 4 sorority girls in one night.

Did the electric chair deter Bundy? *You bet your ass it did*! He sure as hell never harmed anyone after that.

Then there was Arthur Shawcross. He was convicted years ago of killing two children and after pleading guilty he had served only fourteen years before getting out for good behavior. That was when he really began killing ... at least twelve women over a recent two-year period. Did incarceration and psychiatric care cure him? No, it just seemed to have pissed him off big time.

And if those assholes weren't enough, the biggest news event in Seattle had been the almost weekly discovery of another woman's body dumped along the muddy banks of the Green River. Something like forty-eight victims and that sick fuck had still not been discovered. Was there really any hope in rehabilitating him? The reality? *Hell no!*

Forget the social workers and the meds and the tough love. Sue wanted Decatur and all the sonofabitches like him sentenced to the trained hands of an experienced Inquisitional torturer, and then see how long the sick fuck bastard freaks remained faithful to their philosophy of die and let die. The torture rack, the Iron Maiden, the thumbscrew torture, the knee splitter, the breast ripper, the pendulum. Nothing was bad enough for them.

Sue's new-found Ecclesiastical belief, refined and sealed over from her own private visit in hell, was neither dignified nor righteous nor gracious in the least, but it was pure and unadulterated, a Nitro-burning-funny-car fuel that burned with an explosive flame, and it kept her motor purring and her mind focused.

Then, purely by chance, she stumbled on a path that she instantly recognized.

It was the same path on which she had lugged those damned heavy fuel containers from the plane to the cabin.

Sue looked both ways, but had no idea which way to go. Right or left? Damn! *Think!* What had Decatur sung when they first got off the plane? *Wish I was in Dixie. Good times there are not forgotten!* The cabin was to the south!

But which way was south?

Think harder!

Dammit, with all these trees in the way, I can't see the fucking forest.

That's it!

The trees!

On that rare camping trip years ago, Sarge had told her that if she ever got lost in the woods, she could find south simply by looking at the trees. The side of the tree with the most branches was the side that pointed south.

Without hesitating, Sue took the path to the left.

South.

At that moment she knew exactly where she was going, and better yet, for the first time, she knew exactly what she was going to do.

Maybe there was something to that saying after all.

The South is gonna do it again.

THIRTY

UP THE CREEK, LITERALLY, Decatur yanked the first four smoking cigarettes from the tree bark and tossed them one at a time into the creek.

The fifth, he pulled from the bark and savored a long puff before flipping the butt into the rippling waters.

He watched from the bank as all five butts slowly disappeared down the creek.

Decatur scanned the embankment for tracks leading into the woods, but saw none. Then he spotted a broken branch saturated with leaves obscuring something near the mud bank.

Cautiously, he grabbed hold of the branch and lifted it up.

Written in the mud underneath was a message left behind by Sue. It read in shades of nicotine brown:

FUCK YOU!

Decatur kicked the shit out of the message. He was, after all, an experienced and patient hunter, but patience did have its limits.

With no tracks to follow into the woods, Decatur suddenly understood what Sue had done. She wanted to lure him here with the cigarette smoke. Why? What else, to buy time.

He whirled around, waded into the creek and hurried back downstream from where he had just come.

He made his way to the place where Sue's tracks led from the mud bank into the water, where he had dropped the matchstick back into her bootprint.

This time the match was covered in blood.

Yep, the bitch came back here!

There was something else close to the bloodied match. Something new. Another message written into the bank:

> WHICH PART OF "FUCK YOU"
> DID YOU NOT UNDERSTAND?

High overhead, a host of sparrows chirped and sparred. To Decatur, it seemed as though they were mocking him, almost rubbing his face in the mud and its taunting message.

Instinctively, he looked up, following the tree branches hanging over the stream. Then he spotted a smudge of blood on one of the limbs and he smiled.

Shouldering his rifle across his back, he jumped up and grabbed a branch. He pulled himself up into the tree, he imagined, the same way Sue had done earlier.

From the top of the tree, Decatur saw more fresh blood. This was where she had been when he passed by earlier.

Damn bitch is good! This one wants to live. Good luck with that.

Decatur made his way down the tree, then holding onto a low branch, let go, landing in Sue's tracks.

He began walking backward, as Sue had done, until he saw new tracks near the tree line.

"Damn, this could get interestin'..."

As he followed the tracks he noticed, for the first time, she was now paying attention to her environment, not breaking any twigs, walking on boulders or small rocks, not disturbing the grass like she had been doing earlier.

"Very interestin'..."

THIRTY-ONE

IN THE LONG WARM afternoon with sunshine dripping down like honey from the sky, Sue stood waiting in total silence behind an ancient Sitka spruce. For ten minutes now, she had remained still, stiller than Lot's wife, listening and watching from the safety of the tree line.

Some squirrels bickered close by, chirping high-pitch *tackatack-atackas,* as if on speed.

And her own heart, of course, jackhammered as if it was going to leap out of her chest at any moment.

But that was all. There was no other sound, no other movement.

Thirty feet in front of her, across the clearing, stood the cabin.

Sue shot quick last glances to her left and right.

Decatur was nowhere in sight, and he certainly wasn't inside his cabin. She was sure of that. She had to be.

Sue took a deep, labored breath.

Be the woman you know you are.

Then she ran.

She made it quickly across the clearing and onto the porch, then came to a halt. She climbed the steps, careful to walk softly, trying to avoid the loud creaking of the wooden planks beneath her feet.

She paused at the front door.

Jiggled the door knob.

Locked.

She half-expected this, but the time for obstacles to stand in her way were long gone. She picked up Decatur's wooden chair and, without a second's hesitation, smashed it through the window. The glass splintered like a thousand glittering jewels.

Yanking off one of her boots, she used it to hammer all the remaining shards of glass out of the window pane.

All cleared, she jammed the boot back on and hoisted herself through the window and into the cabin.

Sunlight, dark like sepia lamplight, filtered through the window and gloomed into the front room.

Thinking furiously, Sue's first order of breaking and entering was to find a weapon.

She'd remember the previous evening, after supper, that Decatur had put his revolver into what looked like a gun rack built into one of the walls.

She rushed to the rack.

It was locked with an enormous Master padlock.

Figured.

But there were tools, weren't there? She had seen some when Decatur opened the cabinet door beneath the sink.

Sue fell to her knees and jerked open the cabinet. She hurriedly yanked out everything she didn't need, including a bottle of aloe vera skin cream and the largest jar of Vaseline jelly she had ever seen.

217

Yuck!

There, near the back, she found what she was looking for. An 18-inch pipe wrench.

Sue grabbed the oversized wrench with both hands and rushed over to the gun rack.

Lifting the wrench high overhead, she savagely brought it down on the padlock. Hard.

The wood around the lock splintered and she was able to swing the doors open.

Inside was something she instantly recognized.

A .357 revolver.

She grabbed the gun. Blue steel gleamed in her hand.

Beauty!

Finally, she was no longer helpless. She knew her way around guns. Sarge had seen to that at an early age. At the police shooting range, when Sue was only ten, Sarge had begun instructing her in the use of both pistol and shotgun. Although her tiny arms and shoulder had jumped wildly with the recoil from both, Sarge had patiently taught her control and soon she became very proficient. In fact, by the time she turned twelve, she could hit more skeet targets with a .410 shotgun than her father. It just came naturally to Sue.

She flipped the cylinder open. Six rounds were chambered. She flicked the chamber shut and it suddenly dawned on her for the first time that Sarge had done all he could for her. Not comfortable with doing "girly" things with her, he had substituted his affection with what he knew best. And one thing he knew best was guns. He had taught her hope.

Tucking the .357 into her skirt, Sue spotted Decatur's Altoids tin in the broken gun rack.

Sweet Jesus, just what the doctor ordered!

She ripped the lid off, unwrapped the bandage from her severed finger, then jammed the stub directly into the coke.

The numbing effect was instantaneous.

For the first time in hours, the searing pain was temporarily gone.

Sue almost smiled. For a moment, she toyed with the idea of hiding in the cabinet and blowing his sick ass to hell the moment he entered.

She knew she could do it, too. There would be no hesitation in pulling the trigger. None. No remorse. No guilt. No sympathy. No compassion. Decatur's act the previous night and, even more inhumanly, what he had done to the girl with the boots had forever seen an end to any of those privileges.

But she knew that Decatur was too smart to simply stumble inside unaware. The broken window would be like a warning beacon to him.

With the stub of her finger still in the coke, an urgent voice screamed from within her head *Get out now!*

Sue wasted no more time. Moving like a small hurricane around the room, she first spilled the kitchen drawers onto the floor, until she found a First Aid kit. Using gauze and tape, she re-bandaged her finger and made an adequate tourniquet.

In another drawer, she found a box of plastic Baggies.

She placed her severed finger inside, then zipped it sealed.

Moving to the kitchen table, she opened the small cooler. *Thank God*! It was still filled with dry ice.

She placed her baggied finger inside and closed the lid tightly.

Grabbing a backpack off the peg on the front door, she shoved the cooler inside and added a handful of granola bars and bottled waters.

She ripped the map off the wall near the broken gun rack and added it to the backpack.

At the broken window, she knelt down and scanned the treeline across the clearing. The sun felt surprisingly hot on her face as she listened to the far-away sound of birds chirping.

And to the unrelenting pounding of her own heart.

There was no sign, or sound, of Decatur.

She wondered if he was out there, looking at her through his rifle scope, if she would even see or hear him.

Well, if nothing else, she had a weapon.

And with it, some advantage of surprise.

And definitely retaliation.

Big time.

Sue now realized that she had to survive. It was no longer a matter of choice. She had to do it for the girl back in the shallow grave. And she had not only to survive but she had to get off the island to notify her father and the police so that this never happened to another girl. Not to Sunny. Not to anyone else.

Crazy. But she was going to do it.

She just had to keep moving. Movement was safety. Movement was life. It was the reason why she was still alive.

Just keep moving. That's the secret.

For a moment, she entertained the idea of burning the Casa de Sick Fuck Decatur back to hell from where it came, but there was no time.

No.

No time to fuck around.

Decatur was too good at this.

The curtain fluttered lazily in the wind as Sue took one last look out the window, then stepped out onto the porch.

Be the woman you know you are.

And finally, she knew exactly how she was going to get off the island.

THIRTY-TWO

Decatur Kaiser watched as the curtains in the window fluttered lazily in the wind.

He crunched into the sweetness.

Three.

For the better part of twenty minutes, he had been sitting in the camouflaged safety of the tree line counting M&Ms.

As he had so many times before, he sat in a silent, perfected stillness, his assault rifle balanced delicately across his knees.

He was watching his cabin.

Waiting as a stone waits.

Centered.

Focused.

Cobra calm.

Across the clearing, the curtains continued to waver in the breeze.

Sonofabitch! For the first time since he had started his summertime project, he was impressed. The tracks, harder to follow, but still there if you knew where to look, told it all. This one actually went back to the cabin.

Human nature, Decatur mused. He thought back to all those shrinks who had treated him in Arkansas. The ones sequestered in their cluttered offices all day long who thought they knew everything because they'd read a book or two on the subject. Decatur was proof they knew Jack shit about human nature. Not in the real world. Not where it mattered most.

You take sudden death, for instance. Decatur knew from first-hand experience that there were only two options when dealing with sudden death. Either you lay down like a begging dog and accepted it or you ran like hell, fighting it, kicking and clawing it, until your heart and spirit burst and you died anyway.

Those were the choices, black and white, and what further amused him was how they always suddenly discovered God in their last minutes. He found their newborn crutch merely ritual, falsely spiritual.

But this one, this one was different. She had turned and faced death head on.

This one had somehow made it back to the cabin.

How fucked up is that?

This one was either very brave or very foolish. But in the end, it makes no nevermind. Just like shooting fish in a barrel smiled Decatur.

Hell, thought Decatur, maybe I should write a book for those shrinks someday. Teach them a thing or two. Or better yet, take a few of them along on a hunting trip with me sometime.

Crunching into M&M number four, he continued to inspect his cabin from the tree line. He took in the smashed chair and broken window.

Bitch is gonna pay for that window.

Decatur waited, scrutinizing the cabin for another ten minutes. Better safe than sorry.

Still no sound or movement came from within.

Decatur was confident that she was gone.

But there was always the chance that she was right behind the door, waiting for him. With this one, you never knew.

Damn, thought Decatur, *this is some kind of fun!*

He crunched into a blood-red M&M.

Twenty-four.

Without making a sound, he stood up. Five minutes later, he had circled the forest and was standing in the back of his cabin.

He was sure that Sue had not seen the back door in the bedroom. As always, Decatur had a backup plan. Organized and methodical, the only way to be.

Quietly, he unlocked the padlock.

Then kicked the door open and bolted inside.

Gun drawn, commando style, he checked the two rooms.

He was right.

Sue was no longer there.

He quickly inventoried what Sue had taken.

Backpack, map, first-aid kit, some food, bottled water, his .357 and *goddamit* his coke!

"Bitch is gonna pay for that, too," he said to himself.

THIRTY-THREE

FINALLY, THE DENSE FOLIAGE gave way and a blue gap appeared between the trees straight ahead.

There it was!

Just what Sue was looking for.

The beach.

Sue had been half-running, half-walking north on the path for over twenty minutes, praying the whole time that she was going the right way.

And then it was there.

Resurrection Bay.

Thank you, God!

The small mounds of dark earth scattered around the shore looked as though the dead were pushing their way back into the living world. They were crawfish holes, hundreds of them, and Sue stumbled across several, coming damned near close to falling against Decatur's airplane.

Out of frustration, she slammed her good hand hard against the tail, close to the registration markings. 773HZ3NO6.

773HZ3N06. *His idea of a joke…*

For a moment, she cursed herself for not listening to her ex-boyfriend's offer to learn to fly.

But it wasn't the plane that Sue had come for. It was the bay. The life-saving bay. Her one-way ticket off the island.

Standing close to the water's edge, she looked to her right, then to her left, her gaze scanning the beach like a searchlight. Knowing what she basically had in mind, the searchlight continued to swivel along the beach until it stopped on a six-foot-long piece of driftwood silently resting half in, half out of the water some fifty feet away.

Racing to the undulating log, she fell to her knees and, heaving and groaning, slowly shoved it all the way into the bay.

Perfect! It floated like a cork.

Just the life raft she needed off this hell hole.

Stepping into the water, she remembered something.

The .357 digging into her back, tucked behind in her skirt.

No way was she going to risk water-logging her life support system.

Unzipping the backpack, she reached in and pulled out an empty plastic bag. She placed the gun into the bag, then zipped the bag shut, praying that it would keep the gun dry. Securing the baggie inside a compartment within the backpack was the best she could do for now.

Can a wet gun fire? she wondered to herself. That was something she wished she had asked Sarge all those years ago.

Just don't let it get wet and you won't have to find out.

Slinging the backpack high over her shoulders, Sue slipped into the cool blue water with barely a whisper of noise.

She wrapped her hands tightly around several branches protruding from the floating log.

Pushing slime and mud with her body, wading in deeper and deeper, Sue launched the driftwood into the bay, mentally christening it the *S.S. Get Me The Hell Offa This Godforsaken Place Now.*

The cold water stung like a million needles, but that didn't matter. The opposite shore, Kenai Peninsula, appeared less than half a mile away. So close and yet, so close. Sue knew she would make it. There was no other option.

Hugging the log, paddling with her legs, Sue began to move across the bay. The going was agonizingly slow, but little by little, minute by minute, Sue was making progress toward the opposite shore.

Something that moved in the water brushed against her foot. Terrified, she began to kick out with her boots faster and faster. *She was going to make it. She had to.*

A large white bird, a seagull she thought, flew across the sky. Paddling steadily, she watched it disappear and envied its freedom.

Tears touched Sue's eyes.

Soon, she swore.

Soon this will be over. I'll be free.

Half an exhausting hour later, she was.

Shivering from the cold, she flopped onto the shore. Drenched and fatigued. But victorious and alive. She drew in a deep, ragged breath and shook off the water.

She glanced upward, narrowing her eyes against the glint of sunlight visible through the awning of tree leaves overhead. She had at least a couple hours of daylight left. And if she hoped to make any progress toward putting distance between herself and the psycho behind her, she would need to get moving again.

She struggled to her feet, leaning against a tree.

As she rested to catch another breath, she gazed out across the bay looking for any kind of movement on the island.

She saw only the blue glittering water between and a flock of birds flying overhead.

Feeling good, even feeling cocky, she allowed herself a brief smile.

Small victories.

The smile dropped dead in its track when Sue saw the sun reflecting off something on the opposite shore.

It was sunlight reflecting off a sniper scope.

And she knew it was aimed at her head.

Ah, crap!

THIRTY-FOUR

DECATUR SETTLED THE CROSSHAIRS of his scope on Sue's head.

Three minutes earlier, as Sue had fallen down exhausted, spent, and seemingly safe on the opposite shore, Decatur had been watching her every move with his eye pressed up against the 6x48 Trijicon ACOG telescopic sight from across the bay.

He had followed Sue's tracks past his plane to the water's edge. Now the bold optics of the gun sight, capturing every bit of ambient light from the air, threw up Sue's body six times the size of life. Still at over a quarter mile away, her face was just a dot on the other shore. For the first time, Decatur was beginning to feel a palpable sheen of fear approaching. "I'll be goddamn—"

Watching as Sue struggled to stand up, still trying to catch her breath, Decatur had navigated a hemisphere of a tree trunk to use as a brace then slid behind the scope.

He lined up Sue's head in his crosshairs. Raised the gun an inch over her head to allow for the distance.

With his thumb, he flicked off the safety.

Timed his breath.

Fired.

He watched through the scope as the bullet smashed into the tree behind Sue, peppering her face with wooden splinters, but causing no harm.

Before Decatur could get off a second shot, he watched as she had scrambled behind the tree and disappeared into the woods.

"Ah, shit!" yelled Decatur.

Pissed off beyond belief, he ran to his plane parked on the sandbar. Tearing through the cargo hold, he yanked out an inflatable emergency raft.

He dragged it to the shore. Pulled the string on a small canister of CO_2. With a loud hiss, the raft instantly ballooned with compressed gas.

Decatur shouldered his rifle. Wallowed into the raft and pushed off.

He mentally inventoried what Sue had taken from his cabin.

There's no way that crazy bitch can read a map, Decatur pondered and paddled.

THIRTY-FIVE

THANK GOD, I CAN *read a map*, Sue plotted and panted.

Shadows began falling in the late afternoon as she tore through the new forest. Shafts of sunlight pierced the trees, creating zebra patterns across her face as she ran—a sparkling, hypnotic light that made everything seem to fold softly into something else.

Clawing her way through thick underbrush, Sue gasped for a lungful of air.

Stopping for a moment, she leaned against a tree, catching her breath and taking a quick look around. The coast clear for now, she unshouldered the backpack. Unzipping the top, she dug inside. Pulled out the .357 wrapped in the plastic baggie. Surprisingly, the bag had done its job. The gun was bone dry. Thank God for small miracles.

Putting the gun back into the pack, she dug deeper until she found the map. She yanked it out. Opened and spread it across the ground. She studied the topography, then looked up.

As best as she could tell, the map showed a hill close to the bay where she had washed ashore and, on the other side of the hill, the map showed salvation.

A road.

Sue looked up. The hill was directly in front of her. The road, if she was reading the map correctly, was just over the hill on the other side. Could it be that easy?

Shoving the map back inside next to the .357, Sue zippered and reshouldered the backpack. She took a deep, measured breath, then began running up the hill as if her life depended on it.

Which, in fact, it did.

As fast as her legs would take her, she flew up the hill. She struggled for what she thought had to be five minutes. Then ten. The summit was a hundred feet ahead, but still there was no hint of civilization or deliverance. Sue suddenly recalled the sense of eerie aloneness she'd experienced after getting out of her Kia in the parking lot the night before, as if she were the lone survivor of some unknown apocalyptic event. The feeling returned now, even more intense than before. It was just her and this stretch of upward, never-ending thick fucking wilderness.

BAM!

The explosion stopped Sue's heart.

But only for an instant.

She instinctively dropped to the ground and checked for bloody, bleeding wounds. There were none. That was the good news.

Fuck, he found me! That was the bad news.

BAM!

Sue listened intently. She knew that sound. Searching in the deep recesses of her memory, she recalled what it was. She rolled over on the ground onto her back and began laughing insanely. *It wasn't a gunshot. It was a backfire! A fucking car backfire!*

Rolling over, jumping up, she clawed the last one hundred feet to the top of the hill. Way down below, there it was.

The dirt road.

More of a trail than a road, but *what the hell,* a road nonetheless.

She couldn't run down the hill fast enough—

Legs furiously pumping like pistons—

Boots slapping the shit out of the ground, a staccato rhythm.

She tripped. Fell. Staggered back onto her feet.

Determined, she increased her stride. One foot in front of the other. One, two. One, two. Legs scissoring. Eyes glazed dead ahead. Locked on the road.

Huffing, wheezing—

Every muscle aching, burning, on fire—

The road was right in front of her, she could almost touch it ...

Almost, almost—

Then she made it!

Stepping onto the road, as if she was crossing some sort of life-or-death finish line, Sue fell to her knees.

Exhausted and out of breath, but victorious, she looked in both directions, not sure which way to go. No sign of life either way.

Then, from around a bend, the most beautiful thing Sue had ever seen appeared out of the whirling dust in the distance.

The world's most battered pickup truck.

As the beating of her heart ramped to a pulsating frenzy, she astounded herself with an uncontrolled giggle. Melodious, shockingly girlish glee erupted from deep inside her and bubbled forth, a startling laugh, half-joy, half-nervous release.

Then she was simultaneously laughing and sobbing, sobbing and laughing, not with relief, but with a bizarre sense of moral victory.

She slowly, triumphantly rose to her feet, a Phoenix reborn from the ashes of despair and defeat.

Just the physical battle of moving her feet now, one then the other, seemed to be an act of super-human endurance and of bravery comparable to Amelia Earhart flying solo across the Atlantic, Gertrude Ederle spending 14 hours and 30 minutes in frigid water to become the first woman to swim the English Channel, or Junko Tabei battling an oxygen-depraved atmosphere to become the first woman ever to set foot on the top of the world at Mt. Everest. She giggled insanely, giggled as tears rolled down her cheeks.

She continued to laugh as the beat-up truck with an extended cabin in the back bounced toward her. Through the mud and chewing-tobacco juice caked on the side of the cabin Sue could barely make out:

Sturgill Land Survey

Running out onto the road, shouting, screaming, Sue waved her arms above her head like a crazy, broken windmill. "STOP, STOP, STOP, STOP!"

The startled driver had only a second to yell out, "What the hell—" before grounding the truck to a stop in a cloud of dust, stopping inches from hitting her. The three surveyors in the truck took in the tattered and bloodied figure standing at their bumper.

Her reflection in the truck's mud-splattered bumper frightened her. The face was no longer hers. Scratched, battered, bleeding, black and blue. Raccoon eyes, sunken and glazed over. Hair matted, muddied. The woman in the reflection looked insane.

In a way, she was *insane*. Insane with a love of freedom, with an urgent thirst for life. Finally, she was free. Free from Decatur. Free from her own mother. From the past. Free from the need to understand and comprehend. She was insane with the hope that she would hug Sunny once again and at last do more than merely survive. She was going to lead the police straight to that son of a bitch's doorstep, then watch as he fried in hell.

The surveyor riding on the passenger side, a tall, lanky man named Greer, threw his door open and stepped down.

Sue ran to him, screaming, "Get me outta here! He's got a gun! He'll kill us all!"

Greer took his jacket off and wrapped it around Sue, then helped her scramble inside the truck. "It's okay, it's okay." Greer took a cursory look into the woods. Spat a wad of tobacco juice.

Sue pleaded, trying to pull him into the truck, "Please ... get in now!"

Greer took one last backward look, then lumbered back up into the truck and slammed the door shut. He turned to the driver and said, "Let's get out of here."

The worn-out, decades-old cushion springs moaned beneath Sue and the inside of the cab had the repugnant odor of stale cigarettes and freshly masticated chewing tobacco. But to Sue, it held the splendor of a five-star continental hotel. She glanced at the driver. The name patch on his dirty overhauls read: P. Gizzi.

Gizzi ground some gears, the universal groaned loudly, and the truck began to shudder deep in its guts. The twitch eventually passed and the speedometer slowly crawled to twenty-five. A spray of dirt and coarse gravel spurted from beneath the tires.

"Please, go faster ..." begged Sue.

Gizzi looked over at Sue, saw her bandaged hand and missing finger. "My God, what happened to your hand?"

"Son of a bitch was trying to hunt me down like a dog … just … just drive—"

"I'm driving, I'm driving—"

BAM!

A back tire blew out.

The truck lurched to a stop as Gizzi pulled over.

Sue screamed, "NO, DON'T STOP! THAT WAS HIM! FOR GOD'S SAKE DON'T STOP! HE'LL KILL US ALL!"

"Relax," said Gizzi, "it's just a flat, that's all it is. Won't be a minute."

He shut the engine off, taking the key.

"Leave the key," begged Sue. "Please leave the key! Leave the key, leave the key …"

"The spare and jack are locked up in the back, gonna need the key to unlock 'em. There's a med kit back there, too."

"Please," Sue pleaded, tears running down her cheeks, "just drive … on the rim … just drive—"

"Won't make two miles driving on the rim. Not on this jack shit of a road. 'Scuse my fuckin' French. You just stay put and we'll have it fixed in no time," said Gizzi reassuringly.

"'Sides, if someone's out there—" He reached behind the seat, grabbed a rifle and a shotgun off the rack in the back. "—he don't even wanna fuck with the three of us."

The three men got out of the truck.

Gizzi opened the back door, shotgun in hand. He nodded for Greer to take out the spare tire and jack, while he motioned for the third surveyor, Cameron, to stand guard. Gizzi grabbed the med kit and scanned the nearby hills.

Meanwhile, from inside the truck, Sue anxiously watched the three men through the window. A clock on the dashboard ticked the seconds slowly away. Too slowly. "Come on, come on, come on …" Sue begged, nervously rocking back and forth.

Gizzi gave Sue a "don't worry" nod in the side mirror, then walked up to her door with the first-aid kit.

Sue smiled feebly, then nodded back. Even though the windows were rolled up, she could hear Gizzi joke with the other two men. She watched as Gizzi, now standing outside the driver's door with his hand on the side mirror, half grinned then turned to the man standing guard.

'Hey, Cameron,' said Gizzi, "'member that flat we had over that ice flow? I wasn't paying no attention and I damned nearly got killed—"

A 5.56 mm round hole appeared directly in the center of Gizzi's forehead, followed a second later by the near-simultaneous report of the Steyr Aug assault rifle.

BAM!

Gizzi, the half grin still on his mouth, buckled at the legs. He was dead weight long before his body hit the road with a hard thump.

Greer stood up from the jack and was hit just under the chin, the bullet exiting the back of his neck, smashing two vertebrae out of his spinal column.

A second later, Cameron's head sprayed apart in a crimson cloud. His legs spasmed and splayed.

Both bodies began awkward, downward spirals toward the ground followed by two near simultaneous explosions.

BAM!

BAM!

Horrified, Sue looked out the window.

As if in slow motion, Sue watched as Greer and Cameron's bodies slammed against the ground, joining Gizzi's in a large pool of dust, blood, and gore. In shock, she tried to process the three men lying on the ground right outside her window. Dead. Awkward, vicious. And for a moment all she heard was a twitter of birds through the truck's passenger window. It was an almost peaceful moment, in a strange way.

Then, from somewhere in the forest, came Decatur's mocking voice. "Well, well, lookie there! We have us another winner!"

Sue slammed the dashboard with her good hand. "Goddamit!" Instinctively, she slid to the driver's seat and reached for the key. It wasn't there. Then she remembered where it was.

"Gizzi!" She spun around and checked the side mirror. The truck keys were in Gizzi's hand. "Oh, fuck!"

With no other choice, she flung the driver's door open.

Using the truck for a shield, Sue inched her way toward Gizzi's body, inch by careful inch. As best she could, she scanned the nearby hill tops. Saw nothing.

Looking ahead, she spotted the truck keys in Gizzi's death grip just a couple of feet away, but he was in a clearing and there was no protection.

Taking a labored, deep breath she sprinted as quickly as she could over to the dead man's body, then dropped to the ground and tried to take the keys from his hand.

"No, no, no …" screamed Sue as she tried to pry them loose.

The keys were clinched tightly in Gizzi's death grip. Gizzi was a big man and the keys were going nowhere.

SHIT!

Sue took a deep breath and tried to clear her head. *Just work the fucking problem!* She'd come way too far to let this stop her.

Just work the fucking problem!

Then she had it. There was nothing else to do.

Fearing the bullet that would end her at any second, Sue desperately grabbed Gizzi's ring finger with both hands and then threw her weight back on her ass, hitting the ground hard.

CRACK!

Gizzi's ring finger broke with a loud, sickening pop. It sounded to Sue like the sound of a baseball bat breaking.

Sue rolled over in the dirt and tried to get the keys again.

They were still stuck in Gizzi's grasp.

DOUBLE SHIT!

No time to think. Sue hurriedly repeated the procedure. Both hands. Gizzi's middle finger this time. Weight back. Fall on ass.

Another sickening, ear-splitting *CRACK!*

This time it worked.

The keys flew out of Gizzi's hand and landed in a cloud of dust.

Lightning fast, Sue grabbed the keys before the dust could settle and then, just as quickly, she ran back toward the sanctuary of the truck.

On the way back, a bird screamed.

Sue stumbled. Dropped the keys in some shrubbery. *Fuck, fuck, fuck!* It took precious moments of furious searching, but she found them. This time she wrapped the keychain around her finger. Finally, she stumbled back to the truck where she flew through the open door.

Salvation.

Jamming the key back into the ignition, she fired up the engine, popped the clutch and wrenched the gearshift into first.

She jammed the gas pedal to the floor and the truck slowly picked up speed, but now the vehicle jounced and shuddered in a spastic way.

The truck wobbled down the road and Sue felt a sense of small relief. It was slow progress, but it was progress and she was putting distance between herself and *him*.

For about fifty feet.

BAM!

BAM!

Two shots took out two more tires. The truck trembled to a dead stop.

Sue looked up through the mud-stained windshield.

This time she could see him.

Decatur was sitting at the top of a hill high above calmly watching everything down below. He waved at Sue and smiled. Then, over the ticking of the stalled truck engine, his voice, faint in the distance.

Susie Q ... That goddamned song again.

For a moment, Sue tried to will herself away, to another place and another time, much like she had done when dancing.

For the first time in her life, it didn't work.

Then time stopped. Literally.

Glancing at the dashboard, Sue noticed that the clock had broken. Either by one of Decatur's bullet fragments or the hand of God. *Who knew?* The only thing that mattered was that time had come to an end. She cocked her head and ducked down into the seat, hiding, and for a moment, the clock and the world were upside down.

And then, out of nowhere, it came to her.

773HZ3NO6. Upside down.

The registration markings that Decatur had written on the tail of his airplane.

773HZ3NO6. *Upside down.*

What a fucking pisser.

773HZ3NO6 upside down was GONE 2 HELL.

Like everything else, it was just another one of his endless, lame, dumbass jokes. Much like the man, thought Sue.

And Sue had had enough.

The ultimate realization sunk in like a fucking tsunami.

The time for running was over. The time for hiding was over.

This was it. This was the end.

There was nothing else she could do.

One of them had to go.

And after all that she had been through, she would be damned if it was going to be her.

Sue slipped the backpack off. Unzipped the top.

Grabbed the plastic bag inside.

Zipped the bag open.

Took out the .357.

Resigned, enlightened, she tightened her grip around the gun, then opened the door.

Sue stepped out of the truck.

Looked up at Decatur at the top of the hill. She had a clear, unobstructed line of sight.

Sue smiled.

In a surprisingly calm voice, she shouted up at him, "I told you you'd pay for this!"

With a two-handed grip, she raised the .357 into his view.

She thumbed back the hammer.

CLICK!

The ratcheting of deadly metal was menacingly loud in the otherwise-still forest. The sound would scare the shit out of anyone. *Fuckin'*

A. She cherished the occasion of making someone other than herself piss their pants.

Anger ramping into rage, uncertainty morphing into action, surprised by her own courage, she continued to raise the gun higher without hesitation, her hand no longer quivering, rock steady now and certain.

She calmly took a squared-off stance just like her father had taught her all those years ago.

Feet a shoulder's width apart.

Knees slightly bent.

Body squarely facing the target, combat style.

She stretched sideways and then straightened up. Cracked her neck, a relaxing technique of Sarge's. Then slowly, deliberately she brought the gun straight up the hill until the sights were lined up directly on Decatur's face.

The look on his face when she pointed the pistol's barrel straight between his eyes?

Priceless.

Sue felt a gratifying sense of the Karma's mantra *What goes around comes around.* The roles of hunter and hunted were now reversed. *As you sow, so shall you reap.* Sue was now the threat. The terrorizer. The judge and executioner.

And, *fuckit*, it felt great.

Gritting her teeth, she screamed, "Die you fuckin' son of a bitch!"

She took a quick, deep breath.

Held it in.

Then pulled the trigger six times.

BAM!BAM!BAM!BAM!BAM!BAM!

Sue watched as all six bullets drilled a perfect third eye into the middle of Decatur's forehead.

That's what Sue wanted to see.

Needed oh so fucking badly to see.

But the harsh reality was that Decatur had gauged the distance between them with the injurious vision of a sniper's eye.

He knew he was safely out of the range of Sue's handgun.

All six bullets fell pitifully short.

As Sue continued to pull the trigger of the now empty gun, Decatur shouted down from his perch, "Oh, Susie Q ... my gun is bigger than yours."

Raising his cherished Steyr Aug off his lap, he found Sue in his telescopic sight. Then he started to sing again.

The moment Sue saw the sunburst reflection in the scope, she knew it was going to be the last thing she would ever see in this world.

An atom bomb of hopelessness exploded in her soul.

She thought of Sunny. Of their home ...

Who looks outside, dreams.

Who looks inside, awakes.

Then Sue realized it, *Sunny was her awakening, Sunny was her home—*

From up above, the singing stopped.

The 5.56mm bullet exploded Sue's heart almost a full second before the sound of the rifle shot reached her ears. As the bullet ripped through her heart, she was struck by a sharp wave of sadness and regret. She died more frustrated than anything else, haunted by all the space that she would live without her daughter ...

Through his scope, Decatur watched as Sue's blood spilled down the front of her body and splattered the ground. The way her body contorted and convulsed, twisted and turned, made Decatur think of a fish flopping around on the deck of a fishing boat.

"... *I like the way you cry, I like the way you die. Susie Q*," sang Decatur, relishing the moment.

It *was* like the night before Christmas and he wanted to burn every detail forever into his memory.

He sat high on the hill, controlling his breathing using only his nose, savoring the invigorating, late afternoon air, running his tongue over his lips and then across his teeth, deeply inhaling the acrid taste smoldering beneath the lingering umbrella cloud of metal-gray gun-smoke.

He sat there for a long time, processing every nuance of the hunt, reliving the kill-shot, relishing the ambiance of aftereffect.

There was a magical, almost spiritual, quality to the conclusion of his summertime project when it resulted in such a magnificent kill. It reminded him of the needle-dropping quiet of a football stadium in that moment between when a kicker lines up for a game-winning field goal in the last seconds of a playoff game and the frenzied, tumultuous applause when he scores; a sense of accomplishment but also a somber consciousness of eternity, a moment forever frozen in time and sealed over.

With his summertime project completed and the blood pooling down below in the quiet stillness of the dying summer afternoon, Decatur Kaiser was better able to appreciate the cause and effects of his bold accomplishment and to enjoy the quiet intensity of death and the nothingness which was now Sue.

In fact, he'd never felt more alive than at this moment.

This one was particularly sweet. She'd made him work for it, every step of the way. What a trophy. He'd always remember her, better than all the rest.

In fact, looking at Sue splayed out on the dirty road, Decatur was immediately reminded of the first movie he had ever seen. He chuckled to himself. In the Land of Oz, the yellow brick road led to the Emerald City and the promise of a better and happier tomorrow. In Resurrection Bay, it led down green remembered hills to a dusty road and the guarantee of an ethereal insignificance.

Decatur chuckled again. Then, still sitting crossed-legged on his ass, he raised the Steyr Aug.

Took aim.

Fired a second shot into Sue's lifeless body.

The rifle automatically chambered another round. Decatur aimed and squeezed the trigger.

Again.

Again.

Decatur mentally counted the remaining rounds in his clip.

Nine.

Nice.

Always time for a little practice shooting.

He continued to shoot until his clip pinged empty.

Sue had been dead a long time before Decatur finally stopped killing her.

———

With less than three hours of sunlight left, Decatur tossed Gizzi's body into the back of the pickup truck. The bodies of the other two surveyors had already been dragged inside. Decatur slammed the back door shut.

Climbing in behind the wheel, he fired up the engine. Popped the clutch and ground the truck into first gear. The truck lurched forward on three flat tires.

"So … how's my driving?" asked Decatur.

He looked over at the passenger seat.

At Sue's ventilated body.

Decatur smiled at his joke. "No, complaints? Good, I like that in a woman. I like that a lot."

His glance came to a rest on her bloodied blouse pocket. He reached over and took out his six one-hundred dollar bills. "Don't guess you'll be needing these, huh? You don't mind, do you? No?"

He leaned over and feigned waiting for an answer.

There was none.

"Didn't think so," he smiled, stuffing the money into his pocket.

Then he remembered. He leaned over again, ran his hand across the front of her torn, blood-soaked blouse. His fingers brushed the hard metal curve of the Altoids tin. He smiled, dug into the pocket, extracted the blood-covered tin.

"Won't be needing this either, will ya'?"

Decatur had paid special care when emptying his clip not to shoot anywhere near where either his money or his coke was kept.

A man has to have his principles, after all he thought as he checked himself out smiling in the rearview mirror. He had to admit, his hair looked pretty damn good. Then he took a look to his right.

The view from the top of the ravine was the stuff of poets. The gorge was extremely deep and the rock walls unforgiving. Instantaneous vertigo land.

Decatur crawled the truck to a stop at the edge of the gorge. Straight ahead, beneath the rugged gorge, was a steep drop to a riverbed far below. Torrents of water charged over jagged rocks one hundred feet below.

Getting out of the truck, Decatur turned and took one long, last, lingering look at Sue. Suddenly, surprised that he hadn't noticed it before, he spotted her half of the Mizpah pendant, a glimmer of gold sparkling through the congealing blood. He bent back into the cab, grabbed the thin gold chain around her neck—already cold and stiffening up—and crudely, cruelly ripped the pendant away. He held it up to the dying light and studied it.

He smiled, then stuffed it into his pocket.

He looked around and spotted a basketball-sized rock. He jerked the rock up out of the ground, then leaned it against the gas pedal. The engine roared. He set himself, balancing carefully as he leaned into the cab, and threw the truck in gear.

The truck lurched forward.

Off the gorge and down the cliff.

With a huge splash, the truck hit the raging river below.

Decatur watched from above as the truck completely disappeared under the water until the sound of the wild rapids drowned out all other sounds.

Now, that's what I call packing in the fun. Perfectly contented with life, Decatur spat down the cliff, then turned around and walked toward the road. *Yep, sure beats watching the TV.*

He slung his Steyr Aug over his shoulder.

Decatur began to sing the Dale Hawkins classic again as he walked down his very own yellow brick road. In the end, Sue was true to Decatur, and she had not left him blue.

Just like the song said . . .

THIRTY-SIX

BACK IN HIS CABIN, Decatur continued to sing while he punched the eject button on the VCR.

Using a blue felt-tip pen, he carefully scrawled across the videotape label: **Greatest Hits #4**.

Decatur placed the videotape into the wall safe, neatly stacking it next to three other **Greatest Hits** tapes.

Then, venerably, even lovingly, he pulled Sue's bedazzling Mizpah pendant from his pocket. He placed it next to a Claddagh friendship ring, a driver's license, and a pink pair of women's heart-shaped sunglasses.

Reverently fingering his trophy trove, a Pizarro in front of El Dorado, Decatur took a moment with each treasure, reliving each pleasure.

Finally, he locked the safe, twirling the combination dial and covering it with the false wall panel. Still singing, Decatur began cleaning the cabin, erasing all traces of Sue.

His final task, and his most endearing one, was to walk out onto the front porch and hack another large notch into the pine post with his over-sized Ka-Bar hunting knife.

Four. Decatur, the counter, counted to himself, sheathing his knife.

Just looking at the four notches in the pine post gave him an immediate, satisfying erection. He'd killed others—his adoptive parents, the three idiots in the pickup truck, and of course there was Sandra Johnson, who'd quite literally lost her head over him—but this post was the one where he kept the record of the ones he was most proud of: his Summertime Project.

Decatur grinned, or rather half his face grinned; the other half remained austere and rigid. The grin surged across his mouth like a tired wave that could not cross it. Decatur was already counting down the days until next summer.

Three hundred and sixty-five. If only summer lasted year round! Too bad!

An hour later, just as the sun, an orange skull, kissed the horizon, Decatur pushed full throttle on the 140 and gently lifted the plane off the sandbar. In less than a minute, Decatur's plane had vanished into the darkening sky, leaving his island abattoir until the next season.

No stars were visible. Above lay only sullen masses of clouds harried by a cold wind, briefly veined with lightning, pregnant with a deluge.

THIRTY-SEVEN

SARGE WALKED OUT OF the run-down convenience market on Spenard to the stares of three homeless guys passing a Forty around in a paper bag. The three watched him sullenly as he crossed the littered parking lot and climbed back into the prowler. Far to his right, over the landing pattern of Ted Stevens International, the blazing orange sun was just beginning its long slide below the horizon. The bottom of the sphere had just touched the mountains on the other side of the bay and, for only a moment, it looked to Sarge like a giant skull.

He was exhausted beyond words, and growing more worried—even panicked—by the moment. His shift had ended at 3:30, but he kept cruising up and down Spenard, searching for Sue. He stopped in every pawn shop, strip club, porn stand, and bar on both sides of the avenue searching for her. He'd questioned more people than he could remember, hassled a few, gone back to the Bushwhackers parking lot a dozen times to see if the Kia had been moved.

It was still there.

He hadn't gone back into Bushwhackers, though. Chief Kramer made sure of that. In twenty-seven years with APD, he'd never seen a Chief so mad, and no one had ever talked to him like that before. Sarge knew, as did most of the officers under his command, that the Chief was a regular at strip clubs, but he had no idea the boss was in their pocket.

The diatribe went on for twenty minutes. It was all he could do not to deck the fat, slimy s.o.b. right there, but he needed the job and he needed the resources...

If he was going to find Sue.

He sat there with the motor idling for a couple of minutes, gathering his thoughts. People don't just disappear off the face of the earth.

Damn it, he muttered. Something's happened. But what?

He tried as hard as he could, but couldn't think of a single thing left that he could do right now, at this moment. He'd been at it thirteen, almost fourteen hours on about three hours sleep. Maybe the best thing to do was head back to the trailer, let Sunny and Jackie know what was going on, then try and get a little rest.

Tomorrow, he'd be back at it again.

He pulled the squad car out onto Spenard and headed north, back to the other side of town, where his granddaughter was probably about to fall apart.

Sarge had just opened the trailer door when Sunny was in his face.

"Did you find her?" Sunny snapped. "Is she okay?"

She wore a faded pair of jeans and an orange and blue T-shirt with a graphic of a surfer on it and the words *Fun and Sun!* emblazoned across the front in red glitter. She looked like any other thirteen-year-old anywhere else in the world, except in her face. There was suddenly a lifetime of worry in that beautiful young face and in those eyes.

Sarge pulled his jacket off and laid it across the back of a kitchen chair.

"No, sweetie," he said darkly. "I didn't find her."

Sunny let out a shriek of pain and curled up in a ball from the waist up, her head in her hands. She stumbled over to the couch and fell down on it, hard.

Jackie came in from the kitchen. There was darkness on her face as well. "Nothing?" she mouthed.

Sarge shook his head. "We've checked the hospitals, the morgue … Nothing."

At the word "morgue," Sunny let out an anguished moan.

Sarge stepped over and sat down on the couch next to her. He reached out and gently rubbed her back. "Hey, it's good we didn't find her there, right? You gotta admit, that's not where you want to find someone."

Sunny shot up and came into his arms, sobbing. He held her there for a couple of minutes as she heaved and shook. He pulled her into his arms and held her even tighter.

"C'mon," he said, trying to keep his voice soft. "We'll find her. We've got guys watching the bus station, the train station, the airport. I've called in a few favors. Tomorrow, I'll go to the newspaper, the TV stations. I know a few reporters. We'll get the word out. People will help us find her."

Sunny pulled back and looked into Sarge's eyes. Her own eyes shimmered with tears, her cheeks soaked. "No one cares," she said. "No one gives a damn. We're just trailer trash."

"No, Sunny," Jackie said. "That's not true!"

"It is true," Sunny said, almost spitting the words. "You don't think I know where she was working? She was dancing again, in one of those ... What do they call them?"

She stood up and glared at the two grown-ups. "*Gentleman's clubs* ... Well, goddamn it, I can tell you this. There aren't any *gentlemen* there."

Jackie reached for her, but Sunny swatted her hands away. "She's gone and nobody cares. Nobody gives a shit."

Suddenly, Sarge had had enough. He felt his face redden and his blood pressure rise. He stepped toward her and something in his face told Sunny to stand down.

"Now you listen to me," he ordered. "I'm not going to have that kind of talk. Your mother's a good woman. She's my daughter and I'm proud of her. Her life has value and it has meaning and it's precious and I'm not going to stop until I find her. Do you understand me, Sunny?"

Sunny stood stiffly for a moment, and then something in her seemed to finally and completely crumble. She took two steps and fell into Sarge's arms, sobbing once again.

He wrapped his arms around her and held her up.

"Sunny," he whispered into her ear. "I want you to look up at me."

She moved her head a fraction of an inch.

"C'mon, look at me."

She raised her head and looked into Sarge's eyes.

"I'm going to make you two promises right now," he said. "Two promises that I swear to you that I will never break. Never. Do you understand what that means? *Never.*"

She nodded weakly, sniffling

"Here's the first: I'm going to take care of you. From this moment until we find your mother, I am going to take care of you. You are safe and you'll be taken care of. Always. For all time. Understand?"

She nodded again, a little less weakly.

"And here's the second: I will *never* stop looking for your mother. Wherever she is, wherever she's gone to, whoever she's gone there with ... Whether she did it on her own or somebody forced her, I am going to find her. I will *never* stop looking for her."

She put her head back down in the crook of his shoulder. He leaned down and rested his cheek on the crown of her head.

"Do you believe me?" he asked.

Sunny nodded, then pulled away from Sarge and looked him in the eye. He saw something in her eyes, her face, that he'd never seen before. Some reservoir of will, determination.

Iron ...

"I want you to make one small change to that second promise, okay?" she asked.

After a moment, Sarge said: "Okay. One small change ..."

Sunny held her head up and backed away a half-step.

"*We* will never stop looking for her," she said slowly. "*We ...*"

She came back into Sarge's arms and the two stood there, holding each other up, for a long time.

PART THREE

July 3, 2005

He sank so low that all means for his salvation were gone, except showing him the lost people. For this I visited the region of the dead...

—*Dante Alighieri,* Purgatorio

THIRTY-EIGHT

DECATUR KAISER WAS MAKING a killing...
The handwritten sign on the window said it all:

Bagels and donuts.
Round food for every mood.

Thirteen years later and the round food for every mood was bringing him barrels of what he liked to call his folding dough. Business was booming and life, as Decatur would smile his million dollar smile and say, "Life is a *hole* lot better."

Over those thirteen years, Decatur had put the literal frosting on his image as a hard-working provider for his family by expanding his bakery. Seven years earlier, he'd bought the property next to his, a vacant Laundromat, and installed more ovens and cabinets. Additional overhead fluorescent lighting cooled and burned out every shadow. Business was booming, the bakery was packed.

And Decatur? Decatur looked the same, only a bit older, a little grayer. But just a little...

With his horn-rimmed glasses and slicked-back hair, he had the appearance of a gawky teenager who'd grown older but not up.

With such an increase in business, Decatur found it necessary to hire at least two college students part time. At the moment, Cassie was working the checkout counter while Marty was in the back decorating cupcakes with Decatur. Cassie was eighteen and plain, on the verge of nondescript, steady. Marty was twenty, rail-thin, painfully shy, a part-time accounting student at the local community college with all the people skills of an IRS agent. Fading acne scars dotted his cheeks. His hair was already beginning to thin just a bit. Truth was, Decatur hired him because in some ways, he reminded him of himself.

Not *all* ways, of course...

Marty looked at Cassie through the open counter window. He held an icing bag, poised in mid-air over a tray of cupcakes. He stared, in the zone for a few moments. Decatur can't help but notice. He turned, tracking Marty's gaze out into the bakery.

Cassie stood at the cash register, her back to them, making change and small talk for a customer. She'd put on a little weight in the last few weeks, Decatur observed. Probably eating up some of the profits... Her faded jeans were tight against her hips. She wore a tie-dyed T-shirt pulled tight over her muffin top, the outline of the back of her bra and her bra straps straining against the fabric. She's plain, nothing special, Decatur thought, but still...

For a moment, both he and Marty stared at her, zoned out, but in two completely different zones. Marty, Decatur speculated, is fantasizing kissing her over a romantic dinner, dancing close to some slow ballad, and then later making slow, sweet love to her.

Decatur's fantasies are of a decidedly different nature.

"You know, Marty, 'coupla years back," Decatur said, breaking the spell. "I hired a part-time counter girl. She was a real looker, too, just like Cassie out there. But that girl, she had one ... peculiar ... habit. She wore these short skirts and ...," he lowered his voice, "... *no underwear.*"

He smiled as Marty looked down awkwardly at the tray of cupcakes. Decatur took a quick look around to make sure no one could hear him.

"Back in those days, the shop was smaller, so I had to keep some of the specialty breads on the top shelves and she'd have to use a ladder to reach 'em. Now, the item that had previously been least popular but was fast becoming the most popular, with the male customers at least, was raisin bread—which I kept on the very top shelf. So, one day this old man comes in and orders a loaf of bread. Well, without thinking she scurries up the ladder and then realizes she didn't ask the old man what kind of bread he had wanted so she looks down and asks, 'Raisin?'"

"No," he replies. "But it is beginning to twitch just a little."

Decatur laughed. Marty smiled, but said nothing.

"Funny, huh?" smirked Decatur.

"Very."

"See, Marty, that's your problem right there."

Marty gave him a look.

"You talk too much." Decatur smiled.

From the counter, Cassie shouted, "Mr. Kaiser, it's five. Take off, we'll close up tonight. Get an early start on your vacation."

As before, Decatur took off his apron, grabbed a bag of donuts and a bag of money, then walked out from the rear kitchen, into the retail area, and toward the door. He turned back, instructing, "I've left enough in the cash register to open on Monday and you should be good-to-go through the week."

"Mr. Kaiser!" shouted Cassie, grinning. "Go! Enjoy your vacation, you deserve some time away! And don't worry about a thing here."

"See ya," appended Marty.

Decatur shook his head. "There you go again, Marty."

Marty gave him a questioning look.

Decatur smiled, "Talking way too much."

He opened the door holding the two donut bags in hand. Just then, a tourist bus passed by on the street.

Decatur turned to Marty and gave him a wink as he closed the door, "You know, I always wondered why it's called tourist season if you can't shoot 'em?"

THIRTY-NINE

YEAH, LIFE'S BEEN GOOD, Decatur thought as he pulled his brand-spanking-new Jeep Liberty Renegade up to his two-story ranch house at the end of his dead-end street. He drove up to the garage and parked. Even though it was only half-past six, the sun high overhead still burned gold in the early evening sky.

Decatur shut down the engine, sitting in the stillness for a few moments as the motor spooled down into faint ticking. He looked out the windshield into the fading twilight.

Above the garage door, the huge rack of caribou antlers still loomed forlornly like a spectral sentinel, as it had for the last twenty years. *Another trophy…*

Decatur took a moment and mentally calculated how many times he had pulled into the same driveway over the years. At least once a day for twenty years. That came out to a nice round figure—7,300.

7,300 times, minimum.

Unfuckingbelievable.

7,300 times he had entered that door and listened to the never-ending, nails-against-the- blackboard screech that the woman who lived there called a voice.

7,300 times he had killed her in his head. Give or take ten thousand.

But tonight, tonight would make all those miserable, fucking times worthwhile. All 7,300. Decatur's face moved. The right half smiled; the left half remained rigid.

He stepped out of the Jeep, then checked the skies.

The horizon was turning a violent shade of early evening indigo. A storm was brewing, but lucky for him it was blowing north. Shouldn't interfere with his plans at all. Sure was pretty, though. Yep, sometimes you really do have to stop and smell the roses.

He carried the bag of donuts in his right hand as he walked to the house. Decatur wiped his boots on the Welcome mat, then double checked each sole out of habit. For the 7,301st time.

Satisfied, he put on his happy face.

He twisted the doorknob and walked down the dark hallway. He switched the light on. It flickered for a moment, then held.

He didn't make two steps more before he was assaulted. Cindy rushed out of the living room and into the bedroom, histrionically packing a few last-minute items in a suitcase. "Hi Hon, you're late as usual ... It's a good thing we're almost ready ... If you could just check on Hunter and make sure he's packed ... I left you some supper in the fridge ... And when you get some time this week, clean all your dirty piles ... You know I can't stand clutter ... The place is beginning to look like a pig sty ... " she imperiously, incessantly carped.

On and on ...

Decatur poked his head into the living room.

Nadia, tall and willowy, a thirteen-year-old clone of her mother, sat on the couch watching *Groundhog Day* on her iPod. Firmly lodged in Middle School, she was rapidly leaving behind any sense that she was once Decatur's little girl. Her body was beginning its long morph into young womanhood and her attitude, Decatur had observed more than once, was morphing right along with it. She didn't look up as he came in from the garage. Several suitcases and a Powerpuff Girls backpack were stacked nearby.

Decatur walked past her with a cursory, "Hey." It had all the emotional impact of a wet noodle.

"Hey," she replied automatically, not bothering to look up, returning his wet noodle with a limp biscuit.

"All packed?"

"Pretty much."

"How was your day?"

"Good."

"Anything happen?"

"No."

"How's your brother?"

She shrugged. "Ask him ..."

Decatur started to leave.

"You know what's funny about getting old?" said Nadia, watching the movie and still not looking up.

"What?" Decatur asked, confused by the question.

"Do you know what's funny about getting old?"

"Okay, what's funny about getting old?"

"When people get older, they ought to get wiser. But they don't. They just get old. Funny, huh?"

Decatur screwed his round have-a-nice-day face firmly into place and walked into the hallway. "Pretty much."

Decatur found Hunter in his room. Hunter, now seventeen, and an inch taller than his father, was playing NRA Varmint Hunter, a virtual reality shooting game, on his PC. He held a small, plastic rifle which was plugged into the computer and aimed at gophers on the video screen.

Hunter held the rifle left-handed and pulled the trigger. Missed. Shot again. Missed again.

"Hunter!" shouted Decatur. "What have I told you?"

Hunter nervously put the gun down and started to turn the game off.

"Oh, no, you don't! You stay in there until you lose."

Hunter hesitated, then took another shot. Another miss.

The video screen announced in epileptic-inducing, red flashing lights:

Game Over—You're A Loser!

Decatur looked at his son with venom. "Now, how about you do it the right way?"

Hunter restarted the game, then hurriedly, nervously switched so that he was shooting right-handed.

"That's it! If you want to succeed in this world, you've got to get rid of all your faults, got it?"

Hunter squeezed the trigger. Missed.

"Dammit, Hunter. Concentrate!" Decatur grabbed a PSP game from Hunter's desk. "You want to take this one with you? *Grand Theft*?"

Hunter glanced over. "Yep." He took another shot. Missed again.

Decatur tossed the game into Hunter's backpack, plastered with Marilyn Manson patches and stickers. "Your eyes should never leave the target. Ever! You know that! And hold your breath when you pull the trigger, dammit!"

Decatur picked up another game. "*Darkstalkers Chronicles, the Chaos Tower*? Pack it?"

"Yep."

"*Wipeout Pure*?"

"Uh-huh."

"*Twisted Metal*?"

"Yep."

Decatur pushed the games into Hunter's pack.

Hunter took a final shot and splattered gopher guts all over the video screen.

"Nice hit, Hunter! Now that's what I'm talking about! Stay right handed, hear?"

"Sure, Dad ..."

From down the hallway came Cindy's megaphonic voice, "Decatur! Hunter! We need to go! Do I have to do everything myself..."

Decatur turned to Hunter. Handed him his backpack. "Got your toothbrush in here?"

"Yep."

"You're packed. Let's go."

———

At that moment, on the other side of town ...

Six-thirty.

Peaceful.

Pleasant.

Warm and windy.

A storm gathering near the horizon, still hours away. Lightning flashed around inside the distant, globular clouds like a defective light bulb.

She pulled the rental car into the parking space across from Room 219. The Full Thunder Moon was just making its move over the Longhollow Motel; the sun was dying its slow daily death.

She turned off the ignition. Sat listening to the late afternoon silence. She took a large shopping bag off the passenger seat, climbed out, shutting the door behind her. She didn't bother to lock the car.

Carrying the large shopping bag, she made her way toward the motel room. The motel itself was a gray, lifeless building, ultimately cold, in a bad part of town. She stepped over the broken concrete curb and onto a sidewalk littered with cigarette butts and broken glass. Her room was two doors down. She fumbled with the key in the dim light and finally got the door open.

A wave of musty, mildewed air mixed with industrial cleaner wafted over her.

She sighed. Another crappy room in a cheap, crappy hotel in a crappy part of a crappy town.

She set her shopping bag down and pulled the little handle around on the door to keep it from closing. She walked back out to her car and unlocked the trunk. She stood there a moment, staring down at a battered, duct-taped bankers box. There were no markings on the box, no way of telling what was inside.

Hell, it was just paper. If anyone broke into the room, found the box, and bothered to open it, they'd leave it behind. It was just paper, worthless to anyone but her.

But it was her most prized possession.

She picked it up, slammed the trunk lid down and went back to her crappy, cheap motel room. She locked the door behind her, slid the battered hollow-core closet door aside, and put the box in the farthest corner of the tiny closet. On a shelf at the top of the closet, a faded, threadbare, thin blue blanket lay folded neatly. She pulled the blanket down, tossed it on top of the box to cover it up.

She had just gotten into town yesterday and knew exactly what she was getting herself into. What was that saying? Desperate times calling for desperate measures.

Well, her desperate measures were simple. She was going to stay in Anchorage for a week, do what she had come there to do, then catch a plane, any plane, and get the hell out of there.

She had done her research well. She knew this was no place to make a living, but it was the best place to make a quick killing.

She looked once again around the room. It was depressingly small and dingy, but what the hell, she wouldn't be there long. One week and she was out of there.

She turned on the TV, mainly for the white noise. *Jeopardy*. Trebek was asking a contestant how many Alaskas could fit into the lower United States.

"Not many," she said out loud to the television. "Alaska is one big-ass state."

She walked into the bathroom and slammed the medicine cabinet mirror shut. Stared at her reflection in all its plainness.

She picked up the shopping bag, ceremoniously placing the contents of the bag around the room: hair dye, vinegar, makeup, clothes, boots.

The next two hours would have qualified her for a guest shot on Extreme Makeover, The Maxim Edition. Maybe you couldn't judge a book by its cover, but you could sure as hell judge a magazine by its cover.

First, following the instructions on the box, she dyed her hair a Manic Panic Electric Blue. After letting the dye set for an hour she used a blow dryer to dry her hair, allowing the color to penetrate the hair shaft, translating into more intense color. Next, she rinsed her hair with vinegar. This step wasn't meant to actually rinse the dye out, but rather to seal the color in. According to the instruction sheet, think of hair as an Easter egg and the dye as the egg dye tablet. Vinegar, the instructions informed, is added to the tablets to make the color vivid and lasting, and this same principle applies to the dye you are using for your hair.

What a fucking crazy analogy, she thought, *but then who am I to argue with the Manic Panic Electric Blue scientists?*

Finally, she shampooed and blew-dried her hair once again.

She took a look in the mirror. *Damn! Those Manic Panic Electric Blue scientists knew their shit! Marge Simpson would have killed for this blue.*

Her hair done, she skillfully applied makeup and enough black eyeliner to pave a small highway.

Next, she poured herself into Day-Glo colors. Blue high heels, white net stockings, lacy blue bikini top, and the sexiest pink hot pants ever made.

Finally, she checked the results in the mirror. She had to do a double take.

It was a complete transformation. For just a moment, she didn't recognize herself. The woman in the mirror seemed somehow self-possessed ... almost sanguine.

She had to be.

She checked her watch.

Time to go to work.

"Break a leg," she said to the image in the mirror, taking one last look.

She threw on a coat and passed by a cheap nightstand. Yesterday she had clipped a newspaper ad from one of the local papers. Resting next to a Gideon's Bible opened to Romans, the small ad loudly shouted:

Dancers Wanted!
$$$ Make Big Money $$$
Madame Bleau's Bushwhackers Club
No Experience Required

She walked to the door.

Oh!

One more thing. She would need a name.

She had gone through several on the trip to Anchorage. Finally decided on one.

Bambi.

FORTY

DECATUR GLANCED IN THE Renegade's rearview mirror and moved his head to see Nadia and Hunter in the backseat. Hunter was hunched over his PSP; Nadia stared emptily into her iPod. Their faces held little expression. Decatur's face was equally expressionless as he turned his gaze back to the road.

The traffic was still heavier than usual even though twilight had spread over the freeway like a heavy, golden blanket. The turnoff for the Ted Stevens Anchorage International Airport was one-and-a-quarter miles away. Decatur mentally calculated how many more minutes he would have to listen to Cindy's endless nattering.

"...Decatur, don't go so fast! Just slow down a smidge, we want to get there in one piece... Hunter, Nadia, you have your seat belts on? Now where did I put our tickets? How can you see out that windshield, don't you ever clean it? You'd think with a new car..."

Decatur stared out the window, thought briefly of jumping the median and plowing head-on into a tractor-trailer rig that was bearing down in the oncoming lane. It was the only way he could think of to get her to shut the fuck up. To the west, he saw a Technicolor sunset unfolding against the endless barrage of Dolby Digital surround sound harangues raping his left ear from the passenger seat.

"And don't forget to water my plants ... And when you find some time, think about cleaning up the kitchen, I can't live in all that filth ... Oh! Watch out for that truck!"

Decatur returned to counting the minutes until he arrived at the airport. Ten or eleven tops.

Cindy nattered on next to him, but Decatur had long since put her on the snooze button in his brain.

"... Did you remember to empty the garbage in the kitchen? And, really, this time please don't forget to water my plants ... And when you find some time, think about cleaning up the garage, do we really need all that junk? I mean, how many guns do you really need? Oh! Watch out! That guy's changing lanes without signaling! Decatur, are you watching??? I told you we should have left earlier ..."

Nine minutes, and one-hundred and ten henpecks later, Decatur pulled up to the curbside check-in at the Anchorage International Airport.

Everyone got out. Decatur yanked the luggage out of the back, piling it all near the curbside check-in kiosk. He quickly gave Cindy a peck on the cheek. "Give your mom a big hug from me. And now you better check in. You don't want to be late—"

"—and you don't want to get a ticket," interrupted Cindy, right on time. She watched as a jet flew overhead. "Ah, I can't wait to get to the lakeshore! I think all this mountain air is finally disagreeing with me."

I can't see how it would fuckin' dare thought Decatur.

Cindy turned to Nadia. "Sweetie, give your dad a hug."

Nadia didn't hear her mother. She was still plugged into her iPod watching *Groundhog Day* time loop day after day. Bill Murray was asking the Bed & Breakfast maid, "Do you ever have déjà vu, Mrs. Lancaster?" To which she replied," I don't think so, but I could check with the kitchen."

"Nadia! Give your dad a hug!"

Nadia defiantly pulled out her earplugs, gave her father a perfunctory hug, then put the earplugs back in. Cindy turned to Hunter. "Your turn, Hunter. Say goodbye to your father."

Hunter, plugged into his PSP, walked past his dad. "Knock 'em dead, Dad."

A car horn blared from behind Decatur's Renegade. He rushed back into his Jeep just as Sonny and Cher's "I Got You Babe" was waking Bill Murray up for the umpteenth time.

Decatur drove out of the airport departure lane and pulled onto Interstate A1 east back into the city. He cranked the Renegade up to 75, then cracked the window just a trace and breathed deeply of the night air.

Then he reached into his pocket and pulled out the Altoids tin.

FORTY-ONE

THE AGING WALLPAPER LOOKED like the skin of a molting snake. The dim red bulbs gleamed like a low-grade hellfire. The filthy mosaic tiles—the grout between them black with mold and grime—crunched beneath his feet.

In the world's seediest bathroom, Decatur snorted coke from his fingernail. Then again. Carefully washing his face in the diseased-looking sink, he opened the door and stepped out into the thumping heavy metal blaring music and dazzling, kaleidoscopic lights of Madame Bleau's Bushwhackers club.

He made his way over to the bar and ordered a beer so he wouldn't have to tip the girls, then wound and snaked through the crush of bodies to a back table in the shadows. He scrutinized the crowd, scanning the pack of bodies with a practiced eye.

The topless bar was jammed. Most of the working girls were with men.

Then he spotted her.

She was carrying a lacquered tray with drinks. And she was alone.

He instantaneously sized her up, as if she were a trophy Dall sheep in the woods. Mid-twenties. Damned pretty. Hell, beautiful. Electric blue hair. Decked out in Day-Glo colors. Blue high heels, white net stockings, lacy blue bikini top, and the sexiest pink hot pants ever made.

Decatur couldn't take his eyes off her.

Everything about her screamed, "*Come on, I dare you, just try something, make my day!*"

We'll see how long that shit lasts Decatur thought smugly.

Then, from across the room, she looked up and noticed Decatur staring at her.

She began to saunter toward him, while flashing eyes so looming and round they couldn't help but communicate a flirtatious smile.

Their eyes met, for a moment, then Decatur looked down at his beer. When he looked back up, the girl was lost in the overflow crowd.

Then, from over his shoulder, a playful voice boomed out, "Caughtcha'!"

"What?!" asked Decatur, off-guard.

"Caughtcha' checking me out. That's what."

Decatur looked up, quickly opted for the sympathy approach. "Uh, listen … this is the first time I've been in a place like this. I just don't want to get ripped off, you know? I'm a little nervous. I'm putting myself in your hands."

The girl bubbled back, "Well, you're in luck, 'cus I'm new here, too. Just got in last week. Had some … rough times in the Lower 48. Needed a change. Some hide-a-way, this Alaska, wouldn't you say?"

"I'd say."

"Know what else I'd say?"

"What?"

"I'd say this place is just one gigantic license to freak. Want a drink?"

Decatur studied the girl, prey-like. Despite her drop-dead good looks, she seemed a bit naive and a real talker. *She'll do just fine,* thought Decatur. "If you'll sit with me," he said.

"Sure thang, Honey Bun." She sat down, putting the drinks on the table. "Hey, speaking of hide-a-ways, know what I saw on TV today?"

"Got no idea."

"Okay, let's see if I can remember this just right." She closed her eyes, thought for a moment, then opened her deep blue eyes. "Oh, yeah, it was a game show and they said that, uh, you could fit three Alaskas into the lower forty-eight states! Imagine that! But, the real kicker is this —the population here in Alaska is something like six hundred thousand and change. Know what they said that's like?"

"What's that like?"

"They said it was like New York City having only twenty two people living in it. Isn't that amazing?"

"Boggles the mind."

"Oh, man, speaking of boggling, have you seen that new supermarket on Fifth and Muldoon?"

"You mean the new Piggly Wiggly?"

"Yeah! That's the one!"

"I've seen it, haven't been in it."

"Oh my God, you've got to go! It's so cool! The vegetable section has this automatic mist machine to keep all the vegetables fresh. Just before it goes on, you hear the sound of a thunderstorm. And when you walk over to the milk section, you hear cows mooing. And when you walk over to the eggs, you hear hens cackle! I think it's really, really cool, but hell, Honey Bun, so far I've been too afraid to go down the toilet paper aisle. No way, nuh-uh, not me."

Decatur couldn't help but smile. She was babbling continuously, just like Cindy, only with her, it was still cute. "Jesus H. Christ, you remind me of someone."

"Why do people always say that?"

"That you remind them of someone?"

"No, how come people always say 'Jesus *H*. Christ'? Why not 'Jesus *S*. Christ' or 'Jesus *L*. Christ' or something else? Does the 'H' really stand for something?"

"I've heard it stands for 'Hallmark'."

"Huh?"

Looking straight into her baby blues: "Because God cared enough to send the very best."

"Ah, that's so sweet, Honey Bun. So, 'fess up."

"What?"

"Who do I remind you of?"

"Oh, just someone." He snickered, thinking that if he couldn't jam Cindy's head on a pike, hers would do. "Someone who likes to talk a lot. Doggone it, I don't know the word, but I'm sure there's some sort of term for that." He took a drink of beer. "I seem to be drawing a blank on that."

"Hey, can you really do that?"

"Do what"?

"Draw a blank. I mean, how would you do that? You think Van Gogh or Picasso could do that?"

Decatur smiled, then took a drink of beer. "Whadda' they call you here?"

"You can call me Bambi."

"Bambi? The big B. How ... perfect." He finished the beer, then thought for a moment. "Didn't they shoot the mother or something in that movie?"

"Oh, my God, I've seen the movie, like, maybe fifty times and there's so much to it that people don't know. I mean, it's the story of the entire life cycle. You know—birth, death, and re-birth. That's the real story. It's the very basics of life: the 'doe-eyed' innocence of childhood ... parental love ... discovering and learning about the world around us ... both its beauty and its danger ... loss and grief ... joy and tragedy ... developing friendships and loyalties ... growing toward independence and just being at one and in harmony with nature ... Oh! And balancing risk and need. That's what it's all about, Honey Bun!"

"Yeah, well, all I remember is they shot the mother."

"Well, sadness happens, Honey Bun, but I'll tell you something about sadness," she said, leaning in closer and somehow revealing even more cleavage. "I say screw sadness! 'Cause sadness is just another word for inevitable and nothing's inevitable as long as you stick to your guns, face it straight in the eye and say 'Hey! You're *evitable*!'"

She smiled, then pushed one of the drinks from the lacquered tray toward Decatur. "Here's a shot for you, and this one's on the house."

"The way it should be," said Decatur draining the shot.

"The way it is. I'm a free bird and I have to spread my wings."

"Damn straight, get some air under your wings." *Or spread something else ...*

"Damn straight, I have a divine right."

Decatur glanced at her perfect cleavage. "And your left ain't half bad, either, B!" Wolfishly smiled. "Marx Brothers. I've always wanted to say that!" Pointed to the tray of drinks. "How much for the rest?"

"Fifteen should cover it."

Decatur whipped out a twenty dollar bill.

Bambi reached into her cleavage and pulled out a five. Set it on the table close to Decatur.

He pulled out another twenty. Slid it next to the five. Looked up. "You a gambler, B?"

"What else is there?"

Decatur pulled a quarter out of his pocket. "Heads you keep both bills, tails you keep the five." He flipped the quarter. "Call it!"

"Heads!"

Decatur caught the coin. Slapped it on the back of his other wrist. Uncovered his hand. Heads. "Well, lookie there, we have ourselves another winner!"

He pushed both bills over to Bambi. She licked her lips. Leaned forward, showing Decatur even more cleavage. He stared into the valley of her breasts and felt a pang.

"I like tails, but what I really like is heads," she piped.

"You don't say," Decatur said, snapping out of his reverie.

"Just did. I like heads."

Decatur pulled out three one-hundred dollar bills. Fanned them on the table. "Feeling lucky?"

"Bring it on."

Decatur flipped the coin. "Call it!"

"Heads!"

Once again, Decatur caught the coin. Slapped in on his wrist, but this time uncovered his hand so that only he could see it. Then quickly put the coin back in his pocket before Bambi could see what it was.

"Doggone, if we don't have ourselves another winner! It was heads!"

Bambi reached for the bills, but Decatur's hand jerked like a snake grabbing a mouse. He raked in the money and stashed it in his pocket.

"What the hell you doing?" Bambi asked, a pout emerging across her face.

"Oh, the money's all yours. The question is—my place or my place?" Another wolfish grin. "My car's out in the back parking lot. Meet me there in five minutes and you can collect your winnings. House rules."

He stood up. "You won't disappoint me, will you? You said it yourself, heads over tails. Me, I'll take what I can get."

"Disappoint *you*?" asked Bambi with stormy eyes. "Hell no! For three hundred, I'm the fun and only."

FORTY-TWO

THE MOON BURNED GOLD into her hair.

A blonde was smoking a cigarette outside the exit door, calmly unaware, as Decatur nervously bit into one of the M&Ms lined up across his dashboard.

He wanted the blonde long gone, so that if Bambi did come out, there would be no one to see her get into his Jeep.

Sitting behind the wheel, Decatur nervously tapped the steering wheel, willing the blonde away. But the more he willed, the longer she seemed to linger.

Damn it, he thought. *Move, bitch...*

Decatur glanced up at the full moon. Moonlight. *All moonlight really was,* he thought, *is sunlight bouncing off the moon. Right?*

So then, why aren't vampires zapped by moonlight?

By the time he looked back at the exit door, the blonde was gone. Maybe the moonlight zapped her. What the hell? She was gone.

Decatur crunched into the next M&M, number two, and wondered what the night had in store.

He didn't have to wait long. The back door opened. Bambi stepped out, backlit by the light spill.

Decatur blinked his headlights on, then off.

Bambi walked over to his car. Decatur jumped out and opened the passenger door. "Well, well, well, if it's not the fun and only."

"Um, that's me. The fun and only." She smiled as she slid into the passenger seat.

Decatur closed the door behind her, then made his way back behind the wheel. Once inside the car, he hit the button on the driver's door armrest and all four locks clicked simultaneously.

"Come a little closer," he grinned, stuffing the three one-hundred dollar bills into the pocket of her pink hot pants.

She moved over. Decatur hooked his right arm around her shoulders. Began to play with her hair.

Bambi ran her hand across the front of his shirt, then down lower around his waist, until her hand came down to the seat. "Oh! It's … hard?"

"Ain't that the idea, B?"

"No, not you … this!"

She pulled out something between her thumb and forefinger. She looked up with numb surprise. She was holding a .357 Magnum. "What the—"

Suddenly, Decatur grabbed a handful of Bambi's hair and violently jerked her head back. He grabbed the gun out of her hand.

Bambi looked up. Terrified. The barrel of the .357 was planted squarely between her eyes.

"Just had to ruin all the fun, didn't ya', B? Well, we'll have some fun soon enough."

"What are you doing?"

"Just shut the fuck up and do exactly what I say! You cooperate, you get to live. You give me any trouble, I'll stick this gun down your throat and pull the trigger." He cocked the hammer back on the gun. "Got it?"

Horrified, Bambi gave a jerking nod. She could barely get out the words, "I'm so scared." It was a statement, an explanation, a plea, all rolled into one. "Please. Please just don't hurt me and I'll do what you say."

"Good. Now, get down on the floorboard, your face on the seat, your arms behind your back. Do it!"

Decatur forced Bambi onto her knees on the floor of the passenger seat.

Reached under his seat.

Pulled out a pair of handcuffs.

"Look, you don't have to do this," pleaded Bambi, her voice muffled with her face jammed into the seat leather.

"Oh, but I want to!"

"Please, just let me go and I won't say a word—"

"Look, B, you're a professional. I ain't gonna do nothing that hasn't been done to you before. So, you don't get excited, you don't do nothing stupid. You know there's some risk to what you've been doing. If you do exactly what I tell you to do you're not going to get hurt. You're just going to count this off as a bad experience and be a little more careful next time who you proposition. Hell, you may even learn to thank me."

He handcuffed her wrists behind her back.

Bambi remained passive.

"Well, well, well, if I didn't know any better, I'd think you'd been around this block before, B."

For the first time in her life, Bambi, completely helpless, remained silent.

This was the trait Decatur most admired in a woman.

In moonlight or sunlight, it didn't matter.

FORTY-THREE

DECATUR LOOKED UP AND checked his rearview mirror as he pulled into the deserted airfield parking area. Behind him, the lights of Anchorage were winking off in the distance and the night sky glowed crimson, as if the city had been torched by a lost General Sherman.

Up ahead, the Jeep's headlights bathed a patch of daffodils in full bloom in the rough grass at the end of the airfield, making a brilliant yellow splash against the soylent green. The new replacing the old.

Decatur looked to his right. Bambi was still face down on the passenger seat. She'd been there the entire time, not saying one word.

It's funny he thought. *But nothing says attitude adjustment like a good pair of high-tensile steel handcuffs and a quick slap across the face with the business end of a .357.*

Break even the feistiest of fillies. One thing was for damn sure. Nothing about her screamed, "*Come on, I dare you, just try something, make my day!*" any more.

Now it was more like, "*Please, let me go, I'll do anything if you just let me go, I'll make your day, anything you ask.*"

In an odd way, Decatur was disappointed. He hoped he hadn't misjudged her. He thought at first she had a little fire in her. Now the fire seemed to have gone out.

He loved attitude adjustment. Just not too much of it...

Decatur eased the Jeep to a stop near his Cessna 140. He took a quick look around, then killed the lights. There was no one else in sight.

"Man, oh man, are you in for a special treat," he said to Bambi.

"Where...where are we?" Bambi spoke for the first time since the parking lot.

"My little slice of heaven."

Decatur opened his door, then made his way around the Jeep. He opened the passenger door and took hold of Bambi's handcuffs.

"Get out."

He yanked the cuffs, hard, pulling her arms up behind her. Bambi moaned and started to breathe heavily, almost hyperventilating. Decatur dragged her off the seat and out of the Jeep. She almost stumbled, but found her footing. She stood up erect, struggling with the handcuffs behind her, looking around the shadowy airfield in a numbed silence.

"What are we doing here?" she asked quietly.

"Told you. You're in for a special treat." He forced her around so that her back faced him. Then he shoved her and the two began walking toward the plane.

"Now, you do just what I say and everything will be honky dory. You know, I gotta be honest with you … I'm not really sure what 'honky dory' means, but if 'honky dory' means you try anything funny, I'm going to empty my .357 into your skull, then, yep, everything will be honky dory."

"Hunky."

"Say what?"

"It's 'hunky' dory."

His hand shot out and palmed her in the middle of the back, pushing her hard. She stumbled, almost losing her footing in the high, wet grass.

"Whatever, B," he snapped. "Don't go all attitudy on me."

The rest of the twenty yards or so passed in silence. They stopped just under the right wing of the plane. Decatur dug into his pockets, found the keys to the handcuffs.

"You just be cool here, B," he warned. He unlocked the cuff from her right hand, then quickly brought her hands around front and snapped the cuff back onto her right wrist.

Decatur paused a moment, standing there behind her, his arms still wrapped around her. He breathed in deeply through his nose, the cool, crisp Alaskan night air filling his lungs. Decatur smelled something like pine in the far distance. He felt the heat coming off her.

He was always most alive at times like this.

Then he nestled down into the crook of her neck, almost affectionately, and wrapped his arms tighter around her, pulling her to him. In any other circumstances, they would pass for two lovers cuddling sweetly in the night. She stiffened as he buried his face in her hair, then opened his mouth, reached out his tongue, and ran it slowly along the side of her neck to her right shoulder. He brought his hands up her torso, cupped her breasts. He smiled.

She may be scared shitless, he thought, but her nipples can still get hard. He focused his thumb and index finger on her right nipple and gently tweaked it.

Bambi shuddered.

"What's the matter, B?" he whispered.

"No … nothing," she stammered. "I'm just a little chilly."

"Well," Decatur grinned, releasing her from the embrace. "We'll take care of that soon enough."

He reached over and opened the passenger door on the plane. "Get in."

"What!?"

"Did I stutter, goddamnit? I said, 'Get in.'"

"You can't be serious."

"Don't you worry none, B." He smiled at her with his patented acid-sweet smile. "I won't charge you for the ride."

"You don't get it! I'm afraid of heights! I'll throw up! I'll make a mess!"

Decatur shrugged his shoulders. "Messes are made to be cleaned up, B. 'Course, you'll be the one cleaning it up, not me. You just keep that in mind. Now get in, I'm not going to tell you again."

He forced her up into the plane. She clumsily plunked down in the passenger seat.

"Put on that seat belt and be quiet. I have some things to do. Try to run and I'll have to shoot you like a dog."

"I won't make any trouble, I just don't know how to put this thing on. Is it like a car seat belt? Why are there so many straps?"

Decatur let out a small sigh, then reached in and fastened her seat belt. "Not exactly a rocket scientist, are ya, B?"

He slammed her door shut.

As he had done sixteen times before, he lugged two 10-gallon cans and a large cardboard box filled with foodstuff from his Jeep to the plane's cargo hold.

Then he did a quick walk around and, satisfied, released the tie-downs, pulled the chocks.

He climbed into the pilot's seat. Looked over at Bambi. Smiled. Not a pretty sight. "Hope you went before we left."

Once again, he went through his pre-flight check out loud, fiercely, relentlessly: "Pre takeoff and cockpit, check. Trim tab controls, check. Throttle closed. Flap controls full forward. Mixture set to idle. Cutoffs—off. Master battery switch off. Instruments checked and set. Elevator set to neutral. Altimeter set to elevation. Aileron set to neutral. Good. Primer closed and locked. Throttle at one inch. Battery on. Starter switch closed. One, two, three and start."

Decatur turned the ignition key.

The motor coughed in the damp coolness. The propeller spun, grabbing air fruitlessly for a moment. Then the plugs fired in sequence, catching their rhythm, and the engine roared to life.

The plane vibrated as the engine spun up to full throttle, then began rocking gently back and forth as the two big tundra tires began rolling over the grass strip. The plane smoothed out as it gained momentum. Within a minute, they were at the end of the strip. Decatur turned the plane into what little wind there was, then throttled back and checked the magnetos, one at a time.

Bambi stared at him, her eyes wide, as his fingers worked the controls. She tried to see out the windshield, but the taildragger was pitched up at a steep angle.

Decatur turned to her as he pushed the throttle all the way to the panel, smiled again. "Rock and roll..." he said, over the growing noise of the 150 horsepower Lycoming O-320. This time the plane shook and vibrated even harder as it began its takeoff. Within seconds, Decatur pushed the yoke forward and the tail lifted off the ground.

Now Bambi could see out the front of the aircraft, at the line of tall pine trees that seemed to be growing closer by the second. She nervously dug her manicured French nails into the seat cushion.

Suddenly, the violent rocking and vibration stopped as the wheels left the turf strip and slipped in the air. Bambi's stomach leapt into her chest as the 140 climbed out steeply into the night clouds. Decatur moved the wheel and the plane tilted gracefully into a turn. Heading south, he leveled the wing. Anchorage disappeared in the darkness.

Leveling the plane at five thousand feet, Decatur pushed the throttle to cruise power, reducing the noise level in the cabin to bearable. He looked over at Bambi, a human statue.

"Buck up there, B. You gotta think of this here as a vacation. Almost like going to Dollyworld."

Bambi, lit only by the dim light of the instrument panel, looked out the window, then over at Decatur.

Her gazed stopped on something wedged into Decatur's side door, intermittently illuminated by red, then white, flashing lights.

"Yep," repeated Decatur, "almost like Dollyworld."

FORTY-FOUR

Terrified into numbness, strapped in the cramped seat, jammed tightly next to the most repulsive, oily disgusting man she'd ever met, Bambi stared out the windshield as the first glowing fingers of dawn grabbed hold of the horizon and pulled themselves into the day.

The engine noise was deafening, but in the oppressive droning she found a center, a calm that she hadn't expected. She glanced to her left. Decatur's hands were on the yoke, loosely, as the dim glow of the instrument panel bounced off his acne-scarred face.

She looked down in her lap, at the shiny metal handcuffs that held her hands together. Her mind raced. She could grab the yoke, jam it forward, hold it there and just let them both dive into hell.

No, she thought. *Not yet.*

This was bad, but not that bad.

Not yet.

The 140 slipped down through the clouds of dawn like a tumbling coin, reflecting bits of rising sunshine along the white wings, finally dropping through the darkest layer into the murky fog below the mountaintop, a featureless obscurity. A white dark.

Morning light, diffused and fragile, seeped into the interior.

Decatur reached around with his right hand, digging in the pocket behind the seat, and pulled out a folded sheaf of paper. Bambi tried to make it out in the dim light, but could only see a jumble of shapes and unfocused colors. He unfolded the paper and spread it across the instrument panel in front of him. Bambi could see it better now; it's a map, an aviation chart. A sectional ...

The paper was criss-crossed with worn folds and creases.

And dotted around the chart in a random pattern, tiny crosses inked in red, with a circle around each one ...

Like blood, she thought. She tried to count them, but he wouldn't hold the paper still.

He turned to her, grinning, his teeth even more yellow in the dim light. "Almost there, B. Almost there ..."

Bambi, dazed, looked out over the instrument panel, at the morning sky slowly coming to life. She turned to her right, stared out the plexiglass window of the passenger door. Five thousand feet below, the rising sun sparkled off the water like light bouncing off a mirror. Islands covered in pine dotted the immense spread of water.

It's beautiful, she thought. *So beautiful ...*

Out of nowhere, the plane lurched and her stomach was in her throat. She looked down at the instrument panel. The gauges spun crazily for a moment, then the plane dropped again.

Bambi screamed as her head hit the top of the cabin, the straps across her lap straining.

"Oh my God! We're going to crash!"

Over the ear-splitting noise, Decatur's voice rose to a loud monotone. "Just a little thermal. Get these bad boys all the time. That ain't going to kill you."

He turned, grinned to Bambi, trying to reassure her. Missed by a mile.

The plane hit another pocket, dropped about a hundred feet in half a heartbeat, then banked to the right, hard.

Bambi took a quick look at the instrument panel in front of her. Her blank expression transformed to an indignant fear.

Fury.

Confusion.

She couldn't restrain herself any longer. She exploded.

"*Do you know what the fuck you're doing?*" she yelled.

Decatur laughed. "A good pilot flies by feel, by instinct. The only way to live, B!" He looked down. "And a great pilot ... a really great pilot can do this—"

Decatur pushed the yoke forward, hard, and jammed the throttle all the way to the firewall. The engine roared. The plane went into a sudden, stomach-churning dive.

Bambi screamed, jammed her hands against the instrument panel.

The soup of cloud and fog suddenly spread open like a grand theater curtain.

Down below but coming at them fast, Bambi spotted an enormous natural-arch bridge over two rock formations. Decatur flew under the arch with only a few feet to spare on either wing tip, then pulled up sharply and performed a loop over the arch.

Bambi wailed, a long, lung-bursting continuing scream throughout.

Ecstatically, Decatur yelled over the roar of the engine and the rush of air whistling around them, "Am I damned good or what?"

He looked over at Bambi. "Who's your daddy now, bitch!?"

Bambi stared, trembling, out her window in numbed silence.

The plane seemed to float now, the engine throttled back to idle, the flaps extended. Bambi felt her hips pushing into the leather seat as Decatur pulled back gently on the yoke. She gazed outside, the ground seeming to grow larger by the second. All she could see was blue; she wondered if this crazy sonofabitch meant to land in the water.

Then there was a gentle bump as the thick, oversized tundra tires kissed wet sand. Water sprayed up in a rooster tail behind them as the plane settled down, slowed. Bambi could see a little over the nose of the plane: a line of trees in front of them, boulders off to the side growing out of the ground like enormous gray spuds.

Decatur pushed the throttle in. The engine roared again as it dragged the 140 across the sandbar, toward the trees.

Then Decatur pulled the mixture knob all the way out, leaning the fuel/air mix, starving the engine until it coughed a few times and spooled down into sleep. There was an eerie stillness, almost a loud silence, as the propeller spun through a few last revolutions. He turned the ignition off, set the parking brake.

Decatur turned, that blasted eternal grin on his face. "Welcome to paradise, B!"

He dug in his pocket, came out with a tiny key. He reached over, unlocked the handcuffs. Then he climbed out of the plane, reached into the door pocket, pulled out the .357 and stuffed it into his belt.

He circled the plane and opened Bambi's door, released her seat belt, yanked her out. She hit the ground hard, her legs giving way. She was on all-fours, retching. The dry heaves ...

"Guess you weren't kidding me about the fear of flying thing, huh, B? Well, you'll feel better when you get your land legs back."

He took the two cans out of the cargo hold. Put them at Bambi's feet. She struggled to stand. Looked around. Took in the bay, the woods, the distant snow-covered mountains.

"Where … where are we?" she asked.

"My summer house."

He took in a breath so deep he seemed to suck all the air out of the world. "Man, oh man, B, can you believe this fresh air? Clean, pure, virgin, filled with life, filled with hope. Can't you just feel it?"

He took in another deep breath. New life seemed to flow into him. "In the wintertime this whole region is completely frozen over. Nothing but one big damn popsicle. But in the summertime, that's a different story. They don't call Alaska the land of the midnight sun for nothing. This time of the year, we've got us a good eighteen, almost nineteen hours of daylight up here. Yep, this here is strictly a summertime project."

"What are we doing here?" asked Bambi.

Decatur snickered to himself. "I've got a cabin here. That's where we'll spend the day."

He pointed at the two cans. "You take those. Follow that path."

No choice. Bambi grabbed the cans. Two ten-gallon cans. Gas weighs six pounds a gallon, plus the weight of the metal. One-hundred twenty pounds …

Almost her body weight.

Decatur took the large cardboard box of food. As they began the walk along the trail, he suddenly pointed at a bird in a nearby tree.

"You see that Robin Red Breast up there? You know what the scientific name is for that bad boy?"

Bambi shook her head no; she really didn't know.

"'*Turdus migratorius*.' Turdus! Ain't that a pisser? Yep, you can learn a lotta shit out here."

No shit, thought Bambi.

Ten minutes later Bambi was sweating as she lugged the cans through the dense woods. Her feet wobbled under the strain. Decatur followed a safe, leisurely six feet behind.

"Hey, B. You don't look like you're having much fun."

No answer from Bambi.

"I know what might cheer you up some. Know how this place got its name?"

Bambi continued to struggle with the cans. Couldn't really give a shit. "Uh, no. No, I don't."

Decatur looked out at the bay through the trees. "Back when Alaska belonged to the Ruskies, around 1793 or something like that, one of their businessmen name of Alexander Baranov was sailing around looking for a good shipbuilding site when this bad storm blew in and forced old Alexander to retreat into that bay out there. When the storm blew over it was Easter Sunday, so he named the bay in honor of it, you know, 'cus it saved his life and all. Named it Resurrection Bay."

"That so?"

"Yep. And that's why you should cheer up some, B."

"How do you figure?"

"Well, it saved his life. Maybe there's something to be said for this place."

"Resurrection, huh?"

"Yep."

The woods swallowed them up.

FORTY-FIVE

THEY WALKED FOR WHAT seemed like hours, only Bambi knew it was probably less than twenty minutes. No sleep. No water. No food. Her arms were numb, her fingers locked around the carrying handles of the two gas cans, frozen in a clench she wasn't even conscious of anymore.

She did the only thing she knew to do: put one foot in front of the other.

Rinse and repeat.

Then, out of nowhere, the trees thinned and opened and there it was, right in front of them. Sunlight shone down in beams from above, illuminating the stark wooden cabin like a postcard from the Fifties.

"No place like home," Decatur said as he stepped into the clearing that led to his cabin. He turned. "Here, give me those," he said, motioning to the cans.

Bambi set them down and forced her fingers to relax. She felt like she was peeling them off the plastic grips over the wire handles.

He took the two cans from Bambi and walked around the side of the cabin. A portable generator now sat on a pre-fab concrete slab. Decatur set one can down, lifted the other, and filled the tank. He fiddled with a couple of controls, pumped a primer bulb, yanked the starter cord.

Fired it right up.

He adjusted the throttle, gauging the engine speed by the voltmeter.

He turned, grinning.

He went to the front door. Opened the padlock. "I'm starving, c'mon—"

He led Bambi inside as he passed by the porch post with the notches. She glanced down, counted the notches. There were now sixteen hacked deep into the pine.

The cabin looked the same as before, untouched since last summer. Decatur always gave the cabin a thorough cleaning before shutting down for the winter. Not even that much dust.

Only Bambi was blissfully unaware of any of this.

She looked around. There was a large combo TV/VCR on a stand against the wall. On a table next to it was a huge boombox, an external microphone off to the side, with wires leading to two speakers mounted on the wall. She looked at the furniture—the couch, the coffee table in front of it.

"How'd you get all this stuff here?" asked Bambi, as Decatur put the carton of food on the kitchen table. The cabin was open, with the kitchen looking out onto the living room.

"There's a bunch of summer cabins scattered on these little islands all across the bay. If you know where to look for 'em ..."

"You stole all this stuff?" she asked, incredulously.

Decatur shrugged. "Finders keepers."

He walked over to the kitchen sink. The hand-cranked water pump had been replaced two summers earlier. That was the year of the brunette, he thought. Right? Brown eyes, one tit slightly larger than the other, dragon tattoo on her right upper arm.

Yeah, he thought, smiling to himself. *She was a screamer, all right. Begged like a bitch, bargained like a rug merchant.*

She wore dangly turquoise earrings. Decatur had them in the safe.

"Got fresh water," he said, bringing himself out of this reverie. "Comes from a well. Used to have to hand pump it up, but I replaced it a couple summers ago with an electric pump. Gotta go outside to start it up, though. Gotta prime it. I'll go do that in a minute."

He pointed to the stove. "Propane tank's outside, too. Should be plenty for what we're going to need."

Decatur flipped open the top of the carton. "Make ya'self useful, B. Canned food goes in the cabinets above the sink, dry stuff down here."

Bambi stared at him, stunned at the casualness of his conversation, as if they were boyfriend and girlfriend away on a romantic weekend.

Decatur opened the cabinet under the sink, pulled out the ten-foot length of chain bolted to the water pipe and, as before, in one quick fluid motion, wrapped it around Bambi's ankle and snapped the padlock shut.

He straightened up, then took out a couple of steaks boxed in dry ice. "Thought we'd have steak tonight. You like deer, do ya?"

She looked down at her chained leg. Trying to make sense of it. "What the hell is this?"

He ignored her and continued to look at the frozen steaks. "Killed this one myself. Some people hate deer, think it tastes too gamey but I say you can never get too gamey."

She tried tugging at the chain. "I said what the hell is this?"

"Oh, that? Just don't want you wandering outside in those woods. Never know what's out there. Can be downright dangerous."

Bambi looked around the room, uncomfortably. "I have to go to the bathroom."

"What?"

"I have to pee."

"Now?"

"Now."

Decatur smiled. "Didn't I tell you to go before we left?" He threw her a towel. "You can use that."

"You can't mean it."

"Oh, I mean it."

"I can wait."

"Suit yourself." He pulled a tin of seasoning out of the large cardboard box. "Hey! Did you know that you can season meat with gun powder?"

She didn't answer. Decatur continued to pull canned vegetables out of the box. Held up a can of corn. "Oh, you're gonna love this one. Yesterday, I was in this gun shop buying some smokeless powder—I reload my own shells, cheaper that way—anyway, this old man walks into the gun shop and says to the owner, 'I need a big gun to shoot cans.' The owner, he says, 'How about this small rifle?'"

Bambi jerked as Decatur began tenderizing the steaks by pounding them with the back of his Ka-Bar knife. "The old man looks at the rifle and says, 'No, these are really big cans.' 'Well how about this medium-sized rifle?' asks the owner. The old man looks at the larger caliber rifle and says, 'No, these are really big cans.' Finally, frustrated, the owner says, 'What kind of cans are you going to shoot?' The old man replies, 'Oh, you know, Mexi-cans, Afri-cans, Puerto Ri-cans!'"

Decatur howled, then pounded the steaks some more. "Pisser, huh?"

There was a stillness, then Bambi shattered the silence.

"How many before me?"

Decatur stopped pounding the steaks. "How many what?"

"How many have you killed before me?"

Decatur violently slammed the knife into the steak. "B, dog-goneit! I think you got this whole thing down wrong. We're only doing what you get paid to do. I just don't like crowds and there's too many germs in motels, you know? That's all."

"Resurrection Bay."

"What?"

"Resurrection Bay. You made a mistake. You told me where we are. You're not going to let me leave."

"You know, you got some imagination, B," Decatur mused. "When we get back, I say you try to find a job writing for TV or the movies or something. They like people with imagination. Make you some real money."

Bambi was not amused. She took a labored breath. "You also told me all this stuff is stolen."

For once, Decatur was silent.

"Sixteen?" asked Bambi, breaking the silence. "Am I right?"

"Sixteen? Sixteen what?"

"I saw your map. In the plane. You had sixteen crosses circled."

"Chart."

"What?"

"It's an aviation 'chart'. And those are just ... places where I've landed out here, that's all."

"No. I counted the notches on the post as we came in. There were sixteen girls before me."

"Dammit, I told you there had to be a name for someone like you who talks too damn much ... now you're bumming me out here. Okay, think of this as a camping trip. We're gonna spend the day together, get some sleep tonight, and first thing tomorrow, we're outta here. That simple, B. That simple. "

Bambi tugged on the chain and said nothing. The chain was solid, anchored well.

"Hey, take a looksee at this—"

Decatur left the kitchen, crossed the living room, walked over to the boombox. Pushed a cassette in. Picked up the microphone. "I always wanted one of these—"

He flicked the switch, pushed the play button and turned the volume up, then lifted the microphone to his lips. It took her a moment, but then she remembered where she'd last heard the song, crooned by Maverick and Goose halfway through the movie *Top Gun*.

Ohmigod, Bambi thought. *He's doing a bad imitation of Tom Cruise doing a bad imitation of The Righteous Brothers ...*

Bambi fell to the floor, curled into a fetal position, and began to sob. "You're going to kill me, aren't you?"

Decatur reached around, slapped the stop button. The boombox fell silent. "Now why would I do that? We're here to have a good time ..."

"No, you're going to kill me," she whimpered.

"Goddamit, B, I've had it!" He pulled the Altoids tin out of his pants pocket, snapped it open. Snorted a white clump of coke. "It's gonna take some time for those steaks to thaw anyhow. Whaddaya' say let's get down to business?"

He looked down at Bambi and smiled. "Oh, yeah, that wasn't a question."

Decatur walked over to the far wall of the living room, shoved a picture frame aside. Behind the frame was the slate-gray metal safe door. He spun the knob a few times, carefully rotated one way, then another. He pulled the handle and opened the door.

Behind him, Bambi stared through tears. She watched in disbelief as he pulled out a video camera and a tripod. She could barely see, but in the back of the safe she could just make out a stack of VHS tapes.

Decatur attached the video camera to the tripod. Connected a few cables. Turned the TV on. Aimed the camera at Bambi. She turned her head away.

"This bad boy here has a 'loop mode' so that you can play the tape over and over. And now we need us a little mood music..."

He pushed another audio cassette into the boombox.

"Too Late to Turn Back Now." Cornelius Brothers & Sister Rose once again gushed over the speakers. The music lent an even more surreal tone to the scene.

Bambi meanwhile, ashen-faced and trembling, hugged her knees. She sobbed hysterically as if pleading for her life. Close to hyperventilating. "Why do you do this?"

Decatur laughed and replied, "You know, I get that a lot."

He dragged a chair close to Bambi. He took a deep, reflective breath, then leaned forward. "I'm going to tell you something I've never told anybody. I didn't start out hating women, even the ones I've brought out here before you."

He laughed uncomfortably.

"It's kind of funny, I guess, but I felt I was falling in love with them. I just wanted their friendship. I wanted them to like me. But over time, I've discovered that there are only two types of women, you know? Either 'good' or 'bad'. The 'good' I treat with kid gloves of respect, but the 'bad'—prostitutes and strippers, for instance— are the lowest form of life. Fair game for whatever I want."

"That's what we are to you?" Bambi's voice rose to a point midway between hysterical and furious. "*Fair game*?"

Decatur took another deep breath, thinking. "I think society as a whole downgrades these women—prostitutes and strippers and the like. And when one of these girls suddenly disappears from a bar, the whole world doesn't come to a screeching halt. It doesn't mourn the passing of a prostitute who disappears, or even wonders what happened to her. And I'm not just talking out my ass here, I have friends in the Anchorage police. They've discovered that a lot of dancers routinely shuttle on a circuit of bars between Hawaii, Seattle, Anchorage, Kodiak Island, and some Pacific Northwest states. They've told me the supposedly missing girls were probably transferred to Hawaii or one of the other locations on the spur of the moment. Not missed one lick, imagine that?"

Decatur gazed at Bambi. There was a simple prettiness about her, beyond the stripper bling. The thought occurred to him that she was, underneath the makeup, like the girls he wanted in high school.

"By the same token," he continued, "you found that as you were growing up, girls had a certain power over you ... They had something you wanted, but they dictated when you could see it, when you could touch it, and when you could enjoy it sexually. It's kind of nice when you get a little older ... to be able to turn the tables. To be in charge."

Decatur stood up from the chair, taller now, almost puffed up as he took two steps closer to Bambi. Her head was tucked down, still at the end of her chain, huddled on the floor, color drained out of her face, her arms still locked around her knees as if she could protect what he was about to take.

What was rightfully his.

"You weren't allowed to play the leading role or make the big decisions when you were in high school. Now, because you're paying for it, the prostitute can't reject you. As long as you have the greenbacks, she has to do whatever you want."

He squatted down a few feet in front of her and gazed right into her eyes. She looked up right back at him. He had to give her that; she didn't look away.

"Then comes the time you pull out the gun and the binding instrument—shoelace, wire, chain, handcuffs, whatever. Then, you're in control, and for a change it's you who determines what you get ... and when you get it. Like I said, B, the tables are turned."

He paused a beat, and then that miserable hellish grin again.

"You know how a tornado and a woman are alike?"

No answer.

"They both moan like hell when they come and when they leave they take the house."

Bambi squirmed, wrapped her arms even tighter around her knees. "Please, please, please, don't do this ..."

"Don't do what? We're just gonna have a little fun is all."

"You're ... you're going to kill me, aren't you," sobbed Bambi.

"Now why would I ever do that?"

"You're going to fuck me and then you're going to kill me."

Decatur cocked his head, continued with the killer charming smile. "Who says I have to do it in that order?"

"For God's sake, no, no, no, no ..." Bambi was sobbing hysterically now, her lungs pumping violently, her hands shaking uncontrollably, her eyes squeezed tightly shut.

"Got to hand it to you, B, you've got that cowering thing covered. Now, we're just going to pack in a little fun here. Maybe have us a turn on one of these tables here, whaddaya' think? Sound like fun?"

Bambi sobbed, "Turn the tables ..."

"What was that?" asked Decatur.

"You said 'turn the tables,'" repeated Bambi.

"Yeah, so?"

"I think you're right."

"Right? About what?"

She looked up at him, something in her eyes different. "It's time to turn the tables."

"What the hell are you talking about, B?" asked an amused Decatur as he stood up and waltzed toward her in his usual cocky way, a leering grin etched across his gaunt features. He was in his element.

The leer suddenly froze when it happened.

Bambi smiled.

Then held out her hand.

Opened it to reveal a bobby pin.

In the blink of an eye, Bambi stood straight up and kicked her right ankle as if shaking off a cramp. The chain, and the unlocked padlock that held it around her leg, fell to the wooden kitchen floor with a metallic clunk.

Then in Decatur's mind, everything seemed to slow. Like in the movies ... Slow motion.

Bambi, in one fluid, graceful move, cartwheeled! Suddenly, it was like the bitch was ... *airborne.*

Then she was upside down, with her hands on the floor, her legs in the air in a wide arc, swinging up toward the roof and then down toward him.

Before he could even react, her legs shot out and scissored Decatur's head, one leg on each side. He felt incredible, stifling pressure as her legs locked on his skull, his ears mashed painfully into the bone.

Even at this moment, at this point in time when everything in Decatur Kaiser's world was turning as upside down as this bitch plummeting toward him, he was still all about the sex. With Bambi upside down and his head between her legs, his eyes widened as he sought to catch a glimpse of what was almost his...

But now, he instinctively sensed, was not going to be.

It was his last thought.

Her momentum continued and he became airborne himself, out of control, falling...

Then he saw it coming up toward him at ramming speed, Warp Factor 10.

The coffee table, with its thick glass laid over hard wood...

BAM!

The crash was spectacular; there was a loud, agonizing crunch as bone and flesh met glass and wood. Glass and wood won.

The leering quality seeped out of Decatur's expression.

Then the lights went out.

Smash Cut To Black.

FORTY-SIX

THE LIGHT DIDN'T COME back on all at once. When it did, it was all glittery and sparkly, and it came at him randomly, chaotically, from the side, moving in toward the dark circle in the middle of his vision, until it erased it all together and he could—kind of—see again.

Consciousness continued to return to Decatur piecemeal. Once he got past the throbbing in his head, the first thing he discovered was that he was sitting on a chair. The next thing was that he couldn't move. He was tied to the damn thing, his ankles to its legs, his wrists to its arms.

Struggling to regain his senses, his vision came into focus. What he saw was Bambi approaching with a half-filled glass. Almost tenderly, she lifted the liquid to his lips. Delirious with thirst, he drank the glass empty. It wasn't until the last swallow that he realized something was wrong.

The taste was stale, fetid, rank ...

He woke up immediately and spat out the last mouthful. He strained against his bindings. No go.

"What? . . . Where? . . . Where did you get the water, I didn't start the pump?"

"Wasn't water."

Decatur gave her a questioning look.

"Told you I had to pee," shrugged Bambi.

A look of revulsion crossed Decatur's wet face. He drilled his eyes into hers. Seething. "If you were a man, I'd tear you in half!" he screamed.

"If you were a man . . ." Bambi broke out laughing. "Well, we both know that's never gonna happen."

Decatur spat again, shook his head, glared at her.

"Look, I don't know what the fuck you think you're doing, but get me out of this fuckin' chair right fuckin' now!"

Bambi picked up Decatur's oversized knife. Walked over to him. "You know . . . when I was a little girl, I used to think if I died in an evil hell-hole then my soul would stay in that evil hell-hole forever and I would never make it to heaven." She wrapped a rope around Decatur's chest and the back of the chair, then tightened it, hard. He groaned in pain, his hands long numbed.

"Well, fuck," said Bambi, "I don't care where it goes as long it isn't here. Decatur."

He jerked around, crazed surprise written on his face. "How . . . How do you know my name?"

Bambi stared up at a Dall sheep head mounted on the wall. "You know, stuffed sheep heads on the wall are bad enough, but it's worse when they're wearing sun glasses and have streamers and party favors in their horns because then you know they were enjoying themselves at a party when they were shot."

"That supposed to be funny?"

"Nope. I think it's supposed to be karma, Decatur."

"Never believed in that shit. Now how the fuck do you know my name?"

She walked over to the wall safe. Listening to the tumblers as she spun the dial, she opened it with ease. "You'd be surprised what I know."

"Who are you?!"

"You know how the universe tends to balance itself? You know, there's matter and anti-matter. Viruses and anti-viruses. Gravity and anti-gravity. Christ and anti-Christ. Pasta and antipasta."

"What?"

"Well, I'm pretty much the anti-you." She pointed the knife blade toward him. "You. Decatur." She pointed the blade back at herself. "Me. Dick-hater."

She smiled. "Karma."

"What are you talking about? What the fuck do you want from me?"

Bambi casually pointed the knife blade around the room, then violently slammed it into the kitchen table. "Make me make sense of all this."

"Make sense of what?!"

She leaned forward. "Okay, Decatur, this is the part where I ask you nicely and you tell me everything I want to know."

"Know what?"

"I want to know how you killed them."

"You don't know what you're talking about."

"Yes, I think I do. And that's all I want from you, Decatur. Now, I'm going to ask you one more time very nicely, girlie, civilized and all. How did you kill them?"

"Fuck you!"

"Okay, then have it your way." She yanked the knife out of the kitchen table. "This is the part where you bleed."

Using the Ka-Bar's weighted handle, she hit him with a short, shockingly hard punch to the mouth.

Decatur's head snapped back and he yelped, then his head dropped with a moan. He spat again, a goopy puddle of saliva, blood, and mucus onto the floor. He stared down at it, and as his vision refocused, he saw the white chunk of a tooth all mixed in with the goop.

"I wish you'd tell me what you did to those girls."

"Yeah? Well, I wish I had dental insurance." He snickered smugly.

"You know something? I may be the only person who truly understands and gets your humor. That said … you're not funny. Now, I'm going to tell you something about me. I always keep my promises. And if you don't tell me what I want to know I promise you harder, angrier blows will follow. Now, how did you kill them?"

"Fuck you!"

The Ka-Bar struck him again hard enough to elicit a sharp, pained noise that sounded like a bark, followed by something that almost sounded like a boiling tea kettle. But even as he cried out steam-like, Decatur realized she had pulled the blow, striking him just hard enough to hurt and prod him forward without knocking him out again.

"See? I'm a girl of my word. Now, how did you kill them?" she asked.

He spat out another glob of blood. "You are seriously fucked up … but then you are a woman." He smiled. "Let me ask you something, Genius. How you planning on getting out of here? You fly a plane, can ya? You wouldn't last two days out here on your own."

Bambi began to sharpen the blade of the Ka-Bar on a whetstone.

Scrape...

Scrape...

"You know, I appreciate your concern about me, really do..." she said as she continued to sharpen the knife.

Scrape...

Scrape...

Scrape.

"By the way, dumbass," she said, turning to him with a smile. "It's not a *chart*."

"What's not a—"

"It's a sectional, Decatur. Only student pilots and amateurs call it a *chart*."

Decatur stared at her. *How the fuck did she—*

He watched as Bambi inspected the mirrored sheen on the edge of the blade, then picked up a piece of paper. The blade sliced through the paper like warm butter.

What the fuck have I gotten myself into...

She brought the knife over to Decatur's face. "You're sweet to worry about my welfare, D, but the truth is at this point, if I were you I'd be worrying a whole hell of a lot more about myself than what's gonna happen to little ol' me."

"Lookit, just let me go. You keep the damn gun. I'll fly us both outta here and we'll just forget this whole ... misunderstanding. Don't be a doomkoff, just untie me!"

Bambi stopped in her tracks. "Don't be a ... what?"

"Nothing, just let me go. I'll fly you back right now. No hard feelings. Whaddaya' say?"

"Hmm, let me think about it." She kicked it over for less than a nanosecond, then, in a flash, she was in his face, teeth bared, spit spraying: "*No!*"

Decatur glared at her. "If you don't let me go right now, I can't promise that you'll make it back at all, B."

"D, D, D, is that a threat?"

He turned and looked her in the eye. "Abso-fuckin'-lutely."

"Okay, one thing we need to get crystal clear. Threat time is over. When you have the big gun you give the orders. When I have the big gun, I'm in command. It's the new order, D, *capisce*? Now, then, one last time nicely. How did you kill them? Tell me. Pretty please?"

"I don't know what you're talking about ... You're the one who's delusional."

"Yeah, and that's probably my best trait." She continued to hone the blade even sharper. "You ever been to South Dakota? The Bad Lands? The Little Big Horn? General George Armstrong Custer. Now, that, that was one crazy delusional motherfucker."

"What?" asked Decatur.

"What do you know about Sitting Bull?"

No answer.

"Come on, you must know something about Sitting Bull, you being the big-game-hunter-man and all."

Decatur glared at her. Then through gritted teeth he slowly answered, "He ... slaughtered ... Custer."

"Indirectly, D, you get a couple of points. Sitting Bull was a shaman. He was the one who united all those Indian tribes against Custer. Know what a shaman is, do ya?"

"A ... witchdoctor?"

"Um ... something like that. You know what Sitting Bull did the night before the Battle of the Little Big Horn?"

"Bored his tribe to death like you're doing me?"

"Not quite. You see, shamans have visions. That's their job. They can see things that the rest of us can't. Now, to get these visions, the shaman will intoxicate himself. He'll go into a trance by dancing, by whirling around, drinking, taking drugs. However. Then, he'll go on a mental travel and describe his journey to the rest of the tribe. Now, Sitting Bull, he had this ... unique ... way of putting himself into this trance. No dancing for him, no drinking, no peyote. Nope."

She stepped behind Decatur, into the kitchen, and yanked open a drawer. Decatur heard the rattle of utensils in a wooden drawer as Bambi fished around, looking for something. The noise stopped and Bambi came back into the living room with a felt-tipped pen.

She stepped over, rolled Decatur's shirt sleeves all the way up as far as they would go. She yanked the cap off the Sharpie. Carefully sketched a two-inch square box on Decatur's upper right arm. Decatur, uncomprehending, tried to struggle, to no avail. The muscles of his forearm were knotted, tight, hard, but, ultimately ... immobile.

"The night before the battle," continued Bambi, "Sitting Bull had big doubts about attacking the U.S. Army. Unlike some people, he had a conscience."

She looked Decatur directly in the eye. "He understood the consequences of his actions. So, he performed a sun dance and what he did was, he sliced 100—count 'em, 100—notches of flesh out of his arms and legs. Literally skinned himself alive, D. Can you imagine that?"

Decatur looked down in terror at the box drawn in blue ink on his arm.

Bambi continued, "He let the blood run down and endured all that pain, until he had a vision. The vision he had was of white cavalry soldiers falling down, as a voice said to him, 'I give you these because they have no ears.'"

She tossed the Sharpie onto the coffee table and picked the knife back up, placed the point of the blade against Decatur's arm.

"See, the soldiers weren't listening, 'they had no ears.' Decatur, tell me what you did to those girls."

"What ... girls?"

"Decatur, did you not understand what I'm trying to tell you? Did you not get the analogy? The moral of the story? Shamans? Visions? One hundred slices of skin? Hello! Don't you get it, D? Have you got ears?"

"Let me say it one more time for the slow learners in the class. *Fuck you!*"

"Kinda glad you said that."

Following the pen mark, Bambi traced a two-inch by two-inch slice into Decatur's arm, just breaking his skin with the knife.

Blood trickled down his arm in rivulets. Decatur shook, screamed in pain and fright, sweat breaking out on his forehead, his eyes bulging as he watched the knife trace a red trail through his skin.

Bambi began to chant, "One hundred slices of skin on Decatur's arm, one hundred slices of skin ... Take one off ..."

She ripped the piece of skin off his arm.

Decatur howled even louder, his face twisted into a tight, drawn rictus.

Bambi continued her chant. "... pass it around ..." She tossed the piece of skin across the room. It stuck to the wall with a sickening, slapping sound. "... ninety-nine slices of skin on Decatur's arm ..."

Decatur wailed in agony.

"Oh, and, D? That-gun-powder-making-a-seasoning thing? I did know about that—it does contain saltpeter, after all. But let me ask you this. I bet you don't know how to make gunpowder burn twice, do you?"

Decatur continued to scream and cry, wide-eyed.

"No? I didn't think so. Watch this—"

Decatur, sobbing, begged, "No, please ... don't ..."

"Ah, cheer up there, Buckaroo, you're gonna just love this one. It's a real party favorite."

Bambi expertly ejected a shell from the Steyr Aug. Used the Ka-Bar to pry the bullet from the cartridge. Then poured the gunpowder onto Decatur's open wound.

Decatur howled with the newfound pain.

"See? That's how it burns once. Now—"

She lit a match. Held it over the gunpowder on the wound. Slowly, she lowered the match.

Decatur watched in horror. "No, no, no!"

The match ignited the gunpowder in a blinding flash of light and smoke.

Decatur thrashed and wailed.

"That would be twice," said Bambi. "Ready to do this ninety-nine more times?" She started to cut another swath in Decatur's arm. "Decatur, what did you do to those women?"

Decatur started to cry. "I SHOT THEM!"

"Here? In this cabin?"

"NO! I LET THEM GO!"

"You let them go?" It took a moment, then it slammed her in the face like a baseball bat. "You mean ... you ... hunted them down ... out there?"

"Yes!"

"Oh, my God ... You find a girl that no one will miss, you kidnap her, you fly her out here to the middle of nowhere, do whatever you want to her and then you hunt her down for fun. You know, you're not as stupid as you look."

Bambi stood up and ripped a map off the wall, still trying to process everything. "Okay, you're crazy. We established that awhile ago. But I think it bears repeating. You are seriously fucking crazy."

She draped the map over Decatur's lap. "Show me where you buried the bodies."

Decatur leered at her through the film of sweat that had broken out over his face. He was flushed, bright red, furious and in agony, his arm still on fire. The smell of his burning flesh hung in the air. He stared at her for what seemed like a long time, but was probably less than five seconds.

He finally spoke, his voice calm, almost prideful. "I buried the first three here on the island, but the fourth one, she gave me a great idea. I mean why go to all that trouble to dig a fuckin' hole when you don't have to? Fuckin' A. Hell, digging a friggin' hole is too much like … digging a friggin' hole. It's a hell of a lot of work. Where's the fun in that?"

He laughed a gargling kind of laugh.

She savagely raised the knife above her head as if to plunge it through the map and into his groin. "Looney tune time is over. Tell me where they are!"

Decatur screamed, "There! I flushed them all down that gorge!"

With a crazed look on his face, he urgently indicated to a place on the map with a nod of his head.

"Flushed them?" asked Bambi.

"Yes, fuck'n'hell. It was easier than burying 'em. I even went back to dig up the first three, but they were … They were—"

"They were just goop by then," Bambi offered. "Weren't they?"

Decatur grinned his lopsided smile. "It was kinda messy. I just packed the dirt back on 'em."

Bambi leaned over, studying the map. "D, that gorge is across the bay, on that strut out from the mainland. How the fuck'd you get 'em over there? You got a boat hidden on the island?"

His head dropped for a moment, almost as if a wave of fatigue had settled in on him. Then his head bobbed up again and there was a light in his eyes. "That's the part I'm proudest of," he said, his voice way too calm for what he was saying. "I duct-taped 'em in plastic—head to fuckin' toe—and put 'em in the right seat. Strapped 'em in just like a passenger. Then I flew home. On the way back, I buzzed the gorge, maybe a couple hundred feet off the ground. I slowed to just over stall speed, let go their seat belts, kicked open the door and did a hard right bank."

The lopsided, goofy grin widened. "Just let ol' mother gravity do the rest."

For a moment, Bambi found herself stunned. Just when she thought this animal couldn't surprise her anymore. There was a sudden silence in the room as she looked deep into his empty eyes, two black manhole lids covering a cesspool of vileness and depravity.

"You just dumped them overboard like garbage . . ." she said, her voice low.

Decatur smiled up at her again, shrugged his shoulders as much as he could given how restrained he was, and then, oddly, he *winked* at her.

"Did you just fuckin' *wink* at me?" Bambi demanded.

"Just flirtin' with you, B. Just flirtin' with ya."

"That's what you were going do with me, wasn't it?"

Decatur stared at her for a few beats, the grin suddenly gone. "Still am, B," he said. "Still am."

There was a sudden silence in the room.

Bambi stood up. Walked to a window. Looked out at the woods. "Did they get any kind of a head start?"

"What kind of a man do you think I am?" snapped Decatur, seriousness hardened into what little rebuke he had left. "Of course, they got a head start. Thirty... thirty minutes. It was enough—"

"It's enough all right."

She turned and slammed the Ka-Bar's handle into his head. Hard. Violent. No pulling punches now.

Just like she'd been taught...

Decatur heard a crackle of cartilage as his nose gave way, right before he passed out.

Bambi pulled the entertainment center away from the wall and looked at the profusion of dangling wires and cords. She wrapped a hand around several and stepped on the power strip on the floor. They came loose with one savage yank.

Then she quickly crossed to the bear rug in the middle of the floor. Dragged it across the room.

Used the Ka-Bar to rip up one of the floorboards beneath.

Behind her, Decatur hung limp and unconscious against the ropes, his head down, his mouth open and slack-jawed, drooling a mixture of blood, spit, and snot all over the front of his shirt.

Bambi stared at him for a moment, then she went back to work.

FORTY-SEVEN

DECATUR SLOWLY WOKE UP to the smell of—what the fuck was it—*coffee?*

He tried to shake his head, but it hurt too bad. So he just rolled it slowly on his neck.

Coffee?

Disoriented, his eyes strained to adjust. The first thing that came into focus was the sun setting over the distant mountains while the aurora borealis simultaneously began coloring the evening sky.

The fuck is this? he wondered. *It's almost night. Have I been out all goddamn day? And just where the fuck am I?*

Lying like a corpse on the ground, his hair matted, his face grotesquely bloodied and bruised, Decatur turned over and discovered that he was lying in the grass in front of the cabin. Looking up, he saw Bambi sitting calmly in a chair on the porch. Sipping coffee. Percolated coffee, steam rising from the mug.

His mug.

The Steyr Aug rested across her lap.

His Steyr Aug.

"What . . . what is this? What, what are you doing?" asked Decatur, disoriented.

Bambi peeked over the top of the mug, smiled. "My estival project."

"What?" asked Decatur.

"Estival. *Estival*, damn it. Jesus, don't serial killers read, I mean, what's the world coming to?" She smiled. "Estival. It means summertime."

"You can't be serious!"

With sarcasm dripping from her lips, Bambi replied, "Look at it this way, D, you're a professional. I ain't gonna do nothing that hasn't been done to you before. So, you don't get excited, you don't do nothing stupid—you know there's some risk to what you've been doing. If you do exactly what I tell you to do, you're not going to get hurt. You're just going to count this off as a bad experience and be a little more careful next time who you proposition. Hell, you may even learn to thank me."

She lifted the Steyr Aug off her lap. Chambered a round. "Oh, that part about you not getting hurt? Well, I was fibbing a bit on that one."

"You don't have to do this," Decatur reasoned.

"Yeah, well, the thing is you're pretty much in the way of the rest of my life."

"Aren't you going to give me a gun or something?"

"You mean you want to duel? Is that what you're telling me?"

"Just to keep it fair, is all."

"Oh, yeah, right. Like I'm sure you kept it fair with all the other girls you brought this way. Let me quote from Mark Twain: 'I thoroughly disapprove of duels. If a man should challenge me, I would

319

take him kindly and forgivingly by the hand and lead him to a quiet place and kill him.' Call me crazy, but I think the Twain man was onto something there."

"Please, don't do this. For God's sake!" he begged.

"God?" Bambi replied, sitting up straight in the chair, suddenly interested. "Which God are you talking about? There are so many of them."

"Why are you doing this?! Do you want to kill me? Won't that make you as bad as me?"

"Which God are you talking about?" Bambi repeated.

"Any goddamned one you like!"

"Well, I'm guessing the god of compassion would come in handy for you about now. But, me? I'm personally leaning heavy on the god of vengeance. You know. Eye for an eye, tooth for a tooth. Old Testament style … That God."

She took a sip of coffee (*his damn coffee*), then raised her arm. There was a large watch on her arm he hadn't seen before. He started to wonder where she got it, when his thoughts were interrupted by the motion of her hand.

She pushed the start button on the chronometer. "You got your 30 minutes, Decatur."

"You can't be serious?! What did I do to you?!"

BAM!

She shot the ground next to Decatur, inches away. Dirt and gravel pelted his face. "Twenty-nine minutes, fifty seconds."

Decatur calmly turned and faced Bambi. "They say whoever fights a monster becomes one. You do this, B, then you become me. Is that what you really want?"

Bambi faced him down. "Tell you something, D. For almost as long as I can remember, I've been thinking about this. Looking for answers. You know, to the basic stuff. Where do we come from? What are we? Where are we going? Why do people do what they do? Why does evil happen? Who protects the innocent from the bad guys? If there's just a little chance of finding out answers to any of those, yeah, I think it's worth a human life. Don't you, D?"

She checked her watch. "Time's a-burnin'. Twenty-eight minutes and change."

A twisted smile seemed to snake its way across Decatur's face.

"I promise you this, B—I'm gonna put the *fun* in your *funeral*." He calmly turned and entered the woods.

Bambi took another sip of coffee. Looked up at the beauty of the northern lights.

The shadows were long, but Decatur easily made his way through the woods, expertly threading his way through the thick forest even in the scant sunlight filtering through the treetops.

Hell, he thought, *this is my back yard. What the fuck do I have to worry about? So what that bimbo bitch Bambi has a gun, what's she really gonna do with it out here? 'Specially since I ain't gonna be here much longer. Hell, she's gonna die all on her own! All alone!*

He came to a well remembered tree line. A sandbar was on the other side. And resting on the sandbar was his plane. Just waiting to take off.

Hiding in the tree line for a few minutes, Decatur scanned all around for a trace of Bambi.

Finally satisfied that he was alone, Decatur burst onto the sandbar and ran to his plane. Ripping the door open, he jumped behind the pilot seat.

He reached for the ignition key.

It was gone.

A folded note was jammed in its place.

Decatur grabbed the note. Unrolled it. Held it up to the fading light.

It read in bold, spidery handwriting:

Nice Try, Fuckface.

Decatur smiled. Unfazed.

He spoke out loud: "Not too shabby, but any pilot worth his salt has a second key stashed away. Didja know that, you stupid shit?"

He reached underneath the pilot seat. Pulled out a small magnetic key box. Grinned ear to ear.

"Never leave home without it ..." he snickered to himself.

He opened the key box.

Empty ...

Only another rolled up note.

"What the—"

He unfolded the note. This one read:

Hey Numb Nuts, You're Getting
Stupider By the Minute.

The message was followed by a smiley face.

Decatur slammed the instrument panel with his fist. Hard.

"You are so fucking dead!" he screamed.

Jumping out of the plane, he re-entered the woods and fought his way through the clump of trees with a renewed, and pissed-off, effort.

By the time he found what he was looking for, the sun was kissing the mountain tops on the horizon. Decatur, now in his domain, inhabited the lengthening night.

Eyes roaming, he found his shrouded sanctuary with relative ease.

Under a canopy of pines, Decatur stopped at an oversized oak tree, its massive branches weighed down with thousands of acorns.

He had selected this tree years ago out of instinctual hunting expertise. Fresh acorns, Decatur knew from past experience, were key to hunting deer. Deer will eat newly dropped acorns as quickly as they fall from the tree. A good hunter could observe the tops of an oak tree where the acorns are to determine if a given tree will produce enough to attract a deer. The patches of acorns at the top of the tree will begin to hang down as the acorns start to weigh the branches down until they fall. Paying attention to those changes could offer a hunter a distinct advantage. And an edge.

You're right about one thing, B, he thought to himself, *I am smarter than I look.*

Of course, there was another more practical reason why Decatur had selected this oak. In the hollow of the ancient tree, he took out a package wrapped in plastic. The plastic had been weathered by time and yellowed with age.

Decatur ripped the plastic open.

Inside was an emergency backpack that he had stashed there years earlier and had checked each summer. Just in case.

This, he thought, *qualified as that case.*

Decatur took stock of the items he'd stashed in the backpack, taking them out, one item at a time.

MREs, canned water, first-aid kit, clothes, ammunition.

And inside a zippered plastic bag—a Blackhawk .44 Magnum handgun. More of a howitzer than a pistol.

Decatur stuffed the .44 into his pants.

He smiled. Order had been restored.

Opening the first-aid kit, he cleaned, disinfected and bandaged the knife rash on his arm. *Stupid bitch, that's gonna cost you big time!*

His wound bandaged, he tore open a Meal, Ready to Eat and ate the items with the most protein and calories—the beef stew entrée, mashed potatoes, peanut butter spread and pound cake. The M&Ms packet he put in his pocket. He was pretty sure he'd find a good use for them later.

He drank from three twelve-ounce water bottles in the backpack, wanting to hydrate as much as possible.

Finished with both his immediate medical and nutritional needs, Decatur repacked the emergency backpack. He re-wrapped the pack in the plastic covering, then placed it back into the hollow of the oak tree.

Breaking off a few lower branches, he camouflaged the hole, so that when he was finished there was no trace whatsoever of the pack.

In the darkening light, Decatur stepped through the tree line and out onto the water's edge.

The beach on this part of the island was covered in cattails and wild shrubs. Perfect for what Decatur needed.

Using a piece of driftwood about five feet long, he scooped out a one-foot deep trench in the mud among some thick shrubbery by the edge of the bay.

Next, he scooped up handfuls of mud and covered his entire body and face with the icky goo. Then, he laid down, face up, in the trench and buried himself with more mud.

Finally he covered his face and most of his body with branches and cattail shoots.

As the sun sank behind the distant mountains, Decatur looked up through the shadowy green darkness as though from the floor of a living sea. Overhead, there was a rustling of branches, a noise of bats.

Listening to the nighttime noises, Decatur wondered if the girl would get any sleep. He doubted it. That's why it was so important that he be well rested in the morning. It would be his edge.

Sleeping was never a problem with him. Not since Dr. Joseph had prescribed Ambien all those years ago. Decatur took a medicine vial out of his pocket and swallowed one of the little white pills. From past experience, he knew he would be out within ten minutes.

And once asleep, he would stay that way. He never had nightmares. Never.

Bad dreams were for losers who didn't know what they wanted. Who were afraid to live. Losers were ashamed to face their greatest fears and do what they wanted. That's why their pathetic lives revolved around guilt and remorse. Decatur felt neither. Killing Bambi and all the others was like killing any fair game in the woods. They'd never be missed, at least for long, and there certainly would be more where they came from. No, Decatur never had bad dreams because he knew that if something felt right to him, then it was right. Hell, he was doing the world a favor. He was trimming the fat. Taking out the trash. Pruning the leaves. Yes, he was going to sleep well tonight.

As he began to drift off into Ambien-land, he prayed a little prayer, "Rest well tonight, B. Tomorrow you're going to die and never be anymore."

He concluded his prayer with his version of a liturgical acclamation amen. "Bitch!"

Decatur closed his eyes. The mud cracked around his mouth as he tried a smile.

He was having fun again.

His fun.

The darkness absorbed him as he was now completely hidden in the mud trench.

Within seconds of resting his head on a pillow made of the cottony fluff from a handful of cattail plants, Decatur was asleep. From time to time, his legs twitched and cycled through his mud blanket, as if he was after something.

The lambent moonlight cast shadows on the nearby mountain peaks. Storm clouds raging across the Arctic tundra would soon darken the night, turning the silver hills first to pewter and then to the blackest titanium.

Cascades of stars framed, then gave way to a Full Thunder Moon.

FORTY-EIGHT

MORNING BROKE WITH A cobalt sky.

Birds chirped. Fish broke the surface of the bay. Water lapped against the shore. A gaggle of Emperor geese lazily bathed in the golden light. A low mist ghosted, inches over the ground. Peaceful. Serene.

Decatur was fast asleep, still camouflaged in his mud trench. In fact, it was all but impossible to tell where Decatur ended and the muck began.

Then—

BAM!

The early morning serenity shattered with the sound of an explosion.

The gaggle of geese on the shore scattered in all directions.

Decatur jerked up.

Wide-awake.

As the blood roaring in his temples died away, he became aware that he was still encased in his slit trench, still caked in mud. He looked around. In the eerie, ensuing silence, he wasn't sure if the sound was real or just in his imagination.

Finally he allowed himself a smile. Mud cracked around his mouth. "Damn, some dream—"

He stretched quietly. More mud cracked and fell from his clothes.

Then he turned around.

His backpack was right behind him.

The backpack he had left hidden in the hollow of the oak tree the night before.

Its contents had been scattered all over the ground. The MREs, the first aid kit, the ammo, the water. Everything had been emptied from the pack.

But that wasn't all.

There was a huge bullet hole through the center of the pack.

"Fuckin' bitch!" Decatur yelled as he rolled out of the mud trench and ran into the woods for cover.

To make it harder to follow, he worked his way through rugged terrain. The wind was strong, bitter.

The .44 Magnum in Decatur's hand was a legit showstopper up close and personal, but he wanted something with a lot more range. *Altitude is attitude*, he thought to himself. And he knew just where to find the right altitude to make things right.

Half an hour later, Decatur readied his .44.

Cautiously he made his way down the hillside to the cabin. Heart pounding, he twisted the doorknob and pushed the door open. He took a deep breath, then burst inside.

Gun drawn, Decatur held the gun in front of him with both hands wrapped around the grip, his forefinger resting against the trigger.

He methodically checked the two rooms. The cabin was deserted.

Satisfied he was alone, he ripped down a wall panel. Hidden in the recess was a Remington .243 rifle. He lovingly held the high-powered rifle, then locked and loaded a 10-round clip. The metallic click as clip met rifle brought a smile to his face for the first time that morning.

His stomach rumbled. Decatur had forgotten how hungry he was. He opened a food cabinet.

Bambi had pulled a Mother Hubbard, the cabinet was bare. Except for a note that read:

Catchya' Later Honey Bun

Decatur clenched his teeth as he crumpled the message, wishing very much that it was the messenger he was crushing instead. *Soon*, he thought, *real fucking soon.*

Just then, Decatur's heart lurched.

From somewhere inside the cabin a voice boomed out.

Firmly. Loudly.

Bambi's voice.

"Looks like your 'summertime project' is about to come to an end, D—"

He whirled around. Shot twice toward the voice without thinking. Then he realized it was coming from the combo TV/VCR. Bambi had recorded a message.

Decatur watched and listened as the recorded message continued.

"…I guess it's time to stop messing around and get down to the nitty gritty, huh? This is all you think about, isn't it, D? Twenty-four hours a day, I bet. Everything else is just a motion. Your bakery, your marriage, your kids, your normal routine, all motions. Everything is wrapped up with this, huh, D? Your whole life, your whole way of thinking? Your 'summertime project,' huh? Well, soon, very soon, you're going to be no more forever. You have my word on that."

The tape ended, then in the loop mode, began to play again.

"Looks like your 'summertime project' is about to come to an end, D—" Decatur punched the VCR off button.

"Fuckin' hell!"

He took a deep breath. "Okay, get a grip!"

He ripped a pair of binoculars off a peg on the back of the door, next to the pistol crossbow.

He was sneering like his old self as he left the cabin, giving himself a killer pep talk. "Time to set a trap and out-hunt that cunt."

———

Decatur Kaiser had been sitting on top of the crest for most of the morning patiently counting M&Ms.

He sat in a silent, perfected stillness against an ancient Sitka spruce, the Remington .243 balanced delicately across his knees.

Centered.

Focused.

Cobra calm.

He watched the clearing below him, waiting as a stone waits.

After leaving his cabin, Decatur had made his way up to the tallest hill around. It was just what he wanted. High ground. Poplar trees. Good cover. Dark green shade.

From this vantage point he could scan an enormous amount of terrain, including his cabin below.

Picking up the binoculars, he began to glass the area below him.

Decatur inhaled deeply. He was back in his comfort zone.

The trap had been set. Now all he had to do was wait.

He bit into a brown M&M and his heart almost stopped.

From somewhere close, Bambi's voice suddenly boomed out. "Looks like your 'summertime project' is about to come to an end, D—"

Decatur momentarily choked on the small candy as he jerked around. Instinctively, he fired his rifle toward the voice. High above him in a tree.

Silence.

Decatur shielded his eyes. Looked up.

"Fuckin' hell!"

Strapped to a branch some twenty feet over his head was his boombox. Now with two fresh bullet holes.

"That bitch! She knew I'd come here! Fuckin' bitch must die—"

Before Decatur could finish his thought, an explosion got his full attention. Not an explosion, really... More like a *thump*, followed by a *whooshing* sound.

"What the—"

Looking down the hill, he found the source of the blast. Smoke poured out of one of the cabin windows.

"Goddamit!" he yelled. "She's trying to burn the place down!"

He ran down the hill at a dead run. In and out through the trees. Eyes glued to the cabin. More angry than apprehensive.

Arms pumping. Legs pistoning. Faster now, faster than before.

Smoke continued to pour from the window.

Fifty feet from the burning cabin, he hit the ground. Crawled commando style, ground hugging.

Finally he made it to the door, swinging, creaking in the wind.

Gun drawn, he burst inside.

Quickly, cautiously, methodically he checked the two rooms. Bambi was nowhere in sight.

The curtains in the front room danced with orange flames.

Decatur yanked the small fire extinguisher out of its wall cradle. At the same time he noticed that something was missing.

The pistol crossbow wasn't above the front door in its normal place.

Before he could stop his momentum, he noticed the thin wire attached to the fire extinguisher in his hand.

Like some insane Rube Goldberg machine, Decatur instantly traced the wire to the other end.

It was connected to the crossbow, which had been secured to a table and pointed directly at—

Him.

That's when Decatur accidentally dropped the extinguisher.

The crossbow made a *thump* sound as the aluminum bolt was triggered.

Decatur tried to jump for cover.

He was fast.

But not fast enough.

The 14-inch aluminum bolt slammed into Decatur's thigh, just above his right kneecap, knocking him off his feet.

Howling in pain, stunned with shock, Decatur looked at the bolt sticking out of his leg. Something was written on the bottom half of the shaft:

This Shot's On the House

"I'm going to fuckin' gut you!" Decatur screamed. "You hear me!"

That's when Bambi's voice boomed out once again. This time from the back room. "Looks like your 'summertime project' is about to come to an end, D—"

Without thinking, Decatur whirled around and emptied his clip toward the sound of the voice firing through the front room wall.

The kitchen area disintegrated under a hail of fire. Dishes shattered. Cans exploded. The cabinets vomited up their contents.

Decatur snapped in a fresh clip. Emptied it into the back room.

Wood chips filled the air in a cloud. A mist of finely chopped plaster drifted in and out.

Decatur stopped firing.

Through the smoke, he noticed the speaker wires on the floor. Then he reached down, grabbed the wires and followed them.

They led into the back room where the speakers had been hooked up to the VCR.

Decatur began to laugh. A bit insane.

He had shot his speakers all to hell.

Decatur rushed back into the front room. Slammed the eject button on the VCR. Grabbed the videotape. Smashed it to pieces. "That, bitch, is what I'm going to do to you!"

As he continued to smash the videotape, Bambi's taunting voice came through, loud and clear, once again. "Looks like your 'summertime project' is about to come to an end, D—"

"Oh, come on!" Decatur suddenly felt terribly violated, oppressed, observed. This was no longer fun. No fun at all.

Fearful and plagued by doubt, unaccustomed to both of those emotions, Decatur hobbled into the back room, checked for another recording device, when it suddenly dawned on him.

There wasn't one.

His scalp prickled, the flesh on the nape of his neck crawled, his hand tightened on the Remington.

That's when—

From underneath the floorboards Bambi popped up!

Gun in hand, she nodded toward the arrow in Decatur's leg. "See you got my note."

Decatur flicked his rifle up, lightning fast. Pointed it at Bambi's chest. Dried mud cracked on his face as he smiled insanely. "Looks like the situation just accentuated the positive…" He raised the Remington sights between Bambi's eyes. "…'cus you're positively going to be one… dead… bitch."

He squeezed the trigger.

CLICK! The metallic sound echoed through the cabin, bounced off the walls, drilled itself into the very center of Decatur's soul.

The gun, like his soul, was empty.

Nothing there.

Not even a blank. Not anymore.

"Looks like you've shot your load for the last time there, D." She smiled, looked closely at Decatur. He was a complete mess—still covered in mud, blood spilling everywhere. His pants leg below the crossbow bolt was soaked so deeply it bagged.

"You know something else?" she asked.

Grimacing in pain from the arrow in his thigh, he dropped the Remington to the floor, slowly made his way to the .44 in his waistband.

"A mind isn't always a terrible thing to waste," said Bambi.

Decatur looked up in horror.

"I don't want you to take this in a bad way, but you look like shit. And your hair, what a mess. How about a little off the top?"

She pointed her gun at his head. Decatur stared at the black hole in the center of the metal barrel.

"You don't have the balls!" he sneered. "No fuckin' way—"

He grinned.

She squeezed off a shot. The spark of light coming out of the black hole was barely a heartbeat ahead of the *Bam!* that hit his ears right before the bullet found his head.

"Fuckin' way," was the last thing he heard as he saw Bambi standing behind the barrel of the smoking gun.

Scenery spinning, his world reeling, darkness claimed Decatur Kaiser.

FORTY-NINE

At first, it sounded almost like a baby crying, a baby crying far away, in the distance. Then, as the black in front of him faded slowly to gray, and the dim sparkles in his peripheral vision began to give way and become light, the sound likewise gradually became clearer and more focused, as if tuning a radio from static to station.

It wasn't a baby who was crying.

It was a woman.

The quiet, sad, heart-breaking sobbing was somehow vaguely familiar, yet distantly elapsed and misbegotten.

Decatur's eyes slowly fluttered open as he woke up. The pain was beyond pain. It was weight, heavy dark weight on his head, his chest, in his legs and arms.

All over...

He felt nauseous. Even moving his eyes made him want to throw up. Rather than scrape his eyeballs against his eye sockets again, he compromised and slowly turned his whole head to the right, which he discovered was about the only part of his body that he could move.

What he saw was a grotesque face staring back at him. Squinting, trying to focus, Decatur realized the face was his own, reflected back from the stainless steel refrigerator door.

Decatur gagged at his image.

He had a reverse Mohawk, a red, hairless furrow across the top of his head from front to back.

It all began to come back to him—Bambi exploding out of the floor, gun in hand, almost laughing at him. Then, to his complete amazement, she fired.

Bambi's shot had apparently creased the top of his skull, removing a 5.56mm strip of scalp and hair. Messy, painful, burning like a sonofabitch, but not life threatening.

Decatur Kaiser, he thought, *don't die that easy.*

As he struggled to regain consciousness, he discovered something else.

He couldn't move. At all. He could only turn his head from side to side.

Still too zoned to understand why he couldn't budge, he turned his head down, his neck muscles aching from the strain. *Well, there's your problem right there*, he thought to himself.

He was spread-eagled across the kitchen table, his arms and legs tied with rope to the four legs.

He was also nude. He stared down his torso, to his limp penis lying to the left, its bent end almost staring back at him.

"The fuck is this?" he wondered.

The pitiful sound of the sobbing woman continued.

Decatur turned his head to the right.

The sound was coming from the TV. One of his videotapes was playing. He recognized it immediately. It was his *Greatest Hits #4*.

It was Susie Q's tape from thirteen years earlier.

He smiled at the memory. Most of them, he mused, were barely memorable and becoming less so with each passing day.

But that one … That one was sweet. She brought firepower to the game, the first and only one to do that.

Until now.

His smile faded and his jaw tightened.

Bambi. That bitch. He'd remember her, too.

That bitch. Where the fuck is she?

All sixteen videotapes had been taken out of the safe and were stacked up in various piles near the VCR.

Then he caught movement in the far side of his peripheral vision and strained to move toward it.

There she was.

Bambi was busy placing all of Decatur's trophies on the table around him. Susie Q's gold Mizpah pendant, several driver's licenses, women's watches, a pair of heart-shaped sunglasses, assorted pieces of jewelry.

Decatur started to talk, but his mouth was cotton dry. "Wa … water …," he begged.

"Hey, Sleeping Beauty, glad you could make it." Bambi picked up a water bottle and held it up to him.

He started to drink, then had second thoughts.

"It's okay," smiled Bambi. "I already went."

She held the bottle up to Decatur's mouth. While he greedily drank, Bambi nodded toward the TV. "Pretty woman, that one."

Still heavily confused, drifting in and out of consciousness, Decatur slurred, "She was ... the worst fuck of them all. If she had a bitch dog, I'da killed it, too!"

He went back to slurping the water, until it was all gone.

"You know something, Decatur? You never cease to disappoint me." Her voice was eerily, strangely calm.

He sneered. "Didn't have the stones to kill me, huh?"

"Too easy. What's the fun in that?"

Bambi ejected the videotape. Pushed in another one. It was labeled *Greatest Hits #16*. She hit play. On the TV, Bambi watched a very young woman, naked and beaten, her hair splayed stiffly out, cower on the bear rug, the chain around her ankle leading out of the frame.

"Remember this one's name, D?"

"Does it matter?"

"She was very young." She held up a driver's license. There was a tiny, barely postage stamp-sized picture of the girl in the video. "Did you bother to look at her license?"

"No, why?" grinned Decatur. "She a blood donor?"

"Her name was Cheryl Davis. She was only sixteen. I came this close to saving her life last year ..."

She held up two keys. "This close! Recognize these?" Dangled the keys in front of Decatur's eyes.

He looked up. Confused. "Those ... those are the keys to my plane!"

Bambi crossed to the stove. Lit a burner. "That's what they are."

"WHO THE HELL ARE YOU?" he screamed. Decatur lost it for just a second, straining and jerking against the ropes. He stared down toward his left, eyes bulging, as he yanked in panic and fury.

He stopped, eyes wide. She'd wrapped the rope around his wrist, looped it several times, then expertly finished it off with a clove hitch.

Bitch knows knots... he thought.

It was an epiphany as profound and as meaningful as a drunk's moment of clarity. For the first time, he wasn't sure he'd win.

The pain and the rope overwhelmed him, forced the air out of him, and he settled back, defeated, on the table.

"Who the hell are you?" he whispered.

She placed the Ka-Bar blade across the flame on the stove. Heat waves shimmered ghostlike above the blade as the metal began to glow red hot. "They don't call it Mission Difficult, do they? No! They call it Mission *Impossible!*"

She turned to Decatur. "That's something a friend of mine used to say. He was a cop in the Anchorage police department."

He gazed at her as if seeing her for the first time, not knowing what to think.

She shrugged, answering his silent question, "Hey, in my line of work, you meet a lot of people." She turned the knife blade over the flame. "Anyway, he's retired now. But his biggest regret, D, was not solving the one case that he worked the longest on."

She pulled a chair up close to Decatur. Sat down. "You know, the truly pathetic thing is when one of these girls disappears, most guys in the police department assume the girls simply pulled up stakes and moved away. Those kind of ladies aren't real big on leaving forwarding addresses. No one ever misses 'em, do they?"

She looked at Decatur. There was absolutely nothing on his face, as if void of all human emotion.

"Well, D, turns out my cop friend knew one of the missing girls. Knew her well enough to know that she wouldn't just pack up and leave. He knew somebody killed her…"

Bambi stood up and opened a cabinet as if she was at home. Pulled out a first-aid kit. "You made his short list. You were a regular at the club where she disappeared. Where a lot of the others were last seen, too."

She placed the first-aid kit next to Decatur on the table. Pulled out a couple rolls of gauze. "But, because there were no bodies, or even a crime scene, no judge would issue a search warrant against you."

Opening a sewing kit, she took out a needle and a couple spools of thread. Held the spools up. "Which do you want? The red or black?"

He didn't answer.

"Let's go with the black," she said. "Suits you. Now, just when my friend was putting all his facts together, you caught another break."

She threaded the needle. "He came down with Alzheimer's. He had to retire. They put him in a nursing home."

"Gee," seethed Decatur, "if I'd known I would have baked him a cake."

Bambi let the insult slide. All things considered, she was remarkably composed. As if she'd gone through this hundreds of times before in her mind.

She lifted the knife off the burner. The blade glowed an incandescent red. "Which is hotter, D? Red hot or white hot? I always get that confused."

She put the blade back on the burner when he didn't answer. "Let's give it a few more minutes, whaddaya' say? Now, where was

I? Oh, yeah, right before my cop friend retired he Xeroxed his case files and gave them all to me. Why? Guess he didn't want me to end up like all the rest. That, plus I was the only one who seemed to listen to the man."

Decatur looked at the girl, trying to understand.

"That's when I made you my job, D." She sat down in front of him. "Matter of fact, last night was the second time I was ever at one of those places."

"Second time?!"

"After I got your files, I began tracking you."

She took a good look at Decatur. His face a rictus of surprise and incomprehension. Bambi doesn't miss it. "I knew this was your ... what did you call it? Your 'summertime project.' This time last year I followed you to the Anchorage airport. Watched you get your family out of the way ..."

She picked up the Sharpie she had used earlier, uncapped it, then drew a dotted line around Decatur's right shoulder joint.

"... I followed you to your favorite stripjoint, watched you pick up Cheryl and handcuff her in your car. Followed you as you drove away. I was going to stop you then. I was prepared for everything. Everything but that damn plane ..."

She drew a dotted line around Decatur's left shoulder joint.

"Yep, gotta hand it to you ... that was genius. I watched as you put Cheryl in the 140, but I was too far away to do a damn thing. Then you took off and I knew ... I knew I had to be your next summertime project. It was the only way I could find out what really happened to all those girls."

She held the two airplane keys up to Decatur's face again. There's a twinkle in her eye as she recites, "Pre-takeoff and cockpit check. Trim tab controls, check. Throttle closed. Flap controls full forward.

Mixture set to idle. Cutoffs—off. Master battery switch off. Instruments checked and set. Altimeter set to elevation. Elevator set to neutral. Aileron set to neutral. Primer closed and locked. Throttle at one inch. Battery on. Starter switch closed. One, two, three and away we go…"

"What, how did you remember all that?"

"Karma can really be a fickle bitch, can't it, D? It's been a year or so since I had any stick time in a 140, but with a couple hundred hours in the 140 and the Super Cub, it oughta come back to me pretty quick. Imagine that? I can fly out of here whenever I want." She smiled. "Course I'd rather fly something along the lines of a Comanche 250. Now that's one hot mess of an airplane."

She moved farther down his body. "Did I mention karma can really be fickle? And a bitch?" Her voice was relaxed, almost light-hearted.

She drew a dotted line around Decatur's upper right thigh.

"What? You gonna torture me again? Get your rocks off some more?"

"Nope. Playtime is way over."

"Ah, ain't that sad. And you just about had my sinuses all cleared up. Pity, really."

Bambi laughed. "You know, that reminds me. That term you were looking for … when someone talks too much? It's called 'logorrhea.' It means diarrhea of the mouth. And, D, I think I have a cure for that. It's—"

"Logorrhea?" he interrupted.

"I'm thinking about hanging your tongue out there on the porch. Keep those 16 notches company. Now that would be karma."

Bambi gave him a wink. Not unlike the winks Decatur has given her throughout.

Decatur broke down. "What the fuck are you going to do to me?"

"I know you have no control over what you do, D. You've made that clear, what? Sixteen times at least. What I want is to make sure you never do this again."

"And how are you going to do that if you don't kill me?"

"I'm going to box you, D."

"Box me?"

"When you wake up, you're going to fit into one of your big cake boxes. Give or take."

"Give or take?"

She drew a dotted line around Decatur's upper left thigh. Decatur struggled violently against the ropes, straining even against the pain, fighting to turn the pain into energy, into breakout energy.

No go.

"Well, mostly take. Guess I'm going to have to remove a few . . . unessential . . . things first."

"Unessential?"

Bambi smiled down at him, then turned toward his feet. Decatur stared at her back, wishing he could get his hands around her neck for just a heartbeat. Just a heartbeat. That's all it would take . . .

Then he felt it. For a moment, he couldn't tell what it was. Then his eyes widened as realization overtook him. It was the tip of the Sharpie, drawing a wet line of black ink around the circumference of his cock. Right at the base . . .

"Oh, my God, NO! You don't know what you're doing!"

She turned back to him after she finished. "Oh, not to worry, D. I do know what I'm doing. I've even read a couple of books about it." She pointed the Sharpie toward his crotch. "Maybe I'll hang *that* next to the sixteen notches on the porch rail. Now there's your poetic justice."

She hesitated for a beat. "Think it would measure up? I'd hate to embarrass you."

Bambi crossed to the stove. Took the Ka-Bar off the burner. Held it up. The oversized blade glowed white hot.

"Yep, after your tongue goes, I'm going to take off your arms and then your legs and we'll just see from there."

Decatur began to sob. "What . . . Please—"

He stared up at the ceiling. The planks began vibrating and dancing, the straight lines curving and undulating.

Decatur began to slur his words. "Oh, God! Puh . . . please, don't . . . I . . . I don't feel so good . . ."

"Oh, I found these." Bambi held up Decatur's prescription bottle. "Ambien. I mixed a bunch of these sleeping pills in the water you just drank. You should be out for quite some time. Trust me. It's better this way."

She reached for the plastic bottle of rubbing alcohol, unscrewed the cap, tilted it just a bit. "Okay, let's get to it. This can get tricky. Hope your insurance is paid up."

Then she moved to her left, down his body, tilted the plastic bottle and poured nearly the whole bottle of rubbing alcohol all over his crotch, saturating the pubic hair, cascading over his scrotum and penis, puddling between his legs, up into the crack of his buttocks.

"Don't want to run the risk of infection now, do we?" she commented.

It took a few seconds. At first, it felt cool, soothing, as the air wafted over it . . .

And then the burn hit.

Hard.

It was liquid fire on his most sensitive skin.

Decatur screamed, his voice straining to a higher pitch than either of them had ever heard before. He jerked and thrashed against the ropes.

And lost.

"*Goddamit, it burns!*" he howled. "*Shit goddamn you you fuckin' bitch I'm gonna tear your head off and shit down your—*"

Decatur's voice froze solid, mid-threat, and his eyes opened wide in terror as Bambi brought the glowing knife closer and closer. He flexed his arms. No slack. Tried to kick his legs. No deal. Bambi moved the blade closer to the apex of the V his legs made as they joined his torso.

"For … God's … sake … *don't*—"

"You think the alcohol burns," she said, almost matter-of-factly, "wait'll you get a load of this little puppy. Oh, by the way, white hot is as hot as it gets."

"*Please …*"

"*Please,*" Bambi mocked him. "Exactly how many girls asked you the same thing and how many times did you show them mercy? Huh? Name one and I'll put this procedure on hold."

Decatur's face quivered and shook as he began sobbing.

"Nope, didn't think so."

She brought the knife closer. Even through the Ambien fog, he could feel the heat from the glowing tip on his skin.

"Okay, now trust me, this is gonna hurt you a lot more than it is me."

The last thing Decatur Kaiser heard was himself, screaming.

———

The late afternoon air bobbed with the perpetual rumble of the river as it pulsated over the serrated cliff, then broke on the ragged boulders far below.

Bambi stood at the top of the ravine where Decatur had indicated on his map. The ravine where he had 'flushed' the bodies.

She took in the awesome view of the gorge and the roaring river far below.

She bent down.

Picked a handful of flowers. Blue petals. A white inner ring. And a yellow center. The Alaskan state flower.

"Forget-me-not," Bambi said as she smiled fondly, then tossed the bouquet high into the air.

She watched as the flowers carouseled into the raging river below.

FIFTY

THE ENGINE ROARED TO life on the first try.

Bambi looked back from the pilot seat to make sure everything she needed was securely stowed away in the storage area of the Cessna 140. She smiled.

Everything was secure.

Finally...

She looked ahead. Quickly, she effortlessly fastened her seatbelt, scanned the instrument panel, then gently nudged the engine throttle forward.

The pure light of dawn had recently spread over the bay, a spectacular blend of maroon, pink, gold and indigo. The majestic skyscape was sprinkled with fluffy, cotton-ball masses of cumulus clouds; majestically floating snow mountains all tall as Everest, laden with low valleys and towering peaks, endless caves and plunging ravines—strange and mysterious pathways perpetually folding and unfolding in the mapless hemispheres of the sky.

Bambi checked the wind direction by looking at the top of some spruce and maple trees lining the beach. Satisfied, she gunned the engine.

The plane shimmered under the morning sun, then lifted off the sandbar and raced zero feet off the bay, barely kissing the surface as it gained airspeed. Bambi knew instinctively, without even looking at the airspeed indicator, when the right moment came to turn it loose.

Bambi yanked the wheel back abruptly and made a screaming climb, just over stall speed, then banked and circled the island.

Looking through a clearing in the woods, she buzzed the cabin.

Suddenly, the plane was violently buffeted as the cabin below exploded in one enormous fireball.

A mini-Hiroshima.

A tower of fire.

A geyser of smoke.

"Oops, must have forgotten to turn off the propane. My bad."

She leveled off at 1,000 feet. Looked down below. Saw the natural arch that Decatur had looped over earlier.

A smile necklaced across her face.

She applied full throttle and forced the control column down.

The 140 screamed as she looped around the arch, not over it like Decatur. There was no doubt about it; she was the better pilot.

Looking behind her and down, she yelled toward the cabin, now a blazing funeral pyre, "Who's your daddy now? Bitch!"

She drank it all in.

The pulsating thunder of the engine.

The black smoke snaking up from the cabin beneath her.

The cool air on her face.

The beautiful Magritte sky.

The milky coming of the day.

The space without frontiers ahead of her.

She had never felt freer.

For the first time, she knew why they called it *Resurrection Bay.*

The plane climbed into the azure sky, became one with the glimmering northern lights, and then was gone.

FIFTY-ONE

DECATUR KAISER *had his crosshairs trained dead center on a nifty little head shot.*

One hundred fifty yards. Piece of cake. He could make this shot in his sleep.

He set the angle to maximize blood splatter and carnage.

Slid the cross bolt safety from the right side to the left, revealing the red {fire" Dot. Slide to the right, ready to fight.

He had been sitting on top of the hill for most of the morning patiently counting M&Ms.

Centered.

Focused.

Cobra calm.

"You are all mine," he thought, his right eye pressed against the scope, "I've fuckin' earned you!"

He took a long, practiced deep breath. Held it in.

"All right, Miss Bambi, are you ready for your head shot?" Decatur said to himself, grinning ear to ear.

Eased his forefinger around the trigger.

The gun jolted his shoulder.

He knew when the sight in his scope momentarily disappeared in a blur of recoil, that the perfect shot he'd been waiting for all these hours was his.

The bullet screamed toward the girl.

A foot from smashing into her brain, the bullet stopped.

Bambi reached out.

Plucked the stationary bullet out of mid-air.

Tossed it back toward him with all of her might.

The bullet rocketed back, gaining speed like a fucking juggernaut, until it smashed through the scope and into his right eye socket.

Decatur Kaiser woke with a start.

Or at least he thought he woke up.

He wasn't sure if he was awake but not awake. Or asleep but not asleep.

The room was funeral black. It was impossible to make out anything.

He found himself on some sort of chair and when he tried to move, he couldn't.

Still too groggy to completely understand what was happening to him, he remembered Bambi's threat to box him.

In the complete darkness, the anticipation was driving him insane.

Then, the room became dimly lit with blue static, bleeding in minimal light.

Fearing the worse, Decatur looked down. His vision still wasn't right, but what he saw caused tears to pour from his eyes.

Both of his legs were still there. Tied to a chair, but still there.

Looking to his right and left, he found his arms still attached, but equally immobilized.

The next thought shot through his brain like lightning. He looked down. His brain sent his crotch an emergency telegram: *squeeze*. He felt his muscles tighten, the Kegels contracting. He felt his penis brush against some kind of fabric.

Yeah, he thought, relaxing and letting out the longest sigh of relief he'd ever felt. *It's still there.*

The thought only made him angrier.

He tried to shout. Found his voice. His tongue was still there as well.

"The fuck is this?! Where am I?"

As his eyes finally adjusted, he recognized where he was.

"What the hell?!"

He wasn't in his cabin.

He was in his office. At the Heaven Scent Bakery. Tied to his office chair.

Decatur's brain reeled, "Bitch drugged me and brought me back! I knew she didn't have the balls!" he shouted.

He laughed hysterically. "You stupid cunt, I won't be so compassionate when I find you!"

Then there was a sound like a cannon going off, and his office door flew inward in a spray of broken boards and splinters. An explosion of light followed like a flashbulb going off.

And bathed in the globe of brilliant light, half a dozen Anchorage policemen burst into the room. Guns drawn.

Decatur recovered quickly. "The girl! It was the girl. Bambi! She did this to me! She set me up!"

Then, from outside the office came the voice of Decatur's wife. "Let me through! ... I'm the one who got the call ... Let me through! ... Decatur, are you in there? ... What have they done to you?"

She bulldozed her way into the office and past the officers. Rushed over to Decatur.

Decatur stared at her, stunned. "How did ... How did you get here? You're supposed to be in—"

"I got a call last night," Cindy shrieked. "They said you'd been arrested. I got on the first flight."

Cindy stopped, suddenly, as if seeing him for the first time, trussed up in a chair, helpless. Her face went flat, empty. Numb.

Decatur pleaded, "It was the girl! She did this! It's all her fault! She's insane. She tried to rob me. I didn't do anything ... "

Cindy looked down at her husband, bound to the chair.

Scattered around the chair were fifteen of his trophies around his feet—driver's licenses, jewelry, scarves, the heart-shaped sunglasses. And his aviation sectional complete with sixteen crosses circled in red.

Next to it, a stack of videotapes, labeled *Greatest Hits* ...

"I can explain everything," cried Decatur. "She planted all this stuff to make me look—"

The blue static behind Decatur suddenly became a moving image. The TV/VCR behind him flickered, then Greatest Hits #4 automatically started. On the TV screen, Decatur was brutally raping Sue Turnbull for all to see.

Sue was screaming out from hell.

A dreadful howl of pain, horror, groans, and screams like the sounds that might have been heard in the windowless gas chambers at Auschwitz or along ancient Transylvanian roads where Vlad the Impaler skewered countless thousands on sharpened stakes.

It was not a cry for help or even a plea for mercy, but a begging for release at any cost, even death.

After thirteen years, Sue was finally heard.

Decatur looked at the screen in total disbelief.

He looked at the silent cops, their faces grim, hard.

He looked at his wife, her face stricken.

Decatur stared silently, numbly. Time seemed to slow. The cries from the television seemed muted now, everything around him surreal. In the distance, his wife began to wail, her cries mixing in with the sound from the television.

Was it the Ambien, he wondered. Was any of this real?

Then, as if a round from the Steyr Aug had slammed into his head, Decatur Kaiser's brain automatically went into shutdown mode and in a last ditch effort to process something, anything, he did what he always did.

He began to count.

The number of cops in the room?

Twelve.

The number of pissed off wives in the room who would divorce his ass and take everything in no time?

One.

The number of times he was fucked?

Decatur Kaiser stopped mid-thought.

For the first time in his life, he realized he couldn't count that high.

FIFTY-TWO

CADENCING SOLDIERS DOUBLE-TIMED PAST the huge marble, bronze, and granite plaque at the entrance of the army base that bordered the city limits of Anchorage. The plaque read:

United States Army
Fort Richardson
America's Arctic Warriors

In a secluded room in the rear of Buckner Fieldhouse, near the intersection of D Street and 6th, within walking distance of the base's main entrance at Richardson Gate, a group of half a dozen soldiers gathered round, waiting. Men of the 4th Brigade Combat Team (Airborne), 25th Infantry Division. Members of the only airborne combat brigade team in the Pacific Theater, and one of only six such teams in the entire United States Army. Each member of this elite unit had the team's mission committed to memory; they ate, breathed, and lived it every day.

"On order," their mission statement read, "4th Brigade, 25th Infantry strategically deploys, conducts forcible entry parachute assault and secures key objectives for follow-on military operations in support of U.S. national interests."

In other words, these were the guys who jumped out of airplanes so high up you couldn't even hear them, at dawn when you haven't even had your morning coffee yet, fell 30,000 feet and were on top of you before you knew it, then kicked the shit out of you so the pussies who followed on the ground don't have to skin their knees diving for cover.

In a culture of bad-asses, these were the baddest-asses of all. They fell from the sky, came out of nowhere, and they did it in sub-zero temperatures without breaking a sweat. They were in this room to continue their ongoing training in close-quarters, hand-to-hand combat.

The door swung open and Bambi walked in.

She wore a pair of fatigue sweats, a sports bra, T-shirt, running shoes. Her hair, no longer dyed Day-Glo blue but back to its natural, Midwest corn-blonde color, was tied behind her in a loose pony tail.

She shut the door, nodded to the six men, and went to work.

She scanned the room, picked out the tallest, biggest, meanest guy of them all, then took him down with her signature move. The Hurricana. She took two steps forward, dove onto her hands, then cartwheeled into the trainee, locked her legs around his neck, twisted, and slammed him to the mat with a floor-shaking *thud*.

She was back on her feet in a heartbeat, the tall guy on the floor, stunned, groaning. A short, dark-haired guy to the left was grinning. She turned, spun a leg, connected his left ear with her right ankle ...

He dropped, *sans* grin.

Bambi then made her way around the room, taking them down, one at a time. When they got up, she did it all over again.

Just another day at the office.

———

Ninety minutes later, Bambi stepped out of the shower. She toweled off, dried her hair, put on her Class A and topped it off with a maroon beret. She stared into the mirror, at her captain's bars and the four rows of fruit salad, the awards and insignia, the regimental crest.

Five minutes later, she saluted the two soldiers at the Richardson Gate and drove off base. Her two most prized possessions—a weathered book and a duct-taped banker's box—rested beside her in the passenger seat.

Thirty minutes later, she parked in the back lot of the Veterans of Foreign Wars' Nursing Home. As she walked through the front glass doors carrying the banker's box and the book from her car, she was greeted with the augmented fourth, mythic chord strains blasting from a piano.

Checking in at the front desk, then walking into the front lounge, the piano music became recognizable. Scriabin. "Piano Etude opus 8, number 12."

Elderly people, mostly men, moved through the depressing lounge on walkers or pushed themselves in wheelchairs. Some played cards. Others watched TV. A stale smell permeated the place; not exactly unpleasant, but earthy and fecund.

A sole figure with scraggly gray hair, the pianist, sat on a bench, hunched over the piano. He energetically attacked the Scriabin, but he repeated the same opening passage over and over, occasionally struggling to move on, but always returning to the same opening passage.

To Bambi, the sight of the haggard pianist and his repetitive attempts at the syncopated music was nothing short of heartbreaking. She slowly walked over to the piano, listening to the music, reliving a thousand memories. She placed the box and the book down on a chair behind them.

She looked down at the pianist, smiled.

"Very nice," she said.

"You know it?" replied the old man looking up.

"Of course, I do. It's Scriabin." Bambi smiled. "You taught it to me, Sarge. A long time ago ..."

There was a pause, as he looked into her eyes, trying desperately to remember her. He stared at her uniform for a few moments, then finally said: "Hmm ... You ... you a state trooper?"

After all this time, she was inured to this, but it still hurt like hell.

"No, not a state trooper."

"You ... you with APD?"

"No, I'm not with the Anchorage police, either ... but I did hear my mother once say, 'You put the 'anchor' in Anchorage.'"

Bambi took a deep breath as Sarge struggled for some forgotten memory. By the look on his face, she saw that it had been erased long ago.

"I'm your granddaughter, Sarge. I'm Sue's daughter, Sunny."

Sarge looked up at the nameplate on the left side of her jacket: TURNBULL.

The name meant nothing to him.

A shaft of sunlight from the oversized windows spotlighted something glowing sublimely around Sunny's neck, blinding Sarge for just a moment. He squinted, trying to make it out. Then it came into focus.

What was so bedazzling were two gold pendants joined together.

Sarge was transfixed with the pendants. He knew that they should have some meaning, some significance, some importance. He struggled, a kind of strange loneliness across his face, but the exact memory had long since faded and died.

What he was desperately struggling to remember but couldn't was that the two Mizpah pendants hanging around Sunny's neck had been his gift to Sunny and her mother all those years ago.

What he didn't know was that the two pendants were now joined for the first time in thirteen years.

Sunny put her book down on the piano bench, then took a seat alongside Sarge. Effortlessly, she picked up the Etude where he had left off. Talked as she played.

"Sarge, remember that box?"

He looked up, confused.

She nodded over her shoulder. Sarge turned, spotted the box. Nothing.

"You gave me that box ... what? Three years ago? I was just out of Officer Candidate School. They'd just forced you to retire."

He turned to her, stared blankly.

"I know," she said, her voice low. "You're trying. It's okay."

She played a few more measures. "You gave me that box because you didn't think anyone would do anything with it once you were gone."

"Box?" he whispered. "What's—?"

"It's the files," Sunny said. "The files on Mom. All the work you did over the years, trying to find her."

"Mom?"

"Sue, your daughter. My mother."

Sarge nodded, still mostly blank.

"You said you'd never stop looking for her. And you didn't, not until you couldn't anymore. Then you gave me the files. I picked up where you left off."

Sunny hammered down on the piano keys, finishing the piece with a flourish. She stopped, the last notes hanging in the air.

She turned to Sarge. "And now it's over. The guy who took Mom? He's going away forever. He'll never hurt anyone else again."

And for just a brief moment, the image came back to her, of Decatur Kaiser back on the island, in an Ambien coma, wrapped in a sheet, mummy-style, trussed up like a turkey and strapped in the right seat of the tiny Cessna 140. She'd wrapped about fifty feet of duct tape around him, then slung his bony ass over her shoulder and carried him to the plane like a sack of fertilizer.

Or maybe *sack of shit* was a more appropriate description.

Or even better yet, a *blivet*.

She had first heard that expression from Sarge when she was still in high school. A blivet, Sarge had told her, was ten pounds of shit stuffed into a five pound bag. Yep, that pretty much covered it.

In the plane, she had duct-taped his mouth and blindfolded the blivet. She didn't even want to listen to the sonofabitch anymore, and she sure as hell didn't want to have to look into his dead-assed eyes. She'd had as much of his shit as she was taking.

In fact, she smiled, the whole world had.

"Yeah, Sarge. And now Mom's at peace."

Sarge looked down to the floor, sadness like weight pulling the sagging flesh of his cheeks downward. For a moment, there was a beat of recognition and his eyes filled.

"She's a good girl," he said.

"Yes," Sunny replied. "She's a good girl."

She looked down at the piano bench. "I've got something else for you. Something extra special."

"Chocolate?"

"More special," she said, reaching around her, picking up the book and holding it out.

"What's that?" asked Sarge.

"It's mom's diary." She turned to the first page, "Listen to this ... she wrote this when I was only a couple of days old—"

She read out loud: *It's a little after six and you wake up and my new day begins. And, no, Sunny, I haven't solved the Middle East crisis, or discovered the missing mass in the universe. I don't even think I recycled the empty two liter Diet Dr Pepper bottle yesterday. But one thing I do know—to the best of my ability, I did keep you alive and relatively happy and content for another day, and for now, that's all I can ask. And hey, who knows, maybe tomorrow, I'll actually take a shower.*

Sunny smiled. "I wonder if she ever got that shower?"

Sarge looked at the book with searching eyes. Then something clicked and he smiled.

Sunny handed the diary to Sarge. "She asked me to give this to you. There's a lot of you in there ..."

Sarge took the diary from Sunny, held it on his lap for a moment.

Sunny brightened, her voice bringing them both out of reverie. "Hey, Sarge, you remember Edisto Island?"

"Edisto Island?"

"It's off the coast of South Carolina. Blue skies. Green grass. Mild winters."

"Edisto Island?"

"Your sister Jackie lives there. She's got a room waiting for you. A big room. A real room. She wants you to move there."

"But, the police? I've got—"

"You've got to let some things go, Sarge." She looked into his eyes, desperately searching for the rest of him. "You've done your job. It's time to let others do theirs."

Sunny looked around the depressing room. "You need some caring faces, some friendly faces."

"But the piano?"

"We'll get you your very own piano, Sarge." She leaned over, kissed him on his forehead. "We've both been inside way too long."

Their eyes met, held, and he smiled. For just that moment, that brief, wonderful moment, Sunny knew she had him back.

"Captain Turnbull," a deep voice resonated over Sunny's shoulder. She looked around. The nursing home director walked up to her. "Excuse me, Captain, but there are a couple of people here to see you."

Sunny looked up with trepidation. "People?"

"Yes, they're in my office. They said it was important. Told me to tell you they were 'heaven sent.' Said you'd know what that meant."

Heaven sent ... She took a moment, then it hit her: *Heaven Scent.* Decatur's bakery.

Sunny thought for a moment, then turned to her grandfather. "I'll be right back, Sarge, and we'll start packing your stuff."

"Edisto Island?"

"Blue skies."

"Green grass ..."

The nursing home director led her down the hall and to his office. He opened the door for her, then left.

Sunny entered the room with a sense of dread. A man and woman, both in dark suits, were there. They were alone, just the three

363

of them, in the director's office. Sunny instinctively scanned the room for an escape route.

Her gaze suddenly stopped on something she didn't expect to see. Sitting in the middle of the director's desk was a Hostess Golden Cupcake with a single white candle sticking out of its center.

The man in black held a thick folder. He looked directly at her and said, "Captain Turnbull?"

"Yes."

"Have a seat."

"I'd rather stand, thank you."

"Have it your way."

The woman in black struck a match, reached over and lit the single candle on the Hostess cupcake. "Captain Turnbull, according to our records, Happy Birthday is in order." She nodded at the miniature burning cake. "Best we could do on short notice."

Sunny took in the cupcake and burning candle. She looked up at the two strangers. "You know my name. I don't know yours."

The man in black smiled. "C'mon, Captain, you know how this works."

"Your name," Sunny said. It wasn't a question.

"My name is Smith," the man said.

Sunny turned to the woman. "That would make you Jones."

The woman in black nodded, smiled.

Sunny motioned toward the cake on the desk. "Something tells me the government didn't spend all this money just to wish me a Happy Birthday."

"Captain Turnbull," said the man in black, "we're here to offer you a job."

"I've got a job, Mr. Smith."

"Not like this one, you don't. We think it's something that you might be interested in."

"You're not army, are you?"

"Not exactly. But we do have the same employer with a great number of shared interests."

"Shared interests?"

"To protect our country against all enemies, whether domestic or foreign, internal or external."

"And this has what to do with me?"

The man in black tapped his folder. "There has been a great deal of speculation on the recent arrest of a rather prolific serial killer here in Anchorage. While the police are not releasing the complete details, speculation based on your recent activities and initiatives—"

"Alleged activities and initiatives," interrupted Sunny.

"I stand corrected. Based on your recent 'alleged' activities and initiatives, we are authorized to offer you a job working for an organization with no official ties to either the United States armed forces or any government affiliations."

"Okay, I'm going with the black of blackest ops, but you can't say that, correct?"

"That is correct."

"Then can you tell me exactly what it is that I would be doing?"

"We looking for someone who can make problems go away," replied the man in black.

"We're looking for a team leader for what we refer to as unsanctioned 'off-book' missions," filled in Ms. Jones.

"What kind of missions?" asked Sunny.

"Mainly, maximum acquisition and surveillance of select targets ... and if the cause and opportunity arise, a quick and decisive ... let's say ... 'adjustment,'" said the man.

" A 'fix.'" appended the woman.

"A 'fix-it girl', huh? So, what? You're asking me to be an assassin?"

"No, no, Captain, we have plenty of folks for that option," said the man in black.

"What we want," explained the woman, "is someone to 'fix' things before we're forced, as a last resort, to implement that option."

"What we need is someone with your unique … skill sets and initiative … to infiltrate certain restricted areas here and around the world."

"Someone who can quickly assess a threatening situation immediately and then take decisive action, either with a small group, or preferably, on their own." The woman in black held out a card. "Of course, we understand the implication of your decision, so take some time and give it some thought. You can reach us at this number—"

"I need a week to relocate my grandfather."

"Good," said the woman in black. "Take your time and then call us back with your an—"

"Oh, I don't need to call you back. I can give you my answer right now. These are impossible missions, right?"

"Pretty much."

Sunny walked over to the desk. Blew the candle out. Smiled. "That's why they don't call it Mission Difficult, do they?"

The woman in black looked up. "Pardon?"

"Never mind. I'm in."

"Are you sure?" asked the man in black.

"Sounds like fun."

"No," said the man in black. "I mean are you sure you're up to this?"

"Hey, I'm the fun and only."

Sunny walked to the door. The woman in black stood up. "Captain Turnbull?"

Sunny stopped. Turned. "Yes?"

"What'd you wish for?"

Sunny looked at the smoke lingering over the birthday candle. She took a deep breath. She thought back to the last thing her mother said to her, then looked up at the woman in black. "Ah, Sweetie, you're not supposed to tell a wish or it won't come true."

Sunny smiled glibly. A twinkle in her eye. She was alive ... and thirteen once again.

AFTER

It was impossible to talk, to hear, even to think over the roar of the four Rolls-Royce AE2100 turboprops. The wind noise generated by the six-bladed composite scimitar props strapped to each engine was just the audio icing on a very loud cake.

Didn't matter. Sunny and her team were so tightly in synch that the most that was ever needed was a hand signal. Usually, a quick glance was enough.

Sunny leaned against the bulkhead in full military HALO gear: HGU 55/P ballistic helmet, MBU12 oxygen mask, tactical goggles, Airox O_2 regulator, and a pair of Twin53 bailout bottles tucked into her LBE vest. She was decked out in full combat gear, body armor, boots, gloves, with a high-altitude altimeter strapped to her chest.

Strapped next to that was her XM8 Lightweight Assault Rifle. She had a 9 millimeter H&K sidearm on her right side, and cascading down her chest was an array of grenades—a row of M67 fragmentation grenades, a couple of M18 smoke grenades, and a gas grenade to cap things off. Tucked into her boot was the same Ka-Bar knife she'd used on Decatur Kaiser.

All in all, she was carrying nearly 110 pounds of equipment, which was about 25 pounds short of her full body weight.

After all, thought Sunny, *a girl can never have too many accessories.*

The C-130J Super Hercules was the most advanced model on the current flight line. Ordinarily, it had a service ceiling of 28,000 feet, but as lightly loaded as it was today, the aircraft could climb to nearly 40,000 feet.

Almost eight miles above the earth, Sunny mused. From the ground, only a thin wisp of a contrail would be visible ...

From the ground, no one would ever see them coming.

Until it was too late.

She faced the rear of the aircraft, the loading ramp raised to the closed position. Then a red warning light came on, full blast, penetrating the darkness of the compartment, and the ramp began to drop. They were on a heading of 270 degrees, due west. As the ramp continued dropping, a spectacular dawn burst behind them, over the eastern horizon in hues of red, orange, and splashes of white light.

Sunny smiled. They were up so high they were seeing the dawn a full five minutes ahead of the people on the ground. It was like a glimpse of the future. Her heart raced. At this moment, she was completely, insanely, exquisitely alive.

She felt the aircraft's nose raise, as the pilot sought to slow the plane down to just above stall speed. A few moments later, the red light flipped to green and a horn went off that was audible even over the roar of the wind and the engines. Sunny grabbed a handhold on the bulkhead and pulled herself easily to a standing position. Even with all the gear, she was quick and flexible.

She looked down at the only thing slowing her: a pair of composite fins that looked eerily like the swim fins she'd worn as a little girl. She hated walking in them—*waddling* was a better term—but she knew that once in the air, the fins acted like the control surfaces of an airplane, enabling her to do some ass-kicking aerobatics.

She moved into line. She was the mid-person in her team. One by one, they swan dived off the back of the loading ramp into the air blast. A few steps later, it was her turn.

Sunny bit down on the regulator, securing her oxygen supply, and pitched herself forward.

The blast spun her like a top in a tornado. She grinned and screamed through the regulator. She flipped her right foot forward and her left foot back and the fins threw her into a longitudinal rotation that sent her barreling through the sky like an artillery projectile. She was a dervish in a head-down dive, rocketing through the sky at 150 mph.

She grinned so broadly that for a moment, she almost spit out the regulator.

In no time, the meter on her chest harness read 2000 feet. Twelve seconds to impact.

The ground was close enough to see details. Cactus. Sagebrush. Sand. Boulders. Could be Arizona. Could be Afghanistan. Sunny could care less.

She pulled her rip-cord at the last moment.
POOM!

The canopy burst open, an explosion of black spackle mat as her ram air chute fully deployed.

Sunny's eyes were wild; the pupils filled with fire. Ecstatic. A gleeful, adrenalized rush.

She was, after all, the fun and only.

THE END

ABOUT THE AUTHORS

Wayne McDaniel (New York, NY) received an MFA from Columbia University and works as a screenwriter. *Resurrection Bay* is his debut novel.

Steven Womack (Nashville, TN) is the author of the Edgar and Shamus Award-winning Harry James Denton series and the critically acclaimed Jack Lynch series. A member of the Writer's Guild of America, he co-wrote the ABC-TV Movie *Volcano: Fire on the Mountain*. He is also a professor of screenwriting at the Watkins Film School in Nashville, Tennessee.